"*AfroSFv2* is not only as enter... smorgasbord of top-class imagina... superb writing and searing social... of speculative fiction, we're in safe hands." — Sarah Lotz, author of *Day Four*.

"I loved every minute of it. A bouquet with Africa's finest bring futures seen from African perspectives. Refreshing, surprising, magical, grim and beautiful. There is a pulse throbbing through these stories that insists you follow along." — Margrét Helgadóttir, author of *The Stars Seem So Far Away*.

"There was a time when William Gibson said: 'The future is already here, it's just not very evenly distributed.' Then came Ian McDonald who replied: 'The future is actually evenly distributed – as everyone from Nigeria to America, from China to India gets the same iPhone at the same time – it's just that other people are doing more interesting and funky things with it.' So, as the Future arrives everywhere, be prepared to read *AfroSFv2* stories, a brilliant mixture of emerging voices from the vanishing peripheral of the world." — Francesco Verso, author of *Nexhuman* and editor of *Future Fiction*.

AfroSFv2

Edited by Ivor W. Hartmann

CONTENTS

Introduction

Ivor W. Hartmann

First there was the dream, then it became real, and the first volume of *AfroSF* was published in 2012. In the three years since there have been some great strides forward, not only in the number of African writers and publishers exploring SF, but more importantly a great dialogue has been engaged.

Now more than ever we are asking the hard questions about our African futures, what they could be, what they shouldn't be, what are our hopes and dreams, what are the dreams being forced upon us.

This dialogue has taken many forms, to name some: *Lagos 2060* (2013, Ed. Ayodele Arigbabu), *Nigerians in Space* by Deji Olukotun (2013), Rachel Zadok's *Sister-Sister* (2013), Charlie Human's *Apocalypse Now Now* (2013), Dilman Dila's collection *A Killing in the Sun* (2014), the launch of the *Omenana* SFF magazine edited by Mazi Nwonwu and Chinelo Onwualu in 2014, the Jalada *Afrofuture(s)* issue (2015), *Terra Incognita: New Short Speculative Stories from Africa* (2015, Ed. Nerine Dorman), Nnedi Okorafor and Lauren Beukes' many books, and there's more in the making like *Imagine Africa 500* anthology by The Story Club Malawi. And that's just in publishing, in the arts/film/festivals/etc. there's so much going on. Dilman Dila is busy shooting a new SF feature, Neill Blomkamp's *Chappie* came out in March 2015, the Ethiopian *Crumbs* by Miguel Llansó was released in October 2015. The Kenyan BLACK Division Games launched the first-person SF shooter *Nairobi X*, and Kiro'o Games in Cameroon released the RPG, *Legacy of the Kori-Odan*. The artworks of amazing afro future artists such as Cyrus Kabiru, Wangechi Mutu, and Komi Olaf, continue to inspire. There was the Future Fest 2015 in Lagos, and the African Futures festival in Johannesburg, Nairobi, Kenya, and Lagos, simultaneously.

AfroSF as the first truly Pan-African SF anthology has definitely played a part in this exciting new wave of futures exploration, one that is remains entirely vital for Africa. In these increasingly perilous times no longer can we leave our collective futures in the hands of anyone but ourselves. Our futures, our *personal* responsibility.

For *AfroSFv2*, in the spirit of the first volume, I decided we must continue braving new territory and so chose to publish an SF novellas anthology, for quite a few reasons, but mainly: I enjoy the length a novella gives to really get into a story, novellas are the longest story form a print anthology can feasibly comprise, and I wanted to challenge both myself and the writers to see if we could claim another first for African SF writers and publish the first Pan-African SF novellas anthology. And here we are, with a seriously kick-ass anthology.

You might be familiar with Tade Thompson, Nick Wood, and Efe Tokunbo Okogu, from volume one, and if you haven't already come across Dilman Dila, Andrew Dakalira, and Mame Bougouma Diene, be excited.

Superhero face-offs, far future, ancient advanced technology rediscovered, alien invasion, alternate realities, existential crises, and social critiques, are but some of the wonderous, dark, gritty, and beautiful places these five novellas will take you.

Ivor W. Hartmann is a Zimbabwean writer, editor, publisher, and visual artist. Awarded The Golden Baobab Prize (2009), finalist for the Yvonne Vera Award (2011), selected for *The 20 in Twenty: The Best Short Stories of South Africa's Democracy* (2014), and awarded third place in the Jalada Prize for Literature (2015). His works have appeared in many publications. He runs the StoryTime micro-press, publisher of the *African Roar* and *AfroSF* series of anthologies, and is on the advisory board of Writers International Network Zimbabwe.

The Last Pantheon

Tade Thompson & Nick Wood

Prologue

February 18, 1979
Sahara Desert, Africa
My hands are deep in sand, and there is blood on the snow.
 He did not know why there was snow.

 He tried to rise, but it was not time. His breath came in ragged gasps, a death rattle? His ribs grated on each other when he inspired. His jaw felt heavy and swollen. More drops of blood on the snow, from his face. He tried to move his tongue, but it had grown snug inside his mouth and did not budge.

 He was on all fours. He could tell that now, but his right arm was crooked, maybe broken. The left arm held all the weight. Another warm dribble down his face. He pulled the left arm out of the snow and wiped it across his face. It came back smeared red.

 He tried again to stand, but it hurt, a pervasive pain that he had never experienced, his nerves screaming for respite. It seemed like he could feel the individual vertebrae in his backbone.

 What happened? What did I do? What did we do? Why is it snowing?

 He managed to stand. The horizon wobbled and turned, or he may have been turning. It was difficult to tell. Blood still streamed out of him, dripping on his chest and landing on the snow. He felt neither heat nor cold, but the crisp air helped to clear his head and stabilise his vision.

 There were depressions in the snow, footsteps, ending in a lump of a man about fifty yards away. Head bowed, arms by the side, kneeling. His enemy.

Snowflakes gently dropping to earth. Oh, mother. What have we done this time?

He could not find any hatred inside himself, not anymore. He was done. This was over.

He tried to fly away, but his feet stayed linked to the earth. He could not jump because each movement was agony, especially for his right arm.

Maybe he was dying.

He focused on the weather. It should not be snowing. He closed his eyes, coaxed the clouds, and asked the water to disperse. You didn't force weather. You just eased it into doing what it wanted. You said, please don't form precipitation. Sometimes, it listened.

The snowfall stopped but the clouds would not move. Not yet.

Breathing heavy now. The next part would hurt, but had to be done. He held his right forearm and twisted counter-clockwise sharply.

He screamed, and almost passed out again.

His enemy did not stir.

Bastard.

Maybe there was some hatred left after all.

He took strips of his enemy's cape and made a crude sling; then he walked away.

After an hour he came to a gaggle of Algerian troops. By then the sun had returned and the snow had turned to slush. They recognised him and eased safeties off their weapons. He took their fear, absorbed it and fed it to his body for healing.

He spoke Arabic by drawing it out of their minds. "I surrender," he said. "Take me to prison."

1

2015
Lagos, Nigeria

Kokoro had aged well, he thought, but then he missed the question she asked. "I'm sorry, could you repeat that?" he said.

"I said the blogsphere wonders why you chose crime with your abilities, rather than more noble actions like that of Black-Power."

"Ah…I see. Well, I don't think anyone wakes up and decides to be a criminal, Miss Kokoro. A number of things happen, inconsequential nudges, impressions, and time passes. One day you wake up to find out that you are not the hero of your own story. When the newspapers describe you as 'the international criminal known only as the Pan-African' you realise you've been cast and typecast even. There is a power in naming things. You become the name and you convince yourself that it fits like an old coat."

Behind the lights, technicians in the studio moved; dark shadows keeping the television machine going. He saw his own image on one of the monitors. He sat opposite Elizabeth Kokoro and to his left the network had erected a massive black-and-white poster of him from 1975 in his Pan-African war paint. He sported an Afro back then and his expression was feral, possessed. He had a fury that time and prison had leached out of him.

No, it wasn't prison that took the rage away. It was that last time in the Sahara.

"Thunderclap344 from Zimbabwe asks why you didn't break out of prison," said Kokoro. He wondered why she had no tablet or clip board. She had told him this segment of the interview would be a live Q & A from the web. Where was she reading the questions from? Probably the producer was feeding her by a plug in her ear.

"I had no reason to. From the moment I retired I was determined to rejoin society. That meant taking responsibility for what I had done. I surrendered to the Algerian authorities, but it turned out that I had never really committed any crimes in Algeria besides illegally crossing their borders and violating their airspace. They were quite nice to me, considering. Extradition was a nightmare. South Africa tried to claim me, but the whole Apartheid thing meant nobody listened to their noise. Nigeria began extradition proceedings but gave up in 1983 because there was a coup. Ghana, Morocco, Gambia... so many prisons, so little time."

Kokoro adjusted her skirt. She knew all this, but managed to maintain an expression of curious interest. Good interviewers had that quality of not representing themselves, but the listener.

"I ended up incarcerated for twenty years in Edo City."

"When did you leave jail?"

"I've been free since 2003."

"What have you been doing since then?"

What indeed.

2003
Edo City

The clerk was old, way past retirement, and officious. He had one of those Mugabe moustaches that reminded you of Hitler. If he knew who the Pan-African was he did not indicate. He passed forms through the gap in the window with large blue Xs marked at the points requiring signature or thumb print.

"What's this?" asked the Pan-African.

"This confirms that your personal effects were returned to you in the same condition as the day you entered, with the exclusion of any perishable goods and age-related changes."

"I didn't enter with any personal effects."

"So nothing was returned to you. Is the nothing in the same condition?"

The Pan-African stared.

"That was a joke," the clerk said, in a flat voice.

"I see."

"You still have to sign."

The Last Pantheon

He signed.

The clerk gave him sixty-five American dollars.

"What's this?"

"Something the government gives to rehabilitated offenders to help them start off in their new life. Congratulations. Your debt to society is paid. Go forth and live a virtuous life."

The clerk stamped a final form and handed it to him.

Outside. The gates lurched shut with an electronic whine.

Nobody waiting. No friends, no family.

Edo City Prison was technically outside city limits, but nobody cared as long as the degenerates were out of sight. All around him was bush, bisected by a single black-top road which led to civilisation.

I am Tope Adedoyin. I used to be called the Pan-African. I was in prison, but now I am free. I have a piece of paper that says I am free. It has an official stamp on it. I'm free.

He looked at his feet. Black Hush Puppies from aeons ago, fashionable if he were someone's grandfather. He tested something, focused, and left the ground behind. Two, three feet in the air, hovering, testing. Then he fell back down. It was like swimming; you had to relearn how to hold your breath.

He started walking north along the side of the road. Cars and lorries swept past, dusting him. He considered trying to hitch a ride, but thought better of it. He wanted to be alone and charity brought with it the necessity to reciprocate with conversation.

He stopped to relieve himself and noticed a footpath, partly obscured by weed growth, but definitely a walkway. He zipped up and followed it, not knowing why. A whim, a notion of delight or despair. The sound of traffic faded. He passed a yellowed wooden sign, a placard rendered blank by acid rain. He soon came to a settlement. It was a rag-tag collection of shacks, shanties, and lean-tos.

It was probably illegal. The shanty town could not be seen from the road, which meant no taxes or police. There were no estates close by, no legitimate citizens for them to contaminate, and there was no impending property development. These were the criminals, the drunks, the dangerous psychotics, the detritus of society, both victims and perpetuators. The poor were the greatest sinners in a free enterprise society.

Would it be a violation of his parole if he lived here?

He encountered the insensate form of a drunk, whom he stepped over. The first dwelling was a beer parlour with 'No Cridit' stencilled in red paint. A lone male customer drank the local kai kai gin, which was more wood alcohol than ethanol.

"Good evening, uncle," said Tope. "May I join you?"

"Good evening, my son," said the old man. He pulled a seat out by way of invitation. "Sadia! Bring another glass."

Tope sat down, accepted one glass and drank in silence. He called to Sadia and asked for a Stout and another half-litre of gin for the old man. If they noticed his distorted arm they did not draw attention to it.

"I'm looking for a place to stay," said Tope.

"That's what I said when I arrived here," said the old man. "I was twenty and I had just killed a man. Have you killed anyone?"

Tope had a flashback. He...he...

He bunched the ridiculous cape in his left hand and pulled Black-Power towards himself and punched his head into the desert sand. Black-Power's arms twitched in an epileptic fit. The Pan-African stamped on that head. The sand became red with blood.

"No," said Tope. "I haven't killed anyone."

Over the next few days he built a house out of wood from trees he chopped down himself and nails he scavenged and corrugated iron he found. He didn't mind. It kept him busy and was not taxing at all. At first they did not know who he was, but a boy saw him levitating in order to reach a difficult part of his roof.

Once they knew the Pan-African was among them, his power grew and he fixed their weak and wobbly dwellings. He helped till the land on their untaxed farms. The sheer number of the diseased among them complicated matters and added a dark shade to his power. The hepatitis and AIDS dementia, the heart failures and septic abortions. The power from the sufferers was tainted, sick power that could turn him to mischief again if he let it.

2015
Lagos, Nigeria

"I just kept busy with this and that," said Tope.

Elizabeth nodded. "Another question from the forums: what did you learn from your days as the Pan-African?"

"Crime does not pay, stay in school, and never, ever, get into a fight with a man who wears a cape because such a man is insane."

"Now you're just being flippant."

"Only half flippant. Seriously, have you looked at the costume that idiot used to wear? I almost killed him with the damn thing."

"Then why didn't you? You fought many times and both walked away to tell the tale."

"I wasn't trying to kill," said Tope. "I was trying to teach."

"To teach what?"

"That Black-Power, with all his good intentions, was part of the problem, not the solution."

"We'll come back to that, but I have another question, this from Powerfan565. She asks why you were called the Pan-African Coward in 1975."

Tope sighed. He knew this would come up.

"I don't remember."

"Powerfan565 says, was it not because the first time you bumped into Black-Power you ran away?"

"No comment."

"Did you run away from him?"

"No comment." Tope took a sip of water from the glass beside him. He maintained eye-contact with Elizabeth.

"This is supposed to be frank interview," she said.

"I can explain," said Tope, "but I'm not going to. No comment."

"We have a caller on the line. Caller, you're live on Flashback. Go ahead."

The voice came through on the studio speakers and chilled Tope to his core. He could actually feel pain in his chest where he had received the hardest hit in the desert.

"Pan-African, is there something you think you're qualified to say about me?" asked Black-Power.

2015
Cape Town, South Africa
Pain, there was always the pain.

Detective Sipho Cele grunted as he stood up from his desk, holding his arm tightly over the right side of his body. Such an action muted the sharp reminder of shattered ribs from decades ago, the pain at least dulling with the spread of his stomach and the slow creep of age.

He stepped around his broad desk with its bronze name plate, littered with photos and files of low lives, murderers, rapists, and tsotsis. The scum of the Earth, so many of them, a never ending wave that he had spent his life fighting against. But, like the hydra, you take one down and two more step into their place.

Making his way to the window, he smiled at his clever classical allusion; he was no wet-eared plaasjapie, as the Boere used to say, no, he was urban smart—and old, much older than he looked, even though his hair was starting to pepper with grey.

As he stared down seven stories onto the milling street below, he felt yet older still. Offices stretched high into the sky, glass-fronted, left and right, inscrutable—but the street itself below was teeming with people; trade and spill-off from the nearby tourist trap of Greenmarket Square. Of Table Mountain itself, there was no sign, hidden behind tiers of stone and glass.

He watched the people move and bustle, a dance troupe setting up in the paved boulevard, Adderley street flower sellers spilling across for more business as an impromptu crowd gathered.

And, with vision an eagle would have been proud of, he noticed a thin young man spiralling around the crowd's edge, deftly picking back-pockets and coats.

Tcchhaaa, small fry!

There was a time when he would have shown no mercy, when his tolerance was ever set at zero.

Those were old times, gone times.

Sipho turned away with a growl of fury, making his way back to his desk, accidentally brushing past a lurid black, green and yellow cape hanging on the coat stand. He felt a faint frisson of excitement.

No.

Gone times.

Now, at least the pain was dull, hovering in the background, in places he could ignore.

The smaller desk in the corner of the room, with its tiny black swivel chair, was empty.

Where the hell was she? Thembeka took off too much time to go shopping; he would chide her when she got back. He could see the lights on her phone console glowing hot with waiting calls or people depositing urgent messages.

The door opened just as he reached his desk and was about to sit down. He hesitated, flexing his biceps involuntarily as she stepped into the room.

Sure, she was short and on the plain side, but old habits die hard. Still, he'd had to be careful; this new generation of women seemed increasingly less impressed with his towering physique and charm—it could even cause trouble.

And, of course, she was a Xhosa, so not a real Zulu woman.

"Where have you been?" He growled, suddenly and irrationally bored with this dull city.

"Getting information off the street," she hovered in the door, watching him with hooded eyes.

"So," he sat, feeling the chair creak underneath his solid bulk, "What information do you have?"

"There's a new Super-Tik factory being set up just two streets down," Thembeka said. She looked down, as if hoping for praise, but afraid to look him in the eyes.

"Just do your job and answer the phone," he said, turning to his desktop, which was scrolling in news from all across Africa.

18

She sat for a moment in what felt like crushed silence and then with an angry sigh, she picked up the phone and started speaking.

But Sipho wasn't listening. A staccato burst of noise had sprung up from the street below and he knew the sound of that noise.

Trouble.

Big trouble.

In a bound he was at the window again, gaze raking the street, missing nothing. The crowd was disintegrating rapidly, people screaming. No cops of course, a few security guards, but they were running too.

There, the central drama piece, six men standing with automatic weapons, two holding the pickpocket as one large man pistol whipped him, snarling.

The boy had not been careful enough in choosing his victims.

Too bad—Detective Cele was about to turn his back too, when he noticed an old woman sidling up the street with her guide dog.

Dumb fucking dog, he was leading her into Trouble Central.

Without thinking, Sipho reached for the cape.

One of the armed men turned and shoved the woman, who fell, crying. The dumb dog sat down.

Sipho reached for the crumpled mask in his pocket, an old relic he'd never quite managed to let go, a talisman to touch, but not to wear.

The man was lifting his right boot; readying himself to kick the old woman.

Mask and cape on, Sipho Cele threw himself through the window and fell face first in a shower of glass.

Shit, I can't fly.

He panicked as the ground screamed in close to his head.

So it was that his powers finally kicked in again.

Time...

...slowed.

Or, rather, he sped up; spinning his body deftly to land feet first, legs braced.

Fuck, those shoes had been Italian leather. They blew apart on impact, his toes splaying on buckling concrete.

One, two, three steps, and he was there, catching a swinging boot before it landed against the old woman's head. He reversed the force, feeling the man's hip shatter as he was flung over backwards.

Sipho had been gentle. The man landed only ten metres away, but unfortunately on his head—and on bricked pavement.

He did not get up again, nor did he make a sound, lying there like a discarded heap of expensive clothes waiting for a wash that would never come.

Sipho straightened and turned to the other men, who stood stunned, guns dangling at various angles of shock.

No... Black-Power straightened and eyed the miscreants with a stony-faced lack of both mercy and fear.

"Run," he growled.

So they did.

Well, four of them ran, one screaming.

The fifth man stood, a large man tattooed with prison-gang numbers, his one giant hand still holding onto the pickpocket's collar. The young man hung limply, spirit leaking with the blood from his broken nose. Then, abruptly, the tattooed man flung him away like a crumpled piece of paper.

He slowly levelled his machine gun, a reworked AK-47 by the look of it.

His eyes were glowing red, with maddened power. Not just tik, must be the new Super-Tik, thought Black-Power.

"Die, motherfucker..." the man opened fire.

Black-Power covered his eyes with his left hand, bracing his body. Owwwwww, he kept the groans inside his head—he was going to end up with a hell of a bruising on his body.

Abruptly, the firing stopped.

Black-Power removed his hand and grinned at the man's furrowed frown, his gaping mouth.

The Last Pantheon

He gently turned around and picked up the old woman, a little so-called coloured woman, folded in fear.

"You've been a bad boy," he said, "Say sorry to mamma—it's time we all learned to respect our elders again."

The man snarled in frightened rage and rushed forward to launch a punch with his right hand.

Black-Power covered the woman softly with his arms and thrust his face forward to meet the blow, feeling knuckles crumble against his right cheekbone.

The man screamed and stepped backwards, nursing his right hand under his armpit; his shaved head bobbing as he bounced up and down in pain.

Black-Power straightened even more. "Run."

Within seconds, the man had disappeared.

Black-Power put the woman down, and slipped the dog's lead into her hand.

"You're safe now, mamma!" he said.

The woman smiled and nodded gratefully. Black-Power gave the dog a nudge with his toe and they wandered off quietly down the street again.

Sirens started to screech in the distance. Time to go; there was no need to compromise his identity, hidden for so long now.

But a small crowd had already gathered around him.

"Who are you, mister?" an awed youngster asked.

Black-Power noticed the young pickpocket crawling away out of the corner of his eye. He'd more than learned his lesson, by the look of him.

Someone was standing behind him, looking at his cape, which had been relatively undamaged.

"BP," read the man aloud. "British Petroleum probably, with those colours? All done as an advertisement maybe?"

The crowd glanced around, looking for cameras.

"Black-Power!" he snarled, bending his legs, readying himself, scanning for his broken office window above.

Then, with a massive launch of his calves and thighs he was airborne, rocketing upward with explosive power.

Shit, he thought again, crashing through the remnants of his office window, rolling to a halt against the far wall.

Slowly, he untangled himself from his cape and stood up, glass crunching underneath his shredded socks.

Thembeka was standing on her desk, palms across her mouth, looking frightened.

"Who are you?" she whispered, "Who are you really?"

He offered her his hand.

"Power," he said, "Black-Power."

He took her shaking hand, his slightly sweaty palm brushing her skin, and gently lowered her to the floor. "And I think you and I have some Super-Tik factories to visit."

She smiled softly, gaze dropping shyly.

He saw her startle.

He looked down. Sure, his skin was just about invulnerable, but his clothes obviously weren't. There'd been no time to dig his durable bodysuit out. There was very little left of his shirt and trousers.

"Oops," he said, turning around to her embarrassed giggle.

It was then that he heard...him.

He'd know that smooth, honey-tongued voice anywhere. His PC had locked onto a broadcast, somewhere further up the African continent.

He stepped across to his desk, it was an interview from the sound of it, and a sweet feminine voice was chiming in.

Old and very bad pains started to leach back into his body at the sound of the man's voice. His ribs shrieked and his head ached, so much so it was hard to focus on the picture of the man and woman, seated across from each other, in what looked like intimate conversation.

Thembeka stood unnoticed at his shoulder, watching too.

That woman, the interviewer, he thought, she's, she's... Beautiful... He struggled to focus on the words being exchanged between them.

Then he heard his name mentioned.

Without thinking, he reached across for the phone, dialling the number scrolling across the screen.

"....you're live on Flashback," he heard the interviewer's soft words, "go ahead."

"Pan-African," he breathed.

Pain, there's always pain—this time, though, he would rise to greet it.

2015
Lagos, Nigeria
Breathe. Breathe. In, out, in. Not difficult, you've been doing it all your life.

Tope hated this, the nerves. Others might call it fear, but he had already proved himself against Black-Power. Besides, this was verbal conflict, not physical.

Elizabeth Kokoro snorted, a brief, feminine gesture, almost missed but certainly dismissive. She had always favoured Black-Power over the Pan-African and indeed there were rumours. Black-Power had been a pussy hound back then.

"Hello, brother," said Tope, voice calm.

"I am not your brother," said Black-Power, voice vibrating through the studio. Did he sound out of breath? Like he'd been running? "I am Zulu, you are Yoruba."

"And yet I still call you 'brother'," said Tope.

You know why, he thought.

50,000 B.P.
What would later become Southern Africa
"They are barely conscious," said the elder. "I can hear their left and right cerebral hemispheres arguing with each other. They think it's a god, or what they will come to think of as such when they have that concept."

"I don't know if it qualifies as consciousness," said the younger. "At least they have tools."

The primates had taken a warthog and were gutting it. One male primate held its side where the beast had gored him with its tusks. The elder knew he would be dead within a week from infection. They did not have an idea of religion or even the afterlife yet.

"I think we can help them," said the elder. "I want you to-"
"No."
"What?"

24

"I do not wish to take instructions from you anymore. I've done that long enough. This settlement is yours," said the younger. "I'm going further north."

"You do not wish to stay together?" asked the elder. He sounded surprised and perhaps hurt.

"We'll be on the same continent. I will not leave the landmass or planet without letting you know, brother."

"Do not let them begin to worship you," said the elder. "We are not gods."

"I won't," said the younger.

But he did.

2003
Edo City

"Uncle Tope, why is your arm twisted?" asked the boy.

"I broke it one time. It didn't heal well," said Tope. He hammered a nail while he spoke. On a whim he switched the hammer to the right and continued. "Works fine, though, right?"

"Right."

"Pass me the box of nails."

He stepped back and gauged the horizontality of the cross bar. He looked at the boy who nodded.

"Why do you help people?" asked the boy.

"Why do you ask so many questions?"

"My mother says I'm a question bank."

"Indeed you are," said Tope. "I shall call you 'Bank' from now on."

"My mother has tribal marks," he said.

Tope looked across the way where Bank's mother tried to dredge the sluggish stream for something of value. She was twenty-four going on forty and had three horizontal scarification marks and three vertical on each cheek. It was unusual. Nobody had those any more.

"Do you want to hear a secret?" Tope asked.

Bank nodded. He was seven and had already realised that the world of adults was full of secrets. Secrets were the portal between being a child and growing up.

"You see the bar codes on the goods you buy? The black lines?"

"Yes."

"You know how the creation story of Yoruba people is Olodumare lowered Oduduwa down to the Earth with sand and a chicken. The sand became the landmass and the chicken rooted around in it, scattering it all over the Earth."

"I've heard this story in school, Uncle Tope."

"Well…it was a space ship. Oduduwa had something that looked like a barcode on his cheeks. There were already humans here. They saw the code and tried to copy it with their crude instruments. The barcode became the tribal marks."

Bank looked sceptical. "How do you know this?"

"I was in the space ship. I was crew."

Bank squinted, not at all filled with credulity, but still child enough to wonder.

"I'm kidding!" said Tope, though he was not.

He heard someone call his name. It was a verbal call, not a thought, and he looked up. A man was running towards the house he was repairing.

"Tope! There are tractors and police!"

"Calm down," said Tope. "Show me."

There were indeed tractors and police, but in addition there were armed Area Boys who were local toughs usually employed by politicians to beat up the opposition. At the head of the procession was a guy in a black suit sweating in the sun, waving a sheet of paper and speaking through a megaphone. The feedback was such that Tope could not make out what he was saying.

"What the fuck is he saying?" Tope asked the man.

"He says we should all pack up and leave within the hour otherwise the people behind him will forcibly eject us and destroy our dwellings."

"Hmm..." Tope pondered a moment, then said, "Don't worry about it. Tell everyone to return to their homes and go about their daily business."

"We have nowhere to go," said the man.

"You do not need anywhere to go," said Tope. "This is your home."

He walked to the side of the road, under the shade of a palm tree, and he sat down, staring at the column invading the settlement. He began to breathe regularly, timing each inspiration and expiration. He allowed his mind to reach out. *All gods are telepathic. This is how prayer works.*

Sadia brought him a tall gourd of ogogoro without knowing why. He drank it in one long swallow, enjoying the burn, feeling the relaxation and disinhibition. Better than Johnnie Walker and Southern Comfort combined.

Now then.

The official.

Father of three, professional bureaucrat, one mistress currently pregnant, mortally afraid of his boss. A great love for his job, although he did not enjoy inflicting suffering on the less fortunate. *Use that.* The official stopped shouting into the public address system and shouted Marxist slogans, ordering the police to arrest the Area Boys.

Tope spread his mind further.

The Area Boys became confused. They could all see a swarm of flying ants in the air, and they scattered.

Tope nudged the police, and they ran after the Area Boys.

The machine operators screamed as the tippers and tractors became dinosaurs of the carnivorous variety.

The alcohol warmed Tope's belly. He called Bank to him and returned to his carpentry.

2015
Lagos, Nigeria

"I am Zulu," repeated Black-Power. "I am not kin to you."

"You're a fucking idiot is what you are," said Tope. "You weren't helpful in the seventies and you're not helpful now."

27

"Hang on," said Elizabeth Kokoro. "Black-Power was a hero in his time. He was recognised all over the world. He addressed the United Nations. He saved millions from natural disasters, accidents, and criminals such as yourself. How can you justify your statement?"

"Misdirection," said Tope.

"What are you talking about?" asked Black-Power.

"We've had this discussion already," said Tope. "You were too thick then and you're too thick now. You prance about in your cape and mask, a copy of your colonial masters' masks by the way, not drawing inspiration from the African tradition of masking. You fly around in bright colours, puffing up your chest, chasing what? Drug dealers, bank robbers, cannabis cultivators? A volcano goes off and Black-Power is there to save the day. Whoopie. What did you do that was of any long-standing significance? Not one thing. What did you do for social justice? Did you change the injustices that create the petty crime that you policed? No. Do you remember our discussions about Idi Amin? The Congo? Black-Power do you remember me telling you that Murtala Mohammed would probably be assassinated in 1976? What about Kapuuo in 1978?"

"What are you trying to say?" asked Black-Power. He did not sound so certain.

"I'm saying that you're not a hero. You were a tool of the status quo government systems. You kept the poor people in line and turned a blind eye to the real offenders. You allowed the CIA to operate with impunity throughout the continent."

"You could have stopped those same things." Black-Power sounded defensive now.

"I was not and am not a hero. I never claimed to be."

"I didn't know if-"

"Motherfucker, don't you dare. *You knew*. You knew because I told you."

"Do not make me come over there, Pan-African."

The edge in his voice made Tope's momentum dry up and he could not think of anything to say.

28

Elizabeth recovered. "Black-Power, these are serious accusations. Do you have any comment? Any mitigating factors?"

"I have a question for the Pan-African."

"I don't go by that name anymore."

"Nevertheless, I have a question."

"Proceed," said Elizabeth.

"How much are you being paid to appear on television?"

"I-" Tope started.

"That information is confidential, Black-Power. He signed a contract of non-disclosure." Elizabeth uncrossed and crossed her legs.

"I understand. But he is getting paid, no? Is this an instance of crime finally paying off? You criticise my record, but you spent your entire career trying to accumulate money. Without success, I should add. I was always there to beat you down."

"Except one time," said Tope.

"How's the arm?"

"How's your fucking chest?"

"Language, gentlemen. There are children listening," said Elizabeth. "I have a question for both of you. Biohazard344 wants to know which of you is more powerful."

"It depends," they said in unison.

"What does that mean?" asked Elizabeth.

"It means if we fly to the moon and fight we could crack it in two and still not know who is more powerful," said Black-Power.

"Speak for yourself. On the moon I would kill you," said Tope.

"Fool, you don't even have my permission to dream or fantasise about such a fight."

Elizabeth clapped her hands. "Wow! Exciting stuff. Black-Power and the Pan-African, at each other's throats again. Stay tuned: we'll be back after these commercials. If you can't wait log on to our website for behind-the-scenes streaming content."

The producer said something and they were all given five minutes off air. Elizabeth came straight for him.

"That stuff you said, was any of it true?" she asked.

She wore Chanel, but he didn't think it suited her.

"All of it was true."

"Can you prove it?"

"No. Maybe. I think he was employed by the South African government at some point. I have some information that he draws a pension, but it's buried deep."

"You're quite the dark horse, aren't you? I feel we may never really know everything about the Pan-African or his motives." She flicked a hair strand and turned away.

Was she flirting with him?

2015
Cape Town
Detective Sipho Cele was breathing heavily. No, he must remember, <u>Black-Power</u> was breathing heavily, even though his small fracas with the drug gang was receding into the history of the day.

His PC had moved on, circulating others news from Africa in a torrent of chaotic themes; crime, pleasure, sport, business—and money, always money, as the African economic giant awoke slowly, starting to face off the Chinese and the fading Yanks.

But *she* hadn't moved.

Gradually, he became aware of her small but focused presence. Thembeka, his assistant, breathing heavily at his side too—he turned to look at her.

"Was any of that true?"

"No," he said, "They're just lies from a master criminal of the past. Pan-African's super-powers, formidable though they are, don't even come close to the devious sharpness of his deluded brain."

She smiled, but he could see she didn't quite believe him.

The history of the day was just a flicker of moth wings to him.

But the deeper history, well, Pan-African had reminded him of what he was ever avoiding.

Time and accountability.

1961
KwaMashu, South Africa
Now that was a bad year.

Actually, that was an esabeka year, a year so bad it gave him nightmares still.

The year opened gently, with no hint of the tremors and traumas to come. But there were rumblings in the north and—although he was growing comfortable in his Native Affairs

31

job as a clerk in kwaMashu, near Durban—he finally decided that with great power, comes at least some small accountability.

There was a good man—an important man—in trouble, and he needed help.

A new black president, democratically elected as the Continent had started to sweep its way free from former colonial masters. There had not been enough sweeping in this country up north though, where the Belgians and the Yanks remained in place conniving to keep their source of uranium and precious minerals intact for their Frigid Global War.

The Congo Crisis, they called it, capturing the first democratic president of that country.

The president's words rolled across the subsequent decades: *"…what we wanted for our country—its right to an honourable life, to perfect dignity, to independence with no restrictions—was never wanted by Belgian colonialism and its Western allies…"*

So it was with that Gatsha Mchunu—as he called himself then—took leave and headed north. He moved rapidly, hanging on the backs of trains, leaping across borders at night with great strides that took him hundreds of feet into the air.

His face was masked; his body encased in a plain black body-suit for night time camouflage.

Black-Power, he thought, I shall call myself Black-Power.

He looked down at his body and thought again, <u>Black-Power</u>.

And so, at last, Black-Power arrived in Katanga province of the newly independent Congolese Republic.

Elizabethville, generally a quiet and sleepy copper town he'd heard, was humming with activity and military convoys moving in and out. He saw some white faces, overheard some South African accents and knew there were mercenaries and probably South African military, as well as Katangese secessionist forces about.

By this time he was dressed in a poor, ill-fitting jacket and trousers, scuffed shoes, and a hat crammed down on his broad head. Masks would only attract unnecessary attention.

The Last Pantheon

He was given wary directions to the airport by a few locals, who appeared to mistrust both his accent and his size.

The airport was cordoned off, so he waited for night, in nearby bushes. Wet from a sudden furious burst of late afternoon warm rain, he changed out of his sodden attire.

Masked, suited and booted, he waited.

A few distant flashes of lightning lit up the dull runway.

The gods must be about.

It was then that he saw a plane had already landed.

There was no more time to wait.

He hurtled over the fence, bounded once on the tarmac and smashed through the back door of the plane.

It was a small plane, but he could smell blood on board.

Only one man stood facing him, looking startled and bemused. A white man, dressed in pilot overalls, who spoke in French.

"What do you want?" The man looked wan and tired, as if he had been ill recently.

"Where is he?"

The pilot shrugged, "They have taken him somewhere, I don't know…"

Black-Power looked outside, his gaze scanning the horizon for movement. There was a flicker in the distance, a jeep heading off road.

Night fell fast in this area of the world.

He stepped outside, crouched and leapt. In one furious bound, he was soaring over the perimeter fence.

A few troops below opened fire on him, bullets whistling past in the deepening gloom.

As he soared through the air, he watched.

The jeep was parked by a ramshackle house, roof crumbling in disrepair.

He was coming back to earth.

Gunshots.

Within the house.

He crashed through the roof and landed, boots buckling wooden floorboards beneath him.

He could smell death.

Warm and recent death.

Patrice Lumumba lay, broken by boots and bullets, crumpled on his back and bayoneted too, just for good measure.

The other men in the room recoiled as dust and roof debris continued to cascade down.

Black-Power took the scene in, with a cool and gathering rage.

The group were Belgians and Katangese, although they also had the background stench of the CIA hovering about them. Two other men lay dead nearby. The man holding the bloodied bayonet was a Katangese government official he vaguely knew.

"*...They have corrupted some of our countrymen; they have bought others; they have done their part to distort the truth and defile our independence. What else can I say? That whether dead or alive, free or in prison by orders of the colonialists, it is not my person that is important...*"

With one step forward, Black-Power had snapped the man's neck with a flick of the fingers on his right hand.

He caught the dropped rifle and in one smooth motion had slung the bayonet through the torso of a Belgian official, one who had looked the most senior, perhaps even in charge.

The man coughed bright and bubbling blood.

No one moved, stunned and frozen in disbelief.

Without a word, Black-Power stooped and cradled the dead President Patrice Lumumba in his arms.

"*...Neither brutal assaults, nor cruel mistreatment, nor torture have ever led me to beg for mercy, for I prefer to die with my head held high, unshakeable faith and the greatest confidence in the destiny of my country, rather than live in slavery and contempt for sacred principles.*"

With a scream of fury, Black-Power crashed through the roof again, hurtling skywards, wishing he could fly away, far away, from this chaotic, damaged Earth.

Instead, though, he finally found and secretly gave the president's body to his widow, who was grief-faced and quiet, dry of tears, having already received his last words:

"My beloved companion: I write you these words not knowing whether you will receive them, when you will receive them; and whether I will still be alive when you read them...

Do not weep for me, my companion; I know that my country, now suffering so much, will be able to defend its independence and its freedom. Long live the Congo! Long live Africa!

- Patrice"

Nineteen Sixty One, yes, now that was indeed a terrible year. The Sharpeville Massacre in South Africa had followed in March; the white apartheid State of South Africa withdrew from the Commonwealth and called itself a Republic at the end of May; the UN Secretary-General Dag Hammarskjold— he secretly knew—had indeed been shot down in skies that were to become Zambian just three years later, but no, he would not let the litany of that dreadful year go on and on and on.

"...History will one day have its say; it will not be the history that is taught in the United Nations, Washington, Paris or Brussels, however, but the history taught in the countries that have rid themselves of colonialism and its puppets. Africa will write its own history and both north and south of the Sahara it will be a history full of glory and dignity..." (Lumumba, Patrice, 1961)

2015
Cape Town

How he *hated* history and Pan-African's reminders of how little he had changed the course of political events within Africa.

What had Pan-African done, apart from grow fat on his crime?

But Black-Power knew his was an old justification, his fear that taking sides so sharply would end up making the political bloodshed even greater. He had dreaded the sense that he might end up carrying so much more directly the vast weight of a multitude of dead souls, who might have followed him into an ensuing and even greater conflagration.

So instead he had straddled ideological fences through the following decades, concentrating on protecting the innocent from the smaller struggles of crime and the moral simplicities of natural disasters.

But in the process, he had increasingly grown more doubtful of his own mission and sense of self.

The Saharan Battle in the late seventies had been the final straw—broken in body more than he would have liked to admit, he had disappeared into retirement.

Until now.

"Black-Power?" Thembeka's touch on his arm was gentle, querying.

He realised with a start he had been slumped in his chair, brooding, lost in a year that had stripped his hopes and dreams away.

He smiled at her. "We have a drug-factory to break up, don't we?"

She grinned back at him and his heart lifted.

He stood up, old aches reminding him of history yet again. "Pan-African," he swore to himself, "next time I will finish you once and for all!"

5

2015
Lagos, Nigeria

The show was over. It fizzled out after the telephone fireworks with Black-Power, but Elizabeth seemed pleased. She kept taking phone calls and was unable to keep a smile off her face. Tope presumed her friends and co-workers were congratulating her. He sat in the same chair as technicians dismantled the set. They looked bored, as if they had done it a million times. A few people brought him items to autograph; a Wanted poster, an old newspaper article, a 1977 Black-Power comic showing him and Tope locked in combat with a caption that read 'THIS TIME... TO THE DEATH!' He smiled when he signed that.

"Nostalgia?" asked Elizabeth. She was at his elbow and he hadn't noticed her walk up.

"No, not really. Just amusement. These comics were propaganda tools."

"Haba! Now you're being completely paranoid. The comics were harmless fun aimed at children. At most they can be said to be evil for perpetuating bad art and repetitive, clichéd storylines with simplistic moral lessons." She took the comic, with its yellowed paper and handed it to the engineer, then looked up into Tope's eyes.

"You're a journalist, Miss Kokoro-"

"Call me Elizabeth."

"Elizabeth. You're a journalist. I expect better. Examine the facts. I did." He halted the engineer and took the comic back. He flipped open the first page and showed Elizabeth the copyright strip at the bottom. "See this? MKD Press. Do you know what that is?"

"No."

"I checked." Tope dismissed the engineer. "MKD Press had no local offices. The copies of Black-Power comic were shipped in regularly in large quantities every Thursday from England. MKD Press did have a London office, but no association with Fleet Street or the United Kingdom press establishment. I followed the money. It led to Langley, to the CIA. MKD Press was generated out of Project MKDelta. Do you know what that is?"

"No, I've never heard of it."

"Have you heard of MKUltra?"

"Yes, mind control experiments that the CIA ran in the sixties and early seventies? Trying to create Manchurian Candidates, perfect assassins, human automata."

"Exactly. Only MKUltra was domestic, within the United States. MKDelta was the same program, but for foreign countries. They didn't even try to hide the association much because they didn't think anybody would look into their under-priced children's comics."

"What made you suspicious?"

"The details of the storylines were similar to encounters that Black-Power and I had. Watered down, simplified, but with facts that only he or I could know. Black-Power got his abilities from aliens and I got mine when I was struck by lightning as a child. Bullshit. Then I found what I suspected to be subliminal messages in the dialogue. I analysed the paper, the print, the ink, even the poses and body language of the characters. Many of the issues were impregnated with chemicals that might be classified as mind-altering. The comics were not harmless fun, Elizabeth."

"I think I need to know more," said Elizabeth. "Do you have time for a drink?"

"I do."

"Give me some minutes. I'll meet you at reception when I've taken off this."

"You look quite attractive in that outfit."

She waved this away. "Stagecraft. I'm better in my own clothes."

While he waited Bank came up to him. The young man had developed a habit of walking with his face glued to his tablet, assuming he knew where he was going.

"Bank, put that thing away," said Tope.

"The money is in your account," said Bank. "These people keep their promises at least."

"That's reassuring."

"Shall we go home?"

"There's no hurry. Find us a hotel and you can take the rest of the night off."

"What are you going to do?"

"See the sights."

"You're lying."

"Go!"

"Yes, sir." With a mock salute Bank spun and left. He had not made eye-contact once during the conversation. The boy was in love with his computer.

"And call your mother to say you're not coming back tonight. I do not want her wrath."

They had excellent seats in a bar that projected out on to the lagoon. The floor-to-ceiling windows showed the water glittering with the reflection of the city lights. Elizabeth wore a sleeveless jumper and khakis. He appreciated the tautness of her muscles and the smoothness of her skin.

She drank a gin and tonic; he drank mineral water with a twist.

"No alcohol?" she asked.

"It's a school night," he said. "Mind if I ask you a question?"

"Go ahead."

"I'm not going to be so uncouth as to ask your age, but you were a reporter back in the seventies. You must be pushing sixty, but you look about thirty. What is your voodoo and how can I get some of it?"

She laughed like a girl. "Fiendish exercise, a personal dietician, workaholism and a very expensive team of plastic surgeons."

"Expensive, then."

"I forgot to add two ex-husbands."

"I'm sorry to hear that."

"Don't be. One was a cheat and the other was gay."

"I'd have thought they'd have been more discreet."

"There's no such thing, Tope. If it's in the airwaves, if it's digitised, if it's been typed, I can get to it. There are no secrets from me."

"Except in people's heads."

"Except in people's heads," she said. "But you can access that data."

"Sometimes."

"Have you read my mind?"

"No."

"Read it now."

Tope got an image of a parrot with an enormous human penis growing on its back. "Oh, you are so juvenile," he said.

She laughed. "I had to see if you were for real."

"You couldn't imagine pretty flowers and chocolate?"

"Boring."

"I suppose."

"Tope, why did you do the interview?" she asked, serious.

"For the money. You came to me, remember?"

2013
Edo City

Tope was drinking at the beer parlour with Bank, who was just old enough for liquor, and a few men whose names he could not remember. They argued about the Olympics and Usain Bolt's merits when compared with Carl Lewis.

This townie girl came up, followed by a cloud of catcalls and whistles. She wore shorts and was burdened under a backpack, but there was steel in her eyes. On closer look she wasn't a girl, but her beauty was uncontested.

"Which one of you is Tope Adedoyin?"

"I'm Tope," said Bank.

"No, I'm Tope," said a man drunk from oguro.

A few others identified themselves as Tope and the woman sucked her teeth and turned away, generating a roar of laughter. Tope got up and went after her.

"Miss? Miss, don't mind them. I'm the one you're after. Can I help you?"

She stopped, stared him down, and squinted. "Do you remember me?"

"No, sorry," Tope said, dragging the syllables out in his uncertainty.

"Kokoro."

"Ahh, from…you used to do those reports on Black-Power."

"Yes, that's right."

"Why are you here?"

"I want to do a biopic on the Pan-African. It'll be-"

"Fuck off." Tope turned away and went back to his drink.

2015
Lagos, Nigeria

"You are so stubborn! I've never seen a person so unwilling to be handed buckets of cash," said Elizabeth.

"I didn't need any money," said Tope. "I only decided to do it so that Bank and a few of the other kids from the settlement can go to university."

"How is it that the government hasn't bulldozed that settlement to the ground anyway?"

"They've tried. Strange maladies come upon the men who carry out the orders. Sooner or later, squatters' rights will kick in. Some of this money is going to a good lawyer too."

"What happened to all the money you stole when you were the Pan-African?"

"I didn't actually steal a lot of money."

1975
South Africa

When the dust settled in the vault, Tope inclined his head and the men loped inside to fill their bags.

"Ignore the Rands and concentrate on the gold," said Tope. "Be quick. We should be out of here within ten minutes."

The bank officials and security guards seemed oddly calm, and he would have suspected that they had set off an alarm, except, he scanned their thoughts and no such thing had been done. There were no approaching police.

Tope was confused and tired. He had been fighting alongside Cubans and Chinese specialists against the South African Defence Force over Angola. He had spent the last year observing the Angolan independence from the Portuguese. When the whole quagmire descended into civil war it was impossible to decide what side to fight on. MPLA, FNLA, UNITA, what the fuck? Jonas Savimbi was a canny operator, taking support from Communist China and the United States as it suited him.

In the middle of all of this there were starving, diseased, and displaced, women and children. Tope had decided to help them, but he would need money, hence the excursion south to a Cape Town bank.

He heard gunfire and shattering glass.

He left the vault, went into the main banking hall and saw Alamu on the floor, skull caved in and trailing a long smear of blood that led to broken glass doors. His assault rifle was still in his hands, twisted in on itself like a strip of barbed wire.

"What's happening?" said Paulo.

"Your job is to load the gold," said Tope. "I'll deal with this."

Outside on the street the van they had planned for the getaway was flattened, like a car in a junk yard compactor. There was a man standing on it. He wore a mask and black cape and a skin-tight body suit. And he was familiar.

"If you surrender now, you won't taste the might of Black-Power!" said the man.

It was all Tope could do not to laugh. "Brother, is that you?"

The masked man approached and recognised Tope. "What the hell is wrong with your hair?" he said.

"It's called an Afro. You know, like the Jackson Five."

"It looks ridiculous." He looked beyond Tope and saw the rest of the men. "Are you robbing this bank?"

"Brother, will you not greet me with a kiss? I haven't seen you in-"

"You were supposed to stay up north."

"I know. Things happened. I have been travelling around the world. I have much to tell you."

"You can tell me from jail. There can be only one penalty for breaking the law."

Black-Power stamped his foot and the shock wave cracked the floor and disabled the robbers, except Tope.

"Brother, there is no need for violence. This money is going to feed women and children in Angola."

Black-Power's eyes crackled with energy and dark intent. Tope scarcely recognised him. He was heart-broken that his brother would even contemplate aggression.

"You've been with the humans too long," said Tope. He levitated, flew out and up, away from Cape Town.

2015
Lagos, Nigeria

The waiter refilled his glass.

"When they reported it I was some kind of super-criminal coward. The men felt left behind, so perhaps there was some truth to it, but there were tears in my eyes," said Tope.

"Because you were brothers," said Elizabeth.

"Yes." He paused. "He looked so ridiculous in that fucking cape."

"It was kind of stupid, wasn't it?"

They both burst into laughter, loud brays of it which startled the other patrons and drew frowns from the genteel waiters.

"So what did you do?"

"Do? You know what I did. I made a costume of my own and fought back."

2015
South Africa

Black-Power wrapped his cape around him, feeling all the more fearsome for it.

The two men facing him didn't take their cues, one clicking the safety off his pistol, the other steadying his automatic rifle.

He waved Thembeka behind him, so that she was completely hidden behind his massive bulk.

"Please let me through," he asked politely.

"Or what?" laughed the man with the loaded pistol.

Black-Power hit them both with the same punch, a left hook Joe Frazier had once taught him, drilling both men into the wall with sickening thuds.

With a further flamboyant flourish, he kicked the barricaded door, bursting it into flying shrapnel shards of wood.

People turned and gawped at them from inside the large hangar. Most were busy carrying loads of chemicals between vats; several men swung automatic rifles towards them.

Six men, to be precise, thought Black-Power dryly, before exploding into action.

He took all six men out of action in less than thirty seconds.

The seventeen others dropped what they were doing and cowered against the far wall.

Too easy, he thought, I need a real test... I need the Pan-African.

Lost in thought, Black-Power failed to notice a large man enter the room through a door opposite them, a Rocket Propelled Grenade launcher locked and loaded on his left shoulder, which he swung around, but it was too late.

The man fell and curled over, dead. The RPG launcher bounced once on the floor, but did not explode.

Slowly, Black-Power turned to the woman standing next to him, who was lowering a pistol she had picked up earlier.

The Last Pantheon

"I find the heart an easier target than the head," said Thembeka.

Black-Power felt his own heart lurch a little, his head no longer lost in a forthcoming duel with the Pan-African.

Or, indeed, quite so full of that smooth, beautiful interviewer he'd recognised, Elizabeth Kokoro.

"Let's call the drugs and toxicology units in," Thembeka said.

Black-Power felt his rage grow, as he wondered along shelves bubbling with fluids fuelled by caskets of rat poison, methamphetamine, and boxes of anti-retroviral medication.

The Pan-African was wrong. He has—and could still—help this world to be a better place.

Like he had; back in '76.

1976

He had not predicted the death of Hector Pieterson. Indeed, June 16th had come as a huge shock to him. His contacts had warned of growing discontentment from many, but his contacts were mature men, out of touch with the youngsters of the day and the real levels of rage.

Furious youngsters these were, who did *not* want to learn the language of the oppressor, Afrikaans.

On that day, their youthful protests had turned into smoke, teargas, bullets, and blood.

Black-Power stood sombrely on a field nearby, watching, as a white unit of the South African Defence Force gathered with a fleet of military vehicles. They had been called in to support the police, who were running, shooting, and sjambokking youngsters, further away, just outside Phefeni Junior Secondary School in Soweto, their actions misted by teargas and smoke from many fires.

The screams of the schoolchildren had already curdled his blood enough. It took all of his immense will to stop himself launching into the police to halt the mayhem.

A brigadier was briefing his troops.

This, he could stop.

With a few giant strides he was almost amongst them.

Rifles clattered, raised.

The brigadier, moustached and with thick sideburns, turned to him with a pallid face, "You will not stop us, Black-Power."

Black-Power spat on the ground in front of him. "You will not do any more. The police have done more than enough."

The brigadier gave a thin smile and waved to the ranks, which parted.

A man stepped through, close to seven foot of rippling muscle and sinew, his bare chest like a pinkish barrel above his camouflaged trousers and brown leather boots. Tattooed in black on his chest were the words: 'Super-Boer'.

He was blond and bland, a giant of a man who would have made Hitler proud.

The brigadier snickered: "We have bred our own superhero, Weapon Z, with the right balance of steroids and other hormones. Super-Boer can lift a car, you know."

"Oh," said Black-Power. "Well, I'm impressed."

He hit the blond giant then, a right jab into the midriff.

The man's breath escaped in a long whooosshhh of pain and he slowly crumpled in on himself, as his breath almost deserted his body.

Black-Power knew he would not get up.

"This stops now," he said.

The brigadier stepped back as rifles were levelled at Black-Power behind him.

Black-Power flicked his cape in readiness.

Smoke and fading screams drifted across them. Black-Power felt his eyes sting, but kept his gaze steady, his body poised to fight.

The brigadier coughed into a handkerchief, "Okay, okay, you win. We will call off this particular operation, but..."

Black-Power waited tensely for the condition.

"...You will consider a sum to keep yourself in check."

"You will pay me not to act?"

"Sekerlik," assured the man, swallowing.

Black-Power hesitated. Perhaps now was the time to sweep aside the last bastion of colonialism, allied as it was to a particularly ugly ideological racism.

But *that* bloodshed would be huge indeed.

He could conceivably do more, quietly, behind the scenes.

"Private untraceable anonymous account," he said, feeling sick and as if he'd sold his soul to Satan, "...*and* you close the Weapon Z programme."

The troops were heading back to their vehicles. The brigadier hesitated, nodded and left.

Black-Power turned to race across the field to help the injured and dying schoolchildren.

He had surely stopped a complete and final bloodbath.

But at what cost?

Tope would never let me hear the end of this, should he know about this deal, he thought, cradling a young girl's head, feeling for a pulse.

There was none.

He choked in grief and horror.

Her face was twisted in death-pain, bloodied, wet from tear-gas tears; her school uniform torn and smelling of blood and ash.

He cried too.

What will her mamma and tata say and feel? Tope must *never* find out.

But as for the Soweto uprising, this was only just the beginning...

And so Black-Power became the call, eventually finding a fatal focus in Steve Bantu Biko.

As for me, he thought, as he drifted through the decades back to the present, I remain enduringly alive and increasingly tired of living.

2015

Detective Sipho Cele scrolled through pictures of Elizabeth Kokoro on his phone. He found them interesting, captivating, a distraction from work and his incessant pain.

47

They'd cleaned out the Super-Tik factory, but four more had spawned subsequently.

The work of a superhero is never done, he thought absently, marvelling at how well Kokoro had aged over the decades.

He was suddenly aware of Thembeka standing behind him. "She's not bad looking for an old bitch," she said.

Sipho swivelled and scowled in his chair.

"It's not what you think," he said.

She laughed and went back to her desk. "So what am I thinking then, Detective?"

For a moment he toyed with teasing thoughts out of her. He knew Tope as the Pan-African had developed his own talents along those lines, very well indeed.

"Okay," he said, "I have no idea what you are thinking."

But to himself, he thought, Brother (with a sudden chill of recognition and fear), are we to be the death of each other?

Thembeka studied Black-Power from across the room, rustling the papers in front of her PC. Deep inside her, she felt the faintest stirrings of an ancient ancestral power—he's thinking of death, she realised with a sudden and perplexing certainty.

2015
Lagos, Nigeria
Tope could not sleep. It wasn't that he wasn't tired, and it was not insomnia per se. He was sleepy. Elizabeth Kokoro's mind was too noisy for him to get any rest.

She lay naked beside him tangled in the sheets, one breast visible like a Renaissance painting, chest rising and falling with predictable regularity. She looked peaceful.

He could not hear her breathing over the hum of the air conditioner. He idly wondered if she was a millionaire. She did not have a room; she had a suite. Maybe the cable company paid or one of the husbands.

Incoherent nonsense leaked out of her in spurts. Fragments from blogs, tweets, status updates, junk mail headings. It was as if her brain was a web browser.

Ben changed status to it's complicated.
Pictures of my cat.
Ope's thanksgiving photos!
Anselem liked your post!

Banal, banal, banal! Why was this shit on her mind? She must spend hours surfing the net, looking for news stories.

The lovemaking had been surprising, tender. Given her sharp edges he had expected harshness, vigour, pain even. But no. She liked to be held softly and kissed, although she did not resist Flaubert's suppleness and corruption.

His phone beeped. It was Bank.

<Shall I pack? Are we still leaving tomorrow?>

Tope stole a glance at Elizabeth's nipple.

<Call the desk. Book an extra day.>

1975
Tope wandered around the fabric sellers in Idumota, sometimes slipping between adjacent Molue buses. He searched for a suitable length of Ankara cloth.

He needed something durable. Some of the less savoury sellers soaked the fabric in starch so that it seemed stiff. One wash and it would degrade right before your eyes.

When he found what he wanted he haggled and traded insults with the seller. An onlooker unfamiliar with the market would think it was a family squabble, not a transaction. Once they settled on a price, they became best friends and swore eternal fealty for sixteen generations.

Then he hopped on a bus and visited the more upmarket Kingsway and UTC general stores to find a diving suit. Not easy since scuba diving was not a serious pastime in Nigeria, but he found something next to a vicious-looking harpoon gun. The shop assistant said they sold more of the guns than the suits.

It was late so he took a taxi back to his flat in Fola Agoro. On the centre table he had a pencil sketch of a costume completed earlier. He would be everything Black-Power was not. He had that black mask that covered his head with a slit for eyes and an opening for nose and mouth. Tope would not have a mask. He ground up charcoal in a mortar with a pestle and mixed it with Vaseline. This he smeared around his eyes and part of his forehead in an irregular jagged shape. Using a manual Singer sewing machine, which he had owned since 1969, he sewed the fabric into a dashiki. He cut up the diving suit and wore the bottom half as tights.

He would not have a cape. Fuck Black-Power.

He would not have boots like Black-Power. He would go barefoot. Like an African. A Pan-African. *The* Pan-African.

He liked the name. It fit his political ideas.

He stood in front of the full length mirror.

Shit, I look ridiculous too.

2015

"What are you thinking?" asked Elizabeth. She sat up in bed leaving her bosom in full view. He went to the bed and kissed her. Elizabeth's arms came up, circled his neck, and drew him closer still. The flow of internet detritus stopped abruptly.

He broke the kiss. "You want to know what's cooler than a waterbed?"

She raised her eyebrows.

He levitated them both above the bed.

Soon, they were kissing again.

1976
Bol, Chad

My God, he's fast.

The Pan-African barely dodged the fifth punch in Black-Power's flurry of blows. There was an earthquake in his skull. An earthquake with pretty lights dancing across his vision.

The wind and the rain confused him. All Tope could see were grey skies and sheets of water coming into his eyes. Water and the fists of his brother. He was spinning and could not tell which way was up.

Black-Power could not fly, and he was not holding on to the Pan-African. How the hell was he in the air so much? He was gone again. Tope tried to orient himself. There was a crack of thunder and impact. Black-Power was back, digging body shots into the Pan-African's belly. He was seeing black dots. What?

Shit, am I losing consciousness?

It was his ambush. He was supposed to have the advantage of surprise. Black-Power had recovered so quickly, surprise meant nothing.

Headshot. The whole world shook. Even the rain drops fucking shook. He had to get away. Lake Chad was somewhere, above or below.

Fly away. Pick a direction and fly away. The direction doesn't matter. He'll kill you.

Fuck, fuck, fuck.

He flew, fast as he could manage. He knew he was moving, but the wind was so powerful that he couldn't tell where he was. The horizon was gone. No reference point. He heard a thump, and he knew that meant Black-Power had taken one of his powerful leaps.

51

The Pan-African directed himself away from the sound. He tried to take a breath, but it was mostly water and he coughed. His dashiki was tattered.

Fly above the storm.

He spat, and the blood-stained phlegm hit him right back in the face.

He felt a separate rush of air. The sonovabitch missed him by inches and fell back to the earth, sticking his right middle finger out at the Pan-African as he fell.

Tope flew the other way, into the clouds.

2015
Lagos, Nigeria

Tope took a sip of the fresh orange juice Elizabeth offered.

"Well!" said Elizabeth. She was swaddled in the hotel's white fluffy bathrobe.

"What?"

"That was new."

"I bet you say that to all the boys."

"I'm serious."

"I'm hungry."

Elizabeth shoved a buttered croissant in his general direction and poured more juice. She handed him the glass and drank straight from the jar. Room service had delivered two glasses but one had been smashed in a bout of passion.

"You surf the net a lot," said Tope.

"What do you mean? Have you been reading my mind again?"

"Not intentionally. You leaked stuff. Nothing organised, but it kept me awake. All of it was web shit."

"It's a long story. I'm...well, I'm sort of plugged into the web."

A phrase popped into her head, *web witch*, but Tope did not know what it meant. He was about to ask, but her phone rang. She had a Fela ringtone. He knew the song: 'Zombie'—not about the undead, but the soldiers who obey orders without question.

Elizabeth nodded, hummed, hemmed and hawed. "I'll get back to you."

"Who was that?"

"Do you know Lekan Deniran?"

"No."

"He's the biggest promoter in the country, some say on the continent."

"Look at my face. This is my impressed expression. Notice how similar it is to my don't-give-a-shit expression. What does he want from you?"

"Not me. You." She tied a strip of cloth around her hair.

"And?"

"He wants to promote a fight between you and Black-Power."

50,000 B.P.
What would become South Africa

The elder watched his younger brother stride off to the north, with a heavy heart.

Will I see you again, brother he thought to himself. Be safe—and stay good.

He half hoped his brother could pick up his slightly guarded sentiment, but within mere moments he was gone from view, hidden under a forest canopy.

The small group of primates they had witnessed together, returning from a hunt, were gathered around their injured one. The primate was clasping at blood dripping from a red hole amongst his left set of ribs, slowly stumbling to his hands and knees.

The elder—he decided to call himself Umvelinqangi, or Sky God then—watched, with some dispassionate interest, as the group gathered around their stricken group member, now panting his distress into the stubby grasslands.

The largest male amongst them was carrying a squat warthog, oozing serous fluids down his broad back.

Two of the healthy primates picked up short stabbing flint spears, red from their hunt.

What would it be?

Stabbing their injured male or stabbing and eating?

Umvelinqangi caught a flurry of sub-linguistic neural activity, watching postures shift with fluid non-verbal communications; a nod here, a grunt there.

The primates lowered the spears under their injured ones arms and chest at the front, pelvic region at the back. Another group member stepped forward and with forest vine, secured the hafts of the spear to arms and legs.

Four of them shifted to grasp the ends of the spears and hoisted their injured one into the air.

He was now slumped and unconscious, but they were taking him home. The giant with the dead warthog pointed onwards.

The Last Pantheon

The hunting party of eight began their march across the grassy terrain, heading for a large cave at the foothills of the mountains—uKhahlamba thought Umvelinqangi, that shall be their name—towering blue-tall in the distance, clouded or perhaps even snow-capped.

Suddenly, he felt at home, more than he had ever felt in fifty thousand Earth equivalent cycles on his home planet.

With one stride he was amongst the group.

They scattered in terror, for he was much larger and more powerful than they and wearing shining fabric, like nothing they had ever seen.

This primate will not last the journey, bleeding like this, he thought, and removed some healing kenth from a pouch on his belt. He spat onto the brown paste, rubbed it vigorously between his palms and then knelt down to apply it to the primate's broken skin, where a rib gaped through, white and ragged.

The group members were returning, hesitant, baring teeth and with raised arms threatening to stab at him with short wooden spears.

Umvelinqangi stood and spoke with a voice like thunder that made them all cower, including the giant, who had dropped the warthog in their initial scattering. "He will be well."

And, as if on cue, the primate groaned and opened his eyes.

The other primates fell to their knees, but Umvelinqangi knelt with them, heeding his own advice to his younger brother.

I will not be a god, I will live amongst you, he thought, knowing they could not understand him.

Above them, streaks of lights speared across the sky, shattered remnants of their ship.

He felt no loss for *that*.

Umvelinqangi felt his heart grow heavy again.

"Be safe, brother." (Somewhere, unbidden, the name 'Oduduwa' came to mind.)

Umvelinqangi gouged away marks on his cheeks with his fingernails, marks which traced their alien lineage, feeling lacings of his own blood dripping down his scarred cheeks.

And do *not* fail me, brother, he thought, for now I have become human, and we must show these becoming people, the way of good.

So it was that Umvelinqangi nursed an early Khoesaan man back to health—although for some days the treated man was seriously ill with a microbial infection, which reminded Umvelinqangi, just fleetingly, of his home planet.

1976
Bol, Chad

Black-Power watched the Pan-African streak away in the sky above, trailing an erratic spray of moisture and blood behind him.

A tropical storm brooded and flashed intermittently around him, as he cradled a bruised left forearm, feet anchored to the cracked earth waiting for the storm to spill fully.

Bastard's strong and quick, I'll give that to him, he thought, grudgingly.

Deep inside though, there was a wail of despair.

"Brother, *why* have you failed me?"

1976, now that was also a shit year, an esabeka year.

2015
South Africa

Thembeka was persistent in her hunt for the local Super-Tik Drug-Lord.

Detective Sipho could only admire her as she flung clues and tit-bits of information into her software algorithms; Vang-A-Dief©, Catch-A-Thief©, Bamba Isela©. Eventually she narrowed the Street Map search to a lush, loaded mansion in Bishop's Court, perched luxuriously on the rump of Table Mountain. He hurried over to her PC.

The detective sensed a drop in Thembeka's mood and noted her slumped shoulders as the Street Cams panned around the building, bulwarked with razor-wire, deadly electrics, and black-clad men armed with heavy artillery.

"No way through that," she groaned.

"Who said anything about going through?" asked Black-Power, caped and hulking at her right shoulder.

Night fell early in the Western Cape winter, aided by a dull, cloudy sky and a bitter northwester.

Black-Power and Thembeka sat in the back of a marked Eskom van, apparently busy with monitoring faltering electricity supplies to those few who slurped up the most.

But as blackness fell, hardly kept at bay by flickering, pallid, orange street lights, they crept out of the van. Black-Power embraced her protectively with his cape as she finished holstering her pistol, safety off.

"Ready?" he asked, thrilling to her close warmth, the tangy smell of a spicy perfume.

"Ready," she grinned up at him.

He braced his calves and with a light but firm bounce he was soaring over the walls and heading down towards the roof, carefully aiming for the part of the house likeliest (87.4% prediction) to hold the drug lord, only known as Zumba.

They crashed through the roof with an explosive shower of tile, wood, and mortar, Thembeka safely shrouded in Black-Power's Kevlar cape and arms.

He landed with a steely bracing of his booted legs on a meeting room table, crashing through to the marble floor below.

Debris clattered down around them as Black-Power swept the remnants of the table away. Thembeka spun, unfurled from his cape, across the floor, pistol cocked, sliding on her knees, trying to find a target.

Automatic fire opened up at the imposing target of Black-Power. He laughed then, a booming, bursting laugh that dropped the remains of the roof on top of them all; the eight gunmen stopped shooting, confused.

The smoke cleared to reveal a small man in a purple satin suit standing quietly amongst his bodyguards, Zumba. Without warning he broke into a sudden spin, pirouetting like flickering lightning across the empty space, and seized Thembeka from behind with his left arm. He hauled her to her feet, a human shield in front of Black-Power, knife in his right hand at her throat.

"Super-Tik," Zumba said, "speeds you up. Leave, or she dies."

Black-Power hesitated—and blood spilled suddenly from Thembeka's throat.

Bang!

Zumba staggered backwards.

Thembeka had her left arm twisted behind her, her pistol wafting the barest tendril of smoke.

Zumba dropped like a puppet without strings as Thembeka clutched at her throat frantically, staunching the blood.

With one leap, Black-Power had seized her and exploded out of the house.

Landing near the van outside the mansion, Black-Power burst open the back door with a forceful finger, panicking.

Inside, he laid Thembeka gently down, securing the door from the inside.

When he turned around, Thembeka was sitting up and staring at him, a soft and bemused expression on her face

Black-Power noted a drying trickle of blood down the front of her throat.

"You're, okay," he croaked.

She smiled.

He leant across the floor of the van and kissed her.

Softly.

Slowly.

She slapped him.

"What was that for?" He asked, aggrieved, sure for once he had not read her signals wrong.

"That's for thinking of Kokoro while kissing me," she snapped.

He was speechless.

Thembeka stood up and pushed at the door. It buckled outwards and she jumped through the burst metal of the door.

Black-Power could only stare after her.

How did she do that?

How on earth did she know what he was thinking?

And her slap had actually...hurt!

Then a slow and ancient memory came to him. A faintest taste of something he had used up some millennia ago.

Kenth.

He had always marvelled at his anatomical and DNA similarities to emerging humans—life-forms on planets separated by light years, but with puzzling similar evolutionary pathways. Not completely compatible however, his sperm was infertile with humans—perhaps just as well, he thought to himself wryly.

His realisation was clear—Kenth had bound to the DNA of that primate he had helped heal, seventeen millennia back.

And he had kissed that man's very distant long-lost descendant.

Thembeka's thin and dormant strand of alien DNA had somehow become activated...perhaps at their first touch?

...And she had indeed read his mind.

"Thembeka, come back!" he called.

But all he could hear was the gathering sound of police sirens.

2015
Lagos, Nigeria

On the table was a scale model of a modified geodesic dome, although Tope felt sure that Buckminster Fuller never intended his invention for this purpose. Elizabeth squeezed his hand once. He glanced at her briefly, then focused his mind on what Lekan was saying.

"Titanium lattice shell with carbonised steel geodesics, a non-rigid structure which will snap back after impact. One hundred thousand small cameras all around which will give spectators true 3D, not that crap you see in the multiplexes. I plan to project the conflict into stadia worldwide."

Lekan Deniran wasn't a tall man, but he was charismatic and energetic. His eyes burned with that fever that afflicts avaricious men everywhere. He talked with a pace that accelerated when he got to the financial reward. Dark, wiry, relentless. Dressed simple in jeans and a t-shirt because, it was rumoured, he saw Donald Trump dressed like this once in Time magazine.

"Tell me about the kinematics of this thing," said Tope. "I don't want any bystanders getting hurt. What amount of force will this structure resist?"

"Fifty thousand pounds was the limit of testing," said Lekan.

"Is that a lot?" asked Elizabeth.

"Your high performing boxer can punch about twelve hundred pounds," said Lekan.

"Black-Power is an Ubermensch, not a sportsman," said Tope.

"Do you think he can punch with more force than that?" asked Lekan.

"I don't know."

"Can you?"

"I don't know. I don't use force in that way. I don't punch with muscular strength," said Tope.

"Explain," said Elizabeth, ever the journalist.

"My powers are mental. I levitate, and that becomes flight. I lift objects. I detect thoughts. I have a limited force field around my body. When I punch what I do is push with my mind. The mass of the object should not matter, but because I see with my eyes the difference between a pebble and a boulder the effort I apply is different. I should be able to punch a hole in the moon theoretically, but my brain tells me it's impossible, so I can't."

"Can you beat him?" asked Lekan, handing drinks to them.

Tope didn't answer, a brief flash of red desert sand, snow, and a twinge in his malformed arm distracted him.

Lekan shrugged. "It doesn't matter. We'll all be rich at the end of it. We stand to make a gazillion bucks domestic alone."

"How will you get him to agree to the bout?" asked Elizabeth.

Lekan hesitated. "I'm still trying to contact his people."

"Does he have people?" she asked.

"I don't know, but if he does, I'll find them." He emptied his glass and poured another. "I'm flying to South Africa tomorrow. I'll find him."

"How did you get him to the desert?" asked Elizabeth.

"I sued for peace," said Tope. "I offered a truce. I tried to appeal to his rationality by showing the futility of our enmity."

"So how did it turn to a battle?" asked Elizabeth.

"The man has no rationality."

February 18, 1979
Sahara Desert

"This is why you brought me here?" asked Black-Power. "To discuss books and the deranged theories of cocaine-addicted alienists?"

They stood apart from each other, scrub and red sand between them. Eddies carried dust in chaotic ballets.

61

"It's time for this to end," said the Pan-African. "This farce. I've been reading Berne's work. This thing between you and me, it's a game. We're playing 'hero', brother."

"What is this babbling? You sound like a baboon."

"We don't really want to kill each other. I'm trying to educate you and you are trying to chastise a younger brother. Neither of us is playing for keeps. This battle will last forever, with continued attrition and no real resolution. Come the day that this sun goes nova we'll still be standing."

"You're right about one thing," said Black-Power. "I am trying to chastise you. I have done many times."

"I won't fight you this time."

"Then you'll die because I won't hold back."

"Death, then," said the Pan-African. At the time, he meant it.

2013
Edo City

The wedding dress was off-white and the shoes scuffed, but the radiance of the bride's smile did a lot to neutralise the imperfections. The ring-bearer led her to the courtyard, a boy of nine with a solemn expression on his face. The drummers picked up a frenzied beat and barefoot dancers began their performance. The mother of the bride wailed as if someone had died. Everybody sang. A few of the older men were drunk and off-key, but nobody cared.

The bride was pregnant. Tope could hear the proto-thoughts of the growing child. She already recognised her mother's heartbeat and voice. The mother was, as yet, unaware of the life growing in her.

"So, what do you say?" asked Elizabeth Kokoro. She was irritating in the extreme.

"Miss Kokoro, you're not invited to this wedding."

"It's a lot of money."

"We shoot mo gbo, mo ya in these parts, you know."

"We'll get your side of the story. Finally, after all these years."

The Last Pantheon

The groom danced with the little bride. Tope had bought the suit, but it didn't fit the man well. Some men wheeled in gigantic black loud speakers and started playing juju music. In between bowls of jollof rice people took to the dance floor, spraying money on each other.

"It doesn't matter to me if anyone gets to hear my side of the story. I know what happened." He took a bite out of a fried chicken thigh. He deliberately chewed with his mouth open to seem as crude as possible. He offered the drumstick to her, but she ignored it. He bit it again. "Go back to the city, girl. I'm busy here."

"With the society wedding of the century?" she said.

"Do not mock these people. They are poor, but their emotions are genuine. They have dignity."

"Ahh, good. Anger. I was starting to feel that nothing meant anything to you anymore."

"God, you're like a tsetse fly, buzzing around. Go away."

She took the drumstick from him and tore a piece of flesh, then spoke with her mouth full. "I saw you once, you know. In Accra in '77."

Something dawned on Tope. "You took those photographs of me and Black-Power fighting in the water reservoir."

"Yes."

"The first clear photos the news outlets had of me. Not very flattering if I remember." Black-Power had his boot on Tope's chest and his cape flew in the wind. It was a poster and t-shirt graphic and the second major internet meme after 'All your base are belong to us', according to Bank.

"I had to crawl through mud to get there."

"I remember you. Skinny little girl, you looked like a worm."

Not really. She had looked like a snake with breasts.

"Did you hate me?"

"No, I just mildly resented you."

"Come do the TV show."

"No."

But Tope did.

2015
Lagos, Nigeria

On the road back to the settlement, Bank shoved a screen in front of his face.

"What am I looking at?" said Tope.

"That's Black-Power," said Bank.

Tope looked at the tablet and saw the tube video. Mobile phone footage of a few indistinct blurs and a shadow that might have been a cape. Maybe a sub-machine gun in the footage. A woman on the ground. A dog. *A dog?*

"This is blurry," said Tope.

"It's Black-Power. He's back. Read the comments. The guy who was there saw him. It's just a few days ago."

"This is a guy in a mask and cape, Bank. He's wearing a box shirt and chinos. That was never-"

"Trust me. The interweb never lies."

"The interweb lies all the time."

"Whatev. They're bigging up your upcoming bout with him," said Bank. He snatched his tablet back and started moving his fingers around again.

"I haven't agreed to do it."

"Uncle, with that money we can bribe enough government officials to practically own the land on which we live. We won't have to go to court. You can feed people or something. Send more of us to university."

"I know."

"Then what?"

"It's cheap."

"Tens of millions of-"

"Not that kind of cheap. I mean, we're not back street pugilists." We are gods, and we do not fight for your entertainment, he thought but did not say aloud.

Bank said, "Do not think we are unappreciative of you, Uncle. I love you more than my father."

"Your father left before you were born. You've never met him."

"Yes, and I love you more than I love him."

The Last Pantheon

"Go back to your tablet, Bank."

Tope watched the countryside go by.

'*Do not let them begin to worship you*', his brother had said, yet Black-Power was the one who allowed it to happen first.

He felt the hair on his neck rise; Elizabeth was thinking of him. Miles away, but he could still feel her thoughts.

It was time for one last fight. In Lekan's arena they would put it to rest once and for all.

1800 to 1828
Kwa-Zulu Natal Midlands

The boy grew up a bastard, but Dingiswayo—as the elder allowed himself to be known then—recognised something special in that boy. As the boy became a young man, he was prone to angry outbursts to be sure, rising as he did to the frequent challenges of his fully parented peers. One day he had even run a twelve mile return journey through thorn-tree foothills to head off and return seven cattle from the neighbouring Langeni tribe—having silently cut the throat of one of their herders.

So, when that fiery bastard became a full man, his circumcision scars long healed, Dingiswayo gave him an ibutho lempi, his own fighting regiment.

This should channel his energies constructively, thought the elder. Aloud, he said: "Be careful with your men, Shaka, their lives and their families are in your keeping."

The young man respectfully avoided his gaze, as if indeed restrained and finally maturing, "Yes, my Chief."

But, in ongoing skirmishes with the neighbouring tribes, Shaka retained his impulsive and reckless manner, somehow knowing the best times to do so. He was almost always victorious. On the death of their father, Sigujano—Shaka's half-brother—was the rightful heir to the vacant throne. Dingiswayo then helped Shaka to seize military control. The elder was taken by surprise, however, when Shaka had his brother executed.

How can you kill your own brother the elder wondered, thinking of his own younger brother, up north for millennia now.

The elder, using vestiges of his mental manipulation, eventually feigned his own murder as Dingiswayo, at the hands of Zwide, the Chief from the Ndwanwe clan—and waited to see what would happen. He now observed the proceedings as Shaka's bodyguard, his own features additionally altered by the slightest of projected imaginal suggestions.

And as months rolled into years, King Shaka shaped his people around him, the Bodyguard watching, always watching—but sometimes fighting, reining in his strength, so as not to alarm those around him too much, particularly the King.

For the King was building an empire.

Shaka had quickly stopped the initiation rights for boys to men, manhood no longer stemming from wasted strength in circumcision rites, but in active age-cohort regiments, along with training and strategy, military strategy. And weapons, new weapons (throwing spears that are lost on the battlefield, the assegais, were moved to a secondary weapon). A new short stabbing spear, an iklwa, was adopted, alongside a bigger cowhide shield that was used offensively, after Shaka had showed the superiority of these new weapons in bloody training bouts that resulted in some men—even friends—dying.

"From now on, a man who loses his iklwa in battle will lose his life," said the King, as his impi warriors and empire grew rapidly. For this was the start of Mfecane, the 'crushing', the making of a mighty people who expanded into occupying a huge geographical space, absorbing many, leaving many others dead or fleeing into the expanses before them.

Down towards the southern seas of this vast continent...

But, thankfully, some things did not change. Still, mothers and often grandmothers, when they could, sang and recited the old tales that spoke to them all; stories about Why the Cheetah's Cheeks are Stained and even older stories from the very beginning, about how the Sky-God, Umvelinqangi, made the world and how the First Man/God, Nkulunkulu, emerged from watery reeds with his wife, able to draw on thunder and lightning.

I am indeed Zulu, thought the Bodyguard elder on these good evenings, sitting nearby as the women thrilled the children with these tales, enjoying hearing his ancient name being dropped in these living tales, as well as thinking about the brutal genius of his King, who finally defeated and killed Zwide, Dingiswayo's supposed murderer.

In time though, word came to Shaka from startled and shaken scouts, of a new people, perhaps gods or devils, who were as white as crushed limestone.

They too were moving, but moving steadily up towards the amaZulu; slowly, yet inexorably.

Evolutionary brother primates, thought the Bodyguard to himself, perhaps returning from milder climes where their melanocytes have not been so active? So brother will meet brother again at last, reunited.

Ever looking for allies and advantage, Shaka invited some of them in.

But these white brothers and sisters brought firearms, disease, and not the slightest recognition of their long lost family...

As for Shaka, the Bodyguard was deployed elsewhere when his half-brothers Dingane and Mahlangana murdered him in turn.

What is it about brothers, the elder thought grimly on hearing the news.

2015
Strandfontein Beach

There is a place where many wild gulls breed, along a sandy cliff on the False Bay coast of the Cape Town outskirts, just past Strandfontein. The place is protected, a sanctuary for gulls to breed together and fly free, unhindered by humans, searching for fish and scatterings of white and black mussels, which they raise on high and drop, to shatter on the rocks below, exposing pale, delicate meat, ripe for the taking.

From this gull sanctuary, a man or woman, if they are tall enough, can cast their gaze inland across the Cape Flats, where a vast expanse of informal settlements shines in the sun. Mostly shacks cobbled and jury-rigged from tin, aluminium, chipboard, and wire, rain-proofed with black plastic bags or sheets, some sprouting wide and circular satellite dishes. This township is home to over half a million, stitched together in districts such as Mandela Park, Tembani, and Harare.

So it was that Black-Power stood and watched, a man indeed tall enough to see much, who saw with an acute and painful vision, that vast and chaotic spread of Khayelitsha Township. This place was but one of a multitude of the enduring legacies of apartheid, some indeed now improved since liberation.

This place was certainly not one of those that had been hugely improved, despite money swilling around for twenty years since the first democratic elections in South Africa.

Some electrification, surely, to cast light on a dark place... but not enough light! There was indeed a good reason he had chosen mid-day.

Slowly Black-Power shook his head. He preferred to look at the opulent parts of the central metropolis—like the view from his office as Detective Cele—not at this huge broken patchwork of poverty, where TB and the HIV virus continued to wreak their deadly havoc. It was not a good reminder. For all his power, he had actually achieved so little.

His... brother, had never tired of reminding him of this!

Black-Power turned to look at the sea instead, an easier and more pleasant sight, where the incessant roll of surf on white sand soothed his mind, yet also somehow reminded him of how old he had become. Perhaps he should just head home, it was a Saturday after all, or he could catch a movie at the Waterfront, the new Tarantino film was supposed to be brilliant and he had an invite to a VIP preview as Black-Power.

Alone. He would be alone.

Clenching his fist, he looked down at the ripple of muscle along his wrist, underneath his black Kevlar-laced glove. He was Black-Power for fuck's sake, he had stopped volcanoes and faced whirlwinds, he could handle one little paltry... visit.

Steeled, he turned to face the sparkling sea of shiny shacks, alien vision searching for the small bricked day hospital far in the distance, at the locale of Site C, Khayelitsha.

There. Got it. Shit, that's quite some distance, out on the far distant extreme range of his jumps.

But he knew, if he took a slower or more mundane way in a taxi, or bus, his commitment would falter and he would change his route, heading home—or anywhere else. However, the shacks were so densely packed, there was no way he could risk taking more than one jump.

There, that field, next to the hospital, was dusty and open, uninhabited.

Good training too, should he ever need to face his brother again.

Come on focus, bend, brace... No! Not enough purchase here, the sand was shifting beneath his bulk, sliding away under his boots. Perhaps he could have done this in the seventies.

Not now, his stomach was no longer quite so taut, his muscles did not sing quite so beautifully to him, with their clear sense of invulnerable power. So, with one small step, Black-Power bounced onto the empty beach road, legs together, recoil... and JUMP!

He hurtled high into the air like a homing missile, exhilarated by the wind-whistle of his passage and the warm cross-wind buffeting of a berg breeze drifting down from the Mountain. Below him, shacks blurred together in a moving chaotic collage, growing clearer, larger, and more distinct as he headed back towards the earth. He plummeted to the centre of the field near the hospital, his aim indeed true.

But now he could see some boys, six or seven of them, playing football with a small stack of positioned bricks marking their goals, scuffing sand as they chased the ball in the middle of the field.

"No!" he shouted, but the wind whipped his words over his shoulders and up into the sky, as he dropped like a lethal boulder.

One boy looked up and shouted, pointing.

"Is it a bird?" he thought he heard in isiXhosa and then he was dropping onto the stationery boy, whose mouth was gawping wide in sudden frozen shock.

Khayelitsha!

Black-Power landed on one foot, his second leg raised to avoid contact with the cowering boy, pushing away desperately to avoid impact. Sand and dirt exploded from the impact of his landing, showering the boy, as he bounced and rolled away, impelled by the forceful, juddering impetus of his left leg.

Black-Power finally rolled to a halt. Shit, he thought, I'm tangled in my fucking cape—and my leg hurts like hell.

He lay for some moments, trying to catch his breath.

The young boy stood over him, unhurt but sandy, holding a football. "Mister, can you be a referee for us, please?"

Black-Power unleashed a string of invectives in isiZulu, but he knew the boy would understand; they were cousin languages after all, united by the Mfecane. Slowly, he unrolled himself from his cape and sat up.

The field was now deserted.

Sighing with sudden guilt, he stood up gingerly, testing his left leg.

Fine. A bit sore, but it would pass. Not good news for you, my brother, he thought to himself, his gaze tracing a route from the hospital to a mixed spread of brick houses and shacks, some flattened for redevelopment.

There. That was the address. A small brick house just off the bend in the road feeding the hospital, he recognised it from an earlier zoom-in on Google Earth. Modest, but better than many other abodes here, he thought as he made his way towards the house, walking off his slight limp.

A small crowd had gathered on the outskirts of the field, whispering together, gazing at him in awe.

"I told you Black-Power was back," he heard one voice clearly amongst the clamour.

There were other voices, other words...and, and that
FUCKING word again! Even after so many years, it still
ripped deep into his being.

He had reached the road by then, the crowd parting before
him like the Red Sea to Moses, but he turned and roared: "For
the record, I was never an...an... Askari!" He spat the word so
they could see his contempt. "I never betrayed the Struggle...
Amandla!"

He raised his fist.

There was silence.

"Amandla!" he shouted again, louder, more urgent.

"Ngawethu," came a soft reply, from an older voice hidden
amongst the crowd.

"Born Frees!" he sighed with exasperation and, suddenly
feeling slightly foolish, he turned on his heels.

Thembeka was standing in front of him, fists on either side
of a broad-hipped black skirt, her red T-shirt etched with a
slogan in black: 'Pissed Off Woman'.

"Oh-" he took a step backwards. There was no need for her
to be so literal.

"Why couldn't you have just come quietly and knocked on
the door?"

"Uh-"

"My God, but you're inarticulate, even for a man."

"Sorry," he looked down at his dusty boots, feeling a rush of
blood to his face and the faster pattering of his heart.

She smiled then, even if it was gone in a flash.

"So," she said, fists now off her hips, hands opened wide,
"why have you come to see me then?"

A full taxi hooted, on its way to nearby Mitchells Plain.

They stepped quickly off the road, but an older man was
hurrying up to them, holding up a shiny object.

"Eh?" said Black-Power.

Thembeka burst out laughing.

It was an old comic book, glinting in a protective plastic
cover. An early 'Black-Power' comic from '75 that he
recognised, with his first face-off against the Pan-African and

an Angolan war back-story, pointing out the evils of the Cubans and the communist takeover by the MPLA.

"Would you mind signing this for me, Black-Power?" burbled the man, "It's in near-mint condition." The man was dressed in orange council overalls, perhaps a foreman in one of their service departments.

"How much would it be worth then?" Black-Power asked, smiling to himself. He himself had a *Chariots of the Gods* book, personally signed by von Daniken from that very same year.

The man shrugged awkwardly and Black-Power could tell by his lined face and greying hair he was probably upwards of fifty years old. But he was wearing a white #RhodesMustDie T-shirt on top of it all.

He took the offered pen and the opened comic book, braced against its protective backing board that had been part of the sealed package. The pen hovered over the opening splash page with its writing credits. Black-Power looked sharply at the waiting man, who stood, openly holding his breath.

"So," said Black-Power, "what do you think of my role in the Struggle?"

The man looked him in the eyes. "You should be recognised as a Struggle hero, because you challenged the apartheid regime every step of the way. And you only held back from a direct and open confrontation, in order to save many more lives."

Black-Power smiled. "So, to whom should I dedicate this?"

The surf pounded to his left, but they were alone. This stretch of the beach—between Monwabisi and the Strandfontein sewerage outlet—was often deserted, apart from the odd lone fisherman.

Still, Black-Power had never been a man of many words. He had even forgotten the alien language of his birth, only remembering faint echoes of no longer familiar sounds, loosely linked to vague images and objects; smells that tantalised him, that he could no longer name, a black sky and a red sun.

"So?" she said expectantly, hands on hips again, "What is happening to me? Why am I gaining these powers?"

He splayed his hands open to her, with a gesture of helpless ignorance. "My best guess is you may have tracings of an ...er, ancestor of mine's DNA, perhaps inserted into their genome during a microbial infection, which has become activated in the presence of my own powers."

"Oh," she looked down at the beach sand, kicking with her bare right foot at a brown piece of kelp. The kelp shot out over the furthest breaking wave. She looked up again, "Can you take these powers back?"

Slowly, he shook his head, aware she could read his mind anyway.

She turned away and he could tell from the slight shaking of her shoulders, she was crying.

He went over to her and touched her left shoulder gently. "I feel like such a freak," her words warbled back to him.

"Thembeka," he said, "I've always felt a freak."

She turned then and gave him a soft smile, "I'm sorry." Her arms were open, inviting.

He stepped forwards and embraced her.

Lovingly.

"Detective," she said sharply, "I can feel your...interest...and right now, I don't share it!"

He smiled into the nape of her neck. "That's okay, love," he said, "I've got more than enough interest for the both of us."

She kneed him hard...

...and her aim was true.

Slowly, and with much unfamiliar pain, he folded in on himself, until he was curled in a foetal position on the soft sand, clutching his deeply burning—now flaccid—penis and testicles.

She stood over him, legs astride, and he could feel the heat of her rage. "No means fucking NO. Okay? We've had enough of rape, corrective or otherwise, get it?"

74

The Last Pantheon

He lifted his head to look up at her.

Coldness grasped his heart. He could see a distant look in her eyes, as if he no longer existed to her.

"Sala kahle," she said. "Goodbye, Detective."

She looked up at the sun, as if concentrating and...flew.

He sat up, but she had gone, the gulls wheeling and screeching in her wake.

And, with a sudden aching realisation that made the pain in his privates feel trivial, he became aware that she would not come back.

Gone.

Like everyone does, eventually.

Gone.

Alone again.

Thembeka had flown off, just like the Pan-Fucking-African.

He pulled a cellphone out of a small utility clip in his cape.

"I've got more surprises than you'll like in this cape that you dared mock, brother!" He barked at the crashing waves.

Two calls.

One, to request a transfer to Johannesburg.

Jozi—where it's really happening! A real African city, not like this effete Europeanised pretender...

Two, to Phulani, AKA the Sharp-sharp Fixer.

"Get me Pan-African," he said, "Any way you can."

Time to end this, brother.

Finally, once and for all time.

1978
Lagos, Nigeria
Space.
He was not really here. This was a memory or a dream.
Hanging there was a space station, spiky, crystalline almost.
The hull was grown by a layer of bacteria genetically
modified to produce the bulkhead. It was constantly sheared
off and constantly regrown. Inside, there were hundreds of
individuals. Tope was once there. Sleeping for millennia,
aeons, time immeasurable in Earth terms.
 The memory wavers, then there is a skiff, broken off from
the space station, a needle, with dozens on board. A blue
planet. Beautiful. Atmospheric. The needle breaches the
atmosphere, shatters and the people scatter into different
areas of the landmass. Tope and his brother land in what will
be known as Africa. They land, steaming and smoking from
the heat of re-entry.
 Tope woke up.
 At first he did not know where he was. There were empty
Gulder bottles all around him, brown, broken, some half full.
His bottom felt cold and at first he felt he had wet himself,
but no, it was the cold of concrete.
 He had a headache and the world seemed too bright.
 "Pan-African, stay where you are!"
 A loud voice projected by a megaphone. Stern. Loud. Did it
have to be so loud?
 He waved the voice away and tried to open his eyes again.
Tope was in the centre of a crater. This was about a foot deep,
fifty yards wide. Cracked rocks radiated away from him. The
blackened carcass of a twisted bicycle smoked close by.
 What?
He could not remember the night before. There was spent
ordnance all around. He felt his body, nothing damaged. His
force field always kicked in when he was unconscious.
 God, he needed a piss.

He pulled down his Y-fronts and urinated, a long satisfying, steaming stream of yellow. Then he realised he was surrounded by the Nigerian army.

Ah, hence the debris and shells.

"Halt!"

"Please, I beg you, stop shouting," said Tope. "I have a hangover."

A shot rang out and others joined in. Tope's force field stopped the urine and the reflux caused pain to shoot up his pelvis. The bullets also managed to buffet him about. His head throbbed. *Oh, God. Why won't they leave me alone? What did I ever do to deserve this?*

He flew straight up into the sky. At a hundred feet he pissed over all of them.

"Golden shower, assholes!" He shook himself off and giggled. Maybe he was still a bit drunk. Fragments of the night before came back.

From that height he could see the devastation. The crater he woke up in was the tail end of a three-mile serpentine path of destruction which included broken shops, ruptured roads, twisted median strip railings, upturned cars, concertinaed lorries, uprooted street lights (they didn't work anyway!), snapped palm trees, downed power lines, cracked buildings, shattered glass, and clumps of...smouldering matter that he hoped to God were not the remains of human beings.

Fuck.

There were sawhorses and barricades keeping people at bay, and the army was in position with tanks, armoured vehicles, and a mounted multiple rocket launcher.

They fired up at him. He flew higher, then away. Had he done that? He had seen the Nigerian Army use a scorched earth approach in Obalende during the attempted coup in 1976. Tope could remember flattening the trucks. He got flashes of violence and laughter. Smiling lissom women. Booze. More booze. Music. Orlando Owo and Victor Uwaifo. Trumpets and guitars. *Groovy!*

He came down in Oworonsoki, near the Lagos Lagoon. Mostly unpaved streets with pools of relentless mud. Low-income residential area. Barefoot children. He staggered, swayed, and vomited into the stagnant water of the open gutters, disturbing the mosquito larvae as they incubated. A Danfo bus thundered by, spraying him with red mud. He attempted to be angry, but his headache was too severe. He giggled instead.

It was mid-morning and school children in primary colours stared at him as they went to seek an education. He stumbled along to a street called Kiniun-Ifa, and he heard Akpala music come from a kind of grotto. A hand was painted on the wall to the left of the door. An open eye-ball with crude lines spiking away from it lay on the palm. The fingers were all the same size, including the thumb, and they all pointed upwards.

Tope went in.

"Eka'abo," welcomed an old man. He was seated on the floor on a raffia mat, holding a necklace. He gestured to the mat.

Tope sat opposite him. He handed Tope a gourd of water, which went down in almost one gulp. A woman came with food, as if they were expecting him. Which, of course they were. The old man was an oracle, one of the real ones. It wasn't magic; some people were just better plugged into the quantum nature of time. If time was occurring all the time, all moments at once, then travel or prophecy was theoretically possible.

Tope asked to wash, and they led him to a backyard where a pail of water, plastic bowl, raffia sponge, and local ose okpa soap, waited on a sheet of corrugated tin. He took off his clothes and soaped himself. The water was cold, but he didn't mind.

He returned to the first chamber when he was done. He noticed for the first time a shrine off to the left, an earthenware alcove with a lit candle illuminating an information leaflet from W.H.O about small pox immunisation and a statuette of Sopana, the Yoruba god of small pox. With the eradication of small pox from Nigeria this was effectively a dead god.

The old man said some incantations over his necklace, and then held it between clasped hands.

"Ifa olokun, a s'oro d'ayo," the man said. "Blow."

Tope blew over his hands, feeling like a magician's assistant.

The old man threw the necklace to the mat and peered at it. He shook his head.

"What?" asked Tope.

"Iku," said the old man. "Death."

2015
Lagos, Nigeria

"Tell me about your childhood," said Elizabeth.

"I don't remember it," said Tope.

"Any of it?"

"That's right."

"Does that seem odd to you?"

"It does. I don't think Black-Power remembers either. I wonder if we were just created like this, or grown in a vat somewhere and then activated. Or perhaps we had our memories wiped."

"Let me send a car for you."

"…"

"Come on," said Elizabeth.

"I'm in the middle of something."

"The middle of what?"

"I'm writing something," said Tope.

"What a coincidence. So am I. What are you writing?"

He was writing a will, but he did not tell her. Instead he closed the chat window, intending to lie to her about a power failure. His phone rang immediately and it was her so he ignored it.

Tope did not have family among the humans, neither did he have any real money to speak of, but if the bout went ahead he would be rich, or rich and dead. He looked out of his window and saw the settlement. He had virtually built the whole place by hand. A young girl bounced by, revelling in her new pubertal body, a girl Tope had seen squalling and smeared with meconium on the day she was born. Her mother had died, but she had been adopted by the entire settlement. The government had not succeeded in kicking them out and Bank was right. With money they could buy a fucking ministry.

The bout would happen. Lekan had called and was spreading cash around Jo'burg. "No results yet. These motherfuckers are tight-lipped, but there's some guy here or around here called Fulani or something. He may know something. I'm meeting with someone who knows his second cousin tomorrow."

And so on.

He seemed to take for granted that Tope would fight.

February 18, 1979
Sahara Desert

"Fight me, you bastard," said Black-Power.

He smashed into the Pan-African with his right fist while holding him with the left.

Grains of sand rose off the desert floor with each hit, but the Pan-African's force field held fast. He felt no direct pain, but somewhere in his brain he felt weaker.

"I'm not afraid to die, Dingiswayo," said the Pan-African. "Are you?"

Black-Power head-butted him on the nose.

It got through.

And hurt.

2015
Radium Beer Hall, Johannesburg
Jozi, Jo'burg, Johannesburg, iGoli, City of Gold...
Your golden heart is eaten out, surrounded as you are now by huge piles of empty mine debris, smaller splashes of barricaded plushness, and far vaster brooding settlements of cheap brick and shantytown settlements. But, despite the emptying of your beating heart, you continue to burn, to throb...

Detective Cele, AKA Black-Power was here and at rest, with a pint of the finest Charles Glass has to offer—although Phaswane Mpe had expressed this state of being far more eloquently, when he was alive and welcoming people to the Jo'burg suburb of Hillbrow.

Cele was slumped in his old favourite beer-hall from the 1930s—although then he had to put up with drinking in a back-door shebeen section, apartheid well on its way, even before the Nats got to power in '48. He'd even put on his old brown trilby hat from the 50s, sharp end crammed low onto his forehead, dark coat—Wesley Snipes *Blade* style—draped over his formidable bulk.

Still, he was indeed at rest, albeit grudgingly nursing his beer, because alcohol—like so many of the viruses and bacteria around him—had limited impact on his physiology. He envied those who lost control of their speech and functions as they drank, gradually slurping their way into oblivion.Like the young white man sitting opposite him, who was seemingly not frightened by his bulk—or his silence.

The immediate seats around them in the Radium Beerhall were empty, as if people could sense his brooding, fragile peace.

The detective was trying to work out whether the man— apparently Colin Jordaan—was seeking a payoff of companionship or sex.

"So they left me," said Colin, drooping into his emptied beer mug, "and I got no fucking idea why."

Perhaps he's looking for a shrink? The detective, as always, decided to cut to the chase.

"Man or woman?" he asked.

"Eh?" the young man lifted his long orange curls out of his mug, "Uhhhh... Joey's a...dude."

Maybe sex then. The detective smiled to himself. He'd enjoyed a number of male encounters down the decades, but he had been forced to reign in that side of himself—he had an image to maintain, after all.

He patted Colin's hand gently, but the man still winced through his drunken stupour.

As Black-Power, the detective had been attacked by the gender brigade in the past for not embracing more sexual ambiguity and variety, especially in the light of declared Gender Wars and violence. As always, somehow he found himself on what felt like the wrong side, trying to straddle a fence that was impossible to balance on, despite all of his super-powers.

But he knew—from long history—that culture was certainly not set in stone.

Tope's comments had always hurt, when he challenged his asserted umZulu identity—for Cele sensed the truth in this, although he did not want to face the void of identity as to who he really was, underneath the suit and mask...

Brother, yes, maybe a long time ago. So long ago he had no recall of any mother or father, he seemed to have been born old and almost eternal.

The detective had a sudden impulse to whip off his dark overcoat to reveal his Black-Power suit, to don his mask, pick up this young man, and walk past gasping patrons of this restaurant-pub, who would be snapping away at him with cell-cameras.

A pudgy, dark and greying man, suited in tribal Afro-Amani chic, shoved the drunken youth off his chair.

The young man could only say "shitttt...," before falling in a complaining heap on the floor. He had enough control, however, to lever himself up onto a chair at the next table, glowering his discontent.

He was not noticed, the detective and the Suit crouching over their Castles, mumbling.

"You're looking older, Phulani," observed the detective, with the eye of one who misses little.

"And you're fucking not..." scowled the pudgy man, wrinkled and grey, with the air of a man who had seen everything under the sun.

"So," said the detective, "what news?"

"Pan African," said the old man slowly, "wants one last bout. A final decider. To the death, winner takes all."

The detective rocked back on the couch, which creaked its protest at his 200kgs and almost 7 foot of mass. "Really? What's his conditions?"

Phulani looked around the Beerhall slowly and then leaned forward. "We've got to wait for, wait for it, Lekan Deniran."

The detective stroked his chin, smiled, "Ah, the huge fight promoter—Pan-African always did aim big."

He hauled out his cell and opened his messages, but there were none—still—from Thembeka, his phone seemingly blocked to her.

He tapped in a message and sent, but nothing happened. Cursing, he threw it across the Hall, where it clattered in a sprinkle of glass through a closed window.

"Fine," he said, "what time did you set? Is he late?"

A small, dark wiry man stood there expectantly, in jeans and a District 9 T-shirt, with the 'No Humans Allowed' sign and a shambling alien that looked like a Parktown Prawn from the movie emblazoned across his chest. The 'Humans' had been scratched out and replaced with 'Nigerians'.

Phulani stood up and shook hands, "Cute T-shirt, Mr. Deniran."

The wiry man smiled and sat smoothly, as if accustomed to cutting to many chases. "Thank you, Fulani, I take it this big man is Black-Power, in subtle disguise?"

"Phulani, the 'ph' is pronounced like a pee," said Phulani, with creased brows. "Nice T-shirt as I said—what were you, a Blomkamp extra?"

Lekan Deniran laughed, openly and genuinely, "Nollywood would have done a much better job, Phulani, but let's get to the real business at hand, shall we?"

The man turned and focused his intent gaze on the detective; Black-Power could almost see the yen signs rolling across the small man's eyeballs. "So, what are your terms and conditions, Mister Black-Power?"

"I'll fight him any which way I can, I'll fight him in Soccer Stadium, Soweto, I'll fight him on top of fucking Table Mountain, or even in the Tata Raphael Stadium if I have to!"

"Good," smiled Lekan, hauling out a tablet. "There's a contract template on here—what are your conditions?"

"One mill, US dee's, here…" The detective handed over a small square piece of paper.

Lekan looked at the paper and laughed. "Very generous, to allocate all of this to your dead ex-president's charity, ex-prisoner 46664."

"For some strange reason I have an affinity with prisoners," said the detective, signing with an e-pen.

With a nod and a wink, Lekan slipped the tablet into his leather bag and was gone.

"What about my payment?" asked Phulani.

"The usual," said the detective tersely.

"Oh... Can you beat him?" asked Phulani boldly, "Can you beat Pan-African, once and for all?"

The detective stood up, whipping his hat and coat off and—in full regalia, once he'd flicked his cape open and donned his mask—he bent down and kissed the very surprised, drunken white youth at the next door table.

Phulani howled his outrage as cameras began to snap across the hall.

The Last Pantheon

Nothing like the scent of death to focus the mind...

Thud! The young man had flung a drunken upper-cut against Black-Power's chin. Black-Power, stood up, surprised, the punch had tickled, but he'd felt it.

"Just because I'm gay doesn't mean it's all about sex," said the young man, "We're all just *people*, you know."

Humans! Who could understand them?

Phulani slipped a phone into Black-Power's coat pocket and pulled at his arm, "Let's roll," he said, "bigger fish to fry."

Now *fish* he could understand!

February 18, 1979
Sahara Desert

Black-Power slammed him into the side of a mountain. There was a brief rock fall and a tumescence of dust but before the Pan-African could cough there was that grip on the scruff of his neck and…g-forces. Flung into the sky.

The rush of air, the blue sky…

The cold roused him.

It's beautiful up here.

Impact. A light brighter than the sun, then darkness. He woke, then two seconds later he hit the desert ground.

Black-Power landed after him with a heavy vibration. He grabbed the Pan-African's right arm and spun him like a centrifuge, clockwise, then after a half-turn he stopped, then turned counter-clockwise.

The Pan-African's body was still moving clockwise and the bones popped like cheap fireworks. His scream echoed and the involuntary psychic feedback immobilised Black-Power.

In desperation the Pan-African poured his pain into Black-Power's thalamus. As he recovered he saw his opponent recoil in pain. His right arm hung useless at his side and blood poured out of both nostrils. He channelled all of his power in the pain, all his resentment of this hero, this shining one. He punched Black-Power in the centre of the chest. He felt the ribs go, the sternum crack.

The Pan-African reached out with his mind, found the small electric charge that gave rhythm to Black-Power's heart and stopped it.

He held on for as long as he could, and that mighty heart struggled against him.

It got colder. The sun darkened and clouds gathered.

Wind.

Precipitation.

Snow.

The Pan-African collapsed.

2015
Lagos, Nigeria

"I found him," said Lekan. "He spells his name 'Phulani', like Fulani, but with ph. We're on. Black-Power's in."

"He'll fight?" asked Tope.

"He was always going to fight," said Bank, not looking up from his tablet.

"To the death," said Lekan. "Signed the document, which you haven't, by the way."

"I'll get to that," said Tope. "How much did he want?"

"He said he'll fight you for free in a telephone booth in Tafawa Balewa Square, if need be."

"Hmm. Ali, Boma ye."

Bank said, "Is a death match legal? Even in Nigeria?"

Lekan sucked his teeth. "My cousin is a councillor in Surulere. I'll get all the permits I need. We'll say the death match thing is only for publicity. If anything happens and one of you should…accidentally die, well, I'll bury the Lagos State governor in an ocean of Naira. Trust me, the bout will happen."

"And the dome?"

"It'll be a sphere. I've already commissioned my nephew to build it. Parts are already en route."

"How many of you are there?" asked Tope. "Your grandfather was pretty busy."

Lekan laughed. "'*In a land where nepotism is currency, the man with plentiful relatives is rich*'."

"Don't be too sure," said Tope. "Do you know what Operation Deadwoods was?"

"No."

"1975. Nigeria's then Head of State Murtala Mohammed started Deadwoods to purge the corrupt officials from the government bureaucracy. He swept away hundreds of the unscrupulous civil servants and planned to return the country to civil rule."

"Hmm. And where did that get him?" asked Lekan.

February 13, 1976
Lagos, Nigeria
Presidential car, riddled with bullets, Murtala's cap on the back seat. The perpetuators, who hid sub-machine guns in their agbada, were gone.

Tope shook his head and flew away.

You could have kept him alive, brother. I told you. I told you!
This one time, Black-Power responded:

-Fuck off-

2015
Lagos, Nigeria
"An international airport and his face on a twenty-naira bill," said Bank.

Lekan snorted. "Murtala died for similar reasons to Lumumba. You played in that war theatre in the seventies, right? Murtala declared support for the MPLA. Any African leader who even smelled of Soviet or socialist leanings was a target for the CIA. Notice how Nigeria got a U.S style constitution soon after Murtala died?"

"I don't want to think about that time anymore. When is the bout?"

"Six weeks to build the geodesic, five if I can get a hooker to blow my cousin." Lekan guffawed at his own wit.

"Which one?"

Elizabeth stirred and Tope felt the weight change on the bed. He opened one eye. She padded to his desk and opened the laptop. She punched a few keys and gasped.

He allowed himself the pleasure of ogling her fundament, then spoke: "What's wrong?"

She brought the screen to him. It was a tube video. A man forcefully kissed another man in a bar of some kind. Tope recognised the aggressor's face. The scene paused and a voiceover began commentary.

"The man in the video is Sipho Cele, a police detective. The smaller man in the picture is Colin Jordaan, and he has accused Detective Cele of rape. What is more astonishing is that Jordaan has alleged that Cele is the super-powered adventurer from the seventies called Black-Power."

The scene cut to an interview. Jordaan now sported several bruises, a black eye and a torn lower lip. "He walks around with this old, worn black mask in his pocket, fingering it for sexual pleasure. He was…I mean, I go to the gym, but there's no amount of resistance training that would make me strong enough to…" The man burst into tears.

The reporter said Detective Cele could not be reached for comment and it was unclear if he was under arrest.

"What do you make of it?" asked Elizabeth.

Tope didn't speak. He knew Black-Power took male lovers from time to time, but rape? If he raped Jordaan the guy would be in hospital or a morgue, not on a TV show with minor bruises.

"This may not be what it looks like," said Tope.

"What? He's kissing a man."

"Yes, he is. That means he's gay or bisexual, but not necessarily a rapist."

"Will you fly over?"

Tope laughed. "When I went to prison one of the charges was violation of airspace. The other was flying in an urban area without a flight plan. Also, flying in a rural area without a flight plan. Flying without a permit. You get the etcetera? To do that, they first had to classify my body as an aircraft, then retrospectively charge me. It was a work of profound legal gymnastics. Bottom line is none of the Organisation of African Unity countries want me flying. So, no, I will not be flying to South Africa."

"Is it him?"

"The relevant question, Elizabeth, is how you knew about the video. I watched you. You woke and went straight to that web page without a search. What are you not telling me?"

Elizabeth stared at him.

"I can get it out of you if I want," said Tope. "But I want you to tell me."

89

She knelt back on her haunches, swallowed and said, "I have an implant."

"What kind?"

"It… I got it designed and needed thirty hours of surgery to have it inserted." She took his hand, parted her hair and ran his finger over the skin. He felt the bump. "That's the power supply. I have to change it every five years. It's experimental, but I had to have it. It cost fifteen million dollars and change."

"Again, what kind?"

"It keeps me connected to the Net wirelessly and sends the data to my sensory cortex. I can also feed data back down the same route. I see everything that goes on the net. I know everything. I bypass VPN tunnelling, software or hardware firewalls, and one sixty-eight key bit triple DES encryption before breakfast."

"I don't know what that means."

"It means I can go anywhere on the internet, like God intended."

"You have a chip that helps you do that?"

"Yes."

"You're online all the time."

"Yes. Searching, cataloguing, looking for news as it happens. On people's mobile phones, on their fucking e-readers just because. I spent last night talking to eGhosts."

"What's an-"

"You know social media? Well, when people die in real life their online persona still exists, like their profiles, their email accounts, their blogs, their Tweets. This is an eGhost. If you amalgamate all the data, all the status updates, all the Tweets, you can pretty much construct a being who will respond and show quasi-independent thought."

Tope got up.

"Does this freak you out?" she asked.

"I don't know," said Tope. "You could have mentioned it."

"Why?"

"I don't know. I would have wanted…I don't know."

The Last Pantheon

Elizabeth started getting dressed. "You know, you peer into people's heads and I trust you."

"I trust you."

"I don't see that from where I'm standing."

Soon, the door slammed.

She was gone.

14

2008
Alexandra Township, Johannesburg
Killings.
More killings.
Just foreigners, they said, kwerekwere.

This was on a wide open field, stunted bushes bristling across from crumbling shacks and the firmer brick of township houses.

These had been people on their way to work perhaps, or just on their way somewhere, to talk, to have fun—not expecting to die.

Detective Cele bent down, looked at the two twisted, burnt bodies, with gathering rage. The site had been roped off, but a crowd stood watching, silent and sullen. The open field itself was partially scorched and baked a blackish brown, smelling of dirt and charred meat.

He had to be detached and forensic about this. The support squad from his police unit was combing the field for murder weapons; crusted blood from the corpses' ragged head and torso wounds suggested both pangas and knobkieries. Surprisingly, no guns.

Close quarter murders, personal and intimate. Cele gritted his teeth, he needed to be cool and professional, after all.

He stood up and shouted at the milling crowd: "You fucking bastards, why murder your own brothers and sisters?"

A slow growling noise from the mob, a faint echo of umshini wami, bring me my machine gun.

You'll just tickle me with that, Cele thought, and make me angry—and you won't like me when I'm angry. A faint echo in that phrase, perhaps not his own?

A young police-woman came over, neatly uniformed, professional, holding out a partly burned bundle of papers.

"ID documents, sir," she said.

He did not bother to take them. Wearily, "What nationality?"

"Not sure if they're from the victims, sir. Mozambican, Malawian, but mostly Zimbabwean."

Not Nigerian. Not... his brother's people. Not yet, anyway.

He opened a sterile bag for her and she dropped the papers in, with black gloved fingers. He sealed lives away, with one thick brush of his thumb.

"Take this to the van," he said brusquely. "Call the meat squad in."

She almost curtsied in deference—he was a senior detective who had been around for many years, after all. Even more than you think, girl, he thought, watching her bustle back to the van and wishing he could meet someone who would stand up to him, just a bit.

Like this crowd.

He walked towards the end of the plastic rope, pulled taut between two stakes, but with enough give for him to stalk several metres into the crowd, without snapping. The mob moved back slowly, grumbling, ready to strike again.

He smiled, waiting for something to happen, fingering the mask in his pocket.

Slowly, in ragged groups, the crowd dispersed, trailing back to homes and places of meeting, a lucky few perhaps even to various jobs.

Behind him, bodies were removed.

But he could smell the muggy wind picking up now, lacings of moisture in the air as grey clouds boiled in from the horizon.

He stood alone in the field as rain lashed down on his face, cleaning the air and the ground. He could smell damp earth and sense the stirrings of worms beneath the ground, a few broken thorn trees in the distance standing out suddenly in the flares of sheet lightning.

Life goes on, he thought, but is this only the beginning?

All things start, but when will it end?

Shit, he's soaked—his suit will shrink on him if he's not too careful, time to go home.

Or, at least, just a place to sleep.

1975

Cape Town

He could hear sounds on the Foreshore, near the docks, sounds that did not belong; the sound of deep drilling, within a bank filled with gold Kruger rands.

Intel had it that a foreign force had slipped in quietly to town, looking for easy pickings. There were no easy pickings on *his* watch...

There was a security van waiting for pick-up on the kerb outside, but he could tell the markings were fake, they had been sprayed a little too loosely, a little too unprofessionally. It took him one big bound to land on its roof, buckling and crushing it with the pounding weight of his feet and fists. There was a scream from a driver in the front carriage, a scream over breaking glass.

He stepped calmly through the plate glass doors, showers of glass sliding off his impervious skin. The white tellers and customers were calm when they saw him, splayed on the ground as they were, hands clasped above their heads. His mask and cape were well known around here, his power even more so.

A semi-professional operation then, they at least had a man holding the forecourt of the bank, alert and armed, opening fire in fear when he spotted the giant superhero.

Black-Power moved with easy speed—speed that no man could get a lock on. A left jab caved the man's skull, sending him sprawling across the polished floor in a spiral of blood, his gun mangled by a crunch from 'Power's right hand.

Deep inside the vaults, the drilling stopped.

Black-Power bounded outside to land on the wrecked getaway van again, a man crawling away from the wreckage as sirens started to howl. Best keep the fight outdoors, where the chance for collateral damage was less.

A man stepped outside, and Black-Power felt the weight of sudden unease. This man was tall, compactly built and walking with the ease of someone so capable as to fear very little.

"If you surrender now, I will spare you the might of Black-Power," he boomed.

The man started and looked as if he were suppressing a laugh: "Brother, is that you?"

Black-Power stepped off the broken van and approached cautiously. A tall man indeed, not much smaller than he, neatly dressed, but sporting a huge fuzz of head hair. His features were sharp, mobile, familiar...

It had been a long time.

A *very* long time.

"What the hell have you done to your hair?"

Tope smiled: "It's called an Afro, you know, like the Jackson Five?"

Black-Power snorted. "It looks ridiculous...are you robbing this bank?" Three nervous, armed men stood behind his... brother.

"Brother, will you not greet me with a kiss? I haven't seen you in-"

"You were supposed to stay up north."

"I know. Things happened. I have been travelling around the world. I have much to tell you."

"You can tell me from jail. There can be only one penalty for breaking the law."

Cop cars were screeching to a halt nearby, but he waved them to a stop. He had this in hand.

"Brother, there is no need for violence. This money is going to feed women and children in Angola."

Black-Power stamped forward, rippling a force wave through concrete, buckling the pavement, upending the three men, who fell with a clatter of weapons.

Tope stood, several feet above the wrecked concrete pavement, hanging in the air like a mirage. Slowly, sadly, he shook his head, and then with a blur of speed, he was up into the sky, a speck disappearing amongst the few clouds leeching off the cloud cloth of Table Mountain.

Brother, why have you turned back to crime, thought Black-Power pensively, as he strode into the bank hall again, where customers and tellers were picking themselves up.

They looked at him, but no one clapped.

"Ja sure, I know you don't allow black people in here—but your asses just got saved by a black man, so chew on that, honkeys."

He was met with blank looks. Of course, none of them would have seen *Shaft*, or anything like it. He sighed, feeling faintly ridiculous, knowing his brother would not be able to stop laughing if he had watched and heard him just now.

For both our sakes, he thought grimly, don't come back, brother.

The police were moving past him now, careful not to touch him, heading for the vaults. One policeman levelled a gun at the man lying against stairs at the far side of the hall, his broken automatic weapon crumpled like his body.

"Alamu," he'd heard a name mentioned. Yet again, black men die.

Black-Power crouched low and then jumped, bursting through the roof in a spray of wood and brick, heading up and up, towards the Mountain, where no one would find or see him.

At least there, alone, hunched by yellow sandstone rocks and with an orange-breasted sunbird calling nearby in the mountain fynbos, he began to feel somewhat at home again.

But his thoughts brooded north: Brother, after all these... millennia... still the sharp tongue and the patronising tone, even though I am as yet ever the elder...

2015
Somewhere over Africa

Phulani Mabuza sat alongside Black-Power in the specially commissioned SAA jet, loaded with ANC government officials and a small but select press entourage. Black-Power, besides taking up two seats, wore a discreet grey track suit over his bodysuit, stitched in green letters on the back:

'Black-Power'. He was *not* going to be mistaken for a British Petroleum flunkey again.

Phulani nodded at Black-Power's hand-luggage, a subdued but tall Italian leather man-bag, well within luggage allowances.

"What you got in there, BP?"

Black-Power leaned forward and flicked it open with his finger. He took out a cowhide covered shaft and flat blade, about a metre in length, decorated with bright beads on the grip, balancing it on his fingers.

Phulani goggled at him, "What's that, a fucking assegai?"

"No," said Black-Power. "An iklwa. Shaka himself gave it to me."

Phulani laughed then, clasping his suited belly, which had grown with the greying of his hair. "You always were a fucking clown, BP."

Black-Power glowered at him through the mask.

Phulani unlaced his fingers and shifted back in his seat, a little nervously. He knew Black-Power had limits to his tolerance, even though they went back as partners many, many years.

A young aspiring official from Foreign Affairs stood deferentially at their shoulders, a comic book in hand, holding it forward to be signed.

Black-Power took it gently, knowing his fingers could shred the ageing yellow paper with the slightest of heavier touches.

"Ah..." he said. "The last issue." *Battle in the Sahara*. A few pen marks, crumpled spine, VG at best, he thought quietly to himself.

"Is it true the amaBokaboka wanted to sign you, sir?"

Black-Power smiled as he signed the cover page with a flourish. "Yes, they claim they need me at lock forward to beat the All Blacks in the next rugby World Cup in Japan. I said no, because I'm not a transformation token to boost their almost All Whites team."

He handed the man his old comic book back, gently.

The official scurried off hurriedly—but with a pleased smile—holding the scrawled signature across the cover reverentially.

No comic book violence coming up, thought Black-Power drily, and with a faint frisson of fear.

"What else you got in that bag there, BP?" asked Phulani, a little more relaxed, now that Black-Power had signed his name on a collectible so cheerfully.

Black-Power rummaged and pulled out a long cape, slowly and carefully.

"You - have - got - to - be - fucking - kidding - me," said Phulani.

The cape was a bright, luminescent rainbow in colour.

"Just making a statement," said Black-Power.

"What," swallowed Phulani, "That you're representing the fucking rainbow nation?"

"And gay pride."

Slowly, Phulani shook his head, "Tell me it's a secret weapon to kill your brother by laughing until he chokes?"

Black-Power shoved the cape back into the bag, almost bursting the bag's seams.

"You still miss Thembeka, don't you?"

Black-Power was huddled forward, but still shot a sideways glance at Phulani, who had surprised him with the sensitivity in his comment. Not usual, nor in character, but Phulani had showed flashes of insights down the years, which had cemented the bumpiness of their years together. *And* he was a damn good fixer!

"Yes," he said shortly.

"Well, for fuck's sake, kiss another *woman* instead next time, okay?"

The plane's intercom system kicked in, as the aeroplane began to buck up and down with tropical turbulence and the seat belt signs pinged on.

"This is your captain speaking, we're about to head down towards the Murtala Muhammed International Airport."

"Fuck..." said Phulani, clasping the sides of his seat, "I wish we were going to watch Bafana Bafana play the Super Eagles instead."

"Ha!" barked Black-Power, "I stand a much better chance of winning this, than the Bafana would have."

Despite his words, Black-Power suddenly felt very cold indeed, as the plane began its dip down towards Lagos.

2015
Lagos, Nigeria

There was a crackle down the phone line that suggested either wind or that manoeuvre where the device is held between shoulder and ear, freeing the hand for other activities.

"I don't see him," said Bank.

"He's there," said Tope. "I can feel him. Hasn't been this strong in years."

"I'm telling you, I've seen all the flight data from Jo'burg. There is no listing."

"Look for a big Zulu-looking motherfucker with an entourage. He might be wearing sports clothes."

"Isn't he supposed to be under arrest?"

"Maybe, but I doubt it. The case was thin."

"I see him."

Tope took the image out of Bank's head. It took fifteen seconds to resolve the image. While doing that he picked up Bank's fear of being arrested as a terrorist for using field glasses in an airport. Boko Haram had been quiet, so it was reasonable to expect fireworks soon.

Bank was at the airport while Tope stayed home answering mail. Since the bout was announced all kinds of people sent all kinds of things for Tope to sign or touch and send back. They wanted him to contact their dead grandfather. They wanted to know who stole their money. They wanted to know if the baby was theirs, or if the baby was a boy, or if the baby had Sickle Cell Disease. Wasn't there a blood test for that these days? Hadn't these people heard of ultrasound?

It was Black-Power all right. Age had made Cele slightly gaunt, even showing a slight paunch. His muscles didn't pop the way they used to, although nobody but Tope could notice such a difference. He wore a New York City cap and an Addidas tracksuit. Duffel bag hooked around left shoulder. He did not look happy. Actually, he never looked happy.

"Actually, he never looked happy," said Bank.

Shit.

"Bank, I seem to be influencing your thoughts. It's not on purpose, but my control is a bit off. Try to think of a white screen."

"Just ignore the porn."

"I'm going to pretend I didn't hear that."

Weather forecast was good, temperature holding at a steady forty Celsius. Their presence together in the same geographic location hadn't caused any meteorological change. Yet...

"What's that in his hand?" asked Bank.

"It used to belong to Shaka Zulu. It's a weapon."

A priest once told Tope a story about Shaka Zulu. A white soldier told the great king that the manner in which the Zulu troops fought reminded him of the Spartans. He asked if Shaka had heard of them. Shaka asked if the Spartans died like other humans. The soldier asked what he meant. Shaka asked if, when pierced by a spear the Spartans would cry out in pain. The soldier said he thought so. Then Shaka Zulu looked away from the soldier and said he had no use for such soldiers. "If I command it my impi die in silence. These Spartans cry like women and give away their position."

Tope smiled. Only Shaka kaSenzangakhona could call the Spartans pussies.

"Spartans pussies," said Bank.

Tope broke the link.

"Come home, Bank," said Tope.

Lekan hawked and spat. "Yes, he's here. I didn't want to tell you yet because I didn't know if that rape allegation would go forward."

The dome was all but complete. It was a gigantic structure covered in scaffolding and bathed in Klieg lights. Construction continued day and night. Welding sparks floated slowly to the ground. Booms and cranes placed men in unusual positions over a hundred feet in the air.

"How's the foundation?" asked Tope.

"It's wedged in bedrock. Don't worry; it'll hold."

Lekan was happy, and he had good reason. He had already made one hundred million U.S. dollars in pay-per-view bookings alone. Advertising had not collated data yet and the gambling data was astronomical. Merchandising…the figures were beyond what Tope was used to or interested in.

Two men shuffled up in hardhats. They looked harried.

"Tope, I want you to meet Nick Wood and Tade Thompson."

"Pleasure," said Tope, but it sounded like a question. He wasn't sure what their role was. Both were slightly bookish, wore glasses and seemed in awe of him. Tade was black and Nick looked like he might be a Pacific Islander or mixed race, but both had that endomorphic look that Tope associated with academics.

"They're in charge of the novelisation," said Lekan.

"What novelisation?" said Tope.

"*Graphic* novelisation," said Nick. "We're immortalising the bout in print."

"Do you think you have the time to look at some character sketches?" said Tade.

Tope frowned at Lekan. "You know how I feel about this."

"*Pele, o*! Sorry. I know you would prefer Joe Orlando. Look, I couldn't get at Armand Hector-"

"Hector's dead," said Tope.

"That explains a lot," said Lekan.

Indeed. Armand Hector was rumoured to have been a consultant on the early MKDelta-sponsored Black-Power comics, in addition to other African comics like South Africa's Mighty Man and Nigeria's Power Man. The projects all died off when CIA interference in Africa became unfashionable.

"We need some background information on you," said Nick.

"On both of you," said Tade. "The 1970s comics were simplistic bullshit."

They were both sweating and Tope got the impression they were not used to the warm climate. "Let's get some beers…"

The drums kept beating.

The Last Pantheon

Tope was naked.

The Babalawo sliced the cockerel's head off and sprinkled blood on Tope's head, all the while continuing with his monotonous incantations.

It was going to be a long night.

None of these rituals existed eight hundred years ago.

Tope saw Bank into the taxi.

"Uncle, are you sure you don't want me to-"

"I'm not coming back, Bank. One way or the other, this is it. Just share out the money the way I told you."

Bank's cheeks were wet with tears. "We will never forget you, Uncle."

"You better not! I made you all millionaires."

"I-"

"Just kidding. Go. Go now."

"You can win this."

"I can't kill him. He's my brother."

When the taxi pulled away, Tope felt the loss like a knife to the gut.

Question: What do you do on the eve of your death?

Answer: Slot in a DVD and watch John McClane perforate European terrorists in a high rise building over one hundred and twenty frenetic, action-packed minutes!

There weren't many people around the dome. It had no seating and was opaque so nobody could see anything but a dome. A security cordon went up weeks before and there was a desolate circle a mile wide around the area. There were two doors, each coded to admit only one. The north face was for Black-Power to enter, while the south was for Tope. There were no roads, and Tope flew up and dropped straight down by the dome from orbit. The flames of re-entry died quickly against his force field.

He placed both palms against the south door and waited. It opened with a klaxon piercing the silence.

A shining walkway led to a metal platform in the centre.

Tope walked to the centre and sat cross-legged on the floor. He closed his eyes and waited.

A sudden, loud vibration alerted him an hour later.

Black-Power had landed.

Morituri te salutamus.

2015
Geodesic Dome, Lagos
Pan-African sat calmly, eyes closed, meditating.
 But Black-Power knew his presence had been marked...
 ...And that his brother was listening to him.
 There would be no surprising him, they both knew each other
too well.
 Perhaps.
 Black-Power bowed, blanking his mind.
 Jump, swing....
Pan-African rolled with his right hook, a glancing body
blow, but still he gasped. Keep on him—left uppercut, right
jab, scorpion kick, keep the fucker rolling and dodging, no
time to think, no time to use his fucking mind.
 Swivel kick, fucking sweet that one, sent him soaring into
the top of this spherical dome, ramming him against the metal
structure, blood spilling freely from his face. Jump now, nail
the sucker...
Shit, missed, uh!—these bars are titanium hard—losing that
bastard to close quarters was a fucking mistake. Where's he?
 Black-Power grunted as he felt a rock hard fist ram into his
midriff, and he started to fall, blows now raining against his
face. The sky's this fucker's space, air's his power, grab him,
hold him, down to the ground...
 Unhhhh, he's spun on top, using me like a fucking cushion—
bastard's smaller, but still no fucking light weight. Off he
goes again, ha—got his foot, swing him down, hard!
 The ground shook with the impact, blood flying again, as if
in slow motion. Bounce him down hard again, his head
fucking first this time.
 Flashing red stars, stagger back, blink, one eye's puffed and
gone, Pan-African's free again, must have kicked him hard in
the face with his free leg. Tope, his brother, the younger,
hangs on the edge of the cage, crouched, panting, bleeding.

Black-Power could taste sour blood in his own mouth and strained to focus on the Pan-African with his good left eye, wiping blood from a cut leaking on his forehead.

Fucking corny, those fight scenes in comics, when light repartee is exchanged. When it *really* gets down to it, each fucking word will cost you. Just get your breath back...

It was then that he heard them.

A roar from the baying mob outside the cage, heard through speakers, the audience packed in this huge digital stadium, thousands upon thousands, baying them on, to kill each other. Millions more besides—probably several billion, watching, screaming, from across the globe.

Who should I be fighting, Black-Power thought, and *why* am I fighting?

"Lost your balls then?" Pan-African called. "Kissing too many men?"

Fuck you, he thought...fuck everyone!

Black-Power inhaled deeply, settling his weight squarely into his braced legs and haunches, summoning a focus of his strength, sweetly into his favoured left fist.

Pan-African steadied himself on the opposite wall, ready...

But he was not the target.

Black-Power pivoted and drove his fist hard into the structure next to him—it stretched backwards, bent, buckled... exploded...

...and fragments of death flew everywhere...

Black-Power opened his one good eye, feeling the ground beneath him shake and snap.

His brother, the Pan-African, hung in the air, blood pouring from a gaping wound in his chest. He appeared to be crying blood as he clenched his left fist—and Black-Power could feel the ground lifting him up, fragments of the cage hanging like scattered, glowing ingots, caught in the might of the Pan-African's mental force field.

"Where the fuck's he going?" thought Black-Power, as the air grew chill around them and the blue sky deepened into indigo, the ground now a very, very long way below them indeed...

2015
Lagos, Nigeria
Sixty-two miles above the surface
Dick Tiger once told me that boxing fights were abnormal. In fact, all sporting fights were abnormal. Fights in their natural state last seconds. Those that last longer than five minutes are usually between people who are not trying to hurt themselves.
The fight took seconds. Forty-five seconds to cross the Karman line.
Forty-five seconds for Cele to cave the Pan-African's chest in.
I am dying.
I am using micro-sized force fields to keep some of my blood in, but that won't save my life.
It's cold.
Black-Power feels it too.
My mind can keep the platform up here long enough to freeze his blood.
We both die.
Check, mate and fuck you, brother.
Elizabeth…
Elizabeth…

The remnants of the geodesic dome fell to the earth as a meteor shower, red hot chunks of titanium, which set off forest fires and destroyed houses. Families watching the bout on television found their living rooms torn asunder with scant warning. There was no advantage to being outside as crowds pressed against the one-mile security cordon were subjected to the shower and people were reduced to flaming, pulped flesh. A cruise liner traversing the lagoon took a hit to the bow and burned furiously and rich passengers and less-rich crew took to the lifeboats. Those who chanted for blood mere minutes before ran for cover wherever they could find it.

Despite the carnage, the sky looked beautiful with bright orange and yellow streaks.

Seventy-one people lost their lives.

The Pan-African's body burnt up in re-entry, lacking a force field to protect it.

Black-Power was frozen, then burned, then broken against the Earth's surface. His suit was carbonised and the skin blackened and peeled off.

Trees still blazed around him. He tried to stand but his muscles would not obey. He remembered being struck by lightning three times during his descent, each hit like the accusing finger of God.

He could not cry—his tear ducts were gone. He could barely see. His harm-resistant eyelids had been able to protect his corneas only so much. The left was scorched, but the right had better light perception.

He sensed someone close by.

"Are you proud of yourself, old man?" said Thembeka. "A little fratricide to prove you still have lead in your pencil?"

"Thembeka..."

"He was kin to us. I could feel it..."

Black-Power could not see her clearly but he felt the rage coming off her. He tried to speak, coughed instead. The fire had gone down his throat. He could rasp, though.

"Thembeka, fuck off. We are not related to you, Tope and I."

She edged close to his ear. "*Were*, asshole. You mean 'we were not related' not 'are'. Tope is dead, remember?"

The pain threading his nerves intensified and he gasped, clutching at air.

"Shit, Black-Power, you're an absolute fucking mess," she cradled his head then; held him.

"Thembeka," he croaked, "I'm sorry." All he could smell was burning, and the all consuming pain threaded itself tighter and tighter into his body, constricting his throat.

"Shhhhh," she said, "I can hear you. So... you did love him, once."

"Yes," he said, "once."

Black-Power wished he could cry. Instead, he managed a painful croak. Thembeka poured some water onto his lips and tongue. He coughed his thanks.

"You forgive me?" he managed.

"No," she said, "it's not that easy."

A strange weather formation over Africa.

Several listening posts were already turned towards the continent as a precaution in case the bout between superhumans developed complications, so it was well documented. The clouds seemed to be on fire, but it later became clear. A wormhole terminated there and left a ship, some said a shuttle.

It looked like a grand, black metal spider. It flew as if light, but the earth reverberated when it touched down above the spot where Black-Power lay against Thembeka.

The woman tensed for battle.

"At ease," said Black-Power. "I... I know this ship, or it's like. I remember now. It's me they want."

Two constructs emerged, shining ones like Biblical burnished brass men. Black-Power struggled to his feet and accepted the inhibitor bracelets, starting to go with his gaolers.

"What are you?" asked Thembeka.

"A criminal," croaked Black-Power. "Protect them, Thembeka. Protect the people. I always wanted to..."

"When you weren't trying to forcibly copulate with them," she said, but the fire was gone from her eyes, "what was your crime?"

He looked down. "...Forcing myself sexually on others, amongst other things."

She laughed then. And cried. But she did not ask what the other things were.

He held out his blackened mask. "Please, carry on, you will do better than me."

"I don't need that," she said, "I won't hide behind that. But, is there any chance I could get your rainbow cape, the one you never fought with?"

"Phulani told you, the bastard," Black-Power cracked a painful smile, "Sure—sala kathle, Sister."

"Goodbye to you too, Detective."

Black-Power's last words floated over his shoulder, as he entered the ship: "Umuntu Ngumuntu Ngabantu."

Thembeka smiled—a human becomes human, through being with others. "Not bad pronounciation for a kwerekwere," she said.

Black-Power's laughter echoed on, long after the ship's doors closed.

The ship rose, the burning cloud phenomenon happened again, and then it was over.

"…And then it was over," said Thembeka. "That was the end of Black-Power, returned to interstellar incarceration somewhere left of the I-don't-give-a-fuck solar system."

Elizabeth Kokoro stopped typing and saved the document. She switched off the recorder.

"You were in love with him," said Thembeka. "I can feel it."

"I think I loved them both," said Elizabeth. "And hated them too."

They both laughed until they cried.

"What are you going to do?" asked Thembeka.

"A book. *The Last Pantheon.* You just helped me finish it and I already have a publication deal secured. What of you?"

Thembeka went to the window and opened it.

"Fight crime," she said. "What else is there for people like us?"

The curtain fluttered—Elizabeth caught a last rainbow flash of colour.

Thembeka was gone.

Tade Thompson lives and works in the UK, though he is Yoruba. His most recent works include the novel *Making Wolf* and the story 'Child, Funeral, Thief, Death' in Apex Magazine. He is an occasional visual artist.

Nick Wood is a Zambian born, South African naturalised clinical psychologist, with over a dozen short stories previously published in *Interzone*, *Subterfuge*, *Infinity Plus*, *PostScripts*, and *Redstone Science Fiction*, amongst others. Nick has also appeared in the first African anthology of science fiction, *AfroSF* – and now with this collaborative novella follow-up with Tade Thompson here in *AfroSFv2*. He also has a book pending with NewCon Press (2016), entitled *Azanian Bridges*, exploring a current but alternative South Africa, where apartheid survived. Nick has completed an MA in Creative Writing (SF & Fantasy) through Middlesex University, London and is currently training clinical psychologists and counsellors at the University of East London in England. He can be found: @nick45wood or http://nickwood.frogwrite.co.nz/

Hell Freezes Over

Mame Bougouma Diene

1: Hell or High Water

They still talk about the storms…

The bleak landscape stretching behind had nothing on the thunderclouds looming ahead of Ari, and in another few minutes darkness would merge with darkness in a frenzy of hail and ball lightning. He recalled a vague saying about unstoppable forces and immovable objects. In his experience there was no such thing: everything moved eventually; everything could be shaken, torn off, and ripped to shreds. As for unstoppable forces, they stopped too, eventually, and when they did, they left nothing unmoved. He shook his head wondering who the idiot who had thought that up was, and how it had stuck. Different times, probably, and milder winds. Standing by his side, Adi, as if to prove a silent point, had not moved.

In a few minutes it would not matter; in a few minutes the storm would start, and in a few months the winter.

The waters called him, they called her, and they called all of them. Awake and in their sleep, the Fish were the waters.

The Moles' efforts had proven fruitful, or so they claimed. The tunnels of the Divine Undertaking were nearing completion, and the caves would offer a luxury undreamed of on the surface. But few dreamed anymore. Neural synapses would fire at night just as they always had, but you cannot dream if you do not have a past, and you cannot dream if you cannot bring the future to life—when tomorrow is another whirlwind, and the future an endless field of ice…such are not dreams, but fantasies in the void, and in the void there is despair.

He stretched his arms and leaped over the cliff, the friction building up static against the electrically charged air of the storm, and his head closed in on the blue-black waters with barely a splash.

Only the Fish truly Dreamed... Neptune have mercy on their souls.

> *We have been tried by Water and tried by Ice.*
> *We have been carved by its shards,*
> *And moulded by its flows*
> *As Neptune's tribulations pass,*
> *The power of Hades grows.*

Knowing that the Time of Neptune would soon pass, revealing Hades in all of his glory, ushering in the return to the Cave—before humanity wandered into the light and was blinded to reason by the sun—was little comfort from the disdainful looks of the Moles sitting across the aisle. Their time was close, and they knew it. One day, soon now, Hell would freeze over, and it would be their turn to rule in Hades' glory.

The scriptures could not mute the snickering, and even the vision of Hell stretching endlessly outside the church window could not dampen their heckling.

The priest was formal, and the Blank Book of Scriptures, its pages untainted and its message clear, was unequivocal. Millions of years past, a man-shaped demon named Plato, son of the wretched Socrates, Scion of Hell, had led to the fore an Age of Reason, dragging Man from the comfort of the Cave, and into the blinding lights of purgatory.

Upon the surface, man had first experienced the Time of Mars, when wars wrecked the world and billions perished as Hell shaped itself at Man's pleasure. Then came the Time of Hermes, and for a period Man flourished, striking a balance between his aspirations and Hell. In the Time of Narcissus, Man had forgotten his humble beginnings and the comfort of the Cave, and sought his own reflection in the light, his mirror image in Hell. The Time of Neptune had cleansed the world, and Hades would lead us back to the Cave.

Ari shook himself awake, and for a few seconds, the world blended with the Dream before washing it away. Those early moments, growing longer by the day, threatened to rip his sanity apart. As the dreams grew more vivid with each passing night the fragile balance grew more delicate. One day, he knew, like all the other Fish before him, reality would merge with the Dream, and the Dream would win.

"Ari, Ari..."

Jonah had grown accustomed to the dull look in his son's eyes, and the light that grew slowly, alerting him to his return. Just as he had grown accustomed to that same look in his father's eyes, back when he was too young to understand himself. Long before Ari grew accustomed to, recognised, and finally understood, that same look in his own. All the Fish Dream Fish Dreams.

"Ari..."

Stepping into life from the Dream felt like defeat in victory, almost fratricide. There was comfort in the Dream, perhaps the comfort of the Cave. Perhaps. Fish were chosen, after all, chosen to rule under Neptune, and had for five hundred years. Who else would dream of the Cave and know it in their souls?

Ari's sharp intake of air, and sudden rising bolt upright, brought light back to his eyes. He looked around, weighing up his surroundings, making sense of the world as he had known it before going to sleep. Before he Dreamed.

"Father."

His voice was firm and his grip solid, much to Jonah's relief. He should not Dream so young, not with such intensity, but he was one of a generation who sought glory in unfathomable depths, ever darker crevasses, ever more dangerous valleys and canyons and towers. A generation for whom the darkness beneath, the endless echo of whale song, was the melody of the Cave and the enticing murmur of Neptune.

"You're awake. Good. Your mother left some food for you on the table. We need to make the coast before the storm, and we'll have to stay longer beneath than usual."

Ari sensed the tension in Jonah's voice. "It's fine, Father," he reassured him. "Once we're under we can wait out the storm; we'll be needed once it has passed."

Jonah did not respond. Instead he stared out of the window to the cliffs and the thunderclouds creeping over the ocean. He turned and stepped through the doorway. "The storm is a harbinger, Son, and winter is but weeks away…"

"I know, Father." Ari said and looked up, but Jonah had left the room.

The Moles had started work early. Lines of Beasts hauled equipment from Fish coastal outposts to the Colony, coordinated by a few Mole overseers. A storm could lay weeks of work to waste in a matter of minutes and last for days. There was a time when the Fish would have exerted explicitly imaginable violence had the Moles failed in their task and suffered setbacks in the Divine Undertaking.

Ari looked down to the other Fish waiting for his father by the cliff. Only a few had shaken themselves awake but he saw Adi looking over the edge to the ocean, turning her back to it, spreading her arms wide and bending backwards over the edge as if about to dive.

A stone hit him in the shoulder, and a young Mole stood there grinning at him. Times had changed. As the Divine Undertaking progressed, and the Dream took ever-larger numbers of Fish over the edge, the balance of power had shifted, and respect for the Fish dimished. Now they served only a purpose, and that purpose would not last the winter.

His father reached out and patted him on the shoulder. *Let it be*, his expression told him, *let it be…*

They had been prouder than this once. The Fish dared the depths of the seas for months at a time going through towns and cities long submerged. They'd exposed themselves to unknown amounts of radiation and chemical pollutants over

116

generations, swimming the rising waters for food, materials for construction, power sources for the water filters and storage units, and eventually, for machinery geared towards the Divine Undertaking. But those days were gone; the Dream would take over unless the Moles could exact their vengeance first.

His shoulder hurt, his pride a flimsy thing fainter than reality, but he let it be.

He reached the cliff and sidled next to Adi. Caught in the rising winds behind her, and the crash of the waves hundreds of feet below, she did not hear him place a hand behind her back before pulling her back from the edge.

"Aaaaaah!" she opened her eyes, "Ri…"

Her eyes re-focused slowly, and he realised the Dream was taking over her much faster than him. One day he would not be there on time to tease her and no one would stop her fall.

"We're up for a few days, it sounds like," she said matter-of-factly.

Her left eye still bore a small scar below it, an acid burn from a poisoned tentacle. It had seemed trivial at the time, but she had barely survived the infection.

Ari nodded. "When have you ever lied?" he said.

Adi laughed. She loved the depths, their darkness, unexpected poisonous glows and the whisper of giant beings—Neptune's titanic children inside which the legendary Jonah, his father's namesake, had once slept and brought forth the truth of the Cave.

It took a few more minutes for the rest of the Fish to gather by the cliff. Once they were equipped with their suits, propulsion engines, food and energy packs, and fin-shaped oxygen and waste-recyclers on their backs, they resembled the creature they were named after. Not that they would have known—no one in the colony had seen fish before. Only giants and monsters ruled the seas, only the name remained. Fish dove and swam, Moles dug and burrowed.

Not so long ago, a hundred years at most, there would have been a crowd gathered to see them off. But as the Time of

Neptune grew longer, the storms stronger, the winters harsher and more unpredictable, the ice encroaching over more land each year, and with the Dream taking away sanity, authority, and lives, those numbers dwindled.

Jonah stood atop a stone to address the crowd of gathered Fish, and the few on-looking Ants and Bees. "Morning! You've all shaken yourselves out; get ready to stay that way! You ain't blind! You can see it coming just as I do! In all things the mission comes first!

"I have split you into two teams; David will sort you out, and tell you where to go! We have two objectives: fuel for the water filters, and power sources for the Divine Undertaking! The Ants have given me very specific directions as to the kind of power sources they require, so be careful!

"You know the works! Keep your com-units on, communicate findings to each other as necessary!"

Adi raised a hand. "Jonah! This is not a storm, I mean it is, of course it is, but… this feels like winter. A bad one."

"Don't be silly, Adi. We're heading south-southeast. Winter is not for a few months; until then, we have to gather as much fuel as we can. But you're right, the storm will last more than a few days, bet your life on it, and we may have to travel quite far so save on your food and energy packs." He paused to stare back at the clouds. "Just to be safe, keep your eyes open for unusually cold currents and signs of early icing on the way back north. We won't be much use to anybody if we're trapped under… David?"

Jonah's second stepped up to the stone dividing the Fish into two groups. Ari was sent to gather fuel, Adi, autonomous power sources.

The Fish lined up along the cliff, and one after another, in intervals of twenty seconds, leaped off, daring the incoming juggernaut to smash them against the crag, and answering the water's siren call with a kiss on her dark and glowing lips.

Adi had been wrong. It was not winter yet, not quite, and the storm had lasted only fourteen days. Every time they dove the cities and towers had changed. Where the ice had retreated, entire areas were laid to waste, and each year more of the seas stayed trapped under ice.

You could not blame Adi for her caution. Sudden onsets of winter had caught and trapped Fish time and time again, but you could usually read the signs: the permafrost spread its fingers further south, leaving the water-submerged lands frozen out of season, and the currents never lied—blasts of cold water killed as often as they warned, but allowed the Fish to know where to swim and complete their missions safely.

The colony knew of the cold and the snow, but the Fish knew the true meaning of winter. The freezing waters took on a glassy, reflective look moving forward along the city grids, swallowing block after block, turning the waters to solid ice down from the surface and almost to the ground, where water circulation blasted cold currents further ahead; subtle signs of impending glaciation that the Fish learned to recognise as children. Each encroachment sent silent explosions along the currents, forming ice walls several hundreds of feet in height and thousands of miles thick, until the summer came and freed them again, but always shorter summers, and always more ice.

And now, Adi was dead. Ari saw her in the Dream and knew that she had succumbed to her mission. She was in the Dream with him, floating through the depths with the whales and the sharks, spinning through swarms of jellyfish unbitten. He knew she had succumbed to the Dream and merged with it, leaving reality behind for boundless currents and her own freedom.

Mole Councilman Eli Khadivi let himself bask in the tension of the Council, allowing the little give-aways to give, and the tell-tale signs to tell him which way the wind blew.

The Council's currents were only as complex as its members, and the Castes concerns were all the same, and had been so for a century. The ice would trap them if they didn't act decisively and in the thin tremor of panic he saw the opening he needed to support his own agenda.

He cleared his voice. "Councilmen, Councilwomen. I declare this 62nd annual session of the Council of the Divine Undertaking open. As you all know we are nearing completion of the network. As such, the first item on the agenda will be fuel and supplies for the caves."

The Divine Undertaking was ready to embrace them, the network of connecting caves and tunnels was to become the final resting place of a repentant humanity, and the sum of the knowledge it had preserved once the ice covered the world. But he needed to deal with the Fish, they all needed to deal with the Fish, or none of it would matter.

A man raised his hand.

"Yes, Councilman Samadeh, I assume the Bees would have their word as to our supplies, where do we stand?"

The Bees workload had doubled with the Divine Undertaking. Providing food for the colony was an arduous task with every shorter spring, but the Divine Undertaking was a leviathan that required agricultural Bees and labourer Beasts to produce more stock, and engineering Ants to build more storage units and recycle more fuel than the colony had ever needed.

They had grown unaccustomed to the caves after these few centuries on the mountain walls, fields and open seas. They knew they would have to go back to their troglodytic existence, Hades demanded it, but unlike the Moles, they didn't all embrace the future with equal glee.

"Thank you, Head of Council Khadivi," said Samadeh, and looked around the room at the other Caste members assembled for the session. Only the Fish were absent. "As you all know, we have prepared for the coming of Hades with due diligence and hard labour, and within the next few days, with the help of the Ants we will have managed to complete all the major storage units and rehabilitated the old plantation caves. We are prepared for Hell, Head of Council."

"Yes," broke in a young Ant councilwoman. "The fuel supplies the Fish managed to salvage were more potent than we expected after all these years."

"Yes," agreed a Beast councilman, a diminutive fellow in spite of his Caste's name. "Yes they did well, several perished but they did well."

"My fellow friends and colleagues," Khadivi said, "our efforts will not be in vain, none of ours, the Blank Book of Scriptures says so, and so it will be." He paused for effect and added, "But I fear that, in spite of their recent success, the Fish may have outlived their usefulness."

"Again, Khadivi?" sighed the Beast councilman.

"Yes, again?" came another annoyed sigh from the table. "This is not the first time you bring up the Fish and their quirks, but they have their uses Eli, as you well know. Will you Moles ever let bygones be bygones? After all this time?"

A few other voices rose in protest, but they were few.

Khadivi continued, "My fellow councilfolk, you should know me better than this, and you know that my only concern has always and only been for the survival of this colony, of what is left of our humanity, all of us.

"But we must consider the fate of these poor degenerates, if we are to prosper in the warm embrace of the Cave. Would these sad creatures, hopelessly addicted to the freedom of the waters, find peace in the bowels of the earth?

"Those 'dreams' of which they speak, which we naively believed to be Neptune manifested, those dreams, which inevitably, inexorably lead every Fish over the cliff, are nothing more than madness, insanity brought about by their arrogance and vanity. Did we ever really believe that they heard the whales? The Fish thought themselves Neptune's chosen and are paying the price of blasphemy."

"They are paying the price of our survival, Councilman," someone said.

It was true that when the rising waters had drowned civilisation and pushed them inexorably higher into the mountains, the Fish brought food from the sea to complement the meagre meals Bees would scrounge from the caves. Until able-bodied males and females started dying, children were born with deformities, and they realised that they could no longer depend on the sea for sustenance.

The Bees became more adept at sustaining food for the community, and the Ants' steady labour at perfecting remnants of Hermes' gifts allowed the Fish to go deeper and stay longer underwater. Through their alliance the colony made leaps and survived the brunt of Neptune's anger, but it was the Moles who had paid, the Moles who had toiled, bled, and died, at the hands of the ruling Fish. It was the Moles who dug the caves, who had built the houses for the colony. The Moles had been shackled into building the Divine Undertaking, and it was the Moles who had overthrown the Fish a hundred years earlier. It was the Moles whom Hades had called.

Centuries as slaves. All the other Castes seemed to have forgotten but he would not, and neither would the Fish.

"Yes!" a female voice jested slyly. "Perhaps if Moles didn't have so many wives there would be room for a few Fish!"

A few smirks followed, but the councilman saw an overture where the others saw snide.

"Polygamy," Khadivi snapped, "is the legacy of our slavery, when our women were forced into chained pregnancies. Do you wish to see the same happen to you?"

The sudden doubt on her face egged him on.

"Shall we pay the price of *their* survival? The Moles are not angry anymore, but we have not forgotten the whip of the Fish. Do you trust them not to turn on you? Do you trust the madness they leak? The sea calls them, my friends, relentlessly. If we take the heralds of Neptune with us, they will rage and we will perish.

"No, my friends, no.

"They have brought this colony to the brink once before, we cannot allow them to do so again. When Hell freezes over, when Neptune closes his scaly fist upon land and sea, the fate of the Fish must be sealed."

Hell Freezes Over

The Fish quarters lay at the bottom of each settlement along the coast, looking up towards the higher echelons on the mountainside where the Moles and the priesthood resided. Bells rang the hour, and the ending of the Council meeting. Ari thanked his mother for the bread and looked up towards the glinting windows of the Mole district.

His mind was elsewhere. The Dream was stronger since their last mission; laughter mingled with submarine harmonics, and somewhere, Adi giggled at imaginary mermaids. He closed his eyes to get a hold of his senses, wrestling with reality; the table, food and room giving way to dolphins glowing a sickly green around him…

The bread dropped from his hand and he came to, shaken violently by his father.

His mother burst into focus suddenly, tears dampening her cheek. "Even awake, now…wide awake, now!" Her hands clung to her apron and rolled into fists. She was biting her lip, shaking.

How long had he been gone? No more than a few seconds surely.

Jonah rested a hand on her shoulder, and wiped a droplet of blood pearling on her lower lip. "I've turned out alright," he said.

"No, no you haven't, none of you. You don't hear yourselves at night, or maybe you do, maybe you're all together somewhere, but I hear you, loud and clear. The sounds you make…they're not human, Jonah! They're not…"

"We've been over this before; they're just dreams, Zohar, just dreams."

She looked at Ari, spat some blood into her apron, and walked to the window, facing out to the cliff. "One night, the two of you, the two of you were…synchronised. You all were. Every single one of you in every house! The Moles came down with the Priests. No one could wake you. Some Moles even suggested killing you. I left the house. I wandered to the edge." She was visibly shaking, illuminated by the pale light breaking through the clouds. "There were things down there, Jonah. Not the whales, you've shown me those, they spit water. Other things. Strange things. Glowing things. Circling each other until the sun came up. I stayed and watched them spin for hours; made myself sick! I only turned back when they left. When I got home the noises had stopped, you were breathing normally again, both of you, all of you!"

"The scriptures are full of stranger occurrences my soul, they're just dreams…" He threw his son a look.

Ari smiled at his mother reassuringly. "It's fine, Mother, truly." But as he said so the dolphins flickered back into focus. They floated in suspended animation, staring at him silently, and exploded into particles of ice, ripping his mother apart.

When Ari entered the conference room, the tables were laid with maps, marking cities along the usual Fish routes north. The room was full of high-ranking Moles, representatives of the Priesthood and leaders of Fish communities along the coast. The air was heavy with whispers and mistrust; perhaps it was the cigar smoke making eyes squint, but Ari thought otherwise.

His father was leaning over a map, arguing with a Mole councilman, and a silent Priest. "With all due respect, Councilman, we could not have accomplished this mission six months ago. The chances of success were slim then and they are nil now."

"Is there something the Fish can't do, Jonah?" the councilman laughed, slamming a companionable hand on Jonah's back.

"I appreciate the jest, Councilman, and the trust, I do. But most of these cities are caught in the glaciers; everything north of the 49th parallel, in fact, is solid ice from sea to sky, and has been so for years. Even if we could make it that far, hoping some river ways are still navigable and some landmasses are still uncovered, we would need three months to complete this mission, with relays, a network of them." He ruffled his hair and pointed to several spots on the map. "Here around Beirut, Heraklion, and possibly Ragusa. We don't have the human capacity to support an operation of this size. Hauling equipment for transport and relay stations will slow us down significantly. Time is against us, winter will be on us before we can return, and we'd be too busy to keep track of encroachments in the permafrost."

"How much of a delay?"

Jonah paused for thought, cupping his chin and frowning. "We can cover roughly six hundred and fifty kilometres a day in a group, with the extra load, maybe half that, and we would spend half days installing the relay stations. It would be almost twenty days to Central Europe, longer on the way back if the trip is fruitful, which it won't be, Councilman."

The councilman's voice turned to syrup. "How about a… 'hit and run', I believe was the old term. Well how about a hit and swim to the glaciers, we have several seismic charges which the Divine Undertaking will not require, free as much land and town as you can, salvage what you can, and swim back? Three weeks travel time is within reason this time of year, isn't it?"

Jonah shook his head. "Impossible sir, the glaciers are too high and too thick. We could wreak significant damage, here..." He scanned the map for a few seconds. "...and here maybe, around Hannover if we can swim that far, but the repercussions sir. Thousands of tons of ice is a lot of pressure, it could cause giant waves, it *will* bring down water temperature, just enough to allow the glacier to spread faster rather than crumble, it would collapse and solidify farther in a matter of seconds; we'd be trapped under and in, there would be no coming back. A hundred years ago, even fifty, maybe. Today…"

"It is settled then, avoid the deep north, and focus your efforts on these two regions, you-"

"Would need six times the men we have sir."

Khadivi's grin told Ari that his father had fallen right into it. "And you will have them! The Council would never ask the

125

Fish to risk their lives on a suicide mission, nor would we make this unusual request if the Divine Undertaking didn't demand it, and not without significant involvement by the Council."

Jonah looked at Khadivi as if the man had grown a fin. "Sir? It's *all* deep north; it's not a question of where so much as when." Jonah did not like losing, and his face froze as he grappled for arguments to throw off the wrench he had wedged for himself. "We are grateful for your help, but your men aren't trained. There is a reason why Fish pass the tradition down, one generation after another. We would need weeks to train your recruits, and that's barely enough for them to use their equipment, and handle the storage units, sir.

"With all due respect, we are talking about months underwater!" His fist slammed down on the map, and momentarily quieted the buzz of distrust and suspicion bouncing from wall to wall. "Your men, even very well intended, don't have a mind for the depths; they would slow us down further, they're a hindrance, sir, you should know that."

"Didn't you say that you would need relay points along a network, Jonah? That you would be too busy to monitor changes in currents, sudden encroachments of permafrost, marine life, and threats of such nature?"

Jonah stood nonplussed. "Well yes sir, except the last bit, sir, we can handle those, but-"

"It is agreed then, that with enough manpower the mission can be accomplished before the winter, yes? Our men will serve at your command as relays, to monitor submarine activity, and maintain open communication with the Council. If, for any reason, we were to believe your mission could end in failure or death, we would pull back, and wait out the winter. If you have any reason to believe they cannot complete such simple tasks after three weeks of your expert training, we'd be the first to call the operation off. After all, what are a few more years to Hades?"

He turned to Ari's father, but Jonah was staring out the window, his eyes blank and unfocused. Khadivi, looking firmly away from him, smiled and said: "Agreed, Jonah?"

Jonah didn't respond. Everyone in the room had stopped talking, and stared desperately at him, the Fish leaders intimately aware of what was happening, not daring to intervene. All the Fish Dream Fish Dreams, everyone knew by now, Fish, Mole, Priest, Beast, Ant, and Bee. Everyone understood, but none would speak of it. Jonah's last inkling of pride meant that he could not ask the councilman to repeat himself; whatever the councilman's intentions, whichever conditions had been laid out, Jonah had no other choice but to acquiesce if he wanted his honour safe before his life. But even then, the Moles could coerce him into doing exactly what they wanted.

"Agreed? Jonah?"

His eyes shifted back to reality and he looked around, catching the other Fish's eyes, and knew he had lost. "Yes sir. Agreed sir. Of course sir." Embarrassment and shame tinted his voice. "In the name of the Divine Undertaking all Men must labour, and all Men must sacrifice."

Ben Golkar knew he would pass out eventually, but he would never get used to sleeping underwater.

As a child, he had always envied them, but he would never get used to any of it. Ever. He was a Bee; and the Fish…well, they were freakish.

Regulating oxygen levels to induce prolonged bouts of rest was unnatural, decidedly unnatural, so was tying yourself to cliff walls and inside shallow caves, and the way the Fish let themselves get carried away into sleep, oblivious to their surroundings, and the way they sometimes hummed.

How could they? People went missing every other night…

They were all tied along submarine cliffs in small clusters spread over several hundred meters. Some had chosen to break away a little, for whatever privacy the open ocean could offer, but even in the dark you never felt alone, there

were creatures down there that could sense you, even when
you couldn't see them.

Huge things tore each other apart out there...

He couldn't be the only non-Fish still awake. "Einat," he
whispered on the colony's frequency. "Einat, you up?"

Ben sensed something large passing in front of him, the
pressure of water displacement against the cliff, a sudden
warmth as the dark waters went black

On the other end of the line Einat, on the cusp of sleep,
responded. "...Ben? Ben? What do you..."

Einat fell asleep instants before she would have heard a
hungry blare gnawing Ben short.

"How many did we lose last night?" Jonah asked his son.

"Fish or recruits?"

"Recruits."

"Seven..."

Fish Dream on land, and Fish Dream in water. As the weeks
passed, installing markers, trackers, and cables, along the way
west before heading north, Ari's dreams grew deeper.

The waters beneath him swallowed even the darkness. Light
did not fade so much as squeeze to death, leading to the real
bottom, the old ocean floors that would never freeze. Those
depths were the true dark. Somewhere down there was where
all Fish went. The currents rising from them, lashing upwards
to the surface were suddenly drawn back down like giant
tentacles, carrying ripples that spoke of minds.

In the depths, day or night, reality or Dream, who knew? In
his sleep, he could feel other Dreamers circling him. Unlike at
the surface, where the other Dreamers were shadows and
shapes barely glimpsed beneath the surface, underwater he
knew their evil, their care, their disdain, their disinterest, their
love, their amusement; but above all, even in the deepest
Dream, when things he couldn't see and could not bear to,
loomed over and around him in his sleep, he knew that he
was safe.

The recruits were not. Nights could go by without an incident, but one day three never woke up, two were never found, and one could not be identified for missing a head, suit, and skin.

"Do you have any idea what's happening to them, Dad?"

Some recruits spoke of darker shadows, moving faster than the currents, of muffled noises around them on nights when their companions disappeared, of deafening sounds and a stink of decomposing flesh.

The Fish feigned incomprehension; they were too far ahead in the mission to cause further panic by voicing speculations. It helped reassure the recruits that Fish died and went missing too, floating away when the Dream took them.

"I don't know, Son. None of this has ever happened in Fish memory that I know of. Told Khadivi about them. They're trained and they knew what they were getting into, but they're not clawing off their own faces in their sleep or drifting off careless, I can tell you that much…"

What his father did not dare voice was the presence of the Dreamers, the sense of looming beings in the night, the sense of safety the Fish all shared, inevitably translated into one, or several, dead recruits.

Never was a Fish found eviscerated and fed on in the morning. Sea creatures could be as vicious as they were playful, attack with blinding speed in the blind waters. Jellyfish, brainless and indiscriminate in the thousands, and things with mouths… But in the Dream there was always safety, safety until morning.

Chunks of flesh and suit were still tied to the rocky surface, nibbled on by tiny eels working their way around the fibre in the suit, stripping them clean of bits of bone and sinew.

"We found three more partially eaten corpses like this." Ari added, "The other three…gone…"

His father nodded gravely and floated away mumbling "*I told them, I told them…*"

Once they installed the relay stations, the recruits would be safer, and it would be possible for them to keep guard and alternate working shifts. They would be safer.

Mame Bougouma Diene

"West... West... West..." Their teammate Rebecca's communications were erratic, confusing and often rhythmical. For days, between flashes of lucidity, she kept muttering the same word over the com-lines. '*West, west, west...*' he could not shut her out without cutting himself off from the network, so he endured on. They would lose her any day now, and the sooner the better, for them as well as for her.

"Becky, we're heading north-northwest," someone would chime in every now and then, keeping Rebecca focused enough so she would not try to head back southeast in the opposite direction she urged them towards.

It was a burden they all shared, and none of them wanted to be alone when the Dream and reality became indistinguishable, but it had been down to him for several days, and he didn't bother to respond to her anymore, just as long as she kept pace.

Things were easier now that they had left the recruits at the relay stations with supplies. They were swimming over a city called Budapest, or what remained of it. There was nothing left to offer in the city or in the nuclear power plants further north. Bridge foundations remained intact, but everywhere metal frames spiked out of shattered buildings, massive structures open to the waters, with rows of seats surrounding empty stages, flooded plazas covered in rock and algae. From above, you could clearly tell where the river used to flow under bridges and around the central island. All of the city's wealth in wiring, batteries, glass, plastic—anything that could be used, fixed, or recycled—had been plundered by generation after generation of Fish.

They would head northwest from here towards France and with luck, the ice would have retreated far enough that land would be free up to London and most of the old industrial zones that were open to scavenging.

Or so Jonah hoped.

Without luck England would still be under, Northern France would be iced over already, and if the ice had reached the

130

Western Alps then they would have to double back and pray; it would be the last winter before returning to the Cave.

The recruits had held them back more than they'd expected. They were over a week behind; a few more days and it would be the longest Ari had ever spent underwater, and never this long over Europe. He had been as far as Istanbul, and much further southeast for oil, where most Fish missions went. He could have reached here sooner, but this was a different route, further southwest towards Lebanon, then north to Greece to install another relay station before B-Team headed west towards Spain and A-Team caught currents heading north. *We should have sent Rebecca along with them.*

Ari hated himself for thinking that way, but couldn't help it. Before the Dream took you, some of the things you said had meaning. Most of them did not. Sometimes they were prophetic, but prophecy is as much a matter of minutes as of centuries; it will happen sooner or later, and you would lose your mind trying to decipher every random thought.

"B-Team, do you copy? B-Team, do you copy? We have reached Munich and found evidence of deep icing at the bottom. What is the situation in Spain? I repeat, what is the situation in Spain?" Jonah vocalised on the com-lines.

With the winter it was not uncommon for communications to go out for a few days between teams. Any change in the ice cap could muddle communications over very long distances.

Jonah switched frequencies to the recruits at the relay stations. "Relay Station 2, do you copy?"

"We copy, A-Team."

"Relay Station 2, inform the council that ice has encroached to Munich, I repeat, ice has encroached to Munich. By our estimates the glaciers must be no further than 3-400 miles north-northwest. North-northeast might be safer, but not for very long. Water has solidified overhead. Relay Station 2, do you copy?"

"We copy, A-Team. We will inform the Council and communicate their instructions. A-Team, do you copy?"

"We copy, Relay Station 2. On stand-by for instructions."

Ari spun. *"West, Ari! West!"* Rebecca's voice exploded through the com-lines propelling him backwards into a tower. For a second an orca appeared where she floated, swallowed by a lantern-eyed beast the size of the buildings beneath him.

"Ari? What fool games are you playing? If there was anything here we wouldn't be picking ice out of our noses," Jonah said pointing upwards. "See how thin the crust is? It's pretty damn sharp too, so don't tempt it." His father's voice was thick with nerves.

Ari shook himself out of the rubble and floated up to his father. "I'm sorry, did you not see that!?" he yelled through the com-unit, pointing at empty waters.

Jonah followed his finger. "See what?"

"Becky! She was right there, she…" His voice trailed off when he saw nothing behind him but cerulean flows.

Panic registered beneath his father's helmet. He activated a sensor meant for locking arms to half-ton transport cubes, and clamped Ari's shoulders, the sudden pressure nearly breaking bones and sending a flash of searing pain through his skull. "Kid… Becky's gone. Do you understand me?"

Ari started heaving frantically into his breathing unit. Jonah unclenched a hand, turned it, and caught Ari across the face with a blow, while his other hand kept him from spinning.

"When was the last time you saw her?"

"Just a moment ago...she was right behind me before she-"

Ari turned around, looking upwards and downwards; all five hundred Fish left in A-Team were focused on them—some swam in concentric and overlapping circles around the group but all com-units were silent—intent on the conversation. None appeared to have seen Rebecca, or an orca, or a giant stomach with teeth, or heard a Fish burst into whale song.

"When was the last time you remember her interacting with the team? Anybody but you?" Jonah's words were slow, and the deafening silence on the com-waves made the ocean feel like a Priest, his tilted head passing judgement.

"About…four days ago, she kept babbling on, same as she had for days, she started drifting east. I caught up with her, and turned her back our way. Been keeping an eye on her ever since."

"Son, Rebecca was gone in the morning, she drifted off in the night…and she's been behind you since?"

He didn't answer. The A-Team kept floating around them effortlessly. He should have been worried, his father was, but Rebecca's voice in the Dream, while terrified, had sounded helpful.

Jonah shook his head. "It's fine. Night will be on us in a few hours." He raised his voice. "We'll bunk in the buildings and wait for word from the Council. The centre of the city has the most remaining structures; we'll stay in groups of ten within a one-mile radius. We'll reconvene in nine hours if we haven't received word. Understood? Good. Ari, you bunk with me."

The ice was thicker nine hours later. The glaciers had moved southeast enough that the water gleamed with thin particles of ice pushing south.

"Relay Station 2, do you copy? This is A-Team, do you copy?" Jonah said through the network.

"We copy, A-Team. We have just received word from Relay Station 1. You are to stand-by, A-Team; I repeat, stand-by. An emergency session of the Council was called to discuss matters. We have received word from B-Team that significant progress was made in Spain. Stand-by for further instructions. I repeat, stand-by for further instructions. A-Team, do you copy?"

"We copy, Relay Station 2. It's getting rough out here. Ten to twelve hours. Tops. We will expect word from you. In exactly twelve hours I will give orders to consolidate at your location until further communications. Relay Station 2, do you copy?"

"We copy, A-Team. We'll be passing on instructions soon. Hang in tight."

Exactly eleven hours later, just as Jonah was giving orders to double back, Relay Station 2 broke silence. "A-Team, do you copy? A-Team, this is Relay Station 2. A-Team, do you copy?"

"We copy, Relay Station 2. About to lift camp. I repeat, about to lift camp. Relay Station 2, do you copy?"

Temperatures had plummeted since the last contact with the relay station. Where thin particles of ice lit up the dark only a few hours ago, the water was now thick with them, almost slush. Another few hours, less, and the slush would thicken, coagulate, and harden until the moving glacier solidified, creating explosions on the surface, like a giant's thump blowing dust in every direction, blasting ice further south into the waters ahead.

"We copy, A-Team. B-Team is heading back east from Spain. You are to reconvene over Sicily and help with transport. I repeat, reconvene with B-Team over Sicily and help with transport. A-Team, do you copy?"

"We copy, Relay Station 2. Requesting explanation for the delay in communications. Do you copy? Requesting explanation for the delay."

There was a long pause before the relay's response. "We copy, A-Team. A flash storm heading north-northwest hit the colony overnight—communications were disrupted for ten hours. A-Team, do you copy?"

"We copy, Relay Station 2. Relay Station 2, the glaciers are moving faster than anticipated. Conditions over Munich deteriorating exponentially, I repeat, conditions over Munich deteriorating exponentially. At going rates, we will never be more than a few hours ahead of the ice. I repeat; we will never be more than a few hours ahead of the ice. We may have to evacuate Relay Stations after contact with B-Team. Relay Station 2, do you copy?"

"We copy, A-Team, and thank you for fair warning. On stand-by until you make contact over Sicily. Repeat, on stand-by until contact in Sicily. Over and out."

Priority communications shut down and no one spoke until Amir cleared his throat on the com-line and spun a few back flips for show. Amir made everything he said sound like he was coughing up spite. "Haven't heard of a north-northeast storm, flash or otherwise, heading for the colony this season since never. My old man might have said something about that but the Dream took him, and he was drunk most of the time so who knows?"

Laughter rang on the com-line. Amir spun a few more back flips and cleared his throat again. He would die before the Dream took him, and that shouldn't be long. No living Fish had known his father; at nearly sixty Amir was the oldest Fish alive.

"Incoming!" a voice ahead of him rang through the com-lines.

Ari sensed the temperatures drop against his face and barely ducked as a streak of frozen shards, several feet long and sharp as cut diamonds, circumvented a bend in the mountainside along a meddling current, and landed directly in front of him. The two Fish swimming immediately behind were less fortunate, and the waters flashed a momentary red.

The frozen peaks of the Alps towered above the icecap, but beneath, the titanic bodies of the mountains shifted the currents, creating powerful flash maelstroms, yanking Fish into boulders and caves, and smashing them against cliffs.

The ice would move faster in some areas than others, dashing into crevasses and between the stone giants only to reverse its course and rip through the swimmers.

Navigation was difficult, communication worse, and they were getting ever less sleep, never more than a few hours rest when conditions were good, and they seldom were. They doubled down in clear streams and they would wake in pre-glacier slush, but worse, the Dream was free of Dreamers. After weeks of feeling their presence it was discomfiting to sleep without them. On any day, hours could go by without sensing them, but now they were gone entirely.

They rested in cities only twice, and only because the weather conditions made sleeping along cliff walls too dangerous. In both Milan and Naples, buildings came down on the Fish during the night, and the slush infiltrated respirators, oxygen converters, and filters.

By the time they reached Sicily there was no sign of B-Team, but the ice had slowed its rapid progress south, the bulk of the glacier still working its way around the Alps.

"Relay Station 2, this is A-Team, do you copy?" Jonah said.

"We copy, A-Team. Over."

"There is no sign of B-Team, I repeat, no sign of B-Team. The ice is gaining ground, but the mountains are in the way. Evacuate Relay Station 2, consolidate at Relay Station 1. I repeat, evacuate and consolidate at Relay Station 1. Relay Station 2, do you copy?"

"Copy, A-Team. Good luck. Over."

They would need luck. The Dream was taking them in droves, and several Fish would go missing at a time, falling behind and into the deeper slush. Some would emerge and fall back in again, slower in their movements, weaker in resisting the currents.

Ari held on to sanity for Jonah, and Zohar at home, but fear rode the Dream—not his own fear, although it was there too and blurred his vision almost constantly now. Behind him, he caught a reflection of a whale in the ice wall where there was no ice, and no whale.

Around him and ahead of him was thickening slush, even where the waters were clear. His limbs fell numb as he swam, as if they were not his own. Perhaps the other Fish were all feeling the same thing. If it were not for Jonah's constant surveillance, he would have fallen behind too.

Relay Station 2 was deserted as expected; the slush had not reached the station from the north, confirming that the northeast was still relatively quiet, yet the recruits had packed all the equipment, including chargers for the propulsion engines, food and energy packs, and oxygen filters.

"Relay Station 1, do you copy? Relay Station 1?" Jonah asked on the line.

The com-line was silent.

"B-Team, do you copy? This is A-Team, do you copy?"

"A-Team, this is B-Team, do you copy?"

"We copy, B-Team. Over."

"A-Team! This is B-Team, do you copy?" the voice sounded panicked.

"We copy, B-Team, keep calm. Do you copy?" Jonah asked again.

"A-Team, do you copy?! A-Team?! A-Team, head east now! I repeat! Head-" An explosion sounded on the com-line and communication stopped.

"B-Team? B-Team, do you copy? B-Team!"

His father's yelling on the com-line shook Ari out of the Dream long enough for him to assess the situation coldly: B-Team had lost contact, Relay Stations 1 and 2 were deserted, and it took twenty hours altogether, *twenty hours*, for the Council to communicate instructions…

Relay Station 1 was not only abandoned, it was sabotaged. Perhaps, if they hadn't needed to let Amir distract them from the obvious, they would have paid closer attention to what he had said about flash storms this season, and started adding up. *Not since never? Maybe his old man?* No one had ever met Amir's old man; he had been dead forty years or more, and if Amir could not be sure… It took a few minutes for each member of the team to put the last few days together, but someone had to ask.

"Jonah. When you met with the councilman, what were his reasons for this mission?"

Fish missions seldom headed north. Monitoring missions would travel regularly to measure changes in the glaciers and alert the colony to ice moving south. But Europe was always intermittently under ice now, most missions headed south, over the Gulf, for oil reserves that were immediately available and easier to transport. Those waters teemed with submarine life, some benign, some not. But in these waters, abandoned by the Dreamers, sifting through the equipment left behind at Relay Station 2, running out of oxygen, food, sleep, and power, finding only enough propulsion engines to get a handful safely back to a colony that had already decided on their fate…

Jonah gave a start, hesitated, and paused, but Adam cut in. "It's alright, Jonah, we know, we saw you argue this mission best you could."

"Yeah, don't worry about it, Jonah."

"Yeah boss, couldn't have done better myself."

"Yeah, we all saw you, Jonah."

"Yeah…" The com-line was a chorus of agreements.

"It was gonna happen sooner or later, Jonah," Amir proclaimed. "We all saw it coming, we just never said nothing, none of us. We never cared; none of us did, even now. Moles set us up, Council says nothing, Dream kicks in, decisions are made and we're out at sea again, swimming head first into Hell, not 'membering what the hell for or how it is we got suckered in again. None of us care anymore; the Dream'll take us all. Sounds to me like something else got B-Team, and I don't see them caring either. This is the only way for us to go Jonah. So what they say, huh? What can you remember?"

Jonah threw his head back and floated closer to the group. "The only thing that matters every time, Amir: the spouses and kids will be cared for if anything…"

Amir laughed out loud. "That's a nice thought! Not that it matters much either…"

Several voices snapped back at him angrily.

"Easy for you to say, we aren't all married to Fish."

"Yeah, you moron, my wife is a Bee."

"So is my husband."

"My wife was a Mole until they cast her out."

"And so is my wife," Jonah interjected before a fight broke out. His voice had grown firmer. "We made that choice when we married them and we knew what it meant. For Yuri it meant extra ratios of grain, we all know that." Laughter again relieved the tension, but there was little to be wary about anymore. "Those we meet in the Dream we can worry about then, for those we don't…Hades' embrace is warm and comforting…"

Jonah's words afterwards were few and short. The Council had urged the mission forward, in full knowledge of the risks to the Fish, and there was little doubt left that the Moles and Priests were expecting this outcome. Exploiting the last of the resources in Europe before the ice settled over it, and the last winter before the Cave? Right…

Moles…thieves, murderers, and worse, and enslaved for it. To chain a murderer must have made sense when the world fell apart and the waters rose every day; they had needed every hand then, but their children? In perpetuity? In times like those he wondered what kind of masters they had been, or who'd pointed the finger and separated the Moles from the others…

A voice boomed through the waters, part human, part whale song: *WEST*…

A-Team turned west. Ari spun on himself and saw Rebecca again, floating ahead of him, translucent, and glittering with ice flecks, then disappearing once more in a silent blast a few feet from the Fish, rippling through the waters in waves that knocked them back, slammed them into the ice crust, and spiralling towards the bottom. They all felt it this time. Ari tumbled back, regained control, and stabilised himself facing the direction of the blast.

In the distance, the waters were getting darker; gaining ground forward, he focused his visor on a noticeably darker shape caught deep in the incoming slush, and reality caught up with the Dream. Another shock wave threw him back, and another, and another. His visor focused again on the shape, tumble after tumble. He zoomed in on it, and a two-headed white whale was revealed. It was struggling to free itself, tail caught in the western glacier, each new blast ripping chunks of flesh as ice cut through skin and nerve to the bone.

Another blast dislodged ice from the surface, raining several tons of ice blocks, dozens of feet thick, on the scrambling Fish.

Ari felt drawn forward, torn out of his body towards the living ice wall and the dying whale, and yet he remained motionless. He braced himself for impact when, suddenly, the glacier was spreading ahead of him. He could not move, air was freezing in his lungs and the cold numbed the pain from his massive wounds. His entire body trapped, his tail useless, he caught sight of his second head, its eyes black and dead.

Through the ice, he saw human shapes bouncing discordantly in the distance, struggling to stay out of the blast radius. He felt his strength leaving him, his massive heart fading with a final thump, and his eyes zoomed forward again, through the ice, and into the desperate shapes. He saw himself floating lifeless a few yards ahead. Just as he collided with his own body, reality took over and he saw his father was floating above him, one of the metal fixings from the relay station jammed into his ribs, blood twirling into a shield around him as he spun, helplessly bounced around by the blasts, dead underwater.

Ice particles flashed by, cutting through skin suits, and riding only a few seconds ahead of the slush, coagulating almost instantly on disoriented Fish.

Ari floated up to his father and ripped the propulsion pack attached to his back, cursing himself, hoping against luck that there was enough energy left to make it to the colony. No matter what happened, he would see his mother, and he would die taking out as many Moles as he could before they did him. The Dream could claim him then, but not now.

He repeated the operation with three more corpses, attached a food and energy pack to his skin suit, and blasted his way out of the thickening muck, and ahead, faster and faster ahead.

The glacier had changed directions. The Fish had wrongly assumed that its progression was a constant south-southeast. They had never considered that it could have been converging from the west as well. The explosion that silenced B-Team made sense to him now.

Spreading cracks in the icing overhead alerted him to the much larger northern glacier resuming its progress south. If he were not careful, he would be caught in a vice and forced south. If he did not gain speed he would be too far south to reach the colony, if he did not run out of propulsion first. He shot himself towards the surface at an angle, trying to break the thinner ice cap to get a sense of the glacier from the surface.

He projected himself forward at full speed, then up at a spin; to ease the impact with the surface and have a rotating view, catching all the angles before plunging back and repeating the operation again. Cutting through the air rather than the water would keep him out of the slush and explosions, and with luck, he would stay ahead just long enough when he dove back down to allow himself another leap through the surface.

His helmet broke through the ice and into the blearing sunlight. The sun shone bright on the ice, and the sky was a perfect blue, but you could not have guessed from beneath. The spin should have blocked the sun out intermittently, but the reflection on the ice made it worse. He activated his shading unit.

The bulk of the glacier was closing in on him from the west and northwest. The ice cap itself stretched for several hundred yards behind him, until the glacier filled it in from the bottom, and there, the world ended. *A kilometre. Maybe less. Moving at thirty meters a second.*

The surface blew up and settled in sequence. Row after row of frozen eruptions, a cloud of diamonds and glass, stretching north and south further than he could see, settling and rising again in waves.

Where the detonations below were silent killers, the deflagrations outside were shock waves of vertigo. He saw a group of Fish leap through the surface and into the air in the distance, he could not tell who they were, but they were too close to the glacier, much too close. The Fish spun down headfirst into the ice. Ari zoomed out too late. The first Fish's head burst open in blood against it, missing the thinner ice

141

cap by only a few yards. The glacier exploded southward almost as soon as he hit, shredding the body to reddish powder, and slicing the remainder of the group in a detonation of ice spears.

Ari's spin brought him downwards, through the ice cap, into the streaking ice, and up again in hundred meter leaps. It was all he could do to stay ahead, trying to beat Neptune's closing, vengeful fist, leaping and swimming north-northeast towards the colony.

The waters were shallower when he approached the cliff. He could no longer dive as deep nor leap as high. His propulsion pack was running out, and the smaller, more frequent leaps gobbled up all the energy he had left. The glacier moved faster in the hollow waters, blast after blast, threatening almost every leap and every dive, but the familiar cliffs of the colony drew him in.

The smell of smoke caught his nose mid-jump; burning pyres lined the edge of the cliff. He could not tell who they were, but he had little doubt the Moles had kept their word and *taken care* of the children and spouses.

Thousands of voices flooded the Dream. Not the screams of the bodies on the pyres—he was too far to hear them—but a choir of emotions and feelings, none of them painful, all of them accepting. He sought his mother in the jungle of sentience, and could not find her. He probed for his father, and felt him somewhere, and Adi, and Amir...

The smell of smoke, stronger now, broke the spell, but it was too late.

Caught in the dead Fish's Dreams, he tried a leap towards the cliff wall. He would break the surface, he thought, soar over the flames, and find arms somehow, food too, somehow, and then he would wreak havoc, and then and only then, the Dream would take him. He concentrated all the power in his propulsion engines for a final leap forward.

His head broke the ice, but the slush solidified around his feet and pulled him back against his impulse, snapping him in half at the waist. The ice closed in on his body before both halves could fully separate and numbed him to the pain.

He tried to scream and his lungs froze. A low rumble built up underneath him, in useless warning of the eruption to come. The sun faded from his vision along with the smell of smoke and the burning pyres.

The world disappeared, and he saw shapes floating through the depths. Large. Faceless. Floating stomachs with thick tentacles by the hundreds, holding eyes and mouths. Among them he saw dolphins and sharks, glowing in shades of yellow and green. Slowly dying of radiation poisoning, slowly changing into new things. And even smaller, between the dolphins and the sharks, between and around the monsters and the whales, tiny, tiny creatures, shaped just as Fish were when they wore their suits. Small creatures such as he had never seen before, attaching themselves to dolphin, shark, whale and mutant alike, guiding them, drifting gently at their side... He felt himself shrink as the rumble of the glacier grew tenor, then baritone, and saw a giant two-headed white whale in the depths, catching the light glowing off the dolphins, and he swam closer to it, ever shrinking, ever deeper, ever smaller...

...The explosion obliterated his body in a deluge of ice, flesh, and blood, but Ari was already in the depths, in the comfort of the Dream.

2: Hell or High Lava

There was a Time before the world was stone…
There was a Time when birds of flame rose from pits of the same, soaring from cavern to chasm, spreading fire with their wings, nigh invisible in the furnace that was the world. There was a Time when life bled from the earth, burning the ground alive.
Those birds are gone now, and the world has grown old and rigid. Where it was soft and warm, it was now hard and cold. They thought of her as a Mole, but in her heart she was the Phoenix…

The school day had ended early, and the sun was setting over the ocean behind Rina as she walked through the gardens.

Ahead, Bees were covering the fields under electro-photo-thermal protective sheets. When the sun set the sheets would shed light and heat on the plants for the early hours of the night, and then just heat when tended by the Bees working the night shift. Water was channelled through heated capillary tubing from the giant cisterns by the mountain and distributed to the plants through irrigation veins.

The Bees' work was down to five months a year. Her father joked that they would not be busy Bees much longer. She had asked what that meant. An old saying, he'd said. Bees must have been busy someday, go figure.

After the summer the Ants would blast the plantation, bringing up fresh soil. Bees would sow the soil and install the sheets for several weeks, tending to the plants only when there were signs of growth until even artificial heat could not keep the cold out of the ground and the water.

Meanwhile, Bee women and children would secure the produce from the summer and organise it in rations before submitting reports to the Council for distribution. Male Bees would move further southeast, behind the mountain for grazing until the winter.

Rina tripped over a small flowerpot, sending dirt and seeds flying around her as she fell.

A hand grabbed her by the neck, and yanked her off the ground. "Why, you little…" Rina turned to stare into the face of an angry old Bee. "…stinking…"

A young man rushed in, whispering something in the old man's ear. Rina could not make out his words clearly, something about Mole girls, rushed talk, and something about Hades. Whatever it was, it mollified the old man, who put her down, and dusted off his hands. He looked down at her strangely, turned, and walked away without a word.

The younger man patted her on the head. "Don't worry about him, little girl, cold is working his joints, he gets like that sometimes…but, you!" Rina jumped to attention. "What's your name?"

"Rina!"

"Well Rina, I'm Dan, and you need to do two things, one of which is to watch your step—that's food for the colony you just spilled. Understand?" Rina nodded vigorously. "Good. The second is to get home before nightfall. You Moles are really easy with your girls, but besides your mother, you got Beasts to worry about along the way. Now scram!"

"Hey! Watch where you're going!" yelled a teenage Bee carrying roots and berries out of a small store. Rina turned and poked her tongue at him. The alleyways were crowded with Moles changing shifts, and Ants, Bees, and Beasts on their way back from the places they disappeared to while she went to school.

She could get home before her second mother, Chaya, and her sister, Hadar, if she was fast enough. They spent the afternoon at Hadar's husband's house. She was pregnant with his child, and officially married but his first wife had not passed yet, soon, but not yet. He was still in love with her and uncomfortable having Hadar stay in his house, but they visited.

145

Hadar was getting fat. Rina had tried to poke her belly but she'd pulled Rina's head to her stomach to feel the baby's kick. If it was a boy, only four more and Hadar would be finished with her pregnancy duties.

She slowed her pace and hid behind a large wooden cart full of scrap metal as a squad of Fish stepped out of a house dragging two unconscious teenage Moles by the hair, their faces dripping blood, followed by an Ant, his hands tied behind his back. Their leader, a short woman, landed her boot on one of their heads.

The flow of people along the alleyway hadn't stopped, but a few paid attention and many more leaned over from small balconies and windows.

"The two Moles were found attempting to smuggle contraband into the tunnels, and this Ant, abetted them!" said the leader. More people were stopping now, there was something about sentencing that people wanted to hear, if only to have an opinion. One of the boys started struggling. A short, male Fish shocked him with a lancer, and he went numb again. "They will be flogged and thrown over the cliff! The Ant will serve three months penance in the cells and one working the mines! If there are any complaints, log them with the Priests!"

The Ant's knees went weak at the word *mine*, but he managed a steady step as they dragged the two boys away and he followed them guarded by the rest of the squadron.

They walked past the scrap cart but didn't see her crouched at boot-level. She dusted herself off as they rounded the bend curving down between the rows of houses towards the Fish quarters, and followed the smell of smoke around the mountain to where the Moles resided, guarded, and dug the Divine Undertaking.

The common room was empty when Rina cracked the door open. She shut it quietly behind her and rushed to her room, staying there reading until noises drifted through the door.

Hell Freezes Over

She heard Hadar warming up the stove in the small kitchen by the window and talking to Chaya.

Her room was windowless, on the top floor of a three-story house built against and inside the mountain wall. There was just enough room for her bed, a small table for studies, and a string to hang her clothes. Each of her three sisters had rooms of their own, which made her brothers horribly jealous. Boys shared their rooms, and with five brothers, Rina's few square feet were the envy of most of her male siblings.

"Hadar, take some rest, I'll warm up the stove," Chaya said. She heard her sister shuffle her feet to a chair and breathe deeply. The pregnancy was weighing heavily on her, and now that her third mother was between children, she could relieve her of domestic duties.

"Rina?! Get out here!" Chaya's summon drew her into the common room. "How was school?" she asked. Her smile slid from Rina to Hadar and back.

"Fine," Rina said, and smiled back warmly at her second mother. Chaya was a loving woman, and had recovered well from carrying Noah. Her strength was returning, and she could get back behind the stove.

"You're done with your homework?" Hadar grunted.

Rina nodded hesitantly, happy that Chaya had turned her attention back to the stove. Lying to Chaya was half of what she considered homework, and she would have recognised Hadar's grunt for doubt at her sister's honesty. Rina winked at Hadar, who smiled faintly, and pulled herself up to look out of the kitchen window.

Mole quarters spread east and west below the Divine Undertaking. Beneath them stood the Ant, Beast, and Bee neighbourhoods on a lower ridge below the Mole district, opening on the plantations. Stretching all the way down to the lower plateau before the cliff, the Fish quarters still occupied most of the colony, and ended in a perimeter wall that circled the settlement, manned day and night by armed Fish guards. Beyond the wall, smaller Fish communities dotted the edge of the cliff, overlooking the waters that were the world.

From the kitchen window, she could see down past the narrow streets of the Mole quarters, all the way to the furthest Fish settlements, distinguishable only by faint lights in the pitch darkness and dwarfed by the brilliance of the colony.

Rina's mother had died two years earlier. After delivering Rina her health deteriorated, she could no longer bear as many children, nor could she offer any contribution to the Divine Undertaking. Community members had tried to convince her father to let her go, but he had stuck with her.

Dror and Ora, Rina's mother, had had five children. Rina had two younger sisters and two younger brothers from her mother, two older brothers and an older sister, Hadar, from a woman she had never met, whom Dror had married before Ora. With Chaya's baby boy, Noah, asleep in her father's room, they totalled at nine.

Rina's painful memories of her mother, frail and weak, too tired to move some days, were disappearing into Chaya's warm smile and food.

Chaya was happy to have someone around the house helping her, first while she delivered and recovered, and now more than ever with Noah piercing the neighbourhood with screams, to help her stay sane. Rina looked up. Her second mother was leaning over the window, her face tense and hard.

"Rina," she said, without turning away from the street. "Go fetch your little sisters; your father and brothers are coming up. Get the table ready."

Bless the grain from Neptune's winds
Bless the bread from Hades' warmth
Bless the seeds sown by our hands
Freeze the world and warm our hearts.

Dror was pale throughout the blessings and even paler throughout dinner, unable to take more than a bite at a time. He left the table early, followed by Chaya, leaving Rina and her siblings to finish the meal alone.

After a few minutes of silence, Rina asked for permission to go to the bathroom. She walked to the small hallway where her father's room stood across from the bathroom. After pretending to go, she instead tiptoed across the hall and stuck her ear to a small crack in the wooden door.

"...losing it...get worse every day...forget their orders and beat us for not following them, forget why they are beating us halfway through and beat us for it..." Her father coughed heavily, a wet, pulpy sound that made Rina's dinner lurch in her stomach.

"Rest, husband," Chaya said.

Rina checked the hall, and listened for footsteps from the dinner table; when she was sure they were still all seated, she glued her eye to the crack, trying to see her father.

Only glimpses of him were visible in the thick steam rising from a bowl at the foot of the bed by Chaya's toes. She dipped a piece of cloth inside it and wiped his brow and face gently.

Dror caught his breath between fits of coughing. "...Eitan...go get...Eitan..."

The cough was getting worse. Rina could not make out the words her father formed, and stumbled forward when her second mother pulled the door open. "Rina!" she started.

"It's alright," Dror interjected. "It's alright...let her in...you get Eitan...I'll talk to him...later."

Chaya gave Rina a long look, as if her second mother was for the first time, seeing her not as a child to care for, one in a long list of many, but unique, and foreign.

Rina shoved her way into the room, pushing past Chaya, diverting her eyes from her wearying gaze, and up to her father's bed.

The shadows that danced on Dror's face by the dinner's candlelight revealed deep bruises around her father's eyes now that she was close. He coughed up blood and doubled over. Rina yelped.

"It's ok, sweetheart... just Hades...bubbling up... haha... nothing...we haven't seen in the caves....a hundred times..."

149

He attempted a smile, but his lips twisted in a rictus as he tried to stop himself from hacking up more blood.

A knock rang at the door, and her oldest brother Eitan walked in. She ran into his arms and started crying. Eitan rested a hand on her head and ran it through her hair. Hadar was standing in the doorstep, her eyes heavy and wet.

"It's gonna be alright, Rina," Eitan tried to reassure her, but her father chose that moment to go into a bout of damp, raspy breaths.

Hadar walked in to draw her out of her brother's arms. She would not let go. Eitan forced her to the door with Hadar's help, and closed it on them. The sliver of light under the door went out, and Rina heard a whisper coming from the room followed by another fit of coughing.

A storm was brewing on the horizon when Rina walked into the common room in the morning. Sirens rang from the perimeter wall, alerting the rest of the colony to the incoming onslaught of wind and water. From beyond the wall, the wind carried the sound of Fish drummers beating at the storm. Rising and falling with the gusts of wind between sirens, sticks thumped a deep bass rhythm on taut goatskin punctuated by rapid fire staccatos.

Dror, Eitan, and the rest of her brothers, were already underground and would not come back until the tempest had abated. In a few minutes, a Priest would come knocking to home-school the girls for the duration of the storm.

Chaya rose from her chair and shut the window when the wind began to knock candles over and blow cutlery off the table.

Rina sat down with a cup of tea at a table still spattered with red dots from when her father had sat less than an hour earlier. She reached over and found most of the stains were dry though some stuck wetly to her finger. She scrubbed them frantically with her pocket tissue, removing some, while leaving little pieces of lint glued over others.

She scrubbed until the Priest knocked and Hadar went to open the door for him, scrubbed until his hand stopped her, and he sat at the table.

Narcissus leaned over the pond, catching his own reflection in the stillness of the water. Water had not always been still. His Will and his Will alone had made it so. What trees would not bend to it would crack. What water did not still to it would spill. The land would bear forth the fruits of his desires, lest it wither and dry and crumble from sand to dust to powder, dissolving before his Will.

Narcissus leaned over the pond, catching his own reflection in the stillness of the water. But the sun rose high above and reflected in the water, blinding him to his image. So he built walls around the pond and a roof over his head so the sun would bother him no more.

Narcissus leaned over the pond, catching his own reflection in the stillness of the water. But the waters were dark and the weather grew cold. So he set about starting a fire to warm himself and mock the sun.

Narcissus leaned over the pond, catching his own reflection in the stillness of the water, in the shade of the roof, and the warmth of the fire. But the smoke burned his eyes, the roof trapped the air, and the water grew warm. From its depths rose a shape, a shape that was a hand, a hand that was a fist. And Neptune drew Narcissus into the pond, into the boiling waters which bubbled and bled, fiercer and louder and higher until they overcame the fire, burst through the roof, put out the sun, and spilled over the world...announcing a new Time.
— Narcissus' Folly

"Rina! Rina Arfazadeh?!" A short, blond girl walked out of the examination room at the other end of the long hall, behind the Priestess calling out Rina's name, her head low, but smiling faintly. Rina stood up.

Hadar had left only a few days after the storm. Dror had never come back. Eitan's face had been sombre and he'd

151

become unusually dark in the following days, but he'd never said what happened to their father. Even now, almost two years later sitting in the Priestess' anteroom, waiting for her Fertility & Fitness Evaluation, she could still feel the honey-like stickiness of his drying blood on the table tingling under her fingertip. The Priest's dismissive look at it—raising his eyebrows cynically as if telling her to grow up, it was time for Mole female duties—brought something up in her. Trembling with memory she walked into the medical room.

It was her first time seeing the kind of equipment used for Fitness & Fertility testing. These medical facilities were less clustered, and admitted only girls and women. This room had a bed larger and longer than her own or her father's—Eitan's now—and medical equipment she had never seen and did not understand. Everything gleamed with a weapon-like sheen and seemed invasive somehow, angry and intimidating.

A group of Ants was busying around the machines, making last-minute adjustments before leaving Rina alone with the Priestess. She pulled a chair behind a table, and sat in front of a list of names on a sheet.

"Grab a seat, girl... Rina Arfazadeh... have you turned fourteen yet?"

Rina looked down at the paper and smiled inside. *Why else would I be here?* "Yes, Priestess," she answered meekly.

Her inner smile must have broken through, because the Priestess' face hardened suddenly. She slammed the pencil down and grabbed Rina's chin, pulling her forward and madly scanning her face. "Are you fresh, girl?"

Rina struggled with her grip, growing dizzy with the Priestess' antics.

"Are you even fresh?! Girl!"

Rina was fresh. Eitan had refused to keep Chaya after Dror passed, claiming she was not fresh enough. Noah was her only child with Dror, but she had twelve other children from her two previous husbands, and Eitan was right to think she would not be as good a wife or mother as a younger girl. Later, Rina had asked Hadar what not being fresh meant—

Hell Freezes Over

Hadar was pregnant for the third time now, and both of her children were girls—Hadar had told her and Rina had giggled that it must tickle.

The Priestess let go of her face, and she rocked back into the chair. "We'll find out soon enough if you let Narcissus tempt you, girl. Makes my job easier if you have," she said, ticked her name off the list, and nodded over Rina's shoulder. "Head over to that bunk and take off your skirt."

Rina looked up to the door from the couch and put down her drink. There was something familiar about the man who entered the comfort house. She felt an invisible hand pat her head, a sense of confusion and of being admonished. *Dan!*

The man smiled at her; if he recognised her he gave no sign. She remembered falling in the gardens—it seemed long ago but could not have been more than four years— and being picked up and saved from a hideous old man by a handsome young hero. What would her hero turn into inside these walls?

Eventually, you give up on heroes.

"…and then what?"

"Then? Haven't you listened? Then we…"

The conversation had started before she had even left the room. The two Beasts inside were fools, or did they think her as deaf and mute as the couch she lounged on?

Furniture has few privileges, listening in on sex-drunk, over-confident patrons was one of them. She would not be the first girl to curry favour with the Fish by reporting to them things said carelessly by patrons from other Castes.

Life is made of little things. People waste it looking for the one big thing instead of building it themselves out of tiny moments. She was one of those things now, a tiny thing, and a short moment.

The Priestess had confirmed Rina's freshness with a hint of disappointment; it would have made her job easier indeed if she had let Narcissus tempt her, but not by much. The

Fertility & Fitness Evaluation had been conclusive. Rina was barren, and for barren women, the choices were simple. Either leave for another Caste, hoping a male would take an infertile woman for wife and you could live the life of a house slave. Or choose the comfort houses, where you would be cared for, fed, and lodged until you were too old to serve the house's patrons and you would serve as a maid. Un-fresh Mole girls did not get to choose, having chosen Narcissus over Hades.

She had chosen the comfort house as much out of ignorance as out of fear of living her life at the hands of non-Moles and their families—being at the mercy of libidinous husbands, jealous wives, cruel children, and the mockery of other Moles. Her mother had told her about Cast-outs, '*at least you can eat goats; when a goat dies you can skin it for its hide.*' Rina had added that goats were also too stupid to know better. Her mother had liked that, even as she was bleeding internally, dying from a failed pregnancy.

Shutting the door behind her, she stepped onto the balcony overlooking the common room. Rina doubted she would have chosen otherwise even if she had known. An older woman bumped into her, cursed under her breath and disappeared into a room, letting smoke and the hint of string-music drowned in male and female voices drift out into the hallway. She avoided the common room and headed for the staircase.

Rina went to her room in the basement, where all the girls bedded. When she had first seen her room, almost six years earlier, she had giggled again, remembering what Hadar had told her about her freshness, and pounced on the soft, large bed that was to be hers in a room with five other young Mole girls. The room had been empty when the Priestess handed her off to one of the maids to show her to the girls' quarters, and start her training.

There were no windows in the basement, but all the rooms on the upper floors had views over the colony and onto the ocean. The better rooms had verandas, and the best rooms, for councilmen, larger balconies. Girls were only allowed to leave once a year for two weeks to visit their fathers, or oldest male relative, and were thus especially fond of the councilmen.

Training lasted for a year, night after night. Try though she did, there are some things you can never learn, but of the few things she did some could not be unlearned. The body has a memory. Some lessons just stay etched into the skin. No matter how many showers you take, how many drinks you have, no matter how hard you scratch, through the dermis to the raw nerve, some itches never stop, and you learn to live with a prickling under your skin. And when the shaking stops and the sobs subside, either the itch becomes energy, or you scratch yourself to death.

"We can't afford these daily affronts to our authority much longer Amirpour. You and your Caste have assured us that you had dealt with the dissident Moles years ago."

Amirpour wasn't used to being addressed by his surname by anybody outside his Caste, but Supreme Councilman Marandi wasn't one for protocol. "We have, Councilman, which is why nothing happened since we crushed most of their suspected leaders, but you know as well as I how fragile we are. Moles will outnumber the other Castes eventually, but there is no rebellion here I can assure you."

"Then how do you account for the fifty beheadings the first six months this year, and the other fifty since?"

"Copy-cats, Councilman. No doubt we have a killer, killers, on our hands but there is no coordination to any of this, no rise in contraband, no one with enough authority to pick up where we left them. I can assure you, again, for the seventh time I recall, that this is not a rebellion."

The Fish had good reason to worry. Beheading and dismemberment leave an indelible mark. They barely left their quarters except to patrol the colony or patronise the brothels and even the latter seldom anymore. But Amirpour had wasted his last two sentences and admonishments on a mad man.

155

Marandi was an old man. It was amazing in fact that he hadn't dived over the cliff years ago, but in these circumstances... He was staring straight at him, his eyes completely unfocused but his face holding on to its seriousness. He must be well practiced, even though the fish secret had been out of the net for a hundred years now. They were all mad, every last one of them, and they still believed only the priesthood knew the extent of it.

The Councilman's eyes gradually regained their focus, and he nodded absently at whatever had been said. "Do you have a lead? We will crack down on the mines like they've never seen-"

"That might be hasty, Councilman, we do not know who this is yet, and have you considered that it might not be Moles at all? General discontent has spread among the Castes as you well know."

"So you do have a lead?"

"No, Councilman, we do not."

Marandi's face grew hard, and suspicious. "You Priests have always known how to play your hand haven't you? You imply more than you know and yet you seem confident. What do you hide, Amirpour?"

"Nothing, our fate is tied into yours," he said in mock alarm. "If anything were to happen to you we would-"

"It does work for you that way doesn't it? You tried your best to stop us from leaving the caves when the waters receded, then you insisted on the Divine Undertaking, and somehow the Moles still despise us more than they do you. Things always work out for the priesthood."

Amirpour wondered how much of this conversation Marandi would remember. They weren't usually this insightful anymore, but it wouldn't matter, all they needed was some nudging in the right direction. "They will be found, Councilman, they all will, but we can't be everywhere, I would advise you, and its up to you to take it, to apply mild pressure on the other Castes, nothing excessive, just enough to get names, and follow the trail."

Marandi looked out his window to the perimeter wall. Guards changed rotations, trading weapons and shields. In almost four hundred years since they had left the caves they had never encountered anyone else. The Fish guarded nothing, their weapons had always been pointed at the colony. "Yes," he nodded. "Yes, mild pressure, and more when it's needed…that will be all, Amirpour, my regards to Priestess Gilani, we'll reconvene next week."

Even among the Priests, Gilani stood out, a priestess with white-blond hair, red eyes, and almost translucent skin that enabled visions of Hades in the profoundest of unbelievers. Tall as your average Beast, Gilani was a force to be reckoned with among most of the Castes and indeed in the Council.

When Amirpour walked in to her office, he found her staring at her window, also appraising the guards circulating the wall in Marandi's manner, a glass of something deep red in her hand. "Marandi sends his regards."

"As he would…" She turned away from the window. "But the situation is to our advantage if we stir things well, the rebellion might just succeed this time."

Amirpour paused to think, and Gilani smiled. They made a wonderful pair, always at odds in public, or often enough that few suspected their relationship, its efficiency and intimacy.

Amirpour was always the smarter one. "We might. Dror was sloppy, getting rid of him was best, but the elder Moles are corrupt and lazy, they prey on the comfort girls, hoard rations for favours and they will never act. Eitan is…impressive, insane, but impressive, but he is just as reckless as his father, worse even."

She shook her head. "Dror was sloppy, but the boy is a leader. The younger Moles follow him, and kill for him. The Fish abuse the comfort girls, he will not like that. What was your advice for Marandi?"

Amirpour smirked slyly and winked. "To apply mild pressure on the other Castes. I don't know if the Dream makes them violent, or if it terrifies them into brutality, or something else, it doesn't matter. They will overreact, and bloodshed will ensue. That's all they know to do, that's exactly what they will do. We will gain more traction with the other Castes, and turn council members our way… If the boy goes the distance that is."

"Then we will have to advise him somehow, and channel his anger…he is the best chance we have. The Fish have become too dangerous, to the Priests, the Moles, the Divine Undertaking and everybody else." She turned back towards the window. "They will kill us all eventually—I have no doubt about it."

Amirpour walked up behind her and rested a hand on her lower back. "I will have a word with the boy. I might have just what he wants…"

Even the balconies had lost their attractiveness with time. Rina stepped to the thin balustrade, and let the ocean breeze hit her in the face. An Ant Councilman snored behind her, impervious to the cold drafts from the open doors. On a lower level, two Beasts appeared from between a row of buildings running furiously.

"Halt!" someone shouted.

The order preceded three armed Fish in hot pursuit of the Beasts who split down separate alleyways hoping to lose their pursuers. One of them headed back towards the upper level, the second down.

She lit a thin cigarette and lost track of them between the houses until a large crash came from a lower level and a horn rang. The first fugitive had been caught.

From where she stood, she could see the second Beast making his way cautiously between houses, and the two Fish closing in on him from both sides. She saw him pause at the incoming footsteps, turn and pause again at the other, then brace himself to fight.

Both Fish rounded the corners and unloaded their shock lances, the two bright flashes meeting across the alley in seared flesh.

The Fish's crackdown was mostly a rumour to the comfort girls, but from what she'd heard the murders had increased the Fish's brutality which in turn gave way to more murders. The Fish spared no Caste—save the Priests, who appeared to oppose the violence. When they couldn't arrest, beat, or kill someone they took out their energies on the comfort houses. The first runaway and his captor had crashed into another patrol. All seven patrolmen congregated around his companion's corpse. Their voices didn't carry but she saw one give brief orders, three of them walk off handling the prisoner and carrying the body, while the others pointed at her comfort house, and made their way up the streets.

"Eitan, look, it's, it's, it's...whatever they've told you, it's not true, it's not true, Eitan, it's not true!" Mole Elder Nimrod Barghani's falsetto voice rang over the edge of panic.

"We were friends with your father, Eitan...brothers even! And he knew better than to believe the Priests, Eitan, you know he did!" said Avram Sultani. Standing next to him was Elder Gilad Shahzad, his lips sealed in fright staring at Eitan walking up to them in a fire-suit.

"I know you did," Eitan said. "I know. He spoke highly of you that last night, when he took the beating and you held your tongues. Especially you Sultani, he loved you my Father, respected you too..."

The three men standing bound inside the deep cave couldn't feel the blistering heat building up around them, but they could see the lesions forming on their skin nonetheless. The drug cocktail they'd been given would numb them to anything, but knocking them unconscious would defeat the purpose.

"Avram Sultani, he'd say," Eitan went on. "You can depend on Avram, my brother Avram as you put it."

Shahzad and Baraghani were silent now, all three of them old, well fed, and until this morning expecting to hear from the Priests that Eitan had been caught, or killed. They had wanted the overzealous boy dead shortly after Dror had passed, but he had taken it upon himself to stir things up.

He turned to a group of Moles in fire-suits, standing next to one of the walls and nodded at them. They drilled a hole in the bottom of the cavern, directly across from the prisoners who started shaking.

"No!"

"We'll make up for it, we swear!"

"Eitan! For your father!"

He raised a hand and the drilling stopped. "Gag them, and bring the priest."

A short man walked in covered in a suit, followed by two armed Beasts.

"Priest," Eitan asked the newcomer "are these the men who spread rumours about me to the Beast councilmen?"

"Yes," Amirpour answered. "Slander as it were."

He nodded again, and the drilling resumed, releasing a thick stream of lava that washed away flesh and bone. Their eyes bulged above their gags, they writhed against their chains, and muffled screams covered the sound of the wall breaking open to more lava.

"Isn't this somewhat cruel, Eitan? There are people watching, and people talk," asked Amirpour.

"They don't feel a thing," Eitan replied. "They're pumped so full of stimulants and anesthetics they'll live until they've melted to the waist. There's not much you can do after that, but they don't feel a thing."

The Priest pinched his nose, closed his eyes, sighed and said, "The killing must stop, Eitan. We can help, tremendously in fact, but you have to stop the killings, the other Castes won't take this much longer, and we still need to change minds in the Council."

"Agreed," Eitan replied, "in the meantime you turn a blind eye to my operations in the tunnels. We'll have an army, Priest, just as long as you work your way with the council members."

Rina held herself up against the wall by a hand. She could not see through her left eye, but felt the throbbing in her temples; she passed her tongue timidly over the torn flesh above her lips, stinging herself.

She cleaned blood out of her right eye enough to see herself in the mirror. The lower half of her face was covered in it; the bite to her lower lip had torn most of the skin off.

When the Dream took over, Fish could be unpredictable; some would freeze mid-motion, some would drop unconscious for minutes or hours, but they inevitably came to. They knew they were mad and what they hated the most was having someone witness it. They would go limp, they would go crazy. The closer they were to jumping over the cliff the more brutal they became.

On those nights, she needed medical assistance, and several days rest. She used to look for sympathy, but they never apologised, and there was never a measure of pity—just shock, and sometimes a faint echo of her fear. The Dream was all-consuming, and did not allow for even a sliver of empathy. When drums rolled on those mornings she would not hear them; there were no windows in the basement.

She held herself against the sink, leaving bloody fingerprints on the stone. Her vision blurred. She held her hand to the mirror and leaned on it but her fingers slipped and smeared the glass. Some Fish had their favourites, and knowledge that this would be this Fish's last visit helped her cross over into limbo, but it would not heal her wounds.

"This is highly unorthodox!"

"What isn't these days?"

"What if a Priestess came?"

"You're bound to have goggles lying around somewhere. Throw a blue shirt on me and tell them I'm an Ant."

"With that scar on your face?"

"Since when do you care?"

The voices were familiar. Her left eye hurt too much to even try and open, bandaged by the feel of it. Vision out of her right eye was not steady enough to make out the speakers' features, and the lights were dimmed, but she distinguished two voices, one male and one female.

"I like them safe, so did she, and you know exactly what I mean. How do you expect me to handle this?" snapped the female voice.

"It's not the first time we do this. Tell the Priests she died and you handed her over for recycling, pays to have Ants handy, that kind of thing."

"It's not the Priests I'm worried about, the Fish…"

The word Fish sent a jolt of pain through her face. She let go of a moan, lifting herself up from the mattress a brief moment before falling back into the pillow. The man approached the bed, leaned over her and ran his hand soothingly through her hair. Her first impulse was to recoil, but every movement was painful.

"Don't worry, little sister, he's been dealt with, I'm here to take you back." Eitan came suddenly into focus. His face was harder than she remembered; the scar across his left eye was also new, and still healing.

"Good. She's awake." Rina recognised Adina's sharp tone; or rather, she recognised the no-nonsense undertone in the old maid's voice. Adina rose from her chair and approached the bed, but did not spare Rina a glance. She turned to Eitan. "The Fish will come back. You take her now. You might have done this before, but it's the last time you do it with me—understood?"

Eitan nodded at her, and bent down over Rina. "It's gonna hurt." He snatched her off the bed and started walking towards the wall at the far end of the room.

Rina was too dizzy to feel pain. She had not visited her family in four years, and had decided she would never go back. Eitan was barely there, Hadar had died soon after delivering her seventh child, her brothers were either married or dead, and she couldn't be around all the new children, or their revolving mothers.

It was then that she had realised the irony of her circumstances. On the one hand she would never have to suffer the tremendous pressures of childbirth that Chaya had made seem so easy. On the other, she would never know what owning her freedom would mean. If she were going to be passed from man to man until she passed away or was cast away, then it would be the houses for her she'd thought. That was before she had met her first Fish patron.

Adina ran up to them and stuck a syringe in her arm. A surge of energy pulsed through her legs and the dizziness faded along with the numbness in her face. "Careful not to talk, girl. It only feels like you can."

Eitan pushed a stone on the wall and a trap door appeared in the basement floor, sending a gush of hot air up from the tunnel beneath it. Her brother lowered her to the floor, whistled down the tunnel, and footsteps rushed towards them. Eitan lifted her up, and lowered her into the opening.

A group of three Moles was waiting for them with glowsticks. They turned them on and activated glowstrips along the tunnel walls with them. Iridescent strips lining the walls and ceiling spread light and colour down their segment of the tunnel, too intensely for Rina's weak eye to handle.

When she opened it again, the Moles were wearing high-intensity light visors, made for prolonged exposure to lava and drill sparks when Moles dug new caves. They wrapped her in a blanket. Eitan started lowering himself into the tunnel.

She heard Adina's voice through the opening. "Is it worth it boy? Are they any happier down there than in here?"

Eitan paused holding himself up on the edge of the opening. "You can't compare happiness, Adina. How happy are you? Stay safe."

Eitan landed next to her, hitting a dial on the wall. The door slipped shut overhead, followed by the slamming and suction of a plastic seal that barred any air in the tunnel from slipping into the basement rooms. In her six years at the comfort house she had never suspected the tunnel even existed.

Eitan grabbed her shoulder. "We have to hurry, the overseers won't be much longer. Try to keep up. I'll be right behind you. Dov, cover our back, and kill the light." The glowstrips faded to black and the three lifted their visors with relief.

"Ethel, Davi, cover the front. If a Fish or anybody you don't recognise pops their head..." he patted an elongated black metal tube on his left leg, "aim to kill. That's for you too, Dov. We'll deal with bodies later. Now go!"

In the faint light of the cave, sulphur drifted from underground pockets caressing Rina's cheek and tearing up her eyes.

She donned her helmet before placing the drill directly between her legs. A sub-zero draft whistled its way from the mouth of the caves high above and far behind her down the narrow halls, and sent a rare shiver through her neck and shoulders.

The motion of the drill freed stones in small clusters, sprinkling around her feet. The smell of sulphur intensified as a hole started to appear in the rock. A gust of smoke rose through it, revealing the familiar red glow underneath. She raised her helmet long enough to spit through the crack, her saliva turning almost instantaneously to a puff of mist. She thrust her boot heel through the fragile crust, tossed the drill on her back, stretched her arms alongside her body and let herself drop.

Halfway through the fall she activated the cleats inside her boots and landed on the rocky surface, knee down, with a crunch.

She was on a tiny, rocky island inside a smaller sub-cave in the middle of a lava swirl. Left, right, and all around her, boiling lava spun and flowed in a stream leading out of the cave and deeper underground. Her fire-suit and helmet's sensors absorbed the heat, powering her in-suit equipment.

She shot her arms out at an angle in front of her, lodging hooks into the ceiling, swinging herself from the rocky island onto a larger ridge by the cave wall. The hooks shot back into her suit as she landed and she loosened the drill on her back, and tightened her helmet. The helmet was equipped with a light-deflecting visor, but Rina, and the other comfort girls, had no use for them.

Running through the pitch dark tunnels three years earlier, Rina had wondered how her brother and his friends managed, without using the glowstrips, to stay afoot and find their way in the maze of illegal tunnels that seemed to stretch through every quarter in the colony. Eitan had told her that eventually she would not need light either. She had not believed him then, but he had been right.

After centuries in the caves, Moles were genetically predisposed to working in dark environments. Male Moles laboured at the Divine Undertaking from the age of five from sunrise to sundown. Their eyes weren't worth much in the sunlight but had excellent night vision. Mole girls had always carried the trait, but until comfort girls were enrolled in the rebellion, their ability was latent. Not anymore. She could see perfectly in sunlight or darkness.

The helmet was a nuisance. Though necessary, it was uncomfortable, and the light-deflecting function got in the way of her eyesight. Not by much, but it was distracting when passing through different types of lighting. She could not remove it or her face would break out in blisters from the heat. The other comfort girls had the same difficulties. Eitan said they would have to deal with it. Smuggling equipment was a crime, and an unsupervised request for modifications would be suspicious. Ants were discreet, but their discretion might end with a Fish inquiry in their affairs—they had things of their own to hide—or again, it might not. One never knew, but Eitan would not risk failure because his soldiers were uncomfortable.

She didn't see much of him at all come to think of it. He was distant and much darker than she'd remembered as a girl. The sombreness following Dror's death had grown inside of him. It gave him purpose, but sometimes she wondered who he was.

Rina adjusted the zoom on her visor and scanned the cave. The crust she stood on circled it almost entirely, except for two holes on either end allowing the lava to flow. There was no exit she could see except for the hole she had come down through. Rather than circle the cave, she repeated the operation to the opposite wall, bouncing off the central island just long enough to lunge to the other side.

The moment she landed, her suit and helmet registered large volumes of heat radiating from the cave wall directly ahead of her. She applied her hands to the surface; the effect was immediate, her bodysuit's power gauge hit full capacity in less than a second. She was at a dead end though. She stuck her helmet to the surface, powering it and activating audio-sensors, scanning for the slow motion grinding of hot stone behind the wall.

Small fissures were appearing on the rock, and a closer look showed thin cracks reaching halfway around the wall from either opening in the cave base, turning the wall into a spider web of connecting cracks in the rock. She only had a few minutes, likely less, before the magma broke through and inundated the cave.

The rumble deepened, and small flakes of stone started crumbling from the wall. High-pressured sulphur blasted stone chips at Rina and into the lava stream, and droplets of magma leaked through, sending ripples through the cracks with a powerful crunch as the wall gave way to the superheated basalt behind.

Rina landed on the small central island, instinctively sending her hooks through the hole and into the ceiling of the grotto above and shot herself upwards in a spin.

The explosion hurled large chunks of rock across the cave, red-hot slag pouring from one cavern to the other and filling it to the brim. Rina pierced through the hole just as the smaller sub cave's ceiling collapsed under toe, connecting both caves into a pool of fire directly beneath her.

Her options were limited, but her suit and helmet were operating at full power. Her suit could withstand the immense heat and weight of magma for up to fifteen seconds. She should not need that long.

She plunged headfirst into the boiling swirl, supercharging her suit, and propelling herself straight ahead under the surface towards the opening she had drilled to get inside what was then the upper cave. It should remain open above the downpour, but the tremors could bring stones down and leave her trapped outside. She had only a few seconds left before the suit melted, but the magma gave her almost unlimited energy. She shot herself out of the swirl, connected her hooks to the ceiling and threw herself through the hole seconds before it crumbled and closed in on her, catching the hooks' chains, pulling her sharply back, and slamming her hard into the floor.

The suit and helmet glowed hues of orange, red, and yellow on the outside, radiating huge volumes of heat from the magma away from her. Anybody who approached her unequipped would instantly combust. Inside the suit, the effect was of intense cool. She got to her knees and disconnected what was left of her hooks and drill. She turned back to see her suit had burned her imprint into the rock she had landed on.

Rina raised her visor to catch her breath. The suit was cooling down fast, the timer read three seconds. She would need a better suit, and no matter what Eitan thought, she would get the modifications she wanted. Fifteen seconds was not enough for one, and she would do something about that blasted helmet for two. And someone else would finish the tunnel. They would have to slag the rock to glass, seal the hole shut and double back, but they were close, very, very close…

The caves' collapse sent a ripple through the illegal tunnels, opening a large sinkhole directly under the Fish quarters and swallowing up houses, crushing scores of Fish, Beasts, and Ants in the middle of the night.

Conveniently, it was Eitan and his crew who were called in by the Priests to investigate the damage and prevent another crater from opening. They were quick to clear out the debris and even quicker to fill the hole. What could be identified as Ant and Beast would be recycled in the morning; the Fish would tend to their own body parts. He would need someone on the Council to brush off the incident and some Moles would pay for this, but they all knew the risks. Close as they were, time was running short.

> *Do you fear the fire?*
> *Do you feel the flame?*
> — Carvings on the colony walls

"Hmm, you could, sure, you could, you wouldn't be able to move much, but you could. Yes," said Councilman Tamhidi.

Rina turned away from him. No matter how high they rose in the community, Ants rarely climbed above their station in relation to each other. The old man had built his reputation as a personal equipment mechanic, and that alone had gained him enough respect from the other Castes to join the Council, but that was all he would ever be to other Ants: the best personal equipment mechanic in Ant memory.

His underground lab was connected to the illegal tunnels, as were the three maintenance workshops he ran in the other quarters. Tamhidi was one of the few people Rina knew she could trust not to talk to the Fish. Conspiracies have their benefits, although she was not as confident that he would not talk to Eitan, she knew the challenge intrigued him, and she had placed all her chips on his enthusiasm.

The lab was the most cluttered place Rina had ever seen. The ceiling was lined with hanging propeller engines and other large experimental models too heavy for a person to carry. He cleared a table by brushing off all its contents onto the floor and laid out schematics of mole fire-suits and helmets to ponder over, oblivious to Rina's curiosity.

She slipped on a screwdriver, kicked it under a table, and picked up one of the books Tamhidi stacked up in a corner and used as an occasional table or seat. She could not read much beyond the title—there were more symbols than she was used to, some of which were missing entirely, others completely illegible.

"You read the old tongue, girl?" Tamhidi chuckled from the other side of the lab. He left the map and approached her, making his way around a table, stepping over a mechanical hand-drill, and crushing a roll of scrolls on the floor.

"There is not much for you to find in here anyway, unless you're suddenly interested in gravity reversal, but that's not why you're here." He took the book from her hand and put it back on the pile. "Try this. You should understand more." He walked back to the map. "And if you don't," he chuckled again, "why, you made it here once, you'll make it again."

Rina glanced at the cover.

"That first word is guerrilla!" he laughed, without turning his attention from the schematics.

Guerrilla warfare. She put the book down. The old man was irritating. She was not going to ask him what it meant, choosing to nod silently instead.

The councilman raised an eyebrow, but remained silent too.

Tamhidi was one of the councilmen who frequented the comfort houses. Rina had not met him before being dragged into the rebellion, but the old man had discontinued his practice after siding with her brother. Ants were usually distracted, and engrossed in thoughts known only to themselves and understandable only by other Ants and apprentices. She had never heard of an Ant harming one of the girls but she would not vouch for the purity of his thoughts right then and there.

What she was doing was dangerous, forbidden, and much worse according to her brother, frivolous. But if Tamhidi thought he had himself a comfort girl on his hands he would find out how precious his hands were and would never take Rina, or any of the former comfort girls, for granted again.

His long blue robs swished as he spun from the table, grinning at her. "Come back in a week, girl! Come back in a week. You might want to hide, your brother being who he his..." He paused as if about to add something, but changed his mind. "Well he's been kind to you, so I hear, but he wouldn't like your being here you should know!" and winked as he mentioned Eitan.

He would not talk, but he might ask for something in exchange. He was a councilman after all, no matter how hard he pretended otherwise. His robes were soft and thick, unlike the other Ants' blue working shirts and slacks meant for ease of motion, thin-threaded and loose for air and comfort. Ant forges could be scalding hot, barely less than the deeper caves. It was obvious that Tamhidi had not wielded a hammer himself for years; whatever strength he had had in his youth was long turned to fat under his bulky robes.

He pressed a button under the table, and the wall slid into a circular opening onto the tunnel. Rina activated a glowstick and ignited the strips along the walls. She sped down the tunnel shutting down the lights at every intersection, less for the Fish than for Mole patrols. Eitan's sister could get away with a lot, but it would not do for her to set other girls the wrong example.

Running in the dark would have been safer but she had only caught a glance of the map and the maze was complex and booby-trapped, and she had left her helmet behind on purpose.

Tamhidi might talk, but Hades was rising and Mole women would no longer be subjected to comfort houses or pregnancy duties—otherwise what were they fighting for?

She turned a dark corner and slammed head-on into a band of three Moles, two helmetless, heavily armed males and one female with a slit burlap sack hiding her face.

Rina slammed her glowstick on the wall flooding the cavern with light, momentarily distracting both guards. The closest shut his eyes and reached for his glowstick. She spun and caught him in the back of the neck with the flat of her hand, knocking him unconscious before he hit the lights in the tunnel. The second guard was hastily tying his helmet; she tipped her weight on her right leg and slammed her left foot in his face, crushing his visor. He stumbled back and slumped against the wall.

Rina turned to the girl, and ripped the sack from over her head. She did not know her name, but recognised her as one of the former comfort girls. She pinned her to the wall. "Where are they taking you?"

The girl looked her square in the eye and grinned. "Sorry, we're not all privileged enough to be Eitan's sister," she said belittlingly.

Rina slapped her across the face, drawing blood from her lower lip.

The girl spat it on Rina's suit. "Yeah, can't expect any better from you either, can we? There's things you don't understand. Look at you. You're not one of us, Rina Arfazadeh. You never really were."

Rina did not understand what the girl meant, and could not place her. She knew her from one of the teams, but she was not a team leader, so why would she have known? But that was not what she meant. Everybody knew Rina, but she implied that everyone was in on a little secret except for her. And she did not like the scorn in her voice.

The girl kept her eyes locked on Rina's, but her hands took hold of Rina's glowstick and the lights went out. Rina's eyes took only a few seconds to adjust, but not before feet shuffled on the floor and a hand grabbed her by the neck pulling her back, another twisting her arm. A Coil wrapped around and locked her arms, chest, and back.

She leapt in the air, bringing her knee up into the person's chest, bounced back and landed on her ankle, twisting it. Her efforts only made the Coil tighter, and the muscles in her arm were met with twice the resistance every time she flexed. She could feel her chest cave in slowly as her ribs threatened to crack and crush through her heart.

171

She heard Dov's voice as he flipped her over, loosened the Coil, and tied a collar around her neck. "So, causing the death of three djangi was not enough for you? How many more warriors will you take from us? Do you have any idea of the stakes? You've had it easy enough. This time…"

"This time I'll talk to Eitan myself."

He looked at her, his irises flashing through barely noticeable iridescent shades that were not unlike the glowstrips on the walls, his pupils expanding and shrinking frenetically in the dark, filtering the little light in the darkness into an infrared he could make sense of.

"This time you will. This time I think he will want to talk to you himself. You're gonna have to learn some things if you want this arrangement to continue." He turned to the girl. "Are you alright?" She nodded, and placed the sack back over her head.

He turned and kicked his partner awake in the chest. "Get up! Drag her to the secret council hall. I'll deliver this one to Tamhidi and meet you there. Look out for that one; she thinks she's special."

The second guard lifted Rina up and placed a board under her body, tied it to hooks on his shoulder pads, locked his helmet around her head, turned the visor blind, and dragged her behind him down the tunnel.

The hall, a simple, brightly lit circular room, was crowded with members of other Castes resting against walls. A large central table lay covered with maps of the tunnels and reports of weapons caches, sinkhole locations, and designs for explosive devices.

Representatives were seated at the table, each Caste occupying a separate side, with four openings, one on each side, into an open space in the centre.

Ants were nearest to the entrance, in shades of blue. Bees were seated further up on the right in hooded yellow windbreaker coats, some holding cattle poles they also used for stick fighting. The poles were light, hard, and telescopic, they could also be split in two and reattached, and were very flexible. Farming leaves a lot of time for fighting so Bees knew how to put their poles to good use. Across from them, Beast representatives wore their characteristic reddish working clothes. Even without them, their intricate facial tattoos marked them apart from the other Castes. Beasts were after a few hundred years much larger than other members of the colony, but they made it a habit to send only their largest representatives—male or female—to any meeting, secret or public, making them appear intimidatingly more powerful than the other Castes, and occupying much more space at the table.

At the head of the table, Eitan was whispering to a Priest dressed in a white robe. No one had paid any attention to Rina as she was dragged in. Each Caste was busy preparing, agreeing on final talking points; each plotting their seat at the table once the Fish were overthrown.

The guard dragged her through the nearest opening past the Ant delegation, and rolled her onto the floor stopping the buzz of greedy murmur around the room.

Their sudden movement had made the Mole delegation visible. Even with lights, especially with lights, Moles' brown suits and helmets made them almost invisible against cave walls. It was hard to estimate their number until motion made them appear against the background. There must have been a hundred Moles at the meeting, as many as the other Castes put together, but no more than twenty had been visible at the table. The other members reacted with surprise and anger at Moles appearing among them from what they thought was solid wall.

There were only three Priests, two male and one female, but Priests never came in large numbers. At first they had wanted to keep their Caste separate from the rebellion, as advisors, but Eitan insisted on a permanent delegation that could be held accountable if, for reasons of their own, the Priests decided to throw their luck in with the Fish. He could not win the rebellion without the Priests yet there was little sympathy for their presence. Priests were manipulative and deceitful. They had never given the Moles their freedom, instead playing them as pawns in their power struggle with the Fish. But without them the Moles would never sway the entire colony, not even with the help of those present at the meeting and their many cells throughout the settlements.

The slamming of the doors behind the guards was the signal for the clamour to start again. Rina could not make out the individual accusations thrown at her, but she could tell from the few looks she glimpsed curled up on the floor that no one in the room was happy to see her, least of all her brother.

Eitan silenced the room by rising from his chair and stepping into the open space. He flipped Rina over. For a moment the coil tightened and she could feel sharp needles of pain shooting down her arms. The pressure faded as Eitan pressed the coil, removed it, and dropped it to the floor where it recoiled with a whiplash into a small two-inch rubbery circle.

He yanked her up by her braid until her toes touched the floor and then dropped her. Her scalp throbbed under the strain. She jumped up and swung at him, but he caught her blow and sent her tumbling back.

"Three Moles had to die for your carelessness, and you haven't had enough?"

Rina had been told about the executions. The Fish had insisted on them, backed by a mob of Ants and Beasts.

A towering Beast female sprung from her chair, slamming her hands down on the wood and sending a shockwave that lifted her quarter of the table from the ground. "Three Moles?! Three?! We lost twelve Beasts in that 'accident', Mole. Twelve!" Rina did not know her, but had the sense that she had precedence over the Beasts present at the meeting. She leaned over the table glaring down at Rina. "And this one gets to walk? How convenient. No one gets to walk."

"What Councilwoman Majidi means," said a Bee, impervious to Majidi's knuckles grinding on the table, "is that Moles may have suffered a public execution, but Beasts and Ants have their own grievances. Indeed, the Bees-"

"Bees have no business in that neighbourhood at night; likely, he was trading favours for food, yes?" an Ant Rina recognised as Ariel Jafari started. "But we have only a few grievances, three as well as a matter of fact, but they count double, Eitan, for they were children. The adults we recycled, but the children were too young. They will know neither Neptune nor Hades, so how do you expect to compensate us for their souls?"

Eitan spun on him. "Compensate? Compensate? So it is only Moles who should die? Only Moles who should dig, and bleed, and lead the return to the Cave? Your involvement has a cost; you want a seat at the table when we overthrow the Fish? Then pay the price in blood."

He sat back down at the table and stared at his sister. After a pause, he nodded to the wall on either side of the door. Two Mole guards unfolded themselves from the stone, only their faces visible for a short while against the rock. They donned their helmets. "Strip her to her underwear and throw her into one of the sweathouses. Give her one day's supply of water, no more." He turned to Rina, "I tried, but you're gonna have to learn hard. I'll speak to you in three days, if you live. Get her out of here before she starts a riot."

Three days in solitary confinement gives you time to reflect, and despite the pain and thirst, Rina found traces of clarity between blackouts. She was certain of two things: that she and the comfort girls—those who were willing to fight for it—deserved as much respect in the rebellion as the men, and short of Eitan giving it to her, she would take it.

Remembering the comfort girl's scorn and her words in the hallway stung as she shifted uncomfortably from warm rock to warmer rock. She would make sure that changed.

She woke up inside a healing tank. Two Priests were leaning over it with devices that emitted low-level radiation over her burns activating the healing agent in the thick, translucent ointment that glowed on her skin.

Naked under the Priests' scrutiny, a memory of the comfort house flashed across her mind and anger bubbled up under the slight tingling of the ointment binding itself to her burns. It hit her in the stomach and spread throughout her body right to the tip of every hair strand like static. The feeling grew warm, turning her muscles to jelly and making her bones ache. The warmth turned to shaking, an uncontrollable thought-shattering quiver.

Every emotion she had swept away night after night and built walls and lies around, shot through every nerve. A flood of images, of shame, satisfied confusion, blinding pleasure and agonising pain, hit her in waves.

In the midst of mindless sensations, one thought seemed to make its way against the gales of primitive instincts, steadying her with every heartbeat.

Never again.

First it was one thought in the flood of vengefulness and self-loathing, but it started echoing every thought, settling in her spine, answering each trampling of her esteem, each violence endured, each submissive humiliation.

Never again.

When she opened her eyes, the anger was gone; the memories were there, but they read like someone else's story. The shame—the itch under her skin, the prickling she could never scratch—was gone. In its place she sensed a strange sense of calm, of being both supercharged and yet at her most peaceful. She had not felt the electric tingle ahead of a storm for almost ten years, that nanosecond when the wind abated and the world froze before unleashing Hell, but she recognised it in herself. No storm could shake her anymore, and no stone could burn her.

Never again.

"Don't you feel any regret for the lives lost, girl?" asked Councilwoman Majidi.

Across the dais from Majidi standing in a helmetless fire-suit Rina sensed the question was loaded.

Hell Freezes Over

The hulking woman sat on a chair next to Eitan, atop a flight of steps. The room was not completed yet, ending abruptly behind the podium, the walls and ceiling still filled with cracks and holes.

Only the entrance was finished, the stone doors plated with bronze, and the walls smoothed and decorated on the right side with a fresco of Hermes carving a hammer out of a mountain. The lower half of the mountain was hollow, inside a dragon held on a leash by his master blew flames in vain towards the chimney. The tiny puffs of smoke rising from the mountain were barely as large as Hermes' eyes. They all knew the story of how Hermes kept Azhi-Dahaka at bay while he shaped the world. On the left side, Fereydoon, David, and Kaveh, at the foot of the hill left by Hermes' labour, were tying Zahak to two pillars under Maccabee's watchful eye. Whatever the room was, Eitan had big plans for it.

"They died well. We all will," Rina said.

"They died for your recklessness, little sister, there is no glory to this," Eitan interjected.

She focused on her brother. "No, Eitan, they died for yours. What is this place? A throne room? Has Hades crowned you king? We are slaves, Eitan—where's the glory in that?"

Eitan did not move, but his body tensed and the deep scar across his eye crimsoned darkly.

Majidi smirked. "Dror's blood aye?" She looked slyly at Eitan. "Well, girl, we'll find out soon enough if you've learned your lesson. Off to your comfort duties with you-"

Rina launched herself at her. Majidi moved faster than Rina had thought possible, leaving the chair vacant and appearing behind Rina, hands locked onto either side of her head. If she moved, her neck would snap.

"Missing your helmet, girl?" said Majidi with no satisfaction, Eitan's face held even less.

He rolled a leaf into a cone, sparked a match on the chair and lit it. His face had changed. She remembered the gentle giant who had pushed her out of the room the last night she saw her father. That was how she'd wanted to remember him, before he carried her out of the comfort house. This man was not her brother. He might think he still was, but the man sitting in that chair was not Dror's son. He was whatever the Fish had made him, and what he had allowed himself to become: something else, something cold.

Majidi released her grip.

"We never stop being comfort girls," Rina said dejectedly. "That's how you buy your allies." A giggle built up in her stomach and exploded in laughter. "You're a fool to count on those men, Eitan." She could not stop the fit of laughter at the irony and naïve callousness of her brother's plan. "A fool."

Majidi raised an eyebrow. Eitan rose from his chair. "Every man has a price, and once it's paid they're in your debt. They know it. You know it too, every Mole girl pays that price, and you chose the comfort houses, you chose to be a Mole," he said coldly.

"No, Eitan, I was trained to be a Mole. Then I was trained to blow up caves and dig tunnels. Then I was thrown in a pit for following orders. The Fish?" she said softly. "I know where I stand with the Fish."

Eitan did not blink. "And now you know where you stand with me." He smiled. "Councilman Tamhidi would like you, Rina." He looked down at her, head tilted sideways, weighing her like she had seen Bees weigh cattle. "Yes. Yes, he certainly would."

"No." Rina could handle the old man, but she had been caught once. She would only get one shot at meeting with him again, and he was not ready; she needed four more days.

It did not matter what Eitan might do to her. It was too easy for him, using the comfort girls as the Fish did then trading them off for political favours. She did not know that man, and she owed him nothing.

Majidi stayed silent, but seemed to enjoy the exchange. Women in all the other Castes were free. There were no comfort duties for them, no pregnancy duties, no endless stream of raising and bearing children. Majidi was a councilwoman, and she knew what was at stake for the Moles. All Moles.

Eitan snapped his fingers. Two Mole guards unfolded from the walls and clamped her shoulders. "Three more days in the sweathouse, then take her immediately to Tamhidi. She'll wake up there—make sure she does."

Rina smiled up at her brother. "I won't take any less than four."

Eitan's jaw trembled. He nodded slowly. Majidi's eyes appeared to twinkle before they dragged her away.

Never again.

"Let… go of…me…" Rina's hand crushed his throat little by little, making Tamhidi's pleas all the more enjoyable.

She had slipped in and out of consciousness during the four days in the sweathouse, before the heat shut her system down and allowed her to drift into painless sleep.

When she opened her eyes, it was to find the old lecher standing over her naked body. Her first impulse was to struggle with her restraints, but she found that she had none. His mistake, she had thought and thrown her hand up catching the old man in the throat. She could almost see the fat shivering under his plush blue robe, and only released her grip when the colour of his face matched the colour of his clothes. She knew she would have enough time to roll off the table before he could respond to her assault in kind. Tamhidi was still valuable, and killing him would not serve her purposes; he was also valuable to the rebellion.

"Hades, girl," he managed between wheezy breaths, "there is no need for this!" He grasped the table.

Rina would not hear any of his complaining, and leapt over the table, planning to pin him to the wall and get what she had suffered for. She landed, grinning for an instant before her bare foot slammed into a small pin lying on the floor. Her barely healed body felt like it had been dipped in acid from head to toe. Then a sudden jolt of cold numbed her out of pain. Her vision blurred from the shock, but she found

Tamhidi holding her gently, laying her onto the table again, and pulling a syringe out of her arm.

"I told you there was no need for this. Damn you, girl, if I wanted to abuse you, I wouldn't have woken you up. And you know how much your brother would have enjoyed it."

He covered her in a cloak. It was dusty and itched, but compared to the bone searing agony of a moment earlier it was the sweet itch of life returning.

Tamhidi laughed. "Speaking of which...hold on, don't move it will pass...speaking of which, you did show him didn't you? Four days. Ha! Old Majidi was rolling on the floor telling me about it, and you would know just how much a mess that made. Well, you sure impressed him, and impressed her, and that is more important. Ever wondered how you're still alive, girl?"

She did. In the sweathouse, just when she lost consciousness for the last time, knowing her water supply was finished, delirious, and with no real understanding of how much time she had left, she had hoped her death would reveal her brother for what he truly was.

"You're something of a legend now," he said, his back to her, removing pieces of equipment from the ceiling, "and you owe that to the old Beastess. Ha! Yes you do. *I won't take any less than four!*' A steady stream of girls crept in at night, hydrating you at their own risk."

He unloaded the items on a nearby table. His voice picked up with the clang of metal on its surface. "Anyhow, you didn't need to push your luck to prove a point...turns out..." He lost track of his thoughts, engrossed in disassembling the various pieces of equipment on the table. "...Turns out I was already done when he sent you back in."

She let out a groan.

"Yes, yes, would've said something akin to that I reckon."

He lifted her up, gently again. "Think I couldn't see it in your eyes, girl? Thought you were one in a long list of many, didn't you now?"

He walked her to the table. Rina saw what looked like a fire-suit hanging from a wire thread. Something about it was different. She laid a hand on it. It was cold to the touch and seemed to drink in all the heat from her hands. She pulled back. He urged her forward.

"And wait till you try it! Who would have thought liquefying obsidian with lava would create an elastic rubber compound? No one! That's because they don't! Ha!" He cackled at his poor joke, "But Coils now, hmm, that was a finder. See? Turns out they are alive after all, and do extremely well under intense pressure. See? They bond with anything and when melted, they don't die, see!" He got a hold of himself and went on, somewhat calmer. "They transfer their properties to whatever they are melted with and shift shape!"

Rina was not sure she followed, but tried anyway.

"Do you mean to say…the suit is…*alive*?!"

"That's what I said didn't I?" he snapped.

Rina winced but knew he had not meant rudeness. He was always three steps ahead of most people, and in her condition she could not have kept pace with her younger, more naïve self.

"Alive and well, and it will fit like a…well, a Coil I guess, but without any of the discomfort! Wait till you see the helmet!"

How wrong had she been about the old man? As she would find out, comfort girls had been fooling Eitan and his fanatics all along. Not all of them, many were not lucky enough to have landed on Tamhidi's favourite list, but those who were gained a lot from him, and at no charge. Tamhidi offered healing services, food, rest, and care for the girls many had thought he abused over the years. Even in the Comfort Houses, he was not the infamous patron many thought him to be, an image he cultivated carefully even as he supported Eitan.

"Your brother…" he started, as if reading her thoughts, "…your brother is an aberration…" He shook his head. "An aberration! Your father, he had his faults, Hades knows, but your brother is another kind of animal. He will sacrifice everyone to get rid of the Fish. Good people seldom want to rule the world. That tells you something about power, girl..."

Rina knew the truth in his words as she recalled her brother's aura of righteousness, sitting on his makeshift throne, even as he sentenced her to death or rape, or eventually both. A man who could have changed their world, but would not.

"Well?" he inquired, "what are you waiting for? Try it on! Try it on!"

Oblivious to his looks she let the cloak drop from her shoulders and slipped into the fire-suit.

The effect was immediate: she was submerged in intense cold as the suit sucked up all her heat and energy. She began to shiver, but almost immediately the suit started feeding her heat back into her, and stuck tightly to her skin just as the old man had said—tight like a Coil, but with no more pressure than needed to maintain contact with her body.

"What did I tell you? Coils, ha! Who would've thought? Now try this."

He handed over the helmet. It was entirely black, and apparently seamless; you could not distinguish the visor from the rest of the headpiece. She slipped it on and felt the same cooling effect on her skin and through her scalp as with the body suit.

There was a visor, or maybe the whole thing was a visor; if she had eyes behind her head maybe they would... Instantly an image of Tamhidi standing behind her looking appreciatively at her reactions flooded her vision. She closed her eyes, opened them, and saw straight ahead again. She began to turn towards Tamhidi, reconsidered, and thought about what stood behind her, and again, Tamhidi appeared, a much wider grin on his face.

"Getting the hang of it already! Good, very good, it took me a while myself. I'm not gonna lie to you, I'd been working on this for a while before you asked, and it felt like a shame to hand it over to Eitan and his goons, although I would have had to eventually..." he sighed. "Won't go into the details of it, too technical I'm afraid, and truth be told I'm not quite sure how it works myself, but why waste time wondering when it does? Wonderful things, Coils, truly wonderful… what else lies beneath the waters, I wonder, if only the Fish…"

Yes, if only the Fish… she thought, if only they were not mad, if only the winters would shorten, if only…

"The Fish will get what's coming for them," she said aloud, surprised at her own voice. Fire-helmets hardly carried sound at all, and you could barely hear anything through them either. You had to know your mission better than you knew yourself, hope that your teammates did as well, and rely on the heat sensors to warn you in time of a flood of running rock.

She picked up a small match from the table to her left; all she had to do to see it—think *left*—and she struck it on the table, and touched the helmet with it. The match went out: its heat went straight to the helmet and into her skin, and through the whole suit. She felt a surge of power through her entire body, as powerful as full immersion in lava with a regular fire-suit. She grabbed the table with her hand and raised it effortlessly over her head, thought *back*, and saw Tamhidi nodding his head appreciatively.

"Getting the hold of it indeed…"

"Coils again?"

He shrugged. "For some part, maybe the whole of it, maybe something else entirely, the same circuitry runs through fire-suits and with none of these results. Like I said, girl, the *how* isn't always important when it works, and you're in a hurry."

Rina removed, or rather peeled off the helmet; concentrating was making her dizzy, and it snapped, wrapping itself back into its original shape the moment it she let go of it.

"Dizzy already?" laughed Tamhidi. "Don't worry, it will come naturally enough."

His ability to anticipate her thoughts was unnerving, but in spite of her distant demeanour, her respect for him grew with each passing second.

"Your brother is not expecting you to walk out standing upright, girl, you realise that, yes?"

She nodded resolutely. "Hit me," she said calmly. She expected an argument; even after years as a comfort girl, she still believed that it was hard for men to strike women, even after Eitan, but to her surprise, Tamhidi nodded gravely in turn.

"I might have to. I might just. Don't want to blow my cover, anything less than a bruise and your brother won't buy it."

Something strange was happening to her. She used to take pride in hearing people mention Eitan as her kin, but she winced when Tamhidi said it, and knew she would every time from this moment onward.

"Good thing you removed the helmet," he said. He saw the question on her face. "It's shock absorbent. I hadn't mentioned?" He smiled faintly.

His uppercut caught her unexpected in the chin, she flew upwards and back, landing hard on the ground, but could only feel pain in her face and jaw. Shock absorbent indeed, she thought, and the old man still packed a punch and a surprising turn of speed under all that fat. She lifted herself up and his fist crashed into her skull and sent her back down.

"That should do it; anymore and someone might wonder how I could still have a go at you afterwards. Hate doing this every time I have to…"

She felt the bruise growing around her eye, and tasted blood in her mouth from his uppercut. She would not be a pretty sight when she was brought to Eitan, but it was worth it.

"I'll call the guards." He hit a switch on the wall. "Don't worry about the suit. With Majidi on your side, I'll have no difficulty smuggling it. She used to love your brother, you know? Hard to believe from a woman that size, love, but there you have it. Women scorned, ha!"

She limped to the door, and heard the oncoming footsteps through the stone wall.

Tamhidi grabbed her shoulder. "The Fish *will* get what they have coming, girl, you know that as well as I do. But ask yourself, do *you* want what's coming next?"

Rina had let go of herself in the sweathouse, let go of who she thought she was, of who she had been told she was, and for that, she owed Eitan Arfazadeh. Now she had to find out for herself.

It was true she was no longer alone. In the early hours of the morning, before the Fish overseers prodded the Moles into the Divine Undertaking, a stream of former comfort girls would risk their lives to see her. She had few words at first, but her heart did the real talking, or perhaps they were just eager to hear. Hear, and listen.

One morning, one of them brought a small note in Tamhidi's handwriting:

If you live, girl, think well before you act. You'll find the suit waiting for you when he lets you out. Wear it. It will help you heal. Do you know what a phoenix is, girl? Bird from the dawn of Mars, perhaps even before we were blinded by the light; maybe its light shone against the cave, who knows and who cares, a bird of flame, girl, a bird of flame. Think on it. The suit will give you two minutes.

Two minutes! She thought back to the comfort girls who opened up to her, and she knew what needed to be done. *I'm gonna need a hundred.*

The explosion several weeks later caused a small avalanche, killing caste members indiscriminately. She had known that would happen, and as she had told Majidi, they died well. The avalanche sent a signal, and sealed the Divine Undertaking shut. It took the Fish by surprise, and Eitan and the rebels never saw it coming.

The ceiling showered the secret council hall with debris just as the door blew inward and a hundred women shrouded entirely in black, rushed inside.

Majidi smiled and turned to Eitan. "Another one of your tricks?" she said slyly.

Before he could answer, the leading shape leapt across the room, over the table, landed standing upright in front of him, and hit him with a soft blow from the flat of its hand, before turning to face the room, ignoring Eitan while he slammed into the wall on the far end of the cave.

The guards powered their launchers.

"Fry 'em!"

Weapons unloaded electric discharges on the intruders instantaneously. Instead of killing them, they gained speed and strength, appearing and disappearing in front of Mole guards too dumbstruck to fight back. They were everywhere at once, knocking weapons out of their hands, breaking limbs, ripping heads off shoulders, and slicing necks and skulls in half.

The commotion stopped. The dust settled, leaving behind a concussed silence broken by faint groans and the metallic stench of fresh blood.

Eitan rose slowly from a small pile of rubble, the cave wall shattered behind him, his face undecided between rage and surprise. Rage took over, but his step forward, usually unafraid and determined, trembled with a fear he'd thought he'd forgotten.

Rina peeled off her helmet.

Eitan froze mid-motion, his jaw trembled and the tremor spread to his whole body. He charged onward. Rina took a step towards him. Eitan stopped.

She turned her back on him and looked towards Majidi. "No Councilwoman, my *Brother*," all of her contempt carrying through that single word, "has pulled his last trick."

Bees could read the winds. Among the myriad things they did, they had the ability to tell which direction they would come from, and more importantly, how long they would last.

This time they were wrong. The winds *did* blow for three days, and away from the mountain, over the cliffs and onto the oceans, but they did not just blow. Massive gales rocked the colony, carrying the smell of charred houses and burning corpses away from the colony and over the perimeter wall. Fish guards could not tell that the lights gleaming from the more distant Fish outposts along the cliff walls were anything but the night-lights they expected them to be.

It was only when the storm passed and contact was re-established with the colony that they discovered the extent of the slaughter. Five of the ten furthest outposts had been burned to the ground, skeletons of all sizes lay around haphazardly. Eyeless skulls that would never reunite with the Dreamers grinned at them, and the perpetrators hadn't left a trace.

One of the sentinels raised a horn to his mouth, and no sooner had the first note rung out than hooks landed at their feet from over the cliff walls, and strange, black-clad warriors appeared and disappeared among them, tearing them limb from limb.

"They are slaughtering Moles out there!" shouted Rina.

"And what exactly did you expect?" the Priestess responded with a disconcerting cool.

Rina knew her as Gilani, and her acolyte as Amirpour, but Priests would always be Priests in her eyes, only real people had names.

Sitting on the throne, Eitan grinned silently.

In the days that had followed the attacks on the Fish outposts, a civil war had erupted in the colony. Fish soldiers took revenge for their losses the only way they knew how, by killing Moles in droves. Moles had responded by seeking refuge in friendly houses amongst other Castes, drawing them deeper into the century old enmity.

The Fish had not uncovered the secret tunnels, and still did not know how the gruesome attacks had been pulled off, but it was only a matter of time until they did, and then the rebellion would be damned. Surprise was all the rebellion had on their side; lacking that, the Fish with the other loyal Caste members would complete their purge.

Priests outside could not appeal for calm. Their anchor was prophecy, and with their Divine Undertaking shut it never held ground. The Priests inside the caves had received a few relayed messages through the tunnels, but it was clear to Rina that they were biding their time, waiting to see how long the killing on the streets would go on for. Waiting until the inhabitants turned to them in desperation, or better yet, waiting until the Fish found the tunnels and slaughtered the rebellion, handing them the keys to the Divine Undertaking and restoring their power.

They would not give the signal allowing the Bee, Beast, and Ant rebels to rush out of the tunnels and take the fight to the Fish, not with their plans falling apart.

Eitan's authority was gone, even though he still sat on the throne, and all the Castes involved in the rebellion agreed that Rina was too impulsive. The rebellion was effectively leaderless. Her actions had hastened years of quiet preparation, forcing them into action, leading to the slaughter of their families and friends, and jeopardising their victory. Worse, regardless of how much they despised the Fish, they would not take orders from a woman, much less a former comfort girl turned warrior.

A thought tickled the back of Rina's brain, bubbled to the forefront, and hit her between the eyes. She looked up at the Priest's face, calm but betraying a smug self-satisfaction. She caught hold of his neck, lifted him up and turned to her troops. "Kill all the white cloaks," she ordered.

The other Caste members began to move to protect the Priests out of custom, and even her own soldiers seemed hesitant. Seizing the opportunity, he struggled for air and a word. Rina released the pressure on his throat enough for him to speak.

"Blasphemy!" he wheezed. "You can't threaten a Priest... Mole woman!"

The last came out muffled as she tightened her grip, but the Moles gathered in the cave took offense, and converged menacingly on the nearest Priest and Priestess.

"Threaten?" Rina's hand tore through his neck, his body crumpling to the ground, blood dripping down her fingers. His head, slipping from her grasp, hit the ground and rolled to Gilani's feet.

"A sign!" she yelled, dropping to her knees. No one killed a Priest, or a Priestess—one might as well choke Hades to death. "You need a sign, foolish girl!"

"What sign?" she inquired, distrustfully.

Priestess Gilani's eyes flickered from Amirpour's face by her sandals to Rina, "…A sign…a sign of Hades…" she hesitated, staring at the bloody head, its lips reaching for her toes, and gave in. "They, *we*, do not all believe in this rebellion, but we all believe in Hades. They must believe… somehow, that the Time of Hades has arrived."

Rina paused for thought. *A sign? What kind of sign could proclaim Had-*

She looked up at the Priestess and nodded, turned to her brother, who still sat, waiting for the show to go on. "You might be rid of me yet, Eitan, make it worth it."

He stood. "You make it worth it little sister, and there may still be room for you when all is done."

She glared at him. "If I don't make it you're as good as dead, but if I do…" She hesitated as well, unsure of speaking words she could never take back, but it did not matter. Eitan could not, *would not*, rule if she could help it. "If I do, there won't be room for the two of us," she said, and stormed out of the room with her army of sentinels, heading for Councilman Tamhidi's quarters.

"You have two minutes, after that…you should melt, or explode, the latter is preferable, I suppose." He paused and repeated himself. "Two minutes, you do realise what that means don't you?" He read his answer in the flatness of her stare. "And what did I tell you about birds of flame, girl?" He

189

shook his head. "Tsk, tsk, tsk, try metaphors and they fall on deaf ears, I thought you were brighter, girl, but who cares?"

He unrolled an old scroll, showing her the image of what looked like a giant incandescent bird, rising from a pit of flame. "You get the idea, don't you?"

"What are my chances?"

"Of success or survival?"

"Both."

"100% for the former… The latter, who knows, if you make it out in time, and hit the ground before the suit disintegrates… you could also bury the colony in lava."

She weighed his words for an instant. "It sounds acceptable."

"To you certainly, as for myself I would rather avoid another Pompeii."

"Another what?"

"Never mind. Make peace with Neptune before you go, girl. I wish you well."

He clicked the door open.

"Are you in such a hurry for me to die, Tamhidi?"

He laughed, a loud and heavy bass that bounced back against the walls. "You'll live to pester me yet, girl, but you said it yourself, you might only have a few hours left. So far, the Fish have been too busy to dive, but they never let the ocean go too long without them, and when they do…"

She nodded at him. "Thank you, old man," she said, with more emotion than she knew she held.

"Don't thank me, succeed girl. Succeed without killing us. Speaking of which, careful with the charges, you don't want this thing to erupt. Just a nudge."

She nodded and pulled her mask over her head, and started down the tunnel towards the heart of the Divine Undertaking.

Everything in the colony stopped when the ground under them started shaking hard enough to throw Fish sentinels off the walls.

Male Bees abandoned their cattle and ran home to their wives and children.

Ants left the fires in their forges unattended.

Beasts let go of their burdens, and knelt to pray.

Fish looked to the ocean for shelter but did not dare move.

Priests vainly appealed for calm.

But all of them, all as one, looked up to the chimney of the volcano, spitting gusts of coal black smoke and bits of flaming stone into the air, and before their eyes. Hades himself rose from its breath and lit the sky.

Somewhere inside the colony, a Priest stood up, headed to the window and rang a bell, echoed soon after by another, and another, and another, until everyone heard, and everyone knew. Hades had arrived.

The bubbling lava pits at the heart of the Divine Undertaking were waiting for her, daring her to dive and challenge the Gods.

The chimney seemed impossibly high, too high for her to reach, even if the explosion stirred the magma into outraged fury. Grimly determined, she looked back at the few sentinels waiting on her expectantly. This was the only chance they had left. Eitan was right, and so was everybody else. She was too impulsive, too brash, incapable of seeing beyond the immediate satisfaction of revenge to see the bigger—the much, much bigger—picture that had unfolded since her father had started planning the rebellion in what seemed another life now. She alone had led her family, her friends, her fellow conspirators, her Mole Caste, to the brink of extermination; it was only fitting that her sacrifice absolved or ended them. Regardless of the outcome, the centuries of slavery would end, a new order would rise, or all would be wiped clean.

She tore her eyes away from the comfort girls, clad in their black suits, impervious to the heat and faced down into the pit, dropping the payload into Azhi-Dahaka's hungry maw.

The explosion barely registered in the rage of molten lava beneath, but slowly the rumble grew and strengthened in intensity as the embers took on a life of their own and rose to meet her at the edge of the pit. When they were almost at her feet and still building, she felt a glimmer of hope, futile though it was, that she would succeed, and might, just might, live to see the story unfold.

She let the rising semi-liquid guide her into the chimney, it pushed her upward, a tiny thing in the blood of nature.

The rubble shutting the Divine Undertaking blasted outward, taking out the few curious and foolish enough to approach the sealed entrance as Hades blew out of the volcano.

The sound of thousands of underground footsteps made its way from the mountain towards the cliff, and in every neighbourhood, in each Caste's quarters, armed Moles, Ants, Bees, and Beasts, emerged from houses, and popped out of the ground, relentlessly attacking Fish and anyone deranged enough to get in their way.

Hooks landed on the side of the cliff, followed by black-clad female warriors pouring into the Fish outposts, darting furiously towards the colony's outer walls, sucking in the heat and energy from Fish laser beams that only propelled them forward, faster and stronger.

The first woman hit the wall with such strength she bored a hole straight through it, sending stone and those walking along the walls into the battle-torn colony. The others followed in a heartbeat, pounding through the structure until it crumbled and collapsed.

The flow abated in the chimney. Caught in the middle, she focused her vision upwards. The lava was thick but she could make out, still impossibly distant, the mouth of the dragon already roaring with fumes and small hyper-accelerated rocks.

Thirty, maybe forty seconds until the coils melted under the pressure or blew up, making her one with the magma. *At least the colony will be spared.* But the thought, comforting as it was, was not enough. It did not matter that she came out breathing or a writhing ball of flame, unless her body came out for all to see, it would all have been for nothing.

She released one last blast, a little explosive powder wrapped in a pouch made of suit fragments at her side, for one final attempt to reach the exit.

The small detonation was enough for her to accelerate, in seconds her head was peering ahead of the onslaught, her body still caught in the red turmoil, the mouth of the chimney visible intermittently between the gushes of wind that blew smoke away from the mountain.

Twenty seconds, maybe less. She could feel the suit weakening, an odd feeling that disconnected her from her state of hypersensitivity. *At least I won't feel anything.*

Suddenly, air hit her face just as she lost the ability to feel. Only her sight remained clear enough to see the sun break through the smoke, impossibly bright, impossibly close.

Above and around her, bright blue skies conflicted with the blackness beneath, shielding her from the events in the colony, and she soared still further upwards. The weakened suit still shrouded her, but glowed strangely from the heat, giving it shades of purple, streaked with random shots of bright blue where it had weakened the most.

Just as she thought that she would hit the sun and burn inside it, gravity asserted itself, sending her down in an arch back towards the volcano, back towards the colony, and the fight that still had to be fought.

She twisted her body into a spear, heading straight down into the black smoke, through it, and broke out over the confusion of a human eruption.

She thought she was falling back into the volcano and the flames, until she saw it was the colony, burning almost everywhere, accelerating towards her.

She could make out the different coloured hues of the Castes' clothing, fighting Fish, fighting each other, and amidst them, black streaks leaving brushstrokes of carnage behind them.

Brown Mole suits were backed into corners surrounded by Fish black, shooting through them only to be cut down by rebel forces closing in on them. Priests held their heads low, alone or in circles, their robes marred by smoke and soot, surviving as fights danced around them, and succumbing to collapsing structures and warriors too desperate to see them or care for their fate.

Only one target mattered to her, and that one she had to find. She hoped Eitan was dead already, but doubted anything could kill her berserk brother once the smell of death fuelled his madness. She focused harder, using the last of the energy caught in the suit as it slowly started to peel off in little specks of black-purple dust, and found him.

Eitan was in the central plaza, a few yards from where the perimeter wall had stood a few minutes earlier, his blade slashing through Fish and rebels alike.

She aimed herself at him, her body cutting through the air with a shriek. The colony was completely visible now. Eitan's hands were wrapped around a young Ant girl's neck, trying to rip her head off from her shoulders barehanded.

The air caught in her lungs; she tried to scream, and maybe she did, the clamour of battle and the air rushing past numbed her to sound, or maybe the suit had given way entirely.

There was no way of knowing—and it didn't matter at all.

He still had his back to her. He would not survive either way. She might, but not Eitan. Yet she wanted him to see her, and she wanted him to remember her words, remember his deeds, and hopefully, at the last second, remember the brother who'd ruffled her hair.

Eitan pulled up and the girl's neck muscles gave in, tearing away from bone, leaving him holding her reddish haired head, eyes still blinking.

He spun, raising his trophy, and looked up to see a purple-black dash in the sky. The smoke cleared, revealing the shape of a human arrow headed straight for him.

Rina gave a last thrust, one small boost to hit her target before he regained enough sense to dive out of the way. He let go of the head to fall at his feet, transfixed by her sudden apparition.

Two, maybe three seconds. *He still doesn't know, he still...* And then Eitan's eyes widened, a mixture of hate, fear, and respect, growing on his face just as she hit him. Maybe in that last second something changed; maybe terror overcame him, maybe acceptance, but she doubted it was either. Eitan would die believing in his own godliness, just as he had lived, and that was why he had to die.

Eitan exploded on impact as Rina's suit-wrapped head smashed into his torso. The last of the hyper-sensibility left in her clothing sent two fading heartbeats pulsing through her body, before she knew that he was dead.

She hit the ground with a sonic bang, sending ripples through the colony and beyond towards the cliff, lifting air and rock and levelling houses and warriors in its wake. Skidding further, she lost consciousness as the last of her suit peeled off, leaving her naked in a shallow crater a few yards from the cliffs and the endless waters beyond.

A breeze blew stronger through the open windows onto the balcony, carrying a smell of seaweed and iodine into the room.

The 2nd Councilwoman, a young, slender Priestess, wiped the sweat from Rina's brow with a small cloth as she lay in her bed.

The incoming storm felt good, reminding her of her childhood: the green fields in the shade of the volcano, the sun setting over the seas, her father's homecomings on windy nights, and getting herself into trouble.

"You should close your eyes and rest, 1st Councilwoman," the young Priestess suggested.

Rina laughed and coughed. "Ha! My open eyes are all that are keeping me alive. The moment I close them is the moment I'm gone. What do the day's reports read?"

The Priestess gathered a small pile of paperwork from a nearby table. "Which ones, 1st Councilwoman? Of the Divine Undertaking or the expeditions north?"

"Both."

"The Divine Undertaking is progressing well. Overseers speculate that it will take as much time again as since the rebellion before it is complete."

"*Another* fifty years?"

"Possibly, possibly less, 1st Councilwoman, we can always drive the Fish harder."

Rina waved a hand dismissively. "And what of the expeditions north?"

"Northern Europe is under ice, it would seem, large swaths of..." the unfamiliar word twisting in her mouth, "...of *in-ga-land* are now completely out of reach."

Rina nodded. A gust of wind slipped through the window, cooling her fever. "Perhaps, perhaps it is time to rethink the future of the Colony. Perhaps, and I do not say this lightly."

"Of course, 1st Councilwoman."

"But perhaps it is time to start considering how we can bring the Fish back into the fold, back into our community, and find a role for them when the Divine Undertaking is completed and we return to the comfort of the cave."

"Perhaps, 1st Councilwoman."

She took a hold of the Priestess' hand. "Do this for me, 2nd Councilwoman, do this for all of us, so we don't condemn them the way they condemned us."

"Of course, 1st Councilwoman, we will care for the Fish, as the old saying goes, 'Come hell or high water.'"

Rina coughed again. "Hell...hell, or high lava...*1st* Councilwoman...or high lava."

The Priestess seemed to think on her metaphor for an instant and nodded. "Yes, Yes...Or high lav-"

A blast of wind cut the Priestess short. She shielded her face. When she turned back to the bed, Rina's eyes were closed, her smile was gone, and just as she had predicted, so was everything that had been Rina.

196

She clapped her hands, the door opened onto a smartly dressed Beast councilman.

"Yes, 2nd Councilwoman?"

She pointed to Rina's corpse. "It's 1st Councilwoman now. See that the body is disposed of."

"In the pits? As per her wishes?"

She thought it over and shook her head. "No, no, make sure that the proper rituals are observed and that she is recycled; such a great leader should be put to the Colony's benefit, not thrown to the dragon."

She walked towards the window as the Beast councilman had the body lifted onto a stretcher and carried out of the room. A freezing slither of wind cut through the growing storm, chilling her throat and chest.

"And Councilman? Make sure the Fish's working shifts are doubled as of tomorrow, and that expeditions north are maintained until they can no longer swim; kill any protesters." She looked towards the ocean and the storms that sung of endless ice. "Time is running short. One morning, soon now…"

Her voice seemed to linger on her tongue, like a caught snowflake.

"Hell will freeze over, Hades will rise, and we will return to the caves…"

Mame Bougouma Diene

Mame Bougouma Diene is a French-Senegalese American humanitarian based in Paris with a fondness for progressive metal, tattoos, and policy analysis. He is published in *Omenana*, *Brittle Paper* and *Edilivres*, and is in no position to win the Nobel Prize so he can write the hell he pleases until it all freezes over.

The Flying Man of Stone

Dilman Dila

1

He could not tell the colours of the trees. Rocks jutted out of the ground like pillars in the ruins of a prehistoric city, but he could not tell them from the flowers that grew wanton in the valley. Cold tears crawled down his face like maggots. His chest burned as though a fire bomb had dropped in it. He could not tell if it were wind whistling past his ears, or bullets. He could not hear his own footfalls, nor the sound of dead twigs breaking under his soles. The thunder of gunfire deafened him. He struggled to keep up with his father, Baba Chuma, who was nothing more than a shadow fleeing through the vague shapes that he thought were trees and rocks and flowers. They could have hidden in one of the many caves on the slope, but father believed they would be safer on the plateau, if the gunmen would not be bothered climbing a hundred feet to search for them.

The slope became a rock less than twenty feet high. From a distance it looked like an armchair set atop a hill. Kera had climbed it a thousand times before, but now his hands were slick with sweat and he could not find footholds. His father had to help him up. Grass and thorny trees grew out of seemingly bare stone. About fifty meters ahead, at the opposite edge, a grey cliff soared into the sky, forming the back of the chair. Two stone protrusions jutted out of the cliff from each end, hanging above the short trees, giving the illusion of the arms of the chair. They called this plateau Kom pa'Yamo, the seat of spirits.

Kera leaned against a boulder, winded. He squinted down the slope to check if the rest of his family— his mother, little sister Acii, little brother Okee, and elder brother Karama— were coming up the slope too. The tears still made his vision blurry, but he could make out shapes of people running between the trees, ducking into caves to hide. He prayed that some of those shapes were that of his family, though he had seen a grenade ripping his mother apart, though he had seen little Acii lying still on a pavement in a pool of blood, though he had seen Okee beside her, still holding her hand tight, he prayed that he had not seen it right and that they had also escaped the massacre. The prayers brought more tears to his eyes.

He tried to look across the valley to the ledge on which their town stood. He could only see black smoke spewing from burning houses, rolling over the trees and flowers and the beautiful rocks. He closed his eyes and saw the valley as it had been just the day before, as it had always been since the beginning of time as far as he knew. A place he had visited every single day for the last three years since the war forced him out of school. An enchanting place full of boulders, some five hundred feet tall and covered with vegetation, most ranged from the size of a bull to that of a house. Many resembled household goods and animals. One gave the impression of a granary, another looked like a sleeping goat with a pot beside it. There were hundreds of such sculptures. To some people it was a wonder of nature, especially after a group of archaeologists had failed to find evidence of a long dead civilisation, or refused to believe that a civilisation in Sub-Saharan Africa could have had the technology and aesthetics to sculpt giant stones. The locals believed it was the artwork of spirits. Nobody lived in the valley, partly because it flooded for six months during the rainy seasons. Mostly, because they believed spirits lived there, and so they called it Gang Yamo. Shamans had shrines in some of the caverns, and people came from distant districts to worship their ancestors.

When Kera opened his eyes, the tears had cleared and he had recovered some of his vision, but he could still see the nightmare that had befallen his town. Two tanks were rolling down the ledge into the valley, in pursuit of civilians. One turned its barrel toward him, and fired.

Kera saw the missile coming. He fell flat, and an earthquake shook Kom pa'Yamo. He kept his head pressed into the ground, buried under his hands, as pebbles and dust showered him. The world went totally silent. He lifted his head. He could see the grass. He could feel the stones on his skin, the dust in his nose, but he could hear nothing. The two tanks were still on the ledge below the town, their barrels exploded whiffs of smoke every few moments, but the world was silent.

"Baba!" Panic gripped him. He could not see his father. He scrambled to his feet, and ran about, searching the tall grasses, behind boulders, frantic. For a brief moment he feared the shell had obliterated father, just as that grenade had ripped Mama to bits. When Baba Chuma stepped out from behind a boulder, Kera lost his vision again as tears clouded his eyes. "Baba," he cried.

His father said something, but Kera could still not hear.

Baba took him by the arms and dragged him through the tall grass, to a cleft in the cliff that was wide enough for them to hide in. They could cover its entrance with a shrub, which would hopefully conceal them in the event the soldiers came up onto the plateau.

As they neared the cliff, they saw the mouth of a new cave. The tank round had punched a hole in the rock surface opening up a grotto. Kera had never imagined Kom pa'Yamo as a hollow place. He had played on it from the time he had learnt to walk. They had kicked balls against the cliff and chiselled their names on its surface, but not once had it betrayed its hollow secret.

Baba sped to it at once. Kera followed, also seeing it would offer a better hiding place than the open air cleft. They ran over rubble and slid down into the cave. Sunlight fell around its mouth, but the rest of it remained in pitch darkness. Something on the walls made him frown. It looked like

201

charcoal drawings, but it could have been shadows dancing. He took a step back.

Before he could flee, a sound erupted, like the scream of a cricket. He had regained his sense of hearing. He once again became aware of the sounds of soldiers massacring civilians, the rattling of automatic rifles, the thunder of tanks, he thought he could hear a scream.

"Get in!" His father grabbed his arm again, and yanked him into the darkness.

The chill confirmed that something was not right. It was not the kind of cool he enjoyed under a tree in the middle of a scorching day. It was the kind of cold that gripped him whenever he had malaria. He jumped out of the darkness, back into the sunrays, which stopped just inside the mouth of the cave, and he could feel the warmth falling on his skin like something solid.

"Don't be afraid," Baba said.

"It's cold," said Kera.

"Yes. The sun has not touched its inside since the day it was created. Come. We'll be safe in here."

Kera pointed to the walls. He now got the impression that the drawings were wriggling, like earthworms when cut into two, maybe in pain, and he thought they were trying to get away from the sunlight, to slide into the darkness. They were strange patterns, circles that looked like triangles, he could not be sure for the lines shifted endlessly, but it reminded him of the rock art he had seen in Nyero when his school visited pre-historic sites. In the shapes he started to make out animals, strange animals, stranger birds, people hunting, a woman giving birth, a child fishing. It was like watching a silent video, the characters repeating the same actions in an endless loop of agony.

"This is evil," Baba said.

They scrambled over broken stones, climbing out of the cave. Then, a strange sound came from deep behind. It sounded like the hiss of a punctured tire. Kera kept scrambling out, but Baba stopped, and was squinting into the darkness, trying to see the source of the sound.

"Don't stop Baba!" Kera said.

Then he saw it, a shape blacker than the darkness, a human-like creature with a tail. It looked like one of the drawings had come off the wall.

"Baba!" Kera screamed.

Too late. In a split second, the tail shot forward, wrapped itself around Baba Chuma, and yanked him out of sight. The hissing stopped all of a sudden.

Kera froze, wondering if it was all a dream.

The day had started like any other. He woke up to take goats into the valley to graze. His mother was already baking samosas to sell in her kiosk, his little brother Okee and his little sister Acii sat beside her eating porridge. His older brother Karama had left to hoe the gardens. His father was at his garage, forging metals into works of art. They called him Baba Chuma, the father of metals, for he was a gifted artisan.

The war was far away from their town, and there was no hint it would ever come to them. With a population of only about four thousand, stuck in a sea of ancient rocks, they had nothing to offer the warlords. Then, soldiers came for recruits. When no one volunteered, they shot the women and kidnapped the men. Kera had watched a grenade rip his mother apart. He had watched Okee and Acii running hand in hand until bullets sent them crashing onto the pavement. He did not know what had happened to Karama. Maybe he was dead too. Now something that looked like a charcoal drawing had taken the only family he had left.

"Baba," he said, barely able to hear his own voice.

No response. Only a silence. Baba Chuma had not even yelled when the thing took him.

Then he heard the hiss again, like a whispering of wind, like the singing of leaves, and he saw drawings moving in the darkness, like smoke dancing. He fled from the cave. He stumbled over the stones on the plateau. He fell, scraping his knees, but he ignored the pain and ran fast down the slope. It was true, after all. It was not just another fairy tale, not just another superstition. The valley was a home of spirits. He had seen them. They looked like charcoal drawings and spoke like wind.

The tank cannons still pounded away from across the valley, there were still soldiers prowling about, but Kera did not stop to think about that. He would rather end up a captive of soldiers than of that charcoal thing. He sped, aware of the dangers of running fast down a slope, but he could not slow down. Evil drawings had taken his father. Evil drawings wanted to take him too. He stepped on a lose rock, slipped, fell, and went tumbling down the slope, down, down, down, until he crashed against a tree trunk. He struggled to his feet, ignoring the pain that blazed through his body, but he could not continue running for something grabbed him, and pulled him into a cave.

He screamed. A hand clamped on his mouth. He fought, struggling to get away, screaming, even as his brain registered that it was human hands, not a tail, pinning him to the ground.

"Quiet!" someone growled. "The soldiers will hear you!"

He could not stop screaming. He could not stop fighting. Shadows loomed over him. The drawings. The evil spirits. His legs kicked out. His hands broke free, and he threw a punch at a shadow. He tried to wriggle away, but then a rock smashed into his head and the world turned into darkness and silence.

And dreams.

He was with his father in a place without light, yet they could both see, the way cats see in the night. Living pictures materialised on the ragged walls, telling stories of an ancient people, of a magic world where gods still lived with humans. The drawings rippled over the rock face like water. He got a strange feeling that he too was a drawing, a work of charcoal, that he too was made of smoke, not flesh and bones, and that he was living in an ancient world which held the secrets of the universe. It might have been a sweet dream, for this world

The Flying Man of Stone

was a paradise where he could fly, but human-like creatures with tails hissed all around him.

"Baba!" he screamed.

And he woke up, strapped to the ground, supine. Red sun beams fell into the cave, onto roots that had broken through the stone surface and hung suspended like the disembodied fingers of the hissing creatures. He screamed again, but not a sound came from his mouth. He was gagged, the cloth tasted of mud.

"He woke up," someone said. He knew the voice, the man Lafony everybody called Teacher, for he had taught in the primary school for forty years.

"Kera," another voice said. It belonged to Asiba the mayor "Are you okay?"

"Thank God," someone else said. "I feared he'd never awake."

There were about twenty people crowded around him. He recognised them all. He listened for the sound of gunfire. Nothing. A few birds made a racket, a monkey squawked. The sun was going down. He had been unconscious for the whole day, for it had been morning when the soldiers attacked. Darkness would soon come down, and then what? Would the drawings come out of their cave?

Kera fought his bondage, but it came to him that if he wanted to flee he would have to convince the refugees to untie him. They were not the enemy. They kept him tied up to ensure he did not give away their hiding place. He held his breathe for several minutes, gaining control of his nerves, and then lifted up his hands in a gesture begging for them to untie him.

"Will you stay calm?" Teacher asked.

Kera nodded. Teacher removed the gag.

"There are spirits," Kera said, slowly, fighting to contain the panic that threatened to overwhelm him again. He wanted to say more, to tell them that the valley was indeed a home of spirits, that soldiers had knocked open the door of hell and that demons would soon be swarming the place. The only words he could manage were those three.

205

Someone chortled. Teacher frowned at that person and the laughter died out. They had not seen it. Though they called the valley Gang Yamo, no one really believed that spirits lived there. Even Teacher, who openly denounced Christianity and Islam and championed indigenous African faiths, had once said that just as God and Allah did not really live in churches and mosques, the valley was merely a symbolic place of worship.

"I saw them," Kera said. "They took Baba."

This time, more than two people chortled. Teacher smiled at him. "Why are you are scared?" he said. "If you saw spirits then you saw our ancestors. You shouldn't fear them."

Kera's jaws tightened. It would be pointless to argue, pointless to tell this man about the drawings, so he stayed quiet as Teacher untied him.

"I blame the mzungu," Teacher was saying in a low voice. "He has made us afraid of our own ancestors. Maybe this boy has seen spirits, but why should they scare him? I'll tell you why. Christianity has made us so stupid that we think our ancestors are demons. The sad thing is that this stupidity ensures the mzungu continues to rule us. You think this war is because one tribe wants to rule the other? No! It's a direct result of his greed. He created hatred between us so instead of working together we fight each other. The chaos allows him to control the diamond mines and the gold mines and the oil fields. That's what this war is about. We are too stupid to see it. We've become so stupid that we think our ancestors were Jews, and we think our true ancestors are demons."

Now free, Kera rubbed his wrists where the rope had bitten into his skin and examined the entrance. He could not dash out for he was at the back of the cave and there were people between him and the mouth. They would stop him, and tie him up again.

"I have to pee," he said, his voice hoarse with thirst.

The cave was too small for him to use any part of it. They would have to let him out. No one heard his request because

The Flying Man of Stone

Teacher was still going on about wazungu and the war. Kera then stood up, and that got him attention.

"I'm dying," he said. "I have to go."

A man parted the leaves that they had used to hide the entryway and peered out checking for signs of soldiers. The sun had gone down. Smoke from the town tinted the blue of dusk with a black mist.

"Stay close," the mayor said. "Don't scream if you see a yamo."

A few people chuckled, Kera ignored them. Once out, he ran fast down the slope. They shouted at him, but only briefly, for they were afraid the noise would attract soldiers. He knew they would not follow him. This time, he watched his step, and he ran with care. Soon he was off Kom pa'Yamo and running on flat ground, through waist-high undergrowth in a small forest. Though the trees did not grow thick, their shadows made it dark.

He did not stop running until he reached a small river. Being the dry season, it was down to a trickle, deep only to the knees. If he crossed it, and continued northwards up the ledge on which the burning town stood, he might meet the soldiers. Yet to the south were rocky hills bare of vegetation, some a thousand feet high. They formed a wall as though to protect Gang Yamo. To the east and to the west were vast swamps that flooded the valley during the rains. The river ran westwards from one end to the other, dividing the valley into two parts. Since the army barracks were somewhere in the west, the best option was to go east. He would have to stay in the valley until he reached the swamp and either steal a fisherman's canoe to row his way across, or climb the ledge and hope there were no soldiers about. But such a journey would mean passing by hundreds of spirit rock shapes and scores of boulders in which hissing creatures could be hiding. That left him with only one option, to wade across the river and return to town. The soldiers might still be up there, but that was a better fate than the hissing creatures.

Kera, a voice said.

The voice iced through his flesh and froze his bones. He nearly fell into the water. He searched the grass, squinted at the smoke rolling lazily beside the tree trunks, enshrouding the boulders, but saw no sign of Baba Chuma.

Kera, the voice came again, a gentle whisper, a soft and warm cooing. It was inside his head. Yet it was so clear as though his father had spoken aloud.

Then he heard the brush of cloth on grass, gumboots crushing twigs, and a silhouette walked out of the blue haze. Baba's hair always had streaks of grey, his hoary beard always looked like a sponge on his chin, but now white cotton covered his head, and his beard looked like feathers of a bird beaten by the rain. He had grown younger, the muscles were firmer on his biceps, and his eyes, *his eyes*, they shone like metal in bright sunlight.

It could not be Baba. Kera wanted to flee, but fear made his feet sink deep into the mud, rooting him to the banks of the river.

"It's me," Baba said. "Don't be afraid."

Baba had a bag, a heavy bag that visibly strained the muscles of his arm. In the half light Kera could not tell its colour. It looked brown, but it could have as well been blue. It was made from animal skin, maybe a goat. Had he gotten the bag from the cave of hissing creatures?

"I look different," Baba said. "They touched me."

They didn't touch you, Kera thought. They transformed you. He wanted to say this aloud, but he could not find his voice. A metallic ball sat in his throat. Yet Baba heard it, and gave him a slight nod.

"They transformed me, but they are not spirits. They are just people."

People with tails? People who look like charcoal drawings?

"Yes," Baba Chuma said. "They are still people."

Only then did it strike Kera that Baba could read his mind. His mouth became so dry that he could taste fire. He could not feel his body anymore, only his heart beating like a madman banging his head against a brick wall.

The Flying Man of Stone

"The soldiers are gone," Baba said, as he resumed walking. "The town is safe. Come with me. I need your help in the workshop."

Baba did not wait for a response. He lugged the goat skin bag and plunged into the river. The bag seemed to weigh a thousand kilos, though it was no bigger than the basket his mother used to take to the market.

What is in that bag? What makes it so heavy?

Kera did not want to follow his father. Questions whirled in his head, fuelling his terror. What kind of people could change the appearance of a man? Why had they given him the bag? What was in the bag? What work could be so urgent that he had to go to the workshop in the night? There would surely be corpses in the streets. Bodies of people they knew, of their neighbours, their friends, of his mother, of Okee, and of Acii.

Come, Baba said, in Kera's head. *Don't be afraid.*

Kera remembered the dreams of the drawings, and Teacher's talk about Christianity and their ancestors. If the hissing creatures were evil, they would have killed Baba, or turned him into a terrible monster. Instead, they had only changed his hair and his eyes and made him look younger. They had given him telepathic powers and a goat skin bag with mysterious content. There was yet no sign of evil.

Blood resumed circulating in his legs, and now he could feel the mud beneath his feet, warm and ticklish. He did not want to, but he stepped into the river, and followed Baba.

By the time they reached Katong, complete darkness had fallen. Flames leapt high off a vocational school, painting the town orange. Opposite it, the shell of a hotel gaped. A bed sheet stuck in the rubble fluttered like a flag. Burnt vehicles littered the road. A charred hand stuck out of the driver's window of a school van. Kera thought it might have belonged to Musta, who drove Acii to kindergarten. Only two schools, one for primary level and the other for kindergarten, had stayed open through the war. The town folk paid the teachers in kind, mostly with food. Kera's school, a secondary level boarding school, was in another district, sixty kilometres away. It had closed as fighting spread. Apart from Musta, the van was empty. It had not picked up any children when the soldiers came.

They avoided Main Street—where they were sure to find Mama, Okee, and Acii— and used its backstreet, an alley with wooden doors leading to courtyards, some of which were business premises but most were residences. Here, the darkness hid the identity of the dead. They saw a corpse in a gate that stood ajar. Kera luckily did not know anybody who lived in that courtyard. They found another in the gutter, choking the flow of water, and a third beside an overflowing garbage bin.

The workshop stood at the end of the alley. The metallic gate was open and they went in. One side was a graveyard of cars that Baba hauled in to cannibalise their parts and bodies. The other side was a roofed shelter where Baba worked. Since school closed Kera had taken to helping him in the foundry.

"There are no corpses here," Baba said.

How do you know? Kera wanted to ask. He only swallowed, and watched Baba lug the bag to the work table. All along, Kera had stayed behind Baba, so he would not have to see those frightful eyes. Now, Baba wore a pair of black welding goggles. Kera sighed in relief. He would not have to look into those eyes.

Kera flicked on a switch. Several bulbs came on, drawing power from a solar charged battery. Baba opened the bag. Kera froze in anticipation, but it was only full of rocks. Not ordinary rocks, though, they looked like glass with shades of green, yellow, and black, each the size of Baba's fist.

"Start the fire," Baba said, giving him one of the strange heavy rocks. "Melt it."

What are we going to create? Kera wanted to ask. He did not. Like a puppet, Kera followed instructions. They worked all night. Kera melted the strange rocks, as well as iron and steel, and planed timber. Towards midnight, what they were building started to take shape. At first Kera thought it would be a two-wheeled cart, roughly the size of a coffee table.

The Flying Man of Stone

They completed it as the first light of dawn appeared. It was some kind of machine. A tube, whose insides were lined with sheets of the strange glass rock, passed through a box, which had an engine. The box and tube sat on the bed of the cart. At one end of the cart, there were levers, and at the other end there were six projections that looked like arms, complete with fingers.

What does this thing do? Kera wondered. His eyes were dry and aching, eyelids heavy with exhaustion, and muscles throbbing with a dull pain. A wind blew, stinging his nose with the smell of ash, and of bodies that had started to rot. He thought they should go to the street, to gather up his mother, Okee, and Acii, who would by now be swathed in flies. He thought they should give them a decent burial before the worms turns them into obnoxious objects. He had not thought about them all night, and even now he pushed away the horrible images, as though they were something he had seen on TV.

Baba Chuma hooked a battery onto the machine and flicked on a switch. The machine gave a low hum. Kera stepped away, expecting it to transform into a monster and eat him up.

Baba picked a hammer, and pushed it into one end of the tube. The machine sucked the hammer into the box. A rattling erupted. The machine vibrated so much that Kera thought it would fall to pieces. A light flashed inside the tube. It made Kera think of a photocopier. He thought the machine would crush the hammer, shred it, do something to it, but it came out whole at the other end of the tube. Kera frowned. What was the point of passing the hammer through the machine? He got an answer soon, and it turned his bones to ice. The light flashed again, and another hammer, an exact copy of the first, with the same scratches on its head and the same crack on its handle, popped out. Then another, and another, and another, exact replicas of the hammer fell out and piled onto the ground.

A replicating machine?

The technology he knew, like cars and computers, had intricate engines. Even wrist watches had a complex system. His father had built something straight out of a sci-fi movie, yet its system seemed no more complex than that of a rope pulley. It had to be magic, Kera thought as he eyed the glass rocks in the goatskin bag. He had melted only a few of them. The bag was still nearly full. Magic. Nothing else could explain it.

Baba pulled a lever, and the machine went silent. The hammers stopped falling out. He pushed his hand deep into the tube and took out the original hammer. A smile wavered on his mouth. "They are ancient people," Baba said. "They have survived from a very long time ago."

For a few seconds, Kera did not understand what Baba was talking about. Then it came to him. The hissing creatures. Ancient people, Kera thought, recalling the hieroglyphs on the cave, the rock art that was alive with timeless stories.

"They live inside the rocks because they are afraid of the sun," Baba continued. "It kills them. After the tank blew a hole into their home, they feared the sun would wipe them out. They asked for my help. They touched me and gave me their knowledge so that I can seal the hole, but they also want me to protect the valley. Come, let's push this thing to the Kom."

Words welled in Kera's throat, questions, warnings, suspicions, but not a sound escaped his lips. Baba rolled the replicator out of the workshop, not waiting for a response, not looking back to check if Kera was following. Kera wanted to lie on the floor and fall asleep, but again his legs moved of their own volition.

Kera kept his eyes on the back of his father's head, for that would save him from seeing the corpses in the alley, but he could not avoid the smell. It churned his stomach. He did not spit or vomit out of respect. He thought it was a good thing that there were no wild dogs in the area, else they would have mauled the bodies leaving entrails all over the place. There were no carrion crows either, no vultures, not only because they kept their town very clean, but mostly because the war had created hundreds of other feasting sites for the birds.

"Wait here," Baba said when they were out of town. He went back into town and returned shortly after with a small bag of cement and ropes, then they continued their way to Kom pa'Yamo.

The sun kissed the valley. A breeze licked Kera's face. Flowers blossomed and white butterflies floated over the foliage. A wood pigeon sang. The ambience pushed the sight of the burnt town, and the smell of carnage, into the distant memory of bad dreams. Kera caught himself smiling, and almost at once guilt overwhelmed him. He should not be happy on such a morning, but as they pushed the replicator up the steep slopes to the plateau, a macabre happiness gripped him. If Baba could invent a replicator, was he then not able to bring the dead back to life? Could he not invent a machine to resurrect Mama, Okee, and Acii?

They heaved and huffed, and the replicator went slowly up and up. Whenever they stopped for a breath, they tethered it to tree trunks to prevent it from sliding back down.

"I should have built a flying machine," Baba said, during a break.

What about a machine to bring Mama back to life? Kera thought, but said "An aeroplane?"

"No. Aeroplanes pollute the world and cause *climate change*, but I can build a flying machine that truly imitates birds."

Kera saw his reflection in the dark glass of Baba's goggles, an image painted the colour of fire by the sun rising behind him. Maybe Baba is dead, he thought, and something, that hissing creature, has taken over his body. He had never heard Baba talk of pollution, and the only English words he spoke before that morning were *Hullo*, *Fine*, and *Sorry*. Baba never went to formal school. He learnt how to work metal as an apprentice to his grandfather, who bequeathed to him the workshop. Yet here he was talking about aeroplanes and pollution, and saying *climate change* in English. How could this be his Baba? The body might be his, but inside it was someone else, or something else, something that knew about aeroplanes and pollution.

That hissing creature.

Bring Mama back to life, Kera said, but again it was only in his head.

He knew Baba had read it in his mind from the way Baba's face twitched, but Baba did not respond. He resumed pushing the replicator up the slope. Sweat glistened on his skin. Kera pulled the machine. Every muscle ached.

There were people still hiding in the caves. Every time they passed by one, they told them that the soldiers were gone and that it was safe to go back to town. Most crept out silently and started back to their ruined home with only a mild curiosity about the replicator. No one asked aloud why they were pushing it up Kom pa'Yamo, until they reached the cave in which Teacher and the mayor were hiding.

"Is that a gun?" Teacher said.

"No," Baba said.

Teacher's frown deepened. "What is it then?" he said.

"Nothing," Baba said.

"What happened to your hair?" Teacher said. "Did you dye it? Why are you wearing goggles? What is wrong with your beard? Where are you taking this thing?"

"You look younger!" the mayor whispered.

"I'll explain later," Baba said.

He resumed pushing the machine. Kera thought Teacher and the others would follow, but they did not. They stood still, watching, until the trees and undergrowth hid them from view.

By the time they heaved the replicator onto the plateau, the sun had risen high and not a cloud was present to mask its heat. Baba had covered the hole in the cliff with shrubs to protect its secret, but the hissing creatures were lucky for the cliff faced north. If it had faced east or west, the sun's rays would have poked deep into the cave, not just around the mouth.

The Flying Man of Stone

Kera tried to peep into the darkness. The pictures still rippled on the walls, but he could not see the tailed people, nor hear them. He could feel them though, their chilly aura, and he suspected that Baba was communicating with them using telepathy.

 Their work lasted about an hour. They replicated water, which they found in a small puddle, then stones and cement which they used to seal the cave. Now, Kera saw the other function of the machine, particularly the purpose of the six arms. They were builders. Baba manipulated them using the levers, and they piled rocks and mixed cement to seal up the hole. Lastly, Baba replicated a huge pile of rocks and stacked these up to hide the cement.

Katong town was founded in the 1930s, during the construction of the highway from the capital in the west to the mineral rich northeast, as a worker's camp, for it was at a midway point between the two locations. After the highway was complete, Indian traders came to make money off English colonial governors and mine owners, who had set up homes so they could have a place to spend a night on the eighteen hour journey between the city and the northeast. As the town flourished, a quasi-apartheid system cropped up, with a T-junction separating the three different peoples.

The business district had the uninhabited valley to its south and the highway to its north. Here, the Indians lived in little apartments above their shops and restaurants. On the other side of the highway were the two suburbs, separated by a road that led to farms. The English lived in grand mansions in Senior Quarters, which had churches, a recreational complex with a cinema, swimming pool, and golf course. The Africans lived in Chandi, which translates to poverty, or misery, then an overcrowded slum with muddy pavements. While a few rich Indians had mansions in Senior Quarters, and a few poorer Europeans owned shops and restaurants in the business district, Africans could not live in Senior Quarters, nor run any economic activity in the business area. They worked the English owned farmlands, growing cotton and tea, and they supplied Indians with fresh vegetables and foods. They were servants and shamba boys of the foreigners. There were two primary schools, one for the foreigners, and the other for Africans. In the two churches, Catholic and Anglican, both in Senior Quarters, the Europeans took the front rows and the Africans occupied the back seats. Both Indians and Europeans kept to themselves, refusing to intermarry with the Africans, refusing to assimilate, and after Independence they both kept British citizenships and passports.

The Flying Man of Stone

This quasi-apartheid system survived until 1975, when the General assumed power through a military coup. He expelled all foreigners from the country. "You are milking the cow without feeding it," he said. He nationalised the mines, the oil wells, and all foreign owned assets, and gave the Indian shops to Africans. He became an instant hero. Many Africans moved out of Chandi, to Senior Quarters and to the business district. Those who remained had more space for themselves. The slum evolved into a low cost suburb. "That," Teacher once told Kera's class, "is when we got our true independence."

The General ruled for twelve years, until the Americans blew up his plane as he flew to Libya. Five years of turbulence followed. One bloody coup led to another bloody coup, with the country tottering close to an all-out civil war, until one leader undid all that the General had accomplished. He gave the mines and oil wells back to the Europeans and he invited the Indians to reclaim their lost property. Riots broke out, but the President had American money to bribe the opposition to his side. Three hundred civilians died before the rest got the message and stopped rioting. The Indians and the English did not return to Katong.

In the early 1990s, with a loan from the World Bank, the government built a new road to reduce access to the mineral rich region by five hundred kilometres, by-passing Katong. Now, there was nothing to attract anyone to Katong. The English farms had long been abandoned. The population fell from over forty thousand to under five thousand.

The President ruled for over two decades. Then, at the behest of his American masters, who wanted to prove to the world that they were helping the country, he organised elections. And he lost to a soldier, a Colonel who had been the General's vice president. Either he made the mistake of granting the Electoral Commission total independence, or they were aware of the Colonel's power, so they announced the results.

217

Furious, the President annulled the results and ordered the arrest of the entire Commission. Again, riots broke out. This time, disgruntled soldiers who had been kicked out of the national feast sided with the Colonel and with the rioters. Before anyone could understand what was happening, the civil war that had threatened since the General's death finally broke out. A score of different factions cropped up to claim power, and instead fragmented the country into territories under the rule of warlords.

The war did not come to Katong. It had nothing to attract the warlords, no wealth, no military value, it was stuck in the middle of nowhere. They ignored it until they realised it could offer them recruits.

The cemetery lay in a grove about a mile outside town, on the old highway to the city. About five hundred survivors had gathered to bid farewell to the dead. Branches of tall trees intertwined to roof the cemetery, for it was taboo to rest the dead under open skies. The coolness reminded Kera of the chill in the cave. A thick undergrowth of flowers emitted a sweet perfume, but that could not mask the odour of forty three corpses. A hymn, punctured with wails and the sound of digging, wrung tears out of Kera's eyes.

The dead lay in neat rows, wrapped in bark cloth. Though they had adopted the Christian custom of scribbling the name of the deceased on a cross, they never used coffins, and never sealed the graves with cement. Instead, they retained their old rituals of ringing the new home of the departed with stones and flowers. An Anglican reverend led the service. The absence of the Catholic priest was conspicuous.

Kera and his father stood over their three loved ones. Mama's face had grown darker in death, her braids seemed longer than he remembered and her lips appeared a little redder, as though she had applied lipstick. The bark cloth hid the rest of her body, but it was stained with black goo, and Kera could only imagine the damage the grenade had done. Okee and Acii lay beside her, no longer holding hands.

218

The Flying Man of Stone

Bring them back to life, Kera prayed silently, not to God, but to his father.

The replicator could not clone living things. He had experimented with a grasshopper. He got hundreds of insects, but all were dead, and all were made of the glass rock material, rather than of flesh. If he put his mother, or Okee, or Acii, in the replicator, they would not resurrect. Instead, he would create statues.

"Never try to clone a living thing," Baba had said, in a voice so soft, so unlike the alcohol-roughened voice Kera had heard all his life. "You'll only succeed in creating evil."

Please build a machine to bring them back to life, Kera now prayed. Baba frowned at him, but Kera persisted in his prayers. What could be so evil in bringing loved ones back to life?

"You have me," Baba said, "and Karama."

"Where is Karama?" Kera said.

"He's not dead," Baba replied.

That brought more tears, of relief. He still had an elder brother. He did not ask how his father knew. He looked through the trees, to the valley, which lay just beyond the old highway, wondering if Karama was hiding somewhere down there, or if he had joined the small stream of refugees making their way to safer places, wherever they may be. Had Baba had telepathic contact with Karama? Is that how he knew Karama was still alive?

The soldiers took him, Baba said, speaking inside Kera's head. Every time it happened, a breeze blew through Kera's skull, ice made his spine tighter, and a fire hollowed out his belly.

The revelation brought bile to Kera's mouth. If soldiers had taken Karama, he was as good as dead, for the soldiers would turn him into a monster, a rapist, a cold blooded killer, a senseless automaton who saw no value in human life and whose only purpose in life was to fight to the death for the warlords.

He won't turn into a monster. You'll rescue him.

"What?" Kera said.

I'll show you how.

Kera's eyes grew several inches wider. If soldiers had taken Karama, then they held him in an open-air prison with hundreds of guards. How could he, a boy not yet sixteen, rescue his brother?

Baba gave him a smile, and Kera thought an explanation was coming, but the sound of an approaching car broke the moment. A chill spread through the graveyard as a sudden hush fell upon the mourners. The digging stopped. Everybody stood still. The war had created a severe fuel shortage, very few people could afford to drive, and most were soldiers.

"Stay calm," Teacher shouted. "It's only one car."

Teacher was inside a grave, digging, bare-chested, his trousers folded to the knees, his hands and legs covered with dirt, his face smeared with mud and sweat. The slight tremble in his voice did not calm the growing panic. The doubt on his face fanned the fear. A single car could do as much damage as a convoy. It could be a pick-up truck with a machine gun on its bed, or a saloon with a couple of automatic rifles inside.

"Is it soldiers?" Kera asked his father.

"No," Baba said, raising his voice so those around him could overhear. "It's the wazungu from the missionary."

"How do you know?" Okello said. He was a retired policeman with pure white hair.

"From the sound of the engine," Baba said. "I know because I've repaired that car before."

"It's not soldiers!" Okello shouted to stem the growing panic. In spite of his age, his voice boomed with authority. "I know that engine! It's Father Stephen's car!"

People turned to the old man, uncertainty in their stares, and he in turn threw suspicious glances at Baba. Before a stampede could break out, the car came into view, a Landrover with a sleek blue sheen that gleamed like a pearl.

"Father Stephen!" several people shouted at the same time.

"That bastard," Teacher hissed. He climbed out of the grave and started to march toward the Landrover, brandishing a hoe.

"Don't," Baba said, running after him. "He didn't do it."

Teacher did not stop until Baba grabbed him. A vein pounded against Teacher's temple, and Kera thought Teacher would shove Baba aside and charge at the mzungu, but Teacher did not. His fingers tightened on the handle of the hoe.

The car stopped at the roadside. Father Stephen got out and waddled towards them. He had white hair that flowed down to his shoulders and a big white beard that dangled over his chest. His skin was red with sunburn. The frock, hanging lose on his body, could not hide his obesity. His neck had vanished, and his head sat on his shoulders like a melon on a rock. He had lived in Katong for over forty years. When the General expelled Europeans and Asians in the seventies, he stayed as the church had interceded on behalf of foreigners in its service. Father Stephen was fluent in Luo. Two nuns came with him. One Italian, the other French. They had not yet learnt Luo, but they spoke good English. A hymn broke out to welcome them.

"Bastard," Teacher hissed again. But he seemed calm, so Baba released him.

Father Stephen exchanged greetings with many of his congregation as he waddled to the row of corpses. The short walk left him breathless.

"Oh dear," he said. "Oh dear, oh dear."

"Did you send the soldiers?" Teacher said, speaking in English.

Father Stephen's face folded, his eyes seemed to disappear beneath slabs of fat that had once been brows. His lips twitched, searching for an answer, but only a sigh came out. A few people heard the question. They frowned. The majority were out of earshot. They continued to sing and to wail.

"Hello Teacher," Father Stephen managed to say, in Luo. His voice trembled.

221

"Don't foul our language with your tongue," Teacher said in English. "Answer me. Did you send soldiers to kill us?"

"What are you talking about?" Father Stephen insisted on speaking in Luo, and so the exchange happened in two languages.

"Did they attack your church?" Teacher said.

"No," Father Stephen said. "No. Of course not. God protected us."

"God? Are you trying to say there is no God in the Anglican church? The soldiers bombed it. They killed the reverend's wife and his four children. There they are." Teacher pointed at a group of corpses beneath the reverend's feet. "Every building in town has bullet holes. Every family lost something. Why did the soldiers spare you? Is it because you are white? Is it because they are working for you?"

"Nonsense," Father Stephen said, "I came here to pray for the dead and I won't let your madness stop me. This is my home as much as it is yours. Whatever madness has gripped you, I'll pray for God's mercy to touch you."

Teacher's hoe struck Father Stephen in the temple. Blood splashed onto Kera's face. The fat man crumpled to the floor with a yelp of pain. He rolled about on the ground, and he would have fallen into a grave if he were a little smaller. Teacher kicked him, trying to shove him in, and then brought the hoe down intending to hack off the fat neck, but Baba jumped and grabbed onto Teacher. Two other men joined the fray and together they restrained Teacher, who fought back but could not match three men. They pinned him against a tree and took away the hoe.

"You sent them!" Teacher shouted, now speaking in Luo, as he struggled against the men holding him. "You think we don't know your schemes? You want our gold and diamonds and oil! That's why you are here! You bring your stupid religion and you make us stupid and you think we won't ever know the truth? You sent them!"

The nuns helped Father Stephen to his feet. One ripped a piece off her habit and pressed it against the wound to stop the blood. The singing stopped, people were crowding, questions flew about to add to the confusion.

"Oh God," Father Stephen wailed.

"You dirty demon, the soldiers work for you!" Teacher was shouting.

"It's best if we left," one nun said, trying to pull Father Stephen away.

"I'm not leaving," Father Stephen said. "I'm innocent."

"You sent the soldiers because you want our diamonds!" Teacher said.

"Don't blame all wazungu for the crimes of a few," Bondo said. He owned one of the three stationary shops in town. His son was an altar boy.

"Let's go," the nun said, tugging at the father. "You'll bleed to death if they don't fix that wound soon."

"I didn't send them," Father Stephen said. "You are my people. You are my children, how could I hurt you?"

"Hypocrite!" Teacher shouted.

"Don't mind him, Father," the mayor, said. "They killed all his children and his wife. It's the grief making him say such things."

"We are all aggrieved," Bondo said again. "But does that mean that we should blame all wazungu for the crimes of a few? We know about the mines and we know why this war started but blaming Father Stephen for it is sheer stupidity."

"You are the stupid one," Teacher said. "This fat mzungu is a thief! When he came he was so thin that the wind could have blown him away but now, see how fat he has become! He's stealing our wealth!"

"Father," the nun was saying, tugging at his frock, "let's go to the clinic."

"I'm not a thief!" Father Stephen shouted. Blood ran down his face. He wavered, as though about to fall.

"Please go to the clinic," the mayor said. "The Reverend will manage the service. Thank you for coming by, but please leave now."

"I'm not a thief," Father Stephen said.

"Teacher has a point," Timeo said. He was a carpenter. He married hardly a month ago and his wife was with Kera's mother when the soldiers came. She had been pregnant. "Why didn't they attack your church?"

"This is madness," the mayor said.

"How do you know the Catholic church is the only building they didn't shoot at?" Bondo said.

"We searched all houses looking for victims," Timeo said. "The Catholic church was untouched."

A hush fell upon the graveyard. Even the wind seemed to stop, and the leaves fell silent, as though to fuel the accusation. Kera heard a twig break as the carpenter took a step toward the wazungu. Father Stephen's mouth hung ajar, saliva dripped down onto his garb.

"Many other buildings are untouched," Baba said, and every one turned to him. "They didn't attack The Social Centre or the Headmaster's house."

"But they killed the Headmaster," Teacher said. "They wounded Agira. He may not survive the day." Agira was the caretaker of The Social Centre. After the English had gone, the complex had been poorly maintained. The golf course was overgrown, the swimming pool had not had water for decades, and bats infested the cinema.

"Please," the reverend said. "Let's not behave like the soldiers. Vengeance is for the lord. I lost my family. I'm aggrieved. But we've no proof that Father Steven is working with soldiers. No proof at all."

Kera could feel the tension thaw. Sound returned to the world. The wind resumed blowing, the leaves sung, and a murmur spread through the crowd.

"Thank you," Father Stephen said in a weak whisper, finally letting the nuns take him away.

"Don't let them go!" Teacher screamed, fighting the men holding him. "Beat them! Kill them!"

But the crowd parted to allow Father Stephen to retreat to his car.

3

Kera fell into bed early that night. Although nightmares beset him in his sleep, he did not wake until late the next day, when a ray of sunlight fell in from his window and shone through his eyelids. He had a headache.

They lived in Chandi. It was not a slum any more, but it still had a high population density. Every morning he awoke to a cacophony. Women gossiping to each other across the yard, laughing, infants screaming for attention, children playing, the screech of a broom sweeping a compound, the ring of aluminium clashing as young girls washed pans and dishes, the caw of crows. Life.

But that morning he did not hear any noise.

For several moments he could not tell where he was. Then it all came back with such a force that he felt a sharp pain in his heart. There were two other beds in the room, both unmade, as they had been when Okee and Acii had crept out of sleep. Even now it seemed as though they had just walked out, leaving the sheets scattered all over the floor. He watched the dust motes floating on sunbeams, and his tears wet the pillow.

Bring them back to life, he prayed to Baba.

An aroma wafted in from the kitchen. It stirred hunger to bubble in his stomach. A sizzling sound tickled his saliva glands. He drooled a little onto the pillow, and it mixed with the tears. Was it Baba cooking, or had he brought Mama back to life?

Kera scrambled out of bed. The door opened into a short corridor, which had four other doors. One led to the master bedroom, another to the bathroom. Both were closed. The one immediately to his left was ajar. It led to the living room. Kera saw Teacher on a sofa, reading a dog-eared history book. There were two other people with him, but Kera could see only their legs. The fourth door, at the opposite end of the corridor, led to the kitchen. It stood wide open, letting in smoke. If it were Mama cooking, there would not have been so much smoke. He found Baba, still wearing the goggles, straddled over the charcoal stove.

"How have you woken up?" Baba greeted, without turning around.

"I woke up fine," he replied. His voice a croak, barely a whisper.

"Today, I'll build a solar powered stove," Baba said, turning an omelette in the pan. "I hate smoke."

You could simply bring Mama back to life, Kera thought, and Baba finally turned to face him. Baba's face had grown a shade darker.

"Sit," Baba pointed at a three-legged stool.

Kera sat. Baba scooped the omelette out of the pan, put it on a plate, on top of four other omelettes, and then put a kettle on the stove. Without asking, Kera took a slice of bread smeared with odi and wolfed it down. The taste reminded him of Mama. She made him odi whenever he left for another term in boarding school, after he had complained to her that they ate nothing but boiled beans and posho. He mixed odi in the beans, to give it a better taste, and to gain supplementary nutrients from the groundnuts and simsim in the paste. The memories caused something cold to run down his cheeks. He wiped it away quickly.

Baba sat on a stool beside him.

"I can bring her back to life," Baba said. "But I won't. Whatever goes to the other side is not meant to come back. Mama, Okee, Acii, they have gone over. Are they are in a better place or is it a worse off place? I don't know. But it's now their home. Bringing them back will only unleash evil."

Kera ran out through the back door, into the backyard, which they shared with five other families. Laundry fluttered on a wire. A neighbour had washed clothes just before the soldiers came. Behind the laundry stood a small building, which was meant to be a store, but which Karama lived in. Kera sat down on the doorstep, buried his face in his palms, and allowed himself to cry.

The Flying Man of Stone

Nearly half an hour later, Baba brought him breakfast. A mug of milk, slices of bread smeared with odi, and an omelete. Kera wiped his eyes, and ate. Baba went back in without saying a word. After the meal, Kera took the dishes into the kitchen, and caught a quarrel coming from the living room.

"Our gods have woken up," Teacher was saying. "They want us to finish off the mzungu."

"Our gods are more just than that," the mayor said.

"If we spill innocent blood then we are no different from them," the reverend said.

"It's time to revenge," Teacher said.

"Vengeance serves no purpose," Baba said. "I called you to talk about the gift our ancestors gave me and how we can use it to defend ourselves. I don't want to talk about vengeance and bloodshed."

Ancestors? Kera frowned. Baba had insisted that the hissing creatures were not spirits, or gods, just people. A different kind of people. Why then was he telling these men that they were spirits? Was it to protect the secret?

"We can't defend ourselves without weapons," Teacher said.

"Even if I wanted to I can't design weapons," Baba said. "The spirits that possessed me are not warriors. They won't allow me to create things that will end up killing people."

"What ancestors are those? Our ancestors were not cowards. They fought the British. They resisted colonisation."

"Well, I can't build weapons."

"But we need to kill those who try to kill us."

"Weapons are the reason our world is a bad place," the reverend said.

"And you think you will just wish away the badness?" Teacher said. "Get real. Without weapons we won't be able to defend ourselves. Never."

"Yes we can," Baba said. "I can build a wall so high and so thick and so strong that not even a tank will bring it down. I can create a moat of fire outside this wall, a fire that will never go out."

"You talk like a madman," Teacher said.

227

"We've seen his machine," the mayor said. "He can do it if he says he can."

Kera crept away. He wandered about in the empty streets. Even the birds seemed to be staying away from the town. The scars of the massacre glared at him. Burnt vehicles, shattered buildings, bloodstains on the pavement. On Main Street, he saw a family making their way out of town, with a few possessions on bicycles. The stupid ones, Kera thought. Katong had been the safest place before the attack. Leaving it would be jumping from the frying pan into the fire. And if Baba built the wall and fire moat, would they be safe? Probably, but not from artillery fire. The streets had too many painful memories, so he escaped to the workshop, which evoked only metallic memories.

Baba never put a padlock on the outer gate, for the yard had nothing valuable, only scrap and immovable tools. He locked the shop, however, for it contained merchandise, household utensils, iron furniture, and he kept valuable tools in a backroom. But that day, Kera found a padlock on the outer gate, an expensive type that used a combination like a safe.

He stared at the padlock for a long moment, and then climbed over the gate and jumped into the workshop. He found two machines that Baba must have made in the night. One looked like a chair with a wheel. Baba had cannibalised the wheel from an old green bicycle of Kera's, which he had intended to repair and give to Okee. The chair, crafted out of iron and cushioned with red leather and sponge, had been Baba's favourite, a piece of art that Kera's grandfather had made many years ago. Just under the seat, but above the wheel, was a black box made entirely out of the strange glass rock. Two large sheets of leather were attached to the back of the chair. In front of the chair were a bicycle handlebar and a vehicle's gear box. Kera puzzled over the machine until he spread out the leather and the purpose struck him. Wings. '*I can build a flying machine.*'

The second object was a rod twice the length of his arm and just as thick, with four slide switches at the back. It had a slot at the top, with a mirror inside. When he looked into the open end of the tube, he saw a row of mirrors made from the strange glass rock, placed delicately one behind the other, and each caught the image of his eye.

He slid the switches from one position to another. Nothing happened. He left the rod on the table, where he had found it, and crawled into the corpse of a van. He sat behind the wheel and memories of his lost family saddened him.

The sun was high in the sky when Baba came in, alone, still wearing the welding goggles. Kera thought his skin had again grown several shades darker, and now looked as though it was smeared with grease. He gave Kera a smile, and spoke as he strode to his worktable.

"Good you are here," Baba said. "Have you seen that thing?"

"The flying machine?" Kera said, but stayed in the van.

Baba climbed onto the chair, pulled a lever and a pair of six foot wings spread out. He peddled. A whirr filled the workshop. The machine did not move, for a stand prevented the wheel from touching the ground. He peddled harder, and the wheel spun in a blur of motion. Baba kicked away the stand. Instead of the wheel falling to the ground, the machine jumped into the air. Kera gaped. In spite of all he had seen Baba do, he had not imagined it would actually fly. The wings flapped like that of a bird. Baba stayed only a few feet above the ground, within the cover of the wall, and he later told Kera it was because he did not want anyone else to see the flying machine. He circled about for a minute and landed.

"I call it a bruka," Baba said, laughing. "Do you want to give it a try?"

Kera's face tightened. He had just buried Mama, Acii, and Okee. Laughing did not feel right, and certainly flying for pleasure was immoral.

"It's just like riding a bicycle," Baba said. "Give it a try."

Kera shook his head.

"I built it for you," Baba said.

Kera did not reply. He could not bear the weight of Baba's stare. He looked away. He felt more than he heard Baba approach. A strong perfume filled his nose, the smell grew stronger as Baba came closer. Kera turned to him in puzzlement. Baba never used any cosmetics, not even Vaseline, but now he had applied a greasy ointment. It made his skin darker, and it gave him a strong, flowery scent.

Kera looked away, at the rusted wheel, at a spider web on the dash board. His vision blurred.

"I wish I could also cry," Baba said. "I wish tears could roll down my face. But the rock people touched me. I can't sleep. I can't get tired. I can't eat. I pretend to eat in public, but I don't need food anymore. And the sun burns my skin."

You died, Kera wept silently. You died in the cave.

Baba put a hand on his shoulder. It felt like ice. Kera cringed away.

"I'm not dead," Baba said. "I'm only different."

Kera could still not understand. Baba surely had not forgotten Mama's laughter, or how she sung as she ground simsim into odi, or Acii's laughter, or how Okee loved to chase after lizards. How could he remember them and not grieve?

"You still have Karama," Baba said. "You can rescue him before he turns into a monster. I could have done it myself, but these changes." He paused. "I can't see far away things. I can't ask anyone else to do it for I don't want them to know about the flash gun."

Kera stared at the cobweb, at a trapped insect wing glimmering in a drop of sunlight. A cloud swept in and the wing lost its glow, to become just a shrivelled thing with torn edges. He heard Baba sigh, and then walk away. He looked up, to see Baba standing akimbo beside the rod on the table, head slightly bowed, maybe thinking about destroying it.

Kera thought about the flying machine and the flash gun rod for the rest of the day, wondering how a weepy boy of sixteen could rescue an elder brother from an army of savages. He had been eight the last time he had engaged in a fight when a girl had beaten him up for stealing her mango. Karama was the tougher one, with muscles that gave him the nickname

The Flying Man of Stone

Schwarzenegger Commando. If their situations were reversed, with Kera the hostage, Karama would not have hesitated to jump into Baba's flying machine and ride away to rescue his little brother.

But he could not do it. How could he?

He woke up the next morning, from another night of ceaseless nightmares, to find Baba had prepared him breakfast, but no sign of Baba. As he ate, he noticed a candle holder shaped like a dove on the kitchen table. A week before the attack, Mama had asked Baba to make her one because the clay holders she had kept breaking. She had pestered him for it, and Baba had kept giving her excuses, until the night before the attack, when she asked Kera if he heard learnt enough to craft her one. Kera had only smiled in shyness. The dove was warm, and he thought it had Mama's scent. Fighting back tears, he dropped it, and ran to the workshop, where he found Baba making another candle holder.

"What do you want me to do?" he said, trying hard not to sniffle.

Baba gave him a quick smile, went into the room behind the shop, and returned with the rod. "Did you see this?" Baba said.

"Is that the flash gun?" Kera said.

Baba fished a sliver of glass from his pocket and slid it into a slot on top of the rod. "It's the safety, without it the weapon is useless. Do you know what the sun is made of?"

"Fire?"

"Yes. Fire."

Baba picked an empty paint tin from a waste bin and put it on the roof of the van. He then stood several paces away and took aim. Kera waited for a bang, for something spectacular. Nothing happened. He turned to his father with a questioning look, and in that instant he heard a faint sizzling. He turned back to the tin. It had vanished. A whiff of blue smoke wafted lazily, and then thinned out into oblivion.

"You can't see it in daylight," Baba said. "If it were night you would've seen a bluish light." Baba opened a chamber at the back to reveal rechargeable AA batteries. "See? I modified these so they use solar energy to produce a fire so hot that it can punch a hole through a mountain. If you have the patience you can make the mountain disappear, inch by inch."

Heat ray, Kera thought, recalling his favourite book, *The War of the Worlds*. He wondered if the hissing creature was an alien. Some theories had it that human beings originated from outer space, hence their inability to live at peace with the environment. Maybe these aliens found Earth inhospitable because of the sun, so they lived inside caves. Maybe they inhabited apes to survive, and the symbiotic relationship gave birth to humans.

"They are not *aliens*," Baba said, using the English word for he could not find an equivalent in Luo.

Baba pulled out a weird pair of goggles from a drawer. It had two miniature tubes on the glass, one for each eye. He turned a dial, and the tubes elongated with the whir sound of a zoom lens.

"If you wear this at the top of a mountain," Baba said, "you'll see ants walking at the foot of the mountain. With this and the flash gun, you can wipe out an entire army without them knowing what hit them. So you see, the mission will be easy and safe? You stay in the sky all the time and vaporise the soldiers, one at a time. When they are all dead, you fly down and bring your brother back home."

That night, the nightmares did not come. Instead, Kera had vivid dreams of Kibuuka, a warrior who could fly like a bird and shoot arrows at the enemy, and of Luanda Magere, another invincible warrior who was made out of stone. In the dream, Kera was a superhero with the combined ability of Kibuuka and Luanda Magere. He got flying power from his mother, who in the dream lived in the moon, and he got his stone flesh from his father, who lived in a dark cave just outside their home. He darted about in the sky, unleashing lightning onto the warlords, putting an end to wanton rape and murder and all the evils that the war had brought upon his country. The dream was so vivid that, for several moments when he woke up, he could not remember who he was.

Are you ready? Baba said.

The voice added to Kera's confusion, for he was alone in the room. Kera stepped out of bed and got dressed up quickly. As he zipped up his jeans, Baba appeared at the doorway, with the eternal smile. He waved a lunch-box.

"I packed you something to eat," Baba said.

"Thank you," Kera said. "How did you sleep?" he added in greeting, and only after he had said it did he remember that Baba was not capable of sleep anymore. He wondered if he should have instead used the simpler English greeting, Good Morning, or the Swahili one, habari za subui.

Still, Baba replied. "I slept well. Maybe you?"

"I slept well too."

It was still dark when they got to the workshop. Baba had already packed the bruka in a red box, fitted with wheels. Kera rolled it out of the workshop and out of the town into the valley. It was no heavier than a bicycle. He would learn to fly it, and to shoot the flash gun, but the project had to remain a secret for Baba was in a moral quandary. Kera understood his argument, if human beings had not invented weapons the world would be a much safer place. Fist fights were savage and bestial, but surely not as apocalyptic as automatic rifles and atomic bombs. No one could know about the flash gun.

Shortly after he left the workshop, ten men, including Teacher, the mayor, and the reverend, arrived. He could not identify all of them in the half-light, but Baba had told him who would come. They would help build a giant machine to construct a wall and a fire moat around the town. They saw Kera pushing the red box up the street, but he was too far away for them to check its contents. Several people clearing debris from the streets cast Kera curious glances, but did not ask questions.

In the valley, he followed the stream eastward, until he was four miles from town, where he could hope for privacy. He waited until the sun was up before he took to the air.

The first time he flew, vertigo attacked him. He went just above the trees, and nearly crashed in panic. He overcame this fear, and went higher. As Baba had said, it was just like riding a bicycle in the air. The tricky bit was getting the gear lever right. Just under the handlebars, Baba had modified the car gear box. One took the craft up. Two took it down. Three was for hovering. Four fixed the flight horizontally and allowed the craft to run on the ground. Baba called five the autopilot, it enabled the craft to move in a straight line without the rider steering or peddling. Six put the craft in reverse. Seven caused an umbrella-like parachute to pop out, to ensure safe landing in a crisis. Baba had provided a helmet to enable him to breathe in the slipstream as well as the telescopic goggles.

For three days he practiced. He left home before dawn and returned after sunset, hiding the bruka in a cave to preserve its secret. The more comfortable he became in the air, the more he dreamed of Kibuuka and Luanda Magere co-joined to form The Flying Man of Stone. When he slept in the night, and when he took naps during the day, the dreams came with such vividness that he could not be sure they were dreams anymore. He came to believe they were trips he took to another world, where spirits prepared him to save, not just his brother, but the entire country.

After three days, he flew as comfortably as an eagle. He would soar until he was no more than a speck in the sky, then engage the hover gear, and shoot at targets on the ground. The telescopic goggles enabled him to see rats in the fields, even from the height of a mountain peak, and the flash gun vaporised the targets with pinpoint accuracy. At first, he would burn a hole into the ground after hitting a rat, but he learnt how to do it properly. By adjusting the circumference of the rays, he could drill only a tiny hole in the rat's head to kill it.

The Flying Man of Stone

He loved to watch the town from the sky, loved to admire the rooftops of Chandi. It looked like a graveyard of many childhoods. Dolls, toys, bicycle tyres, shoes, bits and pieces of children's things had found their way onto the roofs. A red leather ball, which the sun had bleached to pale pink, had been a birthday gift from Baba when Kera turned ten. It had made him the most popular boy in the neighbourhood, for before that they had played with balls made of polythene bags or banana fibres. This one was leather, and inflatable. For months it had bounced up and down the street, flown over trees in the valley, struck rocks and bounced off the stream. It had broken many windows and earned many boys a thrashing. He could not remember how it ended up on the roof. They must have gotten bored of the imported toy and resumed playing with their homemade gadgets.

In those three days, Baba built a wall around the town, a hundred feet high, twelve feet thick, and a moat of fire twenty feet wide. Machines replicated gas, which fed the fire with an inexhaustible supply of fuel. There were two gates, one in the west facing the city, the other in the east facing the mineral-rich north-eastern region. Since Baba had refused to make a machine to provide an inexhaustible supply of food, the gates opened every morning to let farmers out, and every noon to let them back in.

The miracle wall gave Teacher fame and power, as Baba would not take public credit for the town's defences. Even the handful of men who helped him build the machines did not know who really was behind it. While the mayor and reverend welcomed the idea, for it kept the town safe, their Christian minds associated it with ancestral spirit worship, and hence with devil worship, so they did not openly condone the miracle wall. Thus Teacher gained a springboard.

"Our gods have woken up," he told the townspeople. "They've been asleep all these years as foreign gods laid our land to waste and turned us into slaves but now they've woken up. They heard our cries. They saw our suffering.

They know we are tired of wars and famine so they've come to our rescue."

Teacher became a priest. A messiah. A prophet. A few people gathered at his home every evening to worship, but most of the town folk, though they acknowledged his new status as a spiritual leader, were Christians. Once the wall was up, the Anglicans asked the reverend to pray to rid it of demonic power and bless it with the blood of Jesus Christ.

Teacher attended the service, and just before the reverend's sermon, he gave a speech imploring the town to abandon Christianity and return to the religion of their forefathers.

When the Catholics asked Father Stephen to hold a similar service, and to sprinkle holy water on the wall in a purification ritual, Teacher blew up. His followers disrupted the service, smashing windows and statues, and once again Teacher beat up Father Stephen.

"I have no problem with an African priest leading the prayers," Teacher told the congregation. "But I'll not allow these wazungu to steal our powers! Never!"

The night after the incident, the mayor came to see Baba. "I'm worried about Teacher," the mayor said. "I don't like his actions at all."

They were eating supper, which Baba had prepared, boiled potatoes and chicken. It tasted like nothing Mama ever cooked, but hunger made Kera wolf it all down and lick his fingers.

"I would have no problem if it was just a case of Christianity versus African religions," the mayor said. "But this man is preaching hatred against wazungu."

"What do you want me to do?" Baba said.

"Stop him," the mayor said. "He claims the ancestors have chosen him, but if people knew it's actually you who was blessed, they won't listen to him."

"No."

"Why not?"

"You do it. You are the mayor. You are the politician."

"I'm also a Christian."

The Flying Man of Stone

"So?"

"People listen to Teacher because all along he has preached against Christianity and all kizungu things. They won't listen to me if I told them the ancestors are speaking through me. But you, if you showed people your eyes, they'd believe you."

"I can't do it."

"Why not? You've got to stop the hatred."

"I've never been a political person," Baba said. "All I ever did was work metals. But you are the mayor, and what you are asking me to do is actually your responsibility. You. The reverend. The other leaders. You can convince the town to embrace the new gods without embracing racism."

Kera licked his plate dry, left them arguing, went to his bedroom, and promptly fell fast asleep. He wandered again that night, into the world of superheroes, where he flew with Kibuuka and fought beside Luanda Magere. He dreamed of Mama too, that she had prepared malakwang and they were eating together as a family, in those happy days before the soldiers came.

He woke up to find Baba sitting on one of the other beds, watching him.

"How did you sleep?" Baba said.

"Fine," Kera said, sitting up, pulling the bed clothes to cover his nakedness.

"I'll tell you where they are holding Karama," Baba said.

Kera looked up, wondering about the hoarseness in Baba's voice. Only then did he notice that Baba's skin was peeling off.

"I'm dying," Baba said.

"No," Kera said.

"The sun," Baba said, "it's killing me. I have to go to a place of total darkness."

Like the hissing creatures, Kera thought. He is becoming one of them. Please, no.

237

"You have Karama," Baba said. "Rescue him, and then I'll destroy that gun. I can't leave it behind. You can stay with the bruka."

Kera felt something cold running down his face. He hated himself at that moment. How could he ever be Kibuuka, how could he ever be Luanda Magere, if his tears came as easily as that of a little girl? He buried his face into his palms to hide his shame, but that did not stop the pain that wrecked his heart.

"I don't want to leave you," Baba said. "But the sun will kill me if I stay."

4

Rage propelled him through the sky. The chill bit into his face, his fingers froze on the handlebars. Behind him, the horizon reddened with the waking sun. He flew over the valley of spirits, over the vast swamp, going west, away from home, away from his dying father.

If he failed to save Karama, he would not have any one left. He would be all alone in the world, just a little weepy boy playing superhero.

Doubts plagued him.

Attacking during the day, rather than in the night when the gun's flashes might warn the soldiers, had sounded like a good idea. The flash was invisible in daylight, and the gun made no noise, so theoretically he could kill all the soldiers before they realised what was happening. Yet soldiers would see their comrades falling dead, or vanishing into thin air if he used a wider flash circumference. They were not fools. They would know something was up. They would hide. And then what? Would they sit back like ducks and watch as he took them out one at a time? Some warlords had attack helicopters and anti-aircraft guns. What if someone spotted him in the sky and fired?

Fear fanned his anger. The realisation that maybe he would not save his brother flooded his mouth with the taste of rotten milk. He would soon be all alone. Baba was turning into a shadow. He had a machine that would dig a hole in the bedroom, tunnel under the town, and then into the valley where he would join the hissing creatures. There would be no grave, just a hole under the bed. They still had some days, five at most, Baba had said, and then Kera would have no one left.

Unless he saved Karama.

Villages and small towns appeared far below him. Burnt huts, bombed out buildings, vehicles upturned on the roadsides. Yet, amidst the wounds, life bustled. People crept out of their huts armed with hoes, or jerry cans as they went to draw water. He flew over the ruins of a trading centre. Two men staggered out of a bar. It had a make-shift roof, no windows, no door, and its walls were black from a fire. Kera could not hear the drunks, but he could see them singing, dancing, falling on the road and laughing. An old woman swept the front yard, empty clay pots and beer straws were scattered around her.

Shortly after passing the ruined town, he came upon a bunch of soldiers. There were ten of them on foot patrol. They had stopped four women, two of whom had babies on their backs, one had a suitcase, another had a bundle of clothing. Refugees, Kera thought, in search of a mythically peaceful land.

One soldier used a knife to rip off a woman's dress. She dropped her luggage and tried to cling on to her dress to cover her nakedness. Kera thought she was screaming, as the other women begged, as the infants wailed, and as the other soldiers cheered. The soldier's knife slashed, and slashed, leaving the woman stark naked.

Kera engaged Gear Three. The bruka went into hover mode. He pulled the ray gun from under the seat, just as the soldier threw the naked woman onto the ground. He could use a wider ray circumference to vaporise the boy, but that would take several seconds, as opposed to a bullet-hole sized circumference, which would happen in a split second.

He turned a dial on his goggles. It zoomed in until he could count the pimples on the soldier's face, a boy, about his own age, eyes red with flames of alcohol. Maybe this pimple infested goon had thrown the grenade that ripped Mama to bits. Maybe his gun tore up little Acii and Okee. Maybe he had raped dozens of women old enough to be his grandmother. Kera thumbed the trigger.

The boy fell dead beside the woman. The other soldiers laughed, maybe thinking it an antic, until the blood flowed out of the boy's head onto the tarmac. One soldier stepped closer to examine the dead boy's head. Kera shot him. The others broke into a run, jumping for cover into the drainage ditch at the roadside. Kera swung the gun from one to the other, thinking he was too slow, but a slight press of his thumb was all it took for the gun to flash, one by one, he killed them all.

The women were flat on the road. Kera wanted to go down to them, to comfort them, the way he had not comforted his mother. He could not, but he could show them where to go, so he burned holes and lines on the road, drawing an arrow pointing east, and spelling out the name of his town. Katong.

One woman stood up. She looked about in confusion, at the bodies, at the blood flowing down the grey tarmac, and then at the writing on the road. Kera hoped she could read.

Only when he resumed flight did he hear the pounding of his heart. His fingers trembled. Unable to concentrate on steering the craft, the flight became bumpy, as though he were driving fast over a potholed road, so he set the ornithopter to autopilot and let the emotions wash over him.

He had just snuffled out the life of ten people, ten boys, who in another world might have played football with him, maybe grazed goats with him, boys who were torn away from their parents and turned into monsters. He had punched holes into their heads just as he had done the rats he used for target practice. Did that not make him a monster too? Maybe their mothers were still alive, somewhere, praying for their safe return home. Maybe they had little Aciis and Okees who were waiting for them.

Kera felt faint. Tears blurred his vision. He engaged the hover gear, and cried out aloud, for the first time since he was ten. He wailed for a long time. The sun rode higher into the sky. The day became warmer. He was numbed, unable to go forward, unable to go back.

Then, he saw smoke on the ground, in the horizon, black fumes over the trees. He zoomed in on it, and saw a village burning. There were corpses on the ground, some hacked to pieces, others riddled with bullets. No sign of the perpetrators. He scanned the bushes, the road running from the village, and then he saw whiffs of dust in the air. A car had just passed by. He followed the dust and caught a pick-up speeding away with a machine gun on its back, a dozen soldiers crammed beneath the gun. Blood dripped from their machetes.

He pulled out his gun, and aimed at the soldiers. One of them, whose nascent moustache was smeared with blood, had a frown on his face. Kera moved his gun to the next one, but these soldiers were not cheering as the foot patrol had. The blank expressions probably indicated they derived no joy in their deed. Before he could make a decision, the car plunged into a forest and vanished from his sight.

He took off the telescopic goggles and he thought he would resume crying, that grief would overwhelm him, yet all he felt was a tightening in his stomach. He clenched the handlebars, teeth grinding.

"You are the flying man of stone," a voice whispered, in such a low tone that it could have been the wind singing to him. He looked over his shoulder, expecting to see someone standing on a cloud behind the bruka. Nothing.

"You are Kibuuka," the voice continued. "You are Luanda Magere." He now thought it belonged to his mother. "You are the salvation of your people."

"Ma," he said. It came out a weak whisper.

The voice did not speak again.

He searched the clouds, and only then did the surreal morning strike him. It was something straight out of a dream. Maybe it was all a dream, and anytime now Mama would awake him and give him a mug of hot porridge and a bowl of roasted njugu.

"Ma," he said again, a little louder. "Is that you?"

The clouds did not answer. They did not open up to reveal the gods within them. They sailed by in silence, lazily, on their way to make rain and bless the ground.

Kera felt strangely at peace. The miasma of guilt vanished. He was the flying man of stone. He had just saved four women and two children from rape and death. Why should he feel bad about it? The world lay in ruins. A war raged, filling the rivers with blood and choking the swamps with corpses. The streets bled, homes burned down, dreams turned to ash, and misery flowed in the veins of the people. They needed a god to fight for them. He could be that god, just like Kibuuka and Luanda Magere, he could bring peace back to the land.

Kera donned the goggles and resumed flight.

He sped after the pick-up, eager to vaporise the murderers. But, he did not see it again. Instead, he came upon Kapeto Army Barracks, a sprawling complex of circular huts built in a dozen rings around a three-storied brick structure. The warlord lived in that brick building. A flag waved on its roof. About two hundred meters north of the barracks was a separate ring of huts, encircling hundreds of wooden cages, each about ten square feet, each with about a score of prisoners inside. His brother was somewhere in one of those coops.

Kera zoomed in. The prisoners were eating porridge, which seemed nothing more than dirty water. From their gaunt faces he thought they were probably starving. Maybe the thin porridge was all they ever ate.

In a clearing at the edge of the prison, some of the male captives, cuddling wooden guns, stood in four lines in front of three soldiers. Recruits, Kera thought, out for training. He guessed that those in the cages had not yet yielded. Most bore the signs of beatings, eyes swollen shut, bloated faces, torn lips, broken noses.

He searched from cage to cage, aware of the futility of his mission, for many people were face down, maybe unconscious, maybe dead. When he found Karama, after nearly an hour of searching, for a few moments he failed to recognise him. A bandage wrapped half of Karama's face, covering up one eye. Blood had soaked through the bandage, a smudge where the eye should have been. Had Karama lost his eye? Would Baba invent a machine to cure him?

But even if Baba's dreaded machines could clone life, or generate food, or heal, he would do nothing if he saw Karama's face. He would simply say, 'Your brother is back.

Look after each other,' and then vanish into that dark world inside of rocks.

A soldier stood beside Karama's cage. He had streaks of grey in his hair, wrinkled skin, and a faded green uniform with tattered seams. A rusty AK47 hung on his back on a sisal rope. His hands trembled as he filled mugs with porridge, probably a sign that he drank too much alcohol. The prisoners accepted the meal, seemingly without complaint or thanks. This soldier would be the first to die in the rescue mission. Kera's thumb hovered above the trigger button. He could not shoot. The old man was not doing any harm, and probably had never hurt anyone. He was only feeding prisoners.

Kera instead turned the flash gun onto the frames of the cage, and pressed, vaporising wood. One side fell open. The prisoners scrambled away in confusion. The old soldier dropped the serving jug, splashing porridge, and snatched his gun. He cocked it, but did not shoot. He did not even point it at the prisoners. He stepped away from the cage, confused, and shouted something.

Kera's goggles zoomed out to gain a wider field of vision. Three soldiers were running to the cage. Kera thought he heard the clank of metal as they cocked their guns, but it was only in his head. He could not hear anything. He was watching a silent movie.

A soldier with sergeant's stripes inspected the cage. Then he took out his pistol and pointed it at a prisoner, a man with a bald head. The sergeant asked a question. The bald man shrugged. The gun flashed. A cloud of red exploded from the bald head, splattering the people closest to him. The prisoners dropped their mugs and scrambled away from the sergeant, screaming. They had nowhere to run. The sergeant turned his gun on another prisoner.

Kera's gun flashed.

It was easier when he thought of it as Shooter, a video game he used to play at school.

The Flying Man of Stone

The sergeant dropped. His finger pressed the trigger as he fell. The bullet hit the soldier standing beside him, and again Kera saw an explosion of red.

The other soldiers opened fire, shooting randomly at unseen enemies, shooting at the prisoners, who fell flat onto the bed of the cages. Kera fired and fired, aware that he was too slow, dropping one soldier after another. Panic spread through the camp. Soldiers ran towards Karama's cage in confusion, some took cover behind wheelbarrows, boulders, whatever shelter they could find.

Karama and other prisoners slipped out of the cage and took cover beneath it.

"Run!" Kera screamed, but they could not hear him.

He cut open more cages. Prisoners scrambled out. Some were bold enough to pick up the guns the soldiers had dropped, and now they shot at the uniformed men. The battle intensified.

Not once did anyone look up into the sky. Even if they did, they would not see Kera. He was just a speck in the sky, with the sun behind him. His gun flashed, and flashed, invisible rays, one at a time, searching for men in green and punching holes into their heads, just as the virtual gun had searched for bad guys in Shooter, searching for wooden bars and vaporising them to free prisoners.

It seemed like an hour had passed, but probably it was just a few minutes. He had killed many of the soldiers inside the prison (score twenty six thousand more and he would overtake Odeng who topped the highest score list). The rest were hiding, out of his sight. Tanks and armoured cars were racing from the main barracks, as a host of soldiers ran to the front line. Kera turned his gun on the vehicles, ripping tanks apart, slicing machine guns off armoured cars, vaporising engines, turning them to scrap.

But the foot soldiers were closing in on the prison. If they went in, there would be too many of them. Kera would not be able to stop a massacre, but he could stop them from reaching the prison. He cut a ditch in front of them, moving his gun slowly over the ground, keeping the trigger pressed down. The ditch formed steadily, but too slowly. He wished he could do it faster, but even then it had an effect. Soldiers saw the ground opening up in front of them, no fire, no earthquake, no digging, just a ditch twenty feet deep suddenly appearing, growing longer, and longer. They dropped their guns and fled, only to face fire from their commanders anxious to stop a mass desertion.

Artillery fired, distracting him from the ditch. The shell fell inside the prison. Kera heard the boom. The explosion sent prisoners scampering, trying to get out, but getting out meant passing a ring of sandbags and machine guns, which tore them apart.

For a few seconds, Kera was conflicted. He could not take out the artillery and the machine guns at the same time. Tears spouted afresh, clouding his vision. He was no superman. He could not fight a whole army. His super gun could only kill one soldier at a time. He was not fast enough to stop the massacre.

More shells fell in the prison. Kera turned to the artillery, a row of six guns. He fired. Nothing. The batteries were dead. He ejected them, popped in others, and then he cut the artillery into pieces. Soldiers watched in horror as the big guns broke up in front of them. Then Kera turned to the machine guns. He took out one at a time. Too bad his gun was silent. If it made noise, maybe it would tell the soldiers where he was, and then they would stop shooting at the prisoners.

All of a sudden, the soldiers abandoned the sandbags and fled. Maybe they had finally realised that a ghost was killing them. Their flight enabled the prisoners to get out. Beyond the prison were open fields, bush, and forest. Many prisoners headed for the forest, knowing it would give them better cover.

Seeing that the massacre had ceased, and numerous prisoners now had guns and were fighting off the few soldiers remaining in the prison, Kera spent a few moments etching a message onto the trunk of several trees. Just one word. Katong. It was difficult work, and drained more batteries, but he created enough messages scattered over a wide area. He hoped the prisoners would get it, and head for Katong.

Kera could not be in all places at the same time, but if there were as many people as possible within the walls of his town, it would be easier for him to protect them.

Still, he thought he could instill fear in the soldiers. They would surely be talking about the mysterious attack for a long time, and they would attribute it to ghosts and spirits. He could stress the point, and play on their beliefs, and then maybe it would stop them from harming civilians.

He vaporised the three-storied building, hoping the warlord was inside. The soldiers watched in horror as the building vanished from their sight. He left only one wall standing, on which he wrote, 'Stop Hurting Our People', in Swahili. A small crowd quickly gathered to read the message.

Only then did he remember the mission. Karama. He turned back to the prison. He could not remember where Karama's cage had been. The prison had turned into a mess. There were many unopened cages. Kera cut them loose as he continued to search for his brother. He tried to work as fast as he could. His wrist hurt, his thumb ached. He ejected and loaded more batteries. He hoped Karama was among those who had already made it to the forest, but he had to be sure, so after he had opened every cage he searched the dead and those too wounded to move.

He found Karama. A large part of his head was missing.

He thought grief would rip him apart. He thought he would disintegrate. But the death of his brother only left him with a sense of disappointment. They had not been close. With five years between them, they never had much in common. They did not share friends or play games together. They did not even share the same roof, for as long as Kera could remember, Karama had lived in the little building out in the backyard. He could not remember ever having a one-on-one conversation with Karama. They had never even fought before.

For nearly ten minutes, Kera watched blood flow from Karama's head. He had uncles, aunts, and cousins who he could look to for family support, but none lived in the town. They had not seen or heard from any of them since the war broke out.

His vision blurred. He wiped tears away, and forced his eyes away from the carnage. Soldiers still ran about in their barracks, in utter confusion. Some had jumped into vehicles and were speeding away. Hopefully they would spread word of the terror that had befallen their barracks. The prisoners had all escaped. Kera was glad to see some reading a sign he had etched on a tree trunk, and it warmed his heart to see them heading eastwards, toward Katong.

Salvation, Kera thought. He had failed to save Karama, but he could still bring sanity back to the world. He needed the flash gun. He could not let Baba destroy it.

Kera believed human beings were a cross between the alien hissing creature and apes, that human consciousness and intelligence came from these aliens. Maybe, seeing how humans used this intelligence to ruin the world, they forbade Baba from revealing any knowledge other than what was necessary to protect the valley. But Baba, or the human bit of him still left, had created a supergun to rescue his son.

Kera had failed him. Now, Baba would want to destroy the gun. He would argue that the world was better off without it.

The Flying Man of Stone

Yet Kera had experienced its magic. He had saved four women from rape, and possibly death. He had destroyed a warlord's barracks, and saved thousands of people from being turned into zombies ready to kill, rape, and maim, all for the love of minerals and the illusion of power. With the flash gun he was Kibuuka and Luanda Magere, he could impart fear in the warlords and bring back peace.

He spent the day in the skies, floating, mourning, letting the chill kiss his skin, feeling the wind in his wings, feeling the weight of grief in his heart. When hungry, he ate roasted potatoes and chicken, which Baba had wrapped in banana leaves. He did not zoom in on the details on the ground, for that would make him more miserable. He instead kept the goggles at their widest angle, giving him panoramic views of hills, of rivers flowing through the green, of red dirt roads and grey tarmac roads cutting through the lush vegetation. He stayed up there until the sun started to descend.

He could not keep the gun in the cave. He feared that Baba might communicate with the hissing creatures and that they would creep out at night and destroy it. So he took it to an island in the eastern swamp, and hid it in the reeds.

He knew the futility of his actions, for Baba simply had to read his mind to know where the gun was, but it was worth a try. He then flew the bruka to the cave and walked back home.

He reached the eastern gate well after dark. The fire-ditch threw flames twenty feet up. Beyond the flames, the wall soared into the darkness, glowing in the lights from the ditch. Two watchmen were in a tower.

"Stop!" one shouted. "Who are you?"

"It's me. Kera."

"Baba Chuma's son? What are you doing out at this time?"

"I went to fish."

He showed them a couple of tilapia that he had found on his hooks. The government had started a fish farming project several years back. When war broke out, the market for the fish died, so tilapia spawned wanton in the swamps and streams. It was an easy alibi.

The watchman pressed a button, turning down the flames in the road section of the fire-ditch. The other lowered a drawbridge. By the time Kera reached the gate, he felt singed.

"Only two fish?" one said.

"There are only two of us at home," Kera said.

"Tomorrow, bring more so I can eat too."

"No worry," Kera said. "Baba is waiting for me."

"Refugees came," the other said. "They appeared this evening. Maybe Teacher was right all along. You see they talk of spirits fighting soldiers and telling them to come to our town."

"Oh," Kera said. He had not thought about Teacher.

"Go see them if you want," the man continued. "They are at the police station."

As he hurried to the station, Kera thought he was in a strange town. Even before the war, perpetual darkness had engulfed the town for it did not have streetlights. When war broke out, the electricity supply became erratic, so much so that it would be a miracle for the lights to come on. Baba must have created a generator, for hundreds of bulbs turned the night orange. His machines had repaired the buildings, giving them fresh paint and leaving no signs of the attack. A new police station, three stories high, stood in place of the old colonial structure that had been bombed out during the attack. Kera gaped. The building had gone up in just one day. He could stomach a flying machine, and a flash gun, for these he had seen in a myriad of sci-fi movies, but a three-storied building that appears out of the blue?

About thirty refugees sat on the lawn, bathed in orange lights, eating supper. Steam rose from their bowls, filling the night with the aroma of goat stew and millet bread. Some had bandages. Kera recognised a few faces. When he saw the four women, a smile nearly broke out. The one whose dress the soldier ripped off now wore a green gomesi with yellow flowers and spoon fed her baby.

250

The Flying Man of Stone

About a hundred of the townsfolk had gathered, some sat in the middle of the road, others sat on the pavement, and others stood. Many of them wore clothing made out of bark cloth.

Teacher stood on the steps of the police station, dressed in a bark cloth robe and shoes cut from wood. "I've been telling you that our ancestors are behind these miracles and you've not listened to me," he was saying. "Now listen to these people. Hear them. I tell you it's the god Kibuuka. He has returned to save us from the puppets of the mzungu. Ma-" he started to say Martin, but caught himself, cleared his throat and said, "I'll never mention those kizungu names again. Asimwe, tell us what you saw."

A young man stood up, his hand bandaged, his lips torn, one eye swollen shut. He spoke with a lisp, for several teeth were broken. He was not Luo, but had lived in the town for so long that he knew the language, though he spoke with a heavy accent. "It came from the sky," he said. "I saw the cage burning from the top downwards, which means that the source of heat was up there. The spirit shot the soldiers in the head. Many had holes right on the top of their heads, here." He touched his pate. "I tell you, the spirit was in the sky."

Asimwe sat down.

Teacher grinned. "Kibuuka, the god of war. He can fly. He can hide up there in the clouds and rain arrows upon his enemies. Those soldiers are merely puppets of the mzungu. They care for nothing but minerals. They kill us and rape us and turn our land into ashes for the sake of these useless stones. Now Kibuuka has woken up. He is fighting for us. Maybe soon we'll see Luanda Magere and Aiwel Longar and Jok Olal Oteng.

"Our town is blessed. It sits right beside the home of our ancestors." He pointed toward the valley. "They live there. This is a revival. If the spirits are to grow stronger, we must worship them the right way. They get weak when we use kizungu things, like clothes and kizungu names and kizungu religion. So from today, we must discard everything kizungu. Everything."

251

Each sentence deepened Kera's frown. He wanted to shout that there was no god or spirit, only people who look like charcoal drawings and lived inside rocks, who had no supernatural powers for they needed a machine to mend a hole in their home. He wanted to tell them he was behind it all, and that he had no problem with wazungu. But a lump formed in his throat. The hissing creatures might not be supernatural, but there still could be a spiritual force involved. What else could explain the dreams in which he journeyed to another world to train as a superhero, or his mother's voice in the sky? Maybe there were ancestral spirits involved, and maybe they had possessed Teacher, or maybe it was evil spirits.

Kera walked away in confusion. Teacher's voice fell behind him, growing fainter, but never quiet fading away completely, as though Teacher had become omnipresent. Just as he turned off Main Street into Kaunda Road, which would take him to Chandi, he met two old women dressed in bark cloth. Kera did not know them. He gave them the two fish.

"Thank you," one said.

"This is our ancestors at work," the other said. "We used to share everything freely until mjungu brought money. It spoilt our world."

"Take off those mjungu clothes," the first said. "Ladit Okello is giving out bark cloth. He can make you a nice new shirt."

Like the rest of the town Chandi was bathed in brilliant orange. His neighbourhood had never seen so much light. The houses had always been cramped close together, the walls dirty, the paint peeling off, but now the orange lights made the buildings glow as though it were a scene in an enchanted suburb.

The lights were off at his home. Baba had placed blankets on the window, apparently to keep the tiny bungalow in perfect darkness. At the door, Kera held his nose for a strong smell emanated from the within. He wondered if Baba had died during the day and was already decaying.

"I'm still alive," Baba said from inside. The voice was his father's, but it stabbed Kera with a knife of ice. It no longer was gruff. It had a high-pitched tone that could only mean Baba was losing his power of speech. Soon, Baba would hiss like a snake.

Kera pushed the door open. The smell of decomposition hit him like a gust of wind. Baba jumped away from the ray of orange light that fell in from the door. He hid in the shadows, but Kera had seen a glimpse of him. His skin seemed to have peeled off, revealing flesh full of boils that oozed pus. His hair had fallen off, leaving a few strands on his scalp. It looked as though the flesh had been scraped off to expose a skull as white and as rugged as a rock. He no longer wore glasses, for the strange shine had gone out of his eyes. In its place was something even scarier. It made Kera think of smoke whirling inside a bottle.

"It's not just the sun," Baba said, "all kinds of light hurt me now."

Kera took a step back, putting one foot out of the door. He tried to bear the smell out of respect, but he retched, fled from the doorway, and puked in the street. The door banged shut behind him, but the smell lingered, forcing itself up his nose as though it were a living thing.

Destroy the gun, Baba said.

Kera shivered. He had never gotten used to telepathy. It sparked off a throb in his head, but that was better than suffocating in the smell.

"I failed to save him," Kera said.

I know. Now destroy the gun.

"Did you know he would die?"

I can't tell the future. I only know things that have already happened. But I know that if you don't destroy the gun it will create evil.

"No," Kera said.

You think you are a superhero. You are just a foolish child.

"You can't foretell the future. How do you know the gun will make the world worse?"

253

I know human nature.

"We need it to stop the war. We need it to bring peace."

No. You want glory. You think they'll whisper your name in the stories for thousands of years the way they whisper Kibuuka and Luanda Magere.

Kera walked away from the house.

Please, destroy that gun.

The smell grew fainter, but the puke left a repulsive taste in his mouth. He struggled to keep his eyes dry, but something cold and wet slipped down his face, and he felt as though his heart had been ripped out of his chest.

"Kera," Baba said.

Kera turned around in surprise, to see Baba staggering down the street, covered in blankets from head to toe, and using a crutch. Kera wondered if his bones had turned to jelly. He got some satisfaction from that observation, for Baba would not be able to go to the swamp and get the gun, unless he built a machine. To do that, he would have to use the workshop, and Kera intended to spend the night there, to make sure Baba did not get the gun.

"Please, my son, listen to me."

"Tell me the truth. What are they?"

"You know the answer."

"Are they humans? Are they animals? Are they aliens? Are they spirits?"

"You ask too many questions, but you've already made up the answers. If I tell you our ancestors worshipped them, you'll say they are indeed supernatural. If I say they are aliens, you'll say they brought human life to Earth. If I say they are mortal creatures like you and me, you'll call me a liar and say that I refused to tell you the whole truth. So please don't ask me any more questions. I just beg you, give me the gun. Let me destroy it."

Kera shook his head and ran to the workshop.

The workshop was empty. Machines and dead cars sat silent in the yard, gleaming in the orange lights that washed in from the streets. Teacher's voice seemed to float in with the orange rays. Chanting broke out occasionally. Kera kept hearing the word nywol meaning birth, over and over again. He picked up an overcoat, crawled into the van, his favourite dead car, and waited for his father.

He fell asleep waiting. He dreamed of the ancient heroes again, but in this dream he was an invincible anti-hero, he had committed heinous crimes in order to keep a mzungu warlord in power. His weakness was in his eyes, and Kibuuka shot an arrow made of killer-light right into his pupils.

Kera woke up with a yelp. The sun blazed right into his eyes. Screams came from far off. He threw away the overcoat and scrambled out of the car. Sweat drenched him, his shirt stuck to his skin. He wanted a bath, a dip in the cool waters of the swamp. Had Baba come in the night while he was asleep? Had he destroyed the gun? The door was latched and padlocked, but that did not mean it had stayed so the whole night.

The screaming... It came from the street. Had soldiers attacked again?

He hurried out into the backstreet. People were pouring out of their homes, most dressed in bark cloth, some in crude clothing cut from goat skin. One woman wore nothing but the remains of a raffia mat around her waist. It was stiff and he thought it cut into her flesh. She did not seem to mind. She wielded a machete.

"Sadaka!" she screamed, running.

The other people were screaming the same word. They had their backs to him. Like the woman, they all had pangas.

"Sadaka! Sadaka! Sadaka!"

Sacrifice? Kera's heart stopped. Horror headlines from before the war flashed in his head, photos of children's mutilated bodies, victims of human sacrifice, victims of some rich man's quest for wealth. With Teacher urging the town to worship ancestral spirits, someone might have thought it would please the gods if they sacrificed a child.

Kera followed the screaming maniacs round the corner, into Main Street, where a larger crowd had gathered, all half naked, with bark cloth and animal skin and sisal sacks wrapped around their loins. The men's potbellies poured over the hems of their skirts, while the breasts of the women sagged onto baggy stomachs. Everyone had a panga. Sunlight bounced off the blades.

"Kera!"

Kera turned. A fat man with a bush on his chest waddled toward him, rotating the machete above his head as though to imitate a helicopter's propeller. Atim's father. Atim who gave him his first taste of a woman's flesh, it seemed a million years ago, yet hardly three months had passed. She had followed him into the valley, as he took goats to graze, and she had teased him until he pulled her into a shrub. When he saw her father charging at him, he believed the fat man wanted to pulp him for what he had done.

"Kera you mzungu lover!"

Before he could digest the phrase, someone grabbed his shirt. "Take off these slave clothes!"

An old woman grabbed his sleeve, and tried to rip off the shirt. He knew her face, but he could not recall her names, or how it was he knew her. Maybe she had been a good friend to his mother. Maybe she was his aunt. Maybe she had once been his teacher. All he saw was a wrinkled face, with white hair, and scrawny hands clawing at his shirt.

"Take it off!" Atim's father joined the old woman in tearing his clothes. Within a few seconds, a thousand fingers were on him, ripping off his shirt, ripping off his pants, ripping off his underwear. When the last piece of cloth came off the mob threw up a loud cheer and, almost immediately, lost interest in him. They joined the rest of the crowd in screaming "Sadaka! Sadaka! Sadaka!"

The Flying Man of Stone

Kera seethed in shame, aware of his penis, small and shrivelled, cowering between his thighs. He covered it up with both hands, but no one was looking at him. Their eyes were fixed on the police station, whose walls seemed to glow in the sunlight, as they punched their machetes into the air.

Was the child they intended to sacrifice in there? Whose child was it? Had this child played with Okee and Acii?

"Sadaka! Sadaka! Sadaka!"

Kera ran fast back to the workshop. He stood just inside the gate for nearly ten minutes, listening to the screaming, allowing his heart to gradually slow down. A bitter taste stayed in his mouth, as though he had eaten a lemon rind. He wanted to spit, but his tongue was too dry. He heard the sound of marching and chanting start to grow faint. The crowd was moving. They had probably had their sacrifice and were now heading out to make the offering.

Save that child, Kera heard a voice say. He thought it was Baba, but it could not be Baba, for Baba was far away at home, and Baba's telepathy was effective only in a radius of a few metres.

He could not let them kill the child.

He ran about the workshop looking for something to wear. The only thing available, that would look acceptable to the mob, was a jute sack. His hands trembled as ripped it apart using a shard of broken glass to make a skirt. It pricked his skin when he wore it.

The section of Main Street near the police station was empty. The crowd was about five hundred metres away, pouring out of the western gate, probably heading toward the valley. They no longer chanted sadaka, but were singing a song that would have accompanied boys going to face the knife in a circumcision ritual. Though he was too far to make out their movements, he knew they were stamping their feet and clapping and twisting their waists in what was supposed to be an erotic dance.

Kera ran after them. He soon overtook the stragglers. They limped for they had grown up with shoes to protect their soles, and now with bare feet they staggered in pain.

Kera shoved through the mass of wriggling bodies, over the drawbridge and fire moat, and out of the town. The larger part of the crowd was already going down the slope, into the valley. Vegetation obscured the front of it, but Kera grew increasingly certain that it was a child.

He could save that child. If he got his flash gun, and soared into the sky, he could kill Teacher before he made the sacrifice. The he could etch messages onto the bark of trees, or on the wall of the town, to change the course of the river Teacher had let loose.

Only when he got to the front of the procession did he see it was not a child but three adults. Father Stephen and the two nuns, each stark naked, each tied to a cross, each cross strapped to a cart. Men pushed the carts down the slopes. The sight brought a strange kind of relief. At least they were not going to kill a child who might have been friends with Okee or Acii. Yet the horror only deepened, for they were going to kill three innocent adults.

"Forgive them father," Father Stephen was praying loudly, his voice competing with the roar of the fanatics. "They don't know what they are doing. I don't want to die like your son but these heathens mean to kill me like that. Forgive them, forgive them, forgive them."

The nuns were crying and trying to sing a hymn.

Kera stopped running, and watched the carts go slowly down the slope. People brushed past him as they danced. And then someone grabbed his hand. He pirouetted to face the mayor and Teacher. Like the previous night, Teacher wore a robe of bark cloth, but this time he had a headdress as well, which made Kera think of a crown. At its front was some kind of insignia, an arrow, the sun, the moon, and stars. Was that supposed to be a representation of Kibuuka, the arrow shooter in the sky?

The Flying Man of Stone

"There you are," the mayor said, "we were wondering about you. How is your father?"

The mayor too wore a robe of bark cloth, and he had a headdress, though it was not as tall as that of Teacher. His looked like a skullcap. It had the same insignia, of an arrow in the sky. Kera felt a chill of disappointment washing through his veins. He had thought that if he succeeded in killing Teacher, the mayor would have taken over leadership, and probably would have stopped the madness.

"Glad to see you with us," Teacher said. "But jute is not African. I'll ask Okello to make you a robe. Since you are the son of Baba Chuma our distinguished prophet, you'll get a high seat in the council."

Though they wore wooden shoes, both limped. Kera wriggled away from the mayor's grasp and bolted.

"Kera!" the mayor shouted, but the roar of the mob swallowed up his voice, and Kera did not hear any more.

The grass cut Kera's legs as he sped across the valley. Unlike Teacher and his men, he did not feel the pain of running barefoot. His soles were calloused. He had worn his first shoes only a couple of years ago, and many times when he went down to the valley to herd goats, he had to do it barefoot, or with sandals cut out of car tyres. He soon left the mob far behind him. He could only hear whiffs of their voices.

He retrieved the bruka from the cave where he had hidden it, and flew to the swamp. He no longer cared that someone might see him. He cursed himself for keeping the gun far away. It had seemed like a good idea in the night, but with lives at stake it now felt like a mistake. He prayed that Baba had not got the gun. He pedalled fast. Hunger clouded his vision. He had not eaten. He felt his energy failing. He cursed Baba for not building an engine powered bruka, but Baba's reasoning had been that engines pollute the environment.

Please Baba don't destroy the gun. He prayed, he hoped, he pedalled, he huffed, the wings of the bruka made swooshing noises as they beat the air. He held his breath, knowing his

259

world would collapse if he found Baba had taken the gun, knowing he would never have a good sleep if he failed to save the wazungu. He hoped Teacher would hold a lengthy ritual before drawing blood. That would give Kera enough time.

He reached the swamp, and swooped down on the island, which was nothing more than a rock jutting out of the water. A thick growth of papyrus ensured the rock was visible, and accessible, only from above. Kera saw the bundle of banana fibres in which he had wrapped the gun. He landed, expecting to find the bundle empty, but after all, Baba had not taken the gun.

Kera jumped onto the ornithopter, invigorated, and soared, but now that he was facing the town, he saw three pillars of smoke in the distance. The miasma of failure brought out his exhaustion. His muscles ached with fatigue. He could feel the weight of his own bones. Still, hoping the smoke was no indication of three burning wazungu, he climbed into the clouds and used the telephoto dial to zoom in on the fires.

Father Stephen and the two nuns smouldered on the crosses. Kera thought he could smell burning flesh. The mob stood in a semicircle in front of the fires, screaming, chanting, singing, though Kera could not hear a word.

It had to stop. He had failed to save the wazungu, but he could still put an end to Teacher's madness.

He aimed the gun at Teacher. His thumb trembled on the trigger button. A light press, and Teacher would vanish into thin air. He could not do it. It had been easier with the soldiers, who were strangers, easier to liken them to CGI characters in Shooter, but here was a face he had seen all his life.

He could not do it.

And even if he killed Teacher, he could not be sure the madness would stop. There was the mayor, who he once thought was a good man, but who now seemed to be screaming the loudest with a face distorted in rage. Being a politician, seeing he could not fight Teacher, the mayor must have made a political decision to discard everything he believed in. Even if Kera killed both the mayor and Teacher, someone else might step in. Maybe he could float down into their midst, and tell them that Kibuuka had possessed him. But would that take any power off Teacher? Would that not betray the secret of the flash gun, and possibly of the hissing creatures?

A better option would be to write messages on the town's wall, as he had done in the barracks. They could not argue with such writing. He burned two lines above the western gate. *I hate human sacrifice. I love wazungu.* The two guards atop the gate had no idea what was happening. They chewed sugarcane as they watched smoke rising out of the valley.

Kera did not return to town until after dark. Again, he passed through the gates with the fishing alibi. This night, there were a lot more people in the streets, some stood in clusters talking in whispers, others had lit small fires and were engaging in rituals. Kera noticed many still wore cotton clothing, t-shirts, jeans, coats, ties, khakis, kitenges, dress that Teacher's revolution denounced as kizungu. It warmed his heart that not everyone had joined the madness, but how long was it before Teacher turned his fury on them? Would he burn to death those who refused to denounce Christianity or Islam?

He paused at the door, sniffing for the smell of decay. Nothing. Then he noticed there were no blankets on the windows to block the light.

"Baba?" he said.

He tried the door. It swung open. The living room was empty. He listened. Nothing.

"Baba!" he shouted, as he ran from room to room, flipping on lights, but his father was gone. In his parent's bedroom, there was a hole in the ground, and beside it an A4 sized book.

"Baba!" he shouted into the hole

He shone a torch. It was only a few feet deep. Baba had dug a tunnel to the world inside rocks and sealed it behind him.

261

Kera tried not to cry. I'm a big boy, he told himself. I am Luanda Magere the man of stone. I am Kibuuka the flying god of war. That did not stem the tears. The sound of mourning echoed in the room like a disembodied voice. He listened, as though it were someone else crying.

Knocking on the door roused him and he saw the letter Baba had left in the first page of the book, in the large and careful font of one learning how to write. The letters were spaced out neatly, almost as if the book was printed, rather than handwritten. It was in Luo, so Kera had to read each sentence twice before he could grasp the meaning of Baba's words.

"I was wrong," Baba said. "I thought only weapons stir evil, but Teacher used building machines to gain his power. Maybe you are right. Maybe in the right hands technology can help our people. In this book you'll find designs and instructions on how to create many useful things, but any technology, even something like a plough, can be used for evil. I leave everything in your hands. I hope you are wise enough to discern good from evil."

Kera had flipped through the book, and he saw designs for solar powered stoves, automatic ploughs, pots that could generate water even in droughts. He was reading the letter for the tenth time when the knocks came again.

He tried to ignore it. The knocks persisted. Whoever it was could simply push open the door, but they did not. Reluctantly, Kera staggered to the door, and found Teacher, the mayor, and a dozen others, all dressed in bark cloth. Kera had exchanged his jute skirt for jeans and t-shirts. Now, he regretted it.

"Hello Kera," Teacher said. "What happened to your skirt?"

Kera did not respond. The others glared at him. He felt their fingers twitching with the urge to undress him.

"See?" Teacher turned to them. "I told you, he is a fake. If he was the true Kibuuka, he would not be wearing these clothes."

"We had you followed," the mayor said.

It must have happened as he ran to the cave to get the bruka. He should have looked over his shoulders to check that no one had followed him.

"Where is your father?" the mayor said.

"This pretender stole Baba Chuma's aircraft," Teacher went on. "Baba Chuma is the true messenger, but this one, the Christian demons took possession of him and made him write that blasphemy. Our ancestors can't love wazungu. No way!"

"Where is your father?" the mayor asked again.

Kera quickly stepped back into the house, and slammed the door shut. Before he could bolt it, Teacher and the mayor pushed the door open, overpowering him. He gave up, and fled to Baba's bedroom. He had to keep the book. He could not let them get it. He wished he had his flash gun. He could have vaporised them all. He wished the bruka was nearby. He could then fly away and live in the clouds where no evil existed. He ducked into Baba's bedroom, and again tried to close the door, but the mayor and Teacher were right behind him.

Teacher had a machete. He wondered why he had not noticed that before. The blade sliced through his belly. He did not feel pain, but he felt a warm liquid soaking his t-shirt, soaking his jeans. He tried to stay on his feet. He failed. He crumpled to the floor, falling face downward. He tried to get up. He could not. He was paralysed. He thought he heard a trickling as his blood flowed into the hole Baba had dug.

Someone turned him over. He saw a lizard scrambling across cracks on the ceiling. Faces stared down at him. He tried to speak. Blood filled his mouth and blocked his nostrils, choking him. He could not cough to ease the discomfort. The mayor was flipping through Baba's book, saying something. Kera could not make sense of the words. All he heard was the steady roar of a river.

Dilman Dila

Dilman Dila is a writer and filmmaker. He recently published a collection of short speculative stories, *A Killing in the Sun*. His works have been honored in many international and prestigious prizes. He is currently working on a scifi novel and feature film. He keeps an online journal of his life and works at www.dilmandila.com

VIII

Andrew Dakalira

1

Lake Malawi, Mangochi district, 2023
The lake was calm that day, perfect for hanging out by the beach. Not that it mattered. There was nobody within the group on the beach who was thinking of going for a swim. All eyes were on the sky, waiting, hoping the latest satellite tracking system was as good as the United States government said it was.

Colonel James Banda and his troops had been at the site for nearly six hours. He had never seen a spaceship personally, and he was sure his men had not either. But these Americans have, the colonel thought, looking to his right. The two agents from the CIA were engaged in a serious conversation with their local embassy's security chief, two scientists from NASA who had flown in that morning, and Lieutenant John Phiri of the Malawi Defence Force. The two scientists looked out of place with their lab coats, surrounded by scores of army men.

"What's the word, Lieutenant?" Colonel Banda asked even before his junior opened his mouth.

"Any minute now, sir," replied Lieutenant Phiri.

"Tell me something, Lieutenant. Is the intel reliable? I have over two dozen men on this beach. I do not want the military picking up pieces of their dead bodies just because this spaceship crashed on the beach and not in the lake like they said it would."

"Well, the information is quite reliable, sir," began the lieutenant. "According to the digital satellite trackers, the trajectory the spaceship has taken is going to end here, on this particular side of the lake. And their technology is quite good."

"If the technology was *quite good*, Lieutenant, they would know why this thing altered course in the middle of its mission and why the crew is not responding," the colonel pointed out.

"Yes, well, as a precaution, sir, all the villages within a five-mile radius have been evacuated. The only civilians around are the Americans. Needless to say, the press will be on this. I expect this will make the front page of many local papers."

"Do not worry about that, Lieutenant. It will be taken care of. Now, tell those buffoons to stop moving the canoes."

"Yes, sir."

The lieutenant left and the colonel turned back to the lake. Their country had never dealt with this type of situation before. Things like this only happened in the United States and other superpower countries, he thought. What made the spaceship change its course, and the astronauts to lose communications and control of their own shuttle?

It came from the sky, silent, like a once graceful bird about to meet its end. And in this case, the bird was losing feathers as it fell. The colonel and the other personnel on the beach could see parts of the spaceship ablating from the hull right until the ship hit the water. It crashed into the lake like glass against solid rock.

Colonel Banda and his men were already on the move, the colonel only reminding his men to stay alert in case more debris fell from the sky. Lieutenant Phiri was in the same speedboat as the colonel. They reached the point where the spaceship had crashed about a minute before the rest of the speedboats and trawlers did. It seemed quite clear that no one had survived but the colonel sent divers down to the wreck anyway. Beside him, the two scientists looked on, talking excitedly.

VIII

State House, Lilongwe city

For the first time that day President Moto had time to himself. Done with back-to-back meetings, he was about to call his wife when one of the phones on his desk rang. It was the phone that rarely did.

"Yes, what is it?" Moto asked, warily.

"It was as our American counterparts said, sir," said Limbani Maloto, Principal Secretary in the Ministry of Defence. "It crashed into the lake about three hours ago. Our divers have managed to recover the bodies."

"Three hours? Did I not make it clear that I want to be informed as soon as the vessel crashed?" Moto fumed.

"I asked the colonel to hold all communication to State House, sir. We were hoping to clarify a few things first. Unfortunately, we have not."

"Well, do not keep me in suspense, Secretary Maloto," the president spoke, agitated. "What is it?"

"Well, sir, while retrieving the bodies from the wreckage, the men discovered something else."

President Moto listened, becoming more puzzled as the principal secretary of defence went on. When he finally put the phone down, his face was grim. He then picked up the phone again and said words he had never spoken before, "Get me the White House."

2

Chileka, Blantyre district

"Not too close to the bushes, child! They have thorns," Sir Gregory said. He stood and watched his twelve-year-old stepson Joel guide the goats away from the thorny bushes, smiling as he chased after five kids. The last born of his three stepchildren, Joel had the responsibility of goat-herding during weekends. The boy loved it almost as much as he loved Sir Gregory himself.

Of all his stepchildren, Joel was Sir Gregory's favourite. He was a bright boy and always did as he was told. Sir Gregory was really the only father Joel had ever known, his biological father having left while he was still quite young. Joel reminded Sir Gregory of his late wife, which only made the boy more endearing.

Sir Gregory was interrupted by Father Fletcher, who greeted him in Chichewa. "Good morning, Sir Gregory! How are you today?"

Sir Gregory replied to the greeting also in vernacular, letting out a low chuckle as he did so. The way his mzungu friend spoke the local language always amused him. "Remember our meeting with the school committee today, Father."

"I will be there, Sir Gregory. But right now I must hurry to the river. I am baptising new converts. May the good Lord keep you well."

Sir Gregory grunted a response. Father Fletcher knew very well that he did not believe in God. He watched the man of the cloth get onto his hovercycle, a contraption he disliked. He hated modern technology. It was one of the reasons he was happy to be on this side of the planet; Malawi had not advanced technologically to a great extent. After the hovercycle was out of earshot he noticed a faint buzzing coming from inside the house. Sir Gregory hurried to his room, hoping it wasn't what he thought, but it was.

The signal had finally come. It was time.

VIII

"Mr. President, when I spoke with your ambassador here, we agreed to be completely honest with each other. Your government was supposed to share all the information you have. But it seems you have not adhered to our agreement," said President Moto.

"I am sorry, Mr. President, but I don't follow," replied President Wayne Barry. "To the best of my knowledge, all information has been shared with your military by our agents."

"Then maybe you can explain to me why your agents said nothing about the fourth astronaut," Moto said, impatiently.

President Barry's tone was firm. "I assure you, Mr. President, that the American government had no prior knowledge of this fourth astronaut. I was just as surprised as you are when my secretary of defence told me a few minutes ago."

"Then someone is not telling you the whole truth, sir. A Caucasian male was on board that ship. He tied up, branded and killed your three astronauts, and was then himself killed by my soldiers as he tried to commandeer one of our naval boats. I lost three soldiers in the process, Mr. President. Someone over there must know something."

"And I will keep you informed when we know more, President Moto. But I am afraid we are also in the dark right now. You say this man branded our astronauts?"

"Yes, he did," replied President Moto. "They all had the roman numeral eight on their bodies."

President Barry was silent for a few minutes after getting off the phone with the Malawian president. He had not lied. He really did not know anything. But his counterpart was right. Someone had to know what was going on. He looked around the room, at his chief of staff, secretary of defence, all the generals and senior government staff. "Okay. Somebody start talking."

Andrew Dakalira

Chileka, Blantyre district

Sir Gregory was not really his name, at least, not the 'sir' part. Gregory Tembo was a teacher whose pupils' term of endearment had spread to their guardians as well on account of them hearing it all the time. He had settled in Chileka about twenty years before and married Milcah, his stepchildren's mother, ten years later. Milcah's husband left her when Joel was two, Mavuto five, and Nina—who had now grown into a smart young lady—eleven.

Nobody in the village asked where he came from anymore. He was one of them now and happy here. But now, all that was in danger and he had to act fast. He had to protect his family.

Blantyre city, Blantyre district

"Hello?"

"Nina? It's dad. Did I wake you?"

"It is eleven o'clock at night, Dad. Of course you woke me up," Nina sleepily replied. "What's wrong?"

"I need you to come home tomorrow, Nina. It's urgent," Sir Gregory said calmly.

"Tomorrow? Dad, what's wrong? Are Joel and Mavuto okay?"

"They're fine, Nina. Mavuto will also be here tomorrow. Just come. Please."

"Alright, Dad. I'll see you tomorrow."

"Thank you. Goodnight."

Nina lay wide awake for a while, half-listening to the man breathing heavily beside her, deep in sleep. Her father never called, let alone asking her to visit. She had moved permanently to the city after graduating from college and getting a job. That was almost a year ago. Her father had only visited twice. But never in her life had he summoned her like this. She looked at the muscular, temporarily limp body beside her and sighed. She would tell him about the call in the morning.

State House, Lilongwe city

"So what you're telling me," President Moto finally spoke, "is that Barry and his colleagues at the White House really know as much about this as we do? He was not lying?"

"It would seem so, sir," replied Principal Secretary Maloto. "They do not know what made the spaceship alter its course and they do not know who the fourth person is."

The president's impassive look hid his true feelings. There had to be more to this, he was sure of it. He looked around the room. Military personnel and a few cabinet ministers were there that evening, none of whom seemed to know more than he did at the moment.

"And the Roman numeral on the bodies? Why were the three bodies branded with the number eight? Do we at least know that?"

"I am afraid that is also a mystery, sir," spoke up General Manda, commander of the defence force. "But, I have Colonel Banda here who was commanding officer on site. He may shed more light on the situation." He gestured to Colonel Banda. "Colonel."

Colonel Banda was about to speak when one of the state house staff interrupted with an urgent message for Principal Secretary Maloto. He read it before finally looking at the president, almost as if he was too terrified to speak to the man.

"Mr. President, this message is from the military infirmary, where the bodies were being kept. The fourth one escaped."

"What! What do you mean, *escaped*?" President Moto rose out of his chair. "You told me the man was dead!"

"I am as baffled as you are, sir. And that is not all. He killed eight people in the process. All of them patients, all of them branded sir."

The president sank back in his chair. "What in the bloody hell is going on? I want that man found and I want him found immediately! I do not care if he is found alive or dead. And, if he is dead, make sure this time!"

Everyone stood up to leave at almost the same time. They knew the president's words were as good as a dismissal.

At that point, another message came, this time for the inspector general of the police service. "I am afraid I have more bad news, Mr. President."

Blantyre city, Blantyre district

Nina stepped out of the shower the next morning to find her man sitting on the edge of the bed, wearing only his boxer shorts. She found herself staring dreamily at his bare, muscular chest, before he brought her back from her carnal thoughts.

"Work just called. I have to get back to Lilongwe immediately."

"Oh," Nina's face fell. "I was hoping I would find you here when I get back from Chileka. What is so important that you have to cut your holiday short?"

"I could ask you the same question," he replied, shifting a little so that she could sit on his lap. "What is so important that your old man wants you to go to the village for?"

"I don't know. He did not say," Nina spoke almost to herself as she absent-mindedly ran her fingers through the hair on his chest. "But, whatever it is, it must be important. He has never done this before."

"Alright, well, I guess we will see each other again when you come visit. I told the guys at work that I'd be there in two hours."

"Okay. Wait, Onani. Flying to Lilongwe only takes about forty minutes. Why did you-"

Nina stopped mid-sentence as Onani gently pushed her onto the bed, while at the same time covering her mouth with his. His hands worked skilfully, untying the bathrobe Nina was wearing, revealing a supple body headlined by two perky breasts.

"I figured two hours gave me plenty of time for other things," Onani said, in the few seconds his mouth left Nina's.

She was about to say something but Onani's mouth then went to work on her throat, leaving a trail of kisses down to her breasts. His lips tugged on a nipple and Nina could only manage a soft moan. Then Onani continued to work his way downwards and Nina forgot all about her impending trip to Chileka. At least, for forty-five minutes.

State House, Lilongwe city

"What's the total?" asked President Moto.

"Thirty-eight, sir. All of them prisoners," said Principal Secretary Maloto

"But, it cannot be the same person, surely. The prison is at least thirty miles from the infirmary where he was being kept and these incidents happened at more or less the same time."

"That is true, Mr. President. But, the curious thing is, they were also branded like the others."

"I was hoping you would not say that, Moses," said the president, wearily. "So, what do you make of all this?"

"I believe one word would perfectly summarise my disposition, sir. Dumbstruck."

"I am calling for a cabinet meeting. I know it seems hasty and, dare I say pointless, but I need to brief the ministers. I would like you, the Inspector General and Colonel Banda to be present."

"Very well, sir," replied Principal Secretary Maloto. "And, sir, might I suggest that you call President Barry again. I know I said they know as little as we do but now I'm not so sure. They probably know more than we do. At least, someone over there does. I can feel it."

President Moto was not really listening. He was already on the phone.

4

Lilongwe city, Lilongwe district

The year was 2023 but Malawi, a developing country, was still not used to fCars. Almost everybody still stared when an individual stepped out of an expensive flying car. Only a few individuals and organisations had them. One of those few organisations was, surprisingly, the police service.

Onani parked beside a sleek, black, non-flying sports sedan then crossed the street and into Lilongwe's tallest building.

Preferring to use the stairs, he reached the second floor in a few minutes. It was not hard to find the room he was looking for, there were already a dozen police officers standing around.

The first victim was right by the door. He was wearing a very expensive black suit, white shirt and red tie. The collar and front of his shirt were drenched in blood. His throat had been cut.

"Quite a sight, eh, Detective?" Onani spun around and almost headbutted Masina, his partner, who was right behind him.

"Came here a few minutes before you did. I don't know if you remember this guy." Masina pointed at the corpse by the door. "J.J. Gondwe, Attorney-at-law. The other three are his clients."

"The other three? So there are four victims?"

"Yes," Masina replied, moving past Onani and into the room. Onani followed. "The others were hit with what seems to be a blunt object. And, it seems they were mauled too."

Onani froze. *Mauled? In an office in the middle of the capital city?* "Where was everyone else?"

"This guy was working late. His secretary was home. So was his partner. They're both already at the station giving their statements."

Onani sighed. "So you brought me home for a quadruple homicide. How nice."

VIII

"Actually, you were called back from Blantyre because you know the victims. Well, these three, anyway. See for yourself."

What Onani saw made his stomach churn. The three men in front of him had died violent deaths by the look of things. Two of them were still in their chairs while the third lay slumped on the floor, his back resting on a large bookcase. His cupped hands held his intestines, as well as part of his tongue. The other two had their skulls bashed in, one with his left eye popping out of its socket. Both had hunks of flesh ripped from their chests. Onani's head was spinning. Masina was correct. He deduced who they were, he had arrested them once.

"So, give me a working theory, Partner," Masina spoke up. "Who would want to kill petty car thieves and their lawyer? And, why would they brand the Roman numeral eight on their bodies?"

State House, Lilongwe city

"I am afraid I cannot help you, Mr. President," spoke President Barry from the White House.

"With all due respect, Mr. President, I do not think you are being honest with me," said Moto. "My country has assisted you in every way possible with regard to your spaceship situation. Now all of a sudden people start dying and are branded with roman numerals, all of which was started by a stowaway on your ship. And yet you are still telling me that you know nothing?"

President Barry spoke in an exasperated tone. "As I said, President Moto, I cannot help you. As a matter of fact, I was hoping you would tell me more about what is happening. It could help our own situation here."

President Moto was startled. "Your situation? I do not understand."

"The killings have started here too."

Andrew Dakalira

Lilongwe city centre

She stood outside with the rest of the onlookers and watched as the bodies were brought out from the building and into the waiting police cruisers. She then turned her attention to the two plain-clothed police officers lagging behind—one tall and dark, the other slightly shorter but more handsome. They have no clue as to what's really going on, she thought, but they will find out soon enough.

Nobody would suspect her. They had not even seen her enter the building, in spite of the CCTV cameras. And out here, smartly dressed in a grey suit, no one could suspect her of being a murderer either. She was a woman of social standing to everyone who saw or knew her. And thus it would stay. For now.

The world would know within the next twenty-four hours. The time had come. Things were about to change. The woman smiled to herself as she thought of this. Then leaving the crowd of onlookers, she went and got into a taxi. Her next stop was the city's largest hospital.

Chileka, Blantyre district

Immediately after getting off the bus, Nina felt at peace. The village always had that effect on her. It was quieter than the city, with a lot less traffic and much cleaner air. She took a footpath through the village, smiling and waving in greeting to a few women who were drawing water from the village borehole. She was admiring the freshly-tilled fields near home when she met Father Fletcher.

"Come to visit your family, Miss Nina?"

"Yes, Father. And please call me Nina. Just Nina. We keep talking about this," replied Nina with a smile.

"Alright. I have also seen your brother Mavuto here. He is in his final year of secondary school and is supposed to be in class, isn't he? Is everything alright?"

"I am sure everything is fine, Father. Dad just wanted us all here for a day or two. He has something important he wants to tell us, it seems."

Father Fletcher looked like he wanted to say something else but stopped himself. Instead, he got back on his hovercycle. "Well, now that all of you are here again, perhaps you'll try to convince your father to come to church. I must leave you. I'm conducting mass for the sick this morning. I hope we meet again before you leave, Nina."

She watched the hovercycle speed off in the direction from which she'd come, before she turned and walked the few remaining metres to her father's compound. That white missionary is one of ours now, she thought, and he will never give up on my atheist father it seems, even though the rest of us have. She looked up and there was the atheist himself, standing outside his house staring into space. Sir Gregory looked so lost in thought that for a moment Nina wondered if he had not recognised her. He had.

"Nina, my child. Welcome."

"Thank you, Dad. Where is Mavuto? I need help with these bags."

Her father called Joel instead. "I sent Mavuto on an errand. He should be back soon."

Sure enough, Mavuto showed up just as Nina and Joel were about to enter the house. He waved at Nina but went straight to his father to give him something.

"It's a good thing you are here, Nina," said little Joel. "Dad is not himself. He thinks I have not noticed but I have. Something is bothering him."

Despite the fact that Joel's words only heightened her worry, Nina could not help but smile at her precocious little brother. Nina could also tell her father was troubled.

Mavuto was standing by the living room doorway, arms folded, staring at his two siblings. "How's it going, Sis? Did he call you here too?"

"Yes, he did, although I have no idea why. Do you?"

"No, I don't. It must be pretty important. He would not have called me here otherwise. I start my mid-terms next week. We all know how he freaks out if you don't study beforehand."

Nina pushed past her teenage brother's tall, bulky frame and into the open air. Her father had not moved. She quietly walked over to him, but he must have heard her for he turned towards her as he spoke, "Something is wrong."

And just as he said so, Father Fletcher's hovercycle sped into view. And from the look on the man of God's face, Nina could tell that all was not well.

Kamuzu Central Hospital, Lilongwe city

Onani and his partner were first on the scene. The main hospital building about a hundred metres from the gate looked deserted. But, between it and the main gate stood multitudes, most seemed to be hospital staff and patients.

Onani was out of the fCar even before Masina had unfastened his seatbelt. He asked a nearby nurse where he could find the hospital's administrator. Though visibly shaken the nurse quickly pointed to a portly, bespectacled man with a receding hairline, clad in a dark blue suit.

VIII

"Excuse me, sir, I am Detective Limani and this is my partner Detective Masina. What is going on here?"

"Thank goodness! She is mad, I tell you! All those innocent people! She's killing them all!"

"Who is? Where? The wards?"

"Yes! Main building, to your left!"

Onani was already on the move, Masina not far behind. They dashed past the paediatric ward, which was empty. They were about to pass the male ward when a bloodcurdling scream tore through the hospital silence and was cut short.

Onani signalled to Masina, *keep your eyes open, I'll go in first*. He burst through the doors and into the main ward, gun drawn. Masina came in immediately after, and, like his partner, he also suddenly became immobile, shocked.

The patients had been murdered in their beds. The ones who had not offered resistance were quickly, almost mercifully, killed. Those who had, however, were a different story. Throats had been slit, eyes had been gouged out, stomachs eviscerated and their contents wrenched out. One man had his head severed. The hospital floor was a red, horrifying mess.

"Jesus Christ," Onani said aloud, "who would do something like this?"

Masina was going to say something back but did not get the chance. What came out instead was a squeal of surprise as he was suddenly hit in the chest with huge force and flung back through the doors and out of the ward.

Chileka, Blantyre district

Leaving the distraught Father Fletcher with his children, Sir Gregory hurried to the only church in the village. The wails that could be heard both inside and outside the church only confirmed what Father Fletcher had told Sir Gregory. Death had struck, and it had struck mightily. Sir Gregory walked straight into the church, ignoring the strange looks from almost everyone, including the village chief. The villagers had only seen him inside the church once, at his wife's funeral mass.

Six bodies lay right in front of the altar. Five had their throats ripped open; the sixth had a gaping hole in his chest. But if Sir Gregory was shocked he did not show it.

The chief, on the other hand, could not stop blabbering. "What has befallen our great village? Who would do such a thing? This is a house of worship! It's an abomination! Whoever has done this deserves to be hanged!"

This brought murmurs of agreement from several of his subjects, some of whom were carrying spears and machetes.

Sir Gregory said nothing, but walked out of the church and started to go into the vast orchard behind it.

One of the villagers bellowed out to him, "The police say they are on their way, Sir Gregory! And we have already been in the orchard! You will not find anything!"

Ignoring him, the respected teacher walked a few metres into the orchard. It was cool and quiet in the dense forest of orange, pear, and grapefruit trees. Only a few birds threatened to disturb the tranquillity with their little shrills of delight as they feasted on the succulent oranges now in season. But Sir Gregory knew that someone else was there.

"Show yourself!"

Even before the man's feet touched the ground, Sir Gregory spun around and crouched, quite swiftly for a man his age. His adversary only smiled, his teeth pearl-white, blood drying on his hands and on the white shirt he was wearing. He was barefoot and his shorts revealed well-built calves.

He was still smiling as he spoke. "Hello, *muhiri*."

VIII

6

Kamuzu Central Hospital, Lilongwe city

Instinctively, Onani ducked at the same time raising his weapon in the direction of where Masina had been standing. It was not what he expected at all. Standing in front of him was a strikingly beautiful woman in a grey suit. The high heels on her feet complemented the long, slender legs that disappeared beneath a knee-length skirt. The buttons on her jacket were open, as were the two top buttons on her blue blouse, revealing the cleavage of well-rounded breasts restrained in a lace brassiere.

"Do not move! Keep your hands where I can see them!" Onani barked. She said nothing, but moved towards him. He tried to tell her again but she kept coming. Onani fired. He caught her in the shoulder and she staggered backwards but did not fall. He fired again and, despite the awkward angle, hit her in the chest. This time, she fell and lay still.

Onani rushed out of the room to his partner. Masina's limp body was propped against a large pillar a few metres from the door, unconscious but alive.

Going to get help, he ran to the outer buildings hoping to find medical personnel, but almost ran straight into a troop of soldiers, guns aimed at him, ready to fire. Immediately, he dropped his gun and raised his hands.

"Identify yourself!" came a voice from behind the firing line, in front of a large, dark-green Tata truck.

"My name is Detective Onani Limani! Police Headquarters! I have a police officer who needs medical assistance!" Onani slowly reached into his front trouser pocket and produced his identification.

The man who had spoken came towards him, dressed in a military uniform and looked at Onani's identification. "Alright," he finally said. He pointed towards his men. "You three, with me! The rest of you, secure the perimeter!" Turning back to Onani, he said, "Let's go see to your partner."

Andrew Dakalira

Taking a doctor and two nurses with them, Onani and the soldiers went back to where Masina was. The detective narrated the events to the army men on the way.

"I'm Lieutenant John Phiri," said the man who seemed to be in charge. "And, from what you've told me, my superiors are going to want to talk to you." He turned to his men, "Secure the prisoner!"

Detective Masina was admitted to the same hospital he was injured in. As for his attacker, she was found by the soldiers, alive, thrown into a military vehicle and taken away. Onani and the lieutenant followed.

"Careful. This is the military you are dealing with. Those guys are always hiding something," Masina had warned his partner.

"I'll be fine. You just concentrate on getting better. She really banged you up."

"Yeah, well, at least you got the bitch, right?"

"Yeah, at least there is that." Except to Onani, it was baffling. He had indeed got her. She was in the hands of the military now. But he had put a bullet in her heart, he was sure of it, and yet she was still alive.

Chileka, Blantyre district

"You have amazing agility for someone your age, muhiri. One would think you were as young as I."

"Do not call me that," Sir Gregory spat back. "I am not your brother."

"Ah, but you are, muhiri. We are all brothers and sisters. Muhiris and Chemwas, no? It has been a long time since we last met. But I still remember everything you taught me." Then, for the first time, the man's smile vanished. "They told me I would find you here. Although, I am not exactly sure why they made me travel in that blasted spaceship with those Americans. But that does not matter. I am supposed to bring you back, muhiri. Preferably, alive."

282

VIII

Sir Gregory tilted his head slightly to one side. "My number one obligation has always been to protect the family. Therefore, I am not going anywhere."

"I had a feeling you would say that."

The lithe mzungu moved so quickly that Sir Gregory barely had time to move. He was struck on the left side of his chest and crashed back into an orange tree, scattering a few birds nesting in it. Sir Gregory looked up and just had enough time to avoid a blow to the head by inches that hit the tree trunk behind him. He bunched his fists and hit his adversary in the chest. The man skidded back a few feet then stopped, still on his bare feet.

"Are you sure you want things to be this way, muhiri? Because, if you do not mind my saying so, your strength is clearly not what it used to be."

In response, Sir Gregory launched himself at the stranger, who only shuffled his feet to get out of the way. His cockiness cost him. Sir Gregory's arm connected with his neck, sending him down on one knee. Weakened, he tried to get up but Sir Gregory kicked him in the midriff. The man doubled over but instinctively lashed out. The old man simply moved to one side and that was when he saw it. Someone outside the orchard had thrown a spear, intended for the man on the ground, but now coming straight towards him. In one movement, Sir Gregory caught the spear in mid-air and redirected it into the other man's abdomen.

The man's voice was faint, but his face was glowing, masking the tremendous amount of pain he was feeling. "You cannot stop this, muhiri. You are quite aware of that. You cannot protect your children from what's coming. Not even right now."

When the other villagers, including the man who had thrown the spear, had reached Sir Gregory, the mzungu was dead. Sir Gregory walked past them, hurrying to his family. But not before telling the chief to contact the police again.

Chilinde Barracks, Lilongwe City

"Well, Detective, I think that is all we need from you for now. If there is anything else, we will let you know," said Lieutenant Phiri.

"That is all well and good, Lieutenant, but you still haven't told me what is going on. Why is the military interested in the massacre at a local hospital? That is our job."

Lieutenant Phiri took a long look at the detective before replying. "I am not at liberty to say, Detective Limani. But we really do appreciate your help. As I said before, if there is anything else, we will let you know."

"Fine," said Onani, annoyed, and walked over to the military Land Cruiser that was to escort him off the barracks. Somehow, this was bigger than the lieutenant and his friends in the briefing room had let on. He could feel it. But Onani knew that pressing them for information was futile.

"Excuse me, Detective!" Onani turned around only to see Lieutenant Phiri walking briskly towards him. "I'm afraid you cannot leave just yet."

"What, am I under military arrest now?"

"No, of course not." The uniformed man flicked some imaginary dirt off his shoulder. "There has been a new development. The prisoner. She wants to speak to you."

Chileka, Blantyre district

Mavuto bombarded Sir Gregory with questions even before he sat down. "What is happening? The priest says someone killed people in church. Is that true? Who is it?"

Sir Gregory put up his hand and Mavuto went quiet. He then spoke directly to Father Fletcher. "The police are going to want to talk to you. The Chief is already at the church and sent someone to get the police since the phones no longer seem to be working around here. I will go with you. And, since you live alone, I think you should stay with us for a few days."

"Alright," replied the priest, pleasantly surprised by the offer. "We might as well get going then, carpe diem and all that."

VIII

"Yes, I suppose we should. In the meantime, you three," Sir Gregory's voice was firmer, "under no circumstances are you to leave the house until I get back. And do not let strangers into the house."

"Dad," this time it was Nina, "what is really going on?"

"I will explain when I come back. In the meantime, do as you're told. Look after your brothers."

Father Fletcher spoke again. "Shall I get the hovercycle?"

"You can use it if you want to, Father. I am not getting on that confounded contraption."

Nina watched the two men walk away, wondering what they were discussing. She tried calling her boyfriend again, unsuccessfully. No signal.

"Actually," Sir Gregory was saying, "I asked you to stay with us for selfish reasons, partially. Someone might have to look after the children when I'm gone."

Father Fletcher was confused. "When you are gone? Gone where?"

"The police may want to keep me for a while. I killed a man today."

State House, Lilongwe city

"I am still in control of this country, Mr. Vice President, and I can assure you that I do not require your assistance."

"With all due respect, Mr. President, right now you need all the help you can get," hit back Vice President Chona.

"Might I remind you that you are under house arrest, Mr. Vice President? How do you even know exactly what is going on?" President Moto was beginning to get irritated.

"You may have placed me under house arrest, Herbert, but I still have my ways of keeping in the know. I could be very useful to you right now," replied the vice president, ostentatiously.

"Well, you are still under house arrest. I did not put you under house arrest, the courts did. Let's be clear on that. And, I do not trust you. I am the president. I am the one running this country. Now, if you'll excuse me, I have more pressing matters to attend to."

President Moto slammed down the receiver before the vice president could get another word in. "I have never really liked that pretentious little man," he said, under his breath. Then he turned to his attention back to present company. "Well, gentlemen, have there been any new developments?"

Secretary Maloto and General Manda looked at each other before the former spoke. "You could say that, sir. Fresh incidents. There was a massacre at Kamuzu Central Hospital. Eighteen patients were killed. Also, six people were killed in a church in Chileka. Same fashion."

"But, there is a bit of good news, sir," chipped in General Manda. "We captured the assassin from the hospital, with a little help from the police. She is being interrogated as we speak."

"She? Are you trying to tell me that a woman killed eighteen people?"

"Yes, sir."

VIII

The president cursed under his breath. "Alright. Keep me informed. I want to know everything she tells you."

The president dismissed the two men and called in his spokesperson. "Draft a statement on recent events. Assure the nation, tell them not to panic. Also, remind them that the commemoration tomorrow will go ahead and I shall be in attendance, as previously announced."

"Alright, sir. Is there anything else, sir?"

"Yes. Get President Barry on the phone."

Chilinde Barracks, Lilongwe city

"Nice to see you again, Detective. It is detective, right? I heard them call you that," said the woman in restraints.

"You wanted to talk to me. I am here. You can start by telling me why you killed all those people at the hospital," Onani snarled.

"Straight to the point. I like." Even though her back was against the wall and her arms and legs were in chains, she smiled seductively at the police officer. Her jacket had been taken off; only the blouse and skirt remained. "I will not tell you why, specifically. You know I did it. And, you know my handiwork now, so I do not have to tell you that it was I who got rid of that scumbag that called himself a lawyer. And believe me, Detective, there will be more to come."

"Alright," Onani said. "Let's say I believe you. I've just got a confession. You will be behind bars for life, most likely. Why risk life imprisonment by killing bad men who were already jail-bound and patients who were going to die anyway?"

Onani thought he heard a gasp behind him. He chose to ignore it. The woman looked at him thoughtfully, before she spoke again. "Call it survival of the fittest, Detective. We need only the strong on this planet. Give any theory you like to try and explain what I have done. But, as I said, it will all be explained in due course. And, if you really cannot wait, ask him." Her eyes darted towards the lieutenant then back to the detective. "I just wanted to speak to the man who captured me."

"Well, now you have. The next time you see me is when I testify against you in court." Onani turned and started for the door.

"Detective." The dark, seductive voice came from behind him. Onani froze. The next few words were said in a low tiger-like growl. "It is going to be fun hunting you."

Chileka, Blantyre district

"So Father, you are saying you do not know who killed these people?"

"For the last time, officers," replied Father Fletcher, his tone rather exasperated, "they were already dead when I got here. I got out of the church and raised the alarm, then went to Sir Gregory's. Most of those people were here for the mass I was going to hold for the sick."

But the police officers were persistent. "Father, of all the homes that you could've gone to in the village, why Sir Gregory's?"

Sir Gregory could clearly see that Father Fletcher was not taking the grilling well. The man had turned unhealthily pale and appeared under great strain.

"Excuse me, officers, but could you please leave the man alone? He just came into his church only to find six of his flock murdered. Clearly he is still shaken. Besides, you have already found the culprit in the orchard behind the church. And, what I would like to know is why it took you so long to get here. We reported this in the morning. It is now six o'clock in the evening and you just got here."

The police officer who seemed to be in command glared at Sir Gregory. "You know we have been having persistent fuel shortages in this country for the past few years. Also we are still understaffed at the moment. Anyway, we are here now. And you, sir, will have to come with us to the station. We want to know exactly how this white man was killed."

This time the chief spoke up. "Wait a minute. If Sir Gregory had not acted in the manner he did, the murderer would still be alive! We would all have been slaughtered while you waited for your precious fuel!"

"It's okay, Chief," said Sir Gregory before any of the police officers had a chance to retort. "I have nothing to hide and nothing to be afraid of. I shall go with the officers." Then, almost as an afterthought, "Please tell the people to go home and stay inside, Chief. Immediately." Turning to Father Fletcher, Sir Gregory spoke with urgency in his voice. "Go look after my children. Run. Now." Scared by the dark tone in Sir Gregory's voice, Father Fletcher did not ask questions. He turned and left.

Sir Gregory was not done giving orders. This time it was to the police officer. "If you and your men want to live, get in the car and leave within the next five minutes."

The police officer's facial expression changed from surprise to annoyance and finally defiance. "Is that a threat, Sir Gregory?"

He never got an answer. All of a sudden, the villagers and police officers were shouting in unison. The police officer who was talking to Sir Gregory, and had his back to his fellow officers, quickly spun around. But, Sir Gregory already knew what was happening. He had miscalculated. They were already here.

Seven police officers had turned up at Chileka to investigate the church murders. Now, before everyone's eyes, that number went down to five. Two men jumped from the roof of the police vehicle and landed behind two officers. Two necks snapped and the two officers fell, dead. Galvanised into action, the villagers scattered. Everyone ran, not looking back. Everyone, that is, except the police officers and Sir Gregory.

Ignoring the shocked police officers, Sir Gregory grabbed the nearest officer's handgun and fired. The first man was hit in the abdomen and was dead as he fell, holding his belly. Sir

Gregory fired again and the bullet went through the second man's shoulder. He kept coming.

Sir Gregory gave the police his final orders. "Get in the car and go get help. I will handle him. Go!"

Father Fletcher felt very weak, physically and spiritually. He had run from church today, a place where he and many others praised the Lord. Not once, but twice. Father Fletcher was not young and could not remember the last time he exercised. Had God abandoned them? Maybe He had chosen not to act, not to save those people, Father Fletcher thought, as he slowed down to a quick walk. Well, everything happens for a reason.

"Move!"

Father Fletcher did not even bother turning around. He knew Sir Gregory's voice and the urgency in it made him start running again, although he was only a few metres away from the house.

"We must get home, quickly!" Sir Gregory had caught up with him.

They found Nina and Mavuto standing in front of the house, brother holding sister. Nina was trembling violently. A young man lay in front of them, dead, with a knife in his stomach. Father Fletcher stopped dead in his tracks.

Sir Gregory went straight to his children. "We will talk about what happened later. But right now, we need to get inside the house. Where's Joel?" Nina simply pointed a shaky finger at the house. "Good. Inside. Hurry!"

They went inside the house and, finding Joel, went straight into Sir Gregory's bedroom. Father Fletcher was the one who noticed the blood on Nina's hands, but it was Joel who saw the bright light and heard the faint buzzing first. Before he could say anything, Sir Gregory pressed something and the ground beneath them began to move.

VIII

Chilinde Barracks, Lilongwe City

"Well, Detective," began Colonel Banda after his lieutenant had made the necessary introductions. "Did you learn anything useful from our prisoner?"

"Not really, sir. Most of what she said did not make sense. She talked about herself as a predator. It is almost as if she likes what she did because that is what she is supposed to be doing." Onani paused for a few seconds before continuing. "She says she is going to love hunting me."

"I doubt she will do any more hunting anytime soon," said the colonel. He was thoughtful for a moment and when he spoke again, there were deep furrows across his dark-brown forehead. "This is very disappointing. I was hoping for more. But, we will make her talk. We need to contain this situation. Every piece of intel is vital."

"Well, she did say one more thing, sir. She said if I wanted to know more, I should ask him," said Onani, nodding towards Lieutenant Phiri, who stood impassively.

"I see," replied the colonel emotionlessly. "Well, that'll be all, Detective. I must commend you for your bravery today. I'll assign a sergeant to escort you off the barracks."

"With all due respect, sir," Onani protested, annoyed by the manner in which he was being dismissed, "this is also a police investigation. Now, I need to know exactly what is going on and I feel like there is something you are not telling me."

"With all due respect, Detective," The colonel emphasised each word, mimicking the detective, his tone harsh, "I have more important things to deal with than play cop-informant right now. Already there have been other massacres in Chileka and a few other areas. I hardly have time to..."

He never got to finish. Onani had already rushed out of the door.

Chileka, Blantyre district

"What the hell is this place?" said Mavuto

"Watch your language, child!" Sir Gregory then turned from his eldest son to his other two children. Joel was by his sister's side, frightened. Nina said nothing, still in shock, holding her little brother's hand. Everyone was looking at Sir Gregory as if they had never seen him before in their lives.

The room was almost the same size as Sir Gregory's bedroom but the similarities ended there. This room had a blue light almost like the daytime sky. A large red button was installed on the wall by the bottom of the stairs from where they descended. In the middle of the room were four round chairs. At one end of the room was a bed, at the other, a closet that looked like a locked safe. Sir Gregory pressed the red button. The slit in the floor which had allowed them to go down into the room from the bedroom immediately closed.

"Dad, what is this?" Nina finally asked, her voice hardly obscuring the shock—the fact that she had just killed someone temporarily forgotten.

Sir Gregory was calm. "I built this a long time ago, when you were all quite young. I kept hoping we would never have to use it."

"You built this?" Mavuto's voice rose in pitch. "You built all of this? Did our mother even know what you were hiding beneath her bedroom?"

Sir Gregory was looking at Nina as he spoke. "Yes, she knew. There was nothing about me that your mother did not know. As a matter of fact, we both agreed on this."

Nina was still a bit dazed by it all. "You say you both agreed to it, but what did you build it for? How could you and Mother possibly know that this was going to happen? How could you have known?"

Father Fletcher, who had not said anything until this point, spoke up. "Now, I am sure your father and mother had their reasons for not telling you about this place. Also, I think there is a reasonable explanation as to why they built this place. If we could all just calm down-"

Sir Gregory cut him short, "Yes, Father, there is an explanation. Whether my children will find it reasonable, however, is another matter." He turned to his children. "It is time you all knew the truth. Yes, all of you," Sir Gregory repeated, when he saw Nina glance nervously at Joel. "I suggest you all sit down."

Chilinde Barracks, Lilongwe city

"You won't get anywhere in your fCar, Detective," Lieutenant Phiri called out to Onani, who was getting into an army Land Cruiser. "The military has declared our entire airspace a no-fly zone. Wherever it is you are running to, you won't get there quickly."

"In that case, Lieutenant, may I ask that your man drop me home and not at headquarters? I have something there that can help me."

Lieutenant Phiri looked at Onani thoughtfully for a moment. "Of course, Detective. He will drop you off wherever you need to go. And if you find out more, let me know immediately. You have my number. And Detective—good luck."

State House, Lilongwe city

Principal Secretary Maloto had not slept in thirty-six hours. Not because he did not want to. His job required him to stay up until the man he worked for said otherwise. And it looked like President Moto was not ready to release him yet.

Limbani Maloto had known Herbert Moto long before the latter became president. They attended the same college as undergraduates and had been friends ever since. And many years later Herbert, with a doctorate in economics, had approached his friend about going into politics. Limbani, armed with a masters in public administration, reluctantly said yes. They had built their party from nothing, with Herbert ultimately making it to parliament. Limbani had quit party politics immediately after Herbert was elected to high office, preferring to go back to his old job as a lecturer. But his friend would have none of it. He appointed Limbani principal secretary in the ministry of defence.

We have come a long way from being silly teenagers drinking cheap, homemade rum, Maloto thought. But nothing could've prepared us for this. Absolutely nothing.

"Excuse me, sir." One of the president's aides interrupted Maloto from his reverie. "The United States ambassador is meeting the president as we speak. President Moto has asked that you be present."

"Nobody told me about this beforehand. When did the ambassador arrive?"

"He arrived twenty minutes ago, sir, and was shown straight into the president's office."

Maloto spoke, almost to himself. "Probably concerns recent events. Alright, I'm on my way." He shut the door to his makeshift office at the State House and left for the president's office. He was only a few feet away when he heard the gunshots.

Chileka, Blantyre district

Sir Gregory looked closely at his children. He had always dreaded this moment. He had hoped that it would never come. He suddenly wished Milcah was still alive. He always felt stronger and more confident when she was by his side. She had trusted and believed in him without any reservations. He could certainly have used that during the conversation he was about to have.

"Thousands of years ago, there was a species called metsu. They had their own planet called Mera, which is approximately the same size as Earth, only in a different galaxy. The metsu were hunters, mostly, but there were also other metsus with different occupations. They had homes, with families. In short, their domestic setup was very much the same as that of humans on Earth. They also kept animals. One of those animals was the guma.

"The guma was unique because you could hunt it in the wild, but you could also domesticate it. The guma was more intelligent than the other animals on the planet. Not only could it walk like a metsu but it could also be trained to do simple tasks like starting fires and cleaning its surroundings. Because of this, every female metsu wanted a guma at her home."

Sir Gregory paused; nobody said a word so he continued. "Now, the metsus usually lived in harmony as muhiris and chemwas; that is, brothers and sisters. But there were confrontations. Most of the females wanted all the gumas captured and then domesticated into slaves. They therefore objected to hunting them down and killing them. This, obviously, did not go down well with the other metsus, especially the males, who loved hunting the gumas.

"After a while, it was agreed that some of the gumas be taken off planet and left on other planets in different galaxies to repopulate. That would not be a problem since, due to the metsus' major strides in technology, interstellar travel was quite possible. The gumas left on other planets could be hunted while the ones left on Mera were to be slaves. That way, everyone was happy.

"The hunters agreed to wait until a planet's guma population reached a certain number. When this happened, some of the hunters would be selected for travel to that particular planet. Their sole purpose was to hunt the guma, as a way of curbing overpopulation and getting hunting experience.

"Only one planet in this galaxy was habitable for the gumas, Earth. And it was decided that the hunt could only begin when the population of gumas on earth reached 8 billion. This was because the resources on the planet could only support healthy guma life up to this population threshold. When the guma population had been depleted to a certain point through the hunt, they would then leave the planet."

Although Nina had already figured out where the story was going, she still let out a gasp.

Sir Gregory ignored her and continued. "So, the guma population—or human, as they are called here on Earth—hits 8 billion tomorrow, according to some organisations. Commemorations are even planned, if I recall correctly. Now,

I doubt that will happen because tomorrow, the hunt really starts."

"If this it true then God help us all." Father Fletcher's voice nearly made the children jump. "But Sir Gregory, with all due respect, you cannot expect us to believe such outlandish bits of nonsense! Your story is ridiculous!" An incredulous smile was planted on Father Fletcher's face.

Sir Gregory was not smiling. "Whether you believe me or not, Father, is up to you. But God cannot help you. He does not exist. You see, your god did not put you on this planet. We did. I am one of them."

State House, Lilongwe city

"This is rather unexpected, Mr. Ambassador," began President Moto. "I assume you are here because of what's been happening recently. I have been in touch with your president at the White House. I've just got off the phone with him, actually. It seems all is not well there, either."

The ambassador was a short, rather fat, grey-haired man with a receding hairline. "Indeed, Mr. President. It seems this is happening everywhere. But," the ambassador leaned forward in his chair, "that is not the only reason why I am here."

"Then why exactly are you here this evening, Ambassador, if not because of these killings?"

"Well, it is because of the killings, Mr. President. But I am here because I know why they are happening."

Intrigued, President Moto sat up in his chair while the ambassador explained the same story Sir Gregory was telling his children at that same moment. Slowly, the head of state's features changed from heavy concentration to disbelief to amusement.

"I know that your country is famed for different conspiracy theories amongst its citizens, Ambassador, but I hardly expect a man of your standing to subscribe to them as well," said President Moto, barely able to conceal his laughter.

VIII

"I assure you, Mr. President, this is no theory. It is simple truth. All facts. And I would greatly appreciate it if you took this matter seriously." The ambassador was clearly irritated.

"Forgive me, Ambassador, but you cannot expect me to believe your story. How do you even know all this? I just spoke to your president a few minutes ago and he did not say anything about this to me."

"There are some things that even the White House does not know, Mr. President," said the ambassador, with a menacing glint in his eye.

President Moto caught it. And for an unknown reason the ambassador suddenly made him uneasy. "Do you remember what I told you at the state dinner a few days ago, Mr. Ambassador? About not messing around with my country just because we are still a developing nation?"

"Yes, Mr. President, I remember what you said," replied the ambassador. "But I assure you, everything I have told you is the truth."

"I believe you," said the president. "What I do not believe is that you are indeed the ambassador. So tell me, who are you?"

The ambassador looked startled. The president, now standing, went on. "I have not held a state dinner in over six months upon the United States government's recommendation to cut spending for state residences. So we never had that conversation. But then, the ambassador of the United States to Malawi would know that. So, once again, who are you?"

The ambassador looked up at the president, a smile slowly forming at the corners of his mouth. "Very clever, Mr. President. I was really beginning to think that I had got away with it. But, it does not matter. As I have said, the hunt starts tomorrow. There is nothing you can do to stop it. No human on this planet can."

The door burst open and the president's aide-de-camp came in with two security officers, guns drawn.

"I am going to ask you one more time," President Moto spoke again. "Tell me who you are or my men will fire."

The man posing as the ambassador stood firm. "It does not matter who I am. But know this, Mr. President; hunting season is about to begin." With that, the ambassador literally burst out of his suit.

President Moto stared in horror at the transformation before him. The man he had thought was the United States ambassador was now was standing bare-chested in front of him. He was no longer the overweight, five-foot five, grey-haired gentleman. He was muscular, six feet tall, with dark, close-cropped hair and big, pointed ears. The torn suit barely covered his body. His mouth now an insane grin, he turned to the three men behind him.

One of the security men fired first, and missed. The man jumped towards the ceiling, grabbing the chandelier that hung in the centre of the president's office. Using the chandelier for momentum, he leapt at the three men. This time, none of the security personnel missed. The flying creature took a hail of bullets and fell to the ground with a thud, inches from his killers. Still a bit shaken himself, the aide-de-camp rushed to his president. At the same moment, Principal Secretary Maloto rushed in with more security personnel.

"Sir, are you alright? Are you hurt?" The aide-de-camp carefully examined his boss. Maloto joined him.

"Mr. President, are you alright? What happened?"

President Moto said nothing. He looked like he had aged ten years since the last time Maloto had seen him. After a minute or two, he finally spoke, directly to Maloto.

"Cancel the commemorations. Contact our generals and tell them to put our troops on standby. We may have a war on our hands."

VIII

8

Dedza district

A white 2006 Toyota Corolla sped along the M1, heading towards Blantyre. Onani sat at the steering wheel, Rhythm and Blues playing in the background. The genre always managed to calm him down. Lord knows I need to be calm right now, Onani thought. But it was quite difficult, not only because of what he had seen that day but also because he couldn't reach Nina.

It was by accident that he had even spotted her in college. He, a third-year psychology major putting up a poster of a forthcoming freshman's ball, she, a freshman going to get a copy of the semester timetable. They had started going out two months later.

Onani adored Nina and she loved him. With no siblings and both parents having died in a car accident years before, she was the closest person to family that he had left. He knew Nina's brothers and had even met Nina's father, albeit informally, at her mother's funeral. They wanted to be a family, officially, but as he drove, he worried that this might not happen now.

He glanced at the clock on the dashboard, 9pm. A lot had happened in one day. He still did not really know what was going on. The woman captured by the army, the woman he had shot twice and was still alive, had told him nothing concrete. And the murders continued, with Nina a possible victim.

Onani pushed the thought out of his mind and tried to concentrate on driving. The vehicle's lights cut through the night as Onani passed through Dedza district. He had not driven the Corolla in a long time. It had been his mother's. He knew it would take him a few more hours before getting to Blantyre district but Onani did not care. He had to find Nina.

Andrew Dakalira

Chileka, Blantyre district

Father Fletcher said nothing, but clutched his rosary in his hands so tightly it hurt his fingers. The missionary was both angry and confused. "Sir Gregory, this is insane! I can't believe this. I refuse to!"

Sir Gregory immediately replied, "In all the years you have known me, Father, I have never been one to say things in jest. And I most certainly would not joke about a thing like this."

This time it was Mavuto who spoke up. "If what you say is true, how can we trust you? You've just said you are one of them! Who are you, really, and why are you here?"

"That is enough, Vuto," Nina spoke softly, calmer than she had been all night. "Dad-"

"Don't call him that!" Mavuto snapped at his sister. "We don't even know who he is! We never have and probably never will!"

Nina ignored her brother. "Dad, I know you have a lot to tell us. We are all in shock. But could we please not do this now?" Nina nodded her head towards Joel. The boy not only looked confused but also terribly frightened.

Sir Gregory understood. "You're right, Nina. No need to talk about this further. I need to go back up to the house and check if there is anyone there. I think I heard something."

He went to the locker which Mavuto was now leaning on. Sir Gregory said nothing, only glared at his teenage son. Mavuto grudgingly moved out of the way. Sir Gregory punched a few numbers on the keypad and the closet opened to reveal a vault with different weapons in it. Taking a spear and ignoring the stares, he went back to the stairs, pressed the red button, and cautiously went up telling everyone to remain below.

Back in his room, Sir Gregory found everything untouched. It was when he was about to open the door to the living room that he intuitively felt another presence in the house, one of his kind. Sir Gregory flung open the door, took one sweeping glance across the room and threw his spear. The man sitting on the sofa was dead before he even realised who had killed him.

300

VIII

Sir Gregory calmly removed the spear from the man's stomach and covered him with a tablecloth. Then, after making sure that the rest of the house was secure, he went to call the others, all the while preparing himself for the talk with his daughter.

Chilinde Barracks, Lilongwe city

She was still in restraints, standing with four soldiers, their guns trained on her. But she seemed unperturbed, eyes closed, deep in thought. The soldiers guarding her could have sworn that she had a smile on her face.

There were only a few hours left until the hunt begun. And, captive or not, she would participate. She had lived on this planet for a long time with these gumas. She had even practised killing them over the years. It was easy on this planet; they were more domesticated and even weaker than the ones she used to hunt back on her planet. When she killed on this planet, in spite of their law enforcement agencies, she had always got away with it. Until now.

She was looking forward to the hunt for two reasons now. First, it was her reward for staying on this planet. She had earned it. Second, she now wanted the pleasure of killing the man who had captured her. The man who had shot and almost killed her. She was going to hunt down the detective.

Blantyre city, Blantyre district

The soldier was surprised to see the white sedan approaching the roadblock. He had not seen that Corolla model since he was fifteen. He unslung the rifle on his shoulder, released the safety catch and cautiously approached the window of the driver's seat. One could not be too careful in light of the recent events, especially when a great-looking, but old vehicle approached a restricted area at night.

Behind the wheel was a weary-looking young man. "I'm Detective Onani Limani from Police headquarters in Lilongwe," he said, handing over his identification. "I need to get to Chileka right now."

301

The soldier looked at the man's identification with one hand, the other still on his gun. "I'm afraid that is not possible, sir. We have strict orders not to let anyone through except military personnel. I'm going to have to ask you to turn back."

Onani looked at the soldier carefully. "I have been driving from Lilongwe non-stop for four hours. You have to let me through, it is important."

"That will not happen, sir. You won't get through," the soldier reiterated, handing back Onani's identification. "The road which passes through the power plant has been blocked as well," he said as if reading Onani's mind, "and do not even think about bypassing this roadblock on foot, sir. We already have men in the area who are more likely to shoot you than ask questions."

"Well, aren't you the king of countenance," Onani spluttered sarcastically. He put the car in reverse and parked it by the side of the road, a few metres away from the roadblock. The soldier kept watching him carefully. Onani tried Nina's number again, but still got nothing. It was then that Onani remembered another number.

Chileka, Blantyre district

Sir Gregory left Father Fletcher with Mavuto and Joel, who had calmed down a little, in the boys' room and knocked on Nina's door. The door was already open and Sir Gregory found his daughter sitting on her bed, holding a picture of her mother.

"You should get some sleep," he said, not sitting down. Nina looked up at the man she had called her father since she was little and it was almost as if she had just met him today.

"I killed someone today. Just how do you expect me to sleep? I stabbed him. His blood was all over my hands!"

"It's alright, child," Sir Gregory soothed. "You did what you had to do to protect yourself and your brothers. He wasn't human anyway."

302

VIII

Nina ignored her father's last remark. "Was this all a lie? Did you really love any of us at all or were we just your cover on Earth, to make you look human?"

Sir Gregory sighed. "It was nothing like that at all. I really loved your mother. That is why I married her. And, as time went by, I grew to love her even more. It was the same with you and your brothers."

"Forgive me if I do not believe you," Nina snapped back, with fire in her eyes. "And even if I did, that still does not excuse the fact that you have been lying to us all these years. How could you and mother keep something like this from us?"

"We thought it was best that you not know. We wanted you to go on with your lives as normal, without wondering who was human and who was not."

"Why exactly are you here? You are one of them. You have obviously been on this planet for so long. Why?"

Sir Gregory paused for a few seconds before replying. "When humans were put on Earth, a few of our kind were left here to monitor them. Each of us was supposed to stay here for a few hundred Earth years under different identities until someone came to take our place and we went home. A few years before my time was up, I met your mother so I refused to go home, which made my people angry. And, when I married her, their hatred towards me grew worse. I could not go back, even after your mother died. I love you and your brothers too. I could not leave you."

For the first time, Nina felt like she understood. "You must be really old." That brought a slight hint of a smile on Sir Gregory's face. "So you disobeyed your kind and married outside your species. I guess that explains why they hate you so much."

"Yes, well, the feeling is mutual," said Sir Gregory, moving out of the room. "Get some sleep now, child. I will keep us safe up here tonight. We shall talk further in the morning."

"Dad," Nina could not believe she still called him that. "You said the hatred is mutual. I can understand why they despise you. But why do you hate them?"

Sir Gregory stood by the door and looked at his daughter. In spite of the distance, Nina could see great sadness in the old man's eyes. "They killed the love of my life. They killed your mother."

Sir Gregory sat on his favourite chair in the living room, spear ready. The spear's victim still sat in the chair opposite his, and had probably bled into the cushioning, but Sir Gregory did not care. He did not move, just sat in silence, radiating melancholy.

He had not meant to tell anyone on Earth about what had really happened to Milcah on the day she died. Technically, he still hadn't. But now Nina knew that the metsus had killed her mother, although she did not know how. Milcah's death had seemed natural enough. High blood pressure. But Sir Gregory knew better. Yes, he definitely knew better.

He was interrupted from his thoughts by a low rustling noise in the corridor that led to the bedroom. Sir Gregory did not move. He knew who it was.

Father Fletcher stood by the door that led into the living room, hesitating when he saw the body covered with a bloodstained sheet.

"Do not be afraid, Father. He will not rip your chest open. He is dead. I made sure of that."

Father Fletcher's eyes scanned the dark room, before he finally decided to sit on the chair next to Sir Gregory, grateful for the coffee table which was between them and the dead body.

"Are you sure that thing is dead?"

"Yes, Father, I am. I stabbed it in its heart. You have nothing to worry about."

The priest gave a short, strained laugh. "I have nothing to worry about. Within the last twenty-four hours, my faith has been heavily shaken. Some members of my congregation have been brutally murdered. I have just heard a story about how both the creation and evolution theories championed on this planet are false, how God does not exist. And you say I should not worry."

"Actually, Father, you have evolved, in a way," said Sir Gregory, not looking at the clergyman. "Your appearance has improved and so have your cognitive skills. It seems that this planet agrees with you gumas."

"Well, I suppose we should be thankful for that," snapped Father Fletcher, full of sarcasm. "Do you know what this story of yours could do to this world? How much chaos and irreparable damage it would cause?"

Sir Gregory took the spear from across his knees and leaned it against the chair. "This world is already headed for chaos come morning, Father. I have no doubt about that. And when it comes to my story, I can understand your misgivings.

"However, the hunt starts in the morning, like I said. If we are going to survive, we have to stick together. So believe what you want, Father, because I really do not care. All I ask of you is that we act with the same goal in mind, staying alive."

Father Fletcher knew what Sir Gregory was alluding to. "Well, I can tell you two things right now, Sir Gregory. First, I will never deliberately take another man's life. And secondly, I do not believe your story. Even if I did, you would have to explain how you and your gumas happened to be on your planet in the first place. Quite frankly, I do not think you can. Now, I suggest that that thing lying dead in the chair be removed as soon as possible. You do not want the children to see it."

Deep down, Sir Gregory was forced to admit that he could not explain where metsus and gumas had originally come from. But he did not want to start debating their origins so he sat quietly, waiting for that which he was certain would come in the morning. He would move the body later.

Chilinde Barracks, Lilongwe city

The room her captors had placed her in had no windows, just four walls and an overhead lamp. Her well-honed senses could tell her, however, that it was after midnight, nearly dawn. It was time.

"Excuse me," she addressed one of her guards. "Could I please have some water?"

VIII

The guard looked at her thoughtfully for a moment, then walked over to the table in the middle of the room where a pitcher of water and a few plastic cups stood. Laying his rifle on the table, he filled one of the cups and took it to the prisoner. As if expecting what the captive was planning, he un-holstered his sidearm and pointed it at her forehead. "Drink," he ordered, helping her tilt her head back with the barrel of the pistol.

She drank, concealing her frustration. The plan would not work with a gun to her head. This guma was clever. He had ignored the sense of security the other guards provided, with their guns pointed at her. But, it did not matter. She would try again. The chains she could break. It was the guards that would complicate things.

10

Chileka, Blantyre district

Nina opened her eyes just a few minutes after the first rays of dawn glowed between the curtains of her childhood bedroom. She smiled, happy to wake up at home, in her own bed. Then all the events of the past hours came flooding back. Her smile vanished.

She had killed someone. She had actually murdered someone. And, she had done it up close. Although she kept telling herself that it was self-defence, and an accidental miracle that she succeeded in killing the man who would have killed both her and her brother, she still felt guilty. The man was quite young. He had come out of nowhere and attacked them, knocking Mavuto to the ground and then landing on top of him, beating him mercilessly before turning his attention to Nina. She could still vividly recall how it had felt, the knife slicing flesh and piercing the man's abdomen. Her father had told her that he was not human and was probably hundreds of years old so she should not feel bad about killing him. To Nina, all that provided little comfort.

Her father. Nina shuddered as she recalled the previous night's events. Her own stepfather, the man who had been the most important male figure for most of her life, had just told her that he was not human. Not only that, he'd kept it a secret for all these years, together with her mother. Her mother, who had allegedly been killed by her stepfather's own kind.

Nina had so many unanswered questions. For one thing, she could not understand how her mother, whom the doctors said had died due to high blood pressure, could have possibly been killed by these things. Also, if her stepfather knew about what was currently going on, why had he not warned them sooner? All he had done was confuse Nina even more. He had flatly refused to answer any more of her questions after mentioning her mother's death, leaving Nina seething with rage.

Pushing her ambivalence towards her stepfather aside, Nina got out of bed and dressed. She was glad to be with her family now, with everything that was happening. But right then, there was one person she needed more than anything.

Chileka, Blantyre district

A sharp rap on the driver's side window woke Onani up. He adjusted the seat he had been sleeping in and rolled down the window. In the morning light, Onani thought the soldier he had met during the night looked a lot less menacing as he handed over a satellite phone. "You have a phone call, sir," the soldier spoke with sincere courtesy.

"You are quite the determined lover, Detective," Lieutenant Phiri's voice crackled from the other end of the line. Onani was a bit taken aback. "How did you find out, Lieutenant? I did not tell you why I wanted to be in Chileka this badly."

Lieutenant Phiri laughed. "I have my ways, Detective. When you called last night, I got really curious. Besides, only a woman could make you leave the security of the barracks in such hasty a manner."

Onani said nothing so the lieutenant continued. "Some more of my men are being deployed in the area today. I have instructed them to take you along as our police liaison. Keep in mind, though, Detective, that this is a military operation. Our men will not allow any of your heroics or foolhardiness. Get to your girlfriend and get yourselves out. That's all."

"Yes, Lieutenant, I understand. Thank you," Onani managed to say before the line went dead. He took a few seconds to familiarise himself with his current surroundings. The filling station to his right, taxi rank to his left. The roundabout behind him, with four roads; two led to Blantyre city, he knew. One led back to Lilongwe and the other was the one he was about to take.

The soldier cleared his throat loudly, attracting Onani's attention. "The men are about to leave, sir." Onani nodded, handing back the satellite phone. "Park your car by the roadblock. You will be using army vehicles." When he saw Onani hesitate, the soldier added, "Don't worry, sir. I will personally look after it."

Onani was surprised to see a hint of a smile on the soldier's face, which had seemed quite stiff the night before. He decided to do as he was told. "Hey. What is your name?"

"Chimanga, sir. Corporal Lanjesi Chimanga."

State House, Lilongwe City

President Moto rolled around in his king-size bed and stretched. The clock on his bedside table said it was six in the morning. He had slept for five straight hours. Doctor's orders. The head of state got out of bed and checked himself in the mirror. His face had the haggard look of someone who had not slept in days. So much for resting.

As he showered and dressed, the sequence of events from the last few days played over and over in his head. It had seemed like his country was cursed at first. But now, it was evident that the whole world was.

People were being killed mercilessly. And, if what the 'ambassador' had told him the night before was true, President Moto was sure this was just a practice run. The image of the thing towering over him that night made the president shudder. The Metsu, as it called itself, had managed to infiltrate the American ambassador's well-guarded residence, had killed the diplomat and taken his place without the guards' knowledge. He had also managed to gain access to the State House and, subsequently, an audience with the president!

The president re-evaluated his look in the mirror. The shower, plus the suit and tie gave him a fresh appearance, although his eyes still looked weary. But, he told himself, at least I do not look scared, which, in all sincerity, he was. He had thought he was going to die the previous night.

Herbert Moto's mind drifted to his family. He had spoken to his wife and two children before going to bed. He was glad they were not around to witness what was happening, although he was not entirely assured of their safety. All was not well in the United States of America, either.

VIII

He adjusted his tie and left his room. As president, he had a lot of crises to solve. Moto was sure the Americans would want to get more involved in his country's security affairs now, since one of their own had been killed. But that was only one of the little things. His country, and most likely the entire world, was on the brink of chaos, and it seemed nothing could be done to stop it.

11

Chileka, Blantyre district

"The place you are talking about is about fifteen kilometres from the roadblock. It is halfway between the roadblock and the power plant. As you can see, the road is not in good condition so it might take us a while to get there."

Onani pretended to listen to the sergeant as the Land Cruiser drove along the dusty, potholed road. Besides Onani and the sergeant, there were five other soldiers in the tarpaulin-covered back of the pick-up truck. None of them spoke, except the staff sergeant, whose mouth seemed not to comprehend the meaning of silence.

Onani's mind was still playing the myriad of incidents that had occurred in the last forty-eight hours. So many people had been murdered and Onani still did not know why. His suspect had been of no help, apart from informing him of the fact that she planned to kill him. Onani's policeman instinct, however, told him that the army knew. But he was certainly not going to get any information from them.

"We are going to the power plant afterwards," the sergeant was saying. "We lost communication with the men who were deployed there this morning."

Onani grunted an acknowledgement. The sergeant was about to continue when the pickup suddenly ground to a halt. Cursing under his breath, the sergeant moved to the opening at the back of the truck.

At the same time, the driver spoke up. "Sir, I think you should see this!"

It took less than a minute for all the men to get out, the sergeant being the first. He stood there, speechless. It was one of his men who spoke first. "Dear God, what the hell happened here?"

State House, Lilongwe City

When President Moto walked into the conference room that morning, there was quite a large gathering already. The defence force commander was present with his deputy, as was the inspector general of the police service and his deputy. The president's glare, however, was in a different direction.

"Where the hell have you been?" Moto asked his defence minister, his tone quite the opposite of his outward composure. Thokozani Kanjala rose from his chair. At six foot four, he was easily the tallest man in the room, but as he spoke, it became apparent that he was not the most confident of men at that moment.

"Well, Mr. President... I was in the Southern Region. In Blantyre district. And, with recent events, I felt it was not safe to travel. I just got back this morning. Principal Secretary Maloto has already filled me in."

The president immediately turned to the secretary. "Any new developments, Limbani?"

"A few, sir. There have been isolated incidents in Mvera and Chipoka districts, according to the police and the army, but apart from that, nothing in the past few hours. It has been relatively quiet." Maloto paused and looked at the president to see if he had any questions, he didn't. "The Americans say they want to be more involved now. They say they are sending a few of their personnel to help us with investigations into the death of their ambassador. President Barry is supposed to call around 9am local time so that he can discuss it with you. I believe the Chief of Staff also has a few things to say."

The chief of staff, a thin, hawk-nosed man in his early forties, rose to speak. Nicknamed Mzungu by his juniors because his nose resembled that of a white person, Malango Moyo's shrill voice could be heard from across the room.

"Mr. President, Vice President Chona has been trying to contact you. He thinks that under the circumstances, he could help serve his country. He wants you to speak to the Attorney General and the high court about reviewing the terms of his house arrest."

In spite of everything that was happening, President Moto could not help but be amused by his former confidante's attempt to gain freedom. "Not a chance. He is accused of treason. The man is suspected of orchestrating an attempt on my life. He will stay where he is."

Everyone at the table went quiet. Moyo, not at all surprised by the head of state's answer, continued. "Sir, there is another thing. Crowds are beginning to gather in our two major cities' Central Business Districts."

President Moto immediately turned to Maloto. "Good God, man, did I not tell you to cancel the commemorations?"

"You did, Mr. President," replied the principal secretary, "but these people are not gathering to celebrate the birth of the world's eighth billion person. They are holding vigils in memory of the dozens of people who have been murdered recently and to protest against the country's apparent lack of security. It is actually being broadcast live on our national television station. That is why I had this brought in here." Maloto turned on the plasma screen that looked rather tiny in the wide conference room.

A look of disbelief was pasted across the president's face as he watched multitudes of people gathering at the Lilongwe city centre. In Blantyre, a crowd had gathered at the Clock Tower roundabout, obstructing traffic. "Don't these people know that they are putting themselves at risk?" He then turned to the inspector general and his deputy. "This is a little after seven in the morning. I want those people back in their homes by nine. I do not care how you do it. Is that clear?"

As the two men hurried off to give their own orders, the minister of defence sat next to the president and said quietly, "You know, Mr. President, it might not be a bad idea to leave the people out there. Safety in numbers and all that."

President Moto was about to tell his defence minister how ridiculous his suggestion was when the chief of staff interrupted him. "Excuse me, sir, but are you watching this?"

Chileka, Blantyre district
All over the country, schools were closed. In Chileka, it was no different. At Chigoba Primary School, not a child was in

sight. There were only a handful of soldiers and a few civilians, all lying on the ground, dead.

Onani froze. He had seen this before. "Sergeant, we should leave."

The sergeant spoke back, not looking at Onani but at his dead colleagues in front of him. "I have to report this. They are going to want to know as soon as possible." He stared at a young soldier lying in the dust in front of what seemed to be the head-teacher's office. His eyes were still open, and he had a metal rod harpooned into his chest. To his left lay another soldier, but his death seemed more flamboyant; a Colombian necktie. The gaping wound on his neck, with his dust-caked tongue hanging out through it, gave him an evil second smile.

"Sergeant," Onani tried again, "we cannot stay here. These men are dead. There is nothing we can do for them. But if we hurry, we can save other men and possibly the power plant. We need to go and we need to go right now."

It was at that moment that one of the sergeant's men called out. "We have found one alive, sir! A civilian!"

But the sergeant was not listening to Onani or his man. "What is that? That humming sound, what is it? Where is it coming from?" The sergeant started to look around.

Onani heard it too. It had been faint at first, but now it was very strong, as if made by quite a large swarm of bees. The detective also looked around for a few seconds before finally pinpointing the source.

"You are looking in the wrong direction, sergeant," said Onani, pointing and looking up.

State House, Lilongwe City

The conference room was abuzz with activity. Almost the entire cabinet were now present. Both army commanders were on telephones barking orders, while their police service counterparts were also busy trying to mobilise their men. One thing was clear; everyone in the room now realised the seriousness of the crisis that lay before them.

There was a sense of foreboding in the room as the president and his men watched the news screens, men and women running in different directions, their plans for a day-long vigil destroyed, forgotten. The police had not even arrived at the scenes yet. The people were afraid of something else.

Even on television, the circular flying objects could clearly be seen hovering a few metres above the ground. They were white, their tops flat, and bottoms rugged and ridged like the underside of a muffin.

"What was that about safety in numbers?" President Moto mumbled to no one in particular, but Principal Secretary Maloto heard him. "It seems they also know that principle, Mr. President."

VIII

12

Chileka, Blantyre district

Onani's mind was racing but his body was immobilised. His head was still pointing towards the sky, eyes focused on the spherical shapes above him.

The sergeant recovered faster. "Back to the car! Now!" He slapped Onani hard across the face. "Get moving!" Stunned into action, Onani ran for the cruiser.

One of the soldiers was half-carrying, half-dragging the civilian who was still alive.

The sergeant moved to help him. "For God's sake, man, hurry up!"

The soldier started to hurry, then let out a short scream of surprise. The sergeant staggered back and had already drawn his sidearm even before he saw the bloodied knife in the civilian's left hand. The soldier who had played Good Samaritan dropped to his knees, uttering a few guttural sounds as blood spewed from his mouth. He then fell flat on his face and lay still. Only at that point did the sergeant fire.

The civilian was down on the ground within seconds, two bullets through his head. The sergeant did not take another look. He went straight to the driver of the cruiser. "We are going to the plant. I'm driving."

"Just for how long are we supposed to stay inside? We should be out there fighting those things off!" Mavuto was agitated, fidgeting on the bed he was seated on.

"I have told you before, Mavuto. It is not a good day to go outside. Do not even think of it," Sir Gregory replied, trying to control his temper. His eldest son had enjoyed testing him even before the revelation. "We will stay inside for now."

They had all convened in the boys' room before going back down to the secret room.

Mavuto was clearly against the idea. "These things, whatever they are, are not going to stop. You have said that yourself," he addressed his stepfather. "So what good is hiding in there going to do us? We should be out there, confronting them!"

"Enough!" Sir Gregory's voice was slightly raised. "I am not putting you and your siblings in danger by letting you go out there! You haven't the faintest idea of what metsus are capable of."

Nina jumped in, hoping to calm things down. "You have to listen to him, Mavuto. Those people are dangerous. You saw how strong that man was. Do you really want to put Joel in that kind of danger?"

Mavuto responded in a passive tone. "Nina, those things are dangerous and very strong. But, they can be killed. You have proven that. You have to understand that we can't stay here, no matter what he says. We are dead if we do. They already know we are in here. We stay, we die."

"And what do you know about killing a man? You think it is as easy as in those books you read? Stop behaving like a child and sit down!" said Sir Gregory, his patience expired.

"By the way, you are wrong about one thing, Sis," Mavuto continued, ignoring his stepfather. "I do not have to listen to him." With that, he stormed out of the room.

Everyone stood up at once. "Vuto, wait!" Nina was only a few steps behind Sir Gregory, who had already reached the living room and was just behind Mavuto. She reached the front entrance just as Sir Gregory, now outside, froze.

A few seconds later, he fell to the ground, volts of electricity running through his body. Dazed, Nina looked up at her brother, who was a few feet in front of her.

Mavuto had been staring at Sir Gregory. Now his head moved slowly up, towards his sister. His eyes looked pleadingly at Nina, as if he was asking for forgiveness. The teenage boy who had been defiant just a few minutes before was now a frightened little child.

The man who was holding Mavuto's head in his hands did not seem to care about all that. He was smiling, his pearl-white teeth contrasting against his dark-brown skin. His hands held Mavuto's head firmly, and, as Nina watched, the man's hands twisted slightly. Mavuto's head snapped and he gave a slight convulsive jerk and was still.

"No!" Nina screamed and started running toward her brother but something hard crashed into the back of her head. She started to fall, just as the man in front of her, still grinning, let go of her brother's head. Mavuto's body collapsed to the ground, and so did Nina.

State House, Lilongwe City

Principal Secretary Limbani Maloto looked like someone who had just taken a cold shower against his will. His face was contorted and his whole body was shaking. If anybody noticed, however, they did not show it. At that point, nobody in the room was paying attention to what anyone else was doing. All eyes were on the plasma screen.

It was total chaos. People were now screaming for their lives, and justifiably so. The flying objects were now releasing people. Or, at least, they looked like people. Whatever they were, it looked like killing humans was easy to them. Those who were slow in getting away from the gatherings were being slaughtered.

Thokozani Kanjala, minister of defence, was trying to say something to his boss. The president, however, just stood, paralysed, as he saw a man being bent in half and then torn apart.

The minister then turned to his principal secretary. "We need to move the President. He cannot stay here, it is a security risk. I will coordinate with the generals while you get the president's staff together. We have to act fast."

"Yes, I agree," said President Moto, startling everyone. "We have to act fast. We need to get our men ready and out there." He then turned momentarily to the army generals and police chiefs. "Get your men out there now!"

The president was about to turn his attention back to the defence minister when something on the television caught his eye.

One of the metsus had landed on top of the Clock Tower. Then, stretching itself to full height, it launched itself from the tower like a bird and went straight for a woman below.

The woman was sent crashing onto the tarmac road and the child she was carrying on her back went with her. The metsu was not finished. In one swift movement, it ripped the woman's right arm out of its socket, and with its foot, crushed the toddler's head.

The cameraman had seen enough. As blood gushed from the woman's gaping wound and the baby's head, the camera fell to the ground, still filming. Although the viewers could not hear her, they could tell that the woman was screaming. The metsu then slammed a fist into her neck and she fell back and lay still.

A sharp pain hit President Moto in the right side of his chest just as he was about to speak. It felt as if something was squeezing his heart, catching him off balance, and he put his hands on the large cedar table in the middle of the conference room to steady himself, without success. His chief of staff asked him if he was alright, but he just fell wordless to the floor.

He loved his country. He loved his people and he loved his family. On the day he had decided to run for president, Herbert Moto had made a promise to himself that he would put his country first, that he would do his best to serve and protect his people. And he had done exactly that, to the best of his abilities, until the past few days. Now as he lay face up on the plush carpet with his friend Limbani Maloto shouting for the state house doctor, President Moto was filled with an overwhelming feeling of failure.

VIII
13

When Sir Gregory opened his eyes he was disorientated. The first thing he saw was two of his stepchildren a few feet away from him. His mouth was dry and there was a distinct sound of African drums playing in his head, which brought immense pain. Nina and Joel were not moving.

Sir Gregory tried to go to them but as he got up, something heavy and rubbery slammed into his back, sending him back on the floor.

"I would advise you not to move again, muhiri," said a voice.

Sir Gregory looked up and the face that stared back at him only intensified his rage. With all the strength he could muster, he lunged at the man but only got a few feet forward. The stranger, with coffee-brown skin and a tall, lean body immaculately dressed in a grey suit, only laughed.

"I always did like your combative spirit, Kanoni. I hear the people around here call you Sir Gregory? Quite different from what we used to call you, eh? You still remember that your real name is Kanoni, don't you, muhiri?"

Sir Gregory managed to get up to his knees. "I am not your brother, Mushani. And if I could get to you right now, I would kill you." He looked around. They were in the same church he had been in only hours before. Father Fletcher was there, as were six of Mushani's men.

"You have to learn to let things go, muhiri. You knew this was going to happen. You have always known. It is actually the reason you are on this planet to begin with. The past is the past. Let it go and let nature take its course." Mushani smiled at the last part. "Yes, Kanoni, old friend, I have also been studying the ways of the gumas on this planet and their sayings. Writing the number 'eight' in roman numerals was actually my idea. I was hoping one of the gumas on this planet would figure out what it means. They seem more intelligent on this planet than the ones on ours."

"Let it go?" Sir Gregory was now getting his strength back. "After what you did to my family?"

Andrew Dakalira

"But *we* are your family, muhiri. You are one of us, remember?" Mushani walked over to where Nina and Joel were slowly beginning to stir. "But of course, you mean this family, your gumas. And they are waking up just in time, it would seem. I think they are badly in need of a short history lesson, don't you agree, muhiri?"

Chilinde Barracks, Lilongwe City

She could tell something was happening. Her guards had been cut down to two, and the high-ranking officers who had frequently come to question her were nowhere to be seen. Outside the door, she could hear orders being given and there was the sound of heavy boots hurrying about. It had started. She had to move.

"May I have some water?" She asked in the sweetest voice possible. It was a different guard this time and he brought her a cup without drawing his handgun. It was exactly what she had been waiting for.

She only had to pull and her hands were free of their chains and around the soldier's neck. The second guard, realising what was happening, opened fire. She gripped her captive's body with one hand using it as a shield, drew the soldier's gun with the other and fired. The second soldier fell just as three more men burst through the door.

She did not flinch, even as the soldiers fired at her, hitting her dead-body shield instead. She shot through the chains on her legs and then redirected her aim at the door. As the automatic gunfire cut through the revered men of the defence force, there was a child-like smile on her face and an evil glint in her eye. It was finally happening.

Chileka, Blantyre district

"I am glad you are awake, Nina. It is Nina, isn't it? Do help your brother up. It seems he is having difficulties. He must've been hit a little too hard."

Nina could not move. Her body felt stiff and she willed herself to shift a limb. Who was the man in front of her? All

322

she could see were his shiny black shoes and part of his grey trousers. Nina managed to tilt her head to her left. The back of her skull instantly protested, releasing a sharp pain that made her cry out.

Standing directly in front of Nina, Mushani only shook his head. "Help her up," he ordered two men who were behind him.

The men, also immaculately dressed, hauled Nina up and sat her on a pew. In spite of the headache that threatened to drag her down into unconsciousness, she managed to look around. This time, the scream which escaped from Nina's lips was not due to pain, but horror.

Lying on the cement floor in front of her were Joel and Father Fletcher. The latter was trying to get up, but it seemed that he too had difficulty moving his limbs. Joel had less trouble. He got up slowly, stared directly in front of him and started crying.

At the front of the church, Sir Gregory was being tied to the front of the pulpit, arms outstretched, directly facing Nina. His face a mixture of anger and grief, Sir Gregory looked at the man in the grey suit and then to the altar. There lay Mavuto's limp body flat on its stomach. In this position, he almost looked like he was only asleep, but Nina knew her brother was dead. She had watched while one of the things had broken his neck.

"Truly sorry about your brother," Mushani spoke, as if reading Nina's thoughts. "He was supposed to be alive and witnessing all this. But, I am sure he is with us in spirit, as you gumas on this planet would say. And if he is not," he gestured towards the pulpit, "at least he is with us in body."

"How dare you!" Father Fletcher's voice suddenly rang out throughout the church. The priest was slowly trying to rise to his feet. "You kill an innocent boy and make a mockery of it. Worse still, you make a mockery of God's temple! What kind of person are you? Remove that boy from the altar and untie that man!"

Joel started crying again. Nina, now able to move, went to her little brother.

Ignoring them, Mushani spoke directly to Father Fletcher. "May I remind you, priest, that I am not a person and neither is he." He pointed at the pulpit, but his eyes never left Father Fletcher's. "You have no authority over me. We are the reason you are here, not your god. You came here because we left you here, to breed, to multiply. You are ours, priest, and you would do well to remember that."

Father Fletcher was unmoved. "I am a child of God. By doing this, you incur God's wrath upon yourselves. Mark my words; your punishment shall be severe!"

"I admire your courage, priest, although I hardly see what your faith is based on. You do not wonder why your god has not saved you? Or maybe you need to pray, priest. Pray until something happens. That is what some of you Christians say, is it not? Well, prayer or not, something will happen here, priest." Mushani held Father Fletcher's head in his hands as he spoke. "You are going to die."

"Mushani," Sir Gregory spoke, his voice calm in spite of the rage he felt towards the man he was addressing. "Let them go and I promise to kill you swiftly. You will feel no pain."

Mushani was startled for a moment, then he laughed, the sound echoing in the church. "Kanoni, my friend, I forgot how humorous you used to be. You were quite the jester when we were little." He let go of Father Fletcher's head and turned to Sir Gregory. "But then again, you used to like me back then, before I killed your wife."

The only gasp that was heard in the church was Father Fletcher's, who was still trying to catch his breath after nearly being choked to death. Nina and Joel did not utter a word, even though both their mouths dropped open.

Seeing their reaction only pleased Mushani. "Yes, that story of how your mother was killed and why. Well, I would really like to talk about that, but I'm afraid we have wasted enough time here as it is."

Standing right in front of the pulpit, Mushani took out a knife from his trouser pocket. And then, from his jacket pocket, he produced a shining silver revolver. "The gun is for you, muhiri. But before I kill you, I am going to make you watch me cut their throats." He then turned to the children. "So, who wants to join mother and brother first?"

The answer came in the form of a loud gunshot outside the church. The words "take care of that" were on Mushani's lips when the door at the back of the church crashed open, followed by half a dozen men in military uniform and a civilian. More gunshots rang out and two of the metsus closest to the door fell to the floor.

Mushani was already firing. His revolver barked twice and one of the camouflaged men fell over dead. Then he turned around and fired at the pulpit just as a bullet hit him between his shoulder blades. But that only kept him down for a few seconds. Mushani leapt onto the nearest pew, knocking Nina out in the process, and launched himself at a window. Stained glass sprayed everywhere as he crashed through.

Onani was beside Nina in seconds, focused on her until the sergeant started barking out orders, calling for a medic. He looked up to see Sir Gregory carrying Mavuto in his arms. Onani did not have to be told that Nina's brother was dead.

"You came in the nick of time, son. You and your military friends," said Sir Gregory.

"I wish we had arrived sooner, sir," replied Onani, looking at Mavuto's body. "I do not think you remember me. My name is Onani. Onani Limani."

"I know who you are. You were at my wife's funeral. And Mavuto and Joel kept talking about Nina's police officer boyfriend."

There was an awkward silence for a few seconds as both men looked for something to say. It was only then that Onani noticed the elder man's shirt. Its navy blue colour could not hide the fact that Sir Gregory was bleeding profusely from his right side.

"You need to have that checked, sir. It does not look too good."

Sir Gregory only shrugged. "What I need right now is to take my children home. You should come too. There are a few things you need to know."

Onani shifted his gaze from Nina, who was now beginning to wake up, to her father. "Sir, you can't just walk away from what has happened here. There are a lot of questions that will require answers from all of you. You cannot leave."

"I am quite aware of that," Sir Gregory replied, appearing to be in a great deal of pain. "And I will explain everything to you. I know how to defeat your enemies. Surely that should interest you. Now, leave your army friends here to finish up and let's go home. I do not have much time left."

"I still don't understand. How exactly did you get here? You were supposed to be in Lilongwe, last I checked," said Nina.

Onani, tired as he was, began to narrate his story, leaving out that he was almost killed and that his assailant had every intention of hunting him down and finishing the job. Onani was quite sure that Nina did not want to hear about an attractive but deadly woman, no matter who she was. Not from Onani.

"Anyway, long story short, we saw dead people outside the church and decided to investigate. That's how we found you. Had the church been a little farther from the road, I would probably not have found you," Onani concluded, trying not to move since Nina's head was in his lap.

They made it back to the house and Nina had immediately gone to bed, at her stepfather's insistence. Sir Gregory had then ordered Father Fletcher to stay with Joel while he talked with Onani.

"So where is my father now?" Nina was now trying to get up. Onani gently eased her back onto the bed. "Actually, I wanted to talk to you about him. He is badly hurt but refuses to see a doctor. And," Onani hesitated, "he has told me stories that sound a bit outlandish. I would not have believed him until he gave me this."

Onani reached under Nina's bed and pulled out a large gun, which looked like an ordinary rifle, except this one had a line of blue liquid running along the barrel, making it glow. "All he said was that we will need these later. He gave me quite a few other weapons too. He got them all from his bedroom. Wouldn't let me in, though. He asked that you join him as soon as you woke up."

Nina knew that Onani wanted answers from her, answers which she either currently did not have or was unsure of. But right now, her family needed her. She got up from the bed and was about to leave the room when Onani spoke again.

"By the way, you should probably know that he has Mavuto's body with him."

She found him sitting on the floor in the secret room, cradling Mavuto's body. Only when Nina was right in front of him did Sir Gregory look up. "He always was a stubborn one, wasn't he? Just like your mother."

Nina badly wanted to comfort the man who had played the fatherly role for most of her life. But she could not. Not while he held her brother in his lap, seemingly oblivious to the fact that he was bleeding.

"Dad," Nina managed to speak. "You are bleeding. You need a doctor. We need to get out of here and get you to a hospital."

Sir Gregory looked at the red liquid dripping from his body onto the floor and slowly shook his head. "I do not need a doctor, child. It is already too late for me. But you and your brother need to get to safety. You cannot stay here."

Nina was not listening. "No, Dad, we need to leave, including you! All we have to do is find a hospital and you will be fine! We need you!"

"Enough of that, child! Right now, there are more important things for you to worry about. Joel needs you now. You are all he has. Be strong for him. There is nothing you can do for me but promise me one thing. Promise that you will look after him."

Nina looked at her stepfather and then slowly nodded.

"Tell your boyfriend to remember what I told him. He must relay the message to those in charge. And be more cautious. Mushani will probably have a lot more men with him now. You must be more careful." Sir Gregory paused for a moment. "Onani seems like a good man. I am glad I met him again, despite the circumstances." Nina now in tears managed a smile.

Father Fletcher descended the steps into the room. "I do not mean to interrupt, but the army people are outside. They say we need to leave." He went quiet as he took in the scene.

VIII

Sir Gregory looked at his only daughter, then at Father Fletcher. "Take care of my children for me, Father."

The priest looked at Sir Gregory, and he understood. "I will. God will look after us all."

Sir Gregory only smiled. "One more thing. Watch out for Salamona. Very dangerous, that one."

"Salamona? Who is he, one of your people?" Father Fletcher was genuinely alarmed.

"Not he, she. Try to avoid her at all cost. She is quite vicious, relentless. She does not believe in clean deaths." Then, remembering that his daughter was still present, Sir Gregory said no more. He looked at her one last time. "Go."

Nina and Father Fletcher came out of Sir Gregory's bedroom to find Onani holding little Joel's hand, a large bag slung over his shoulder. Onani immediately knew Sir Gregory was not coming with them.

Little Joel, however, did not. "Where's Dad?"

Father Fletcher said nothing, but sadly looked at Nina before going outside.

Nina knelt next to her brother, filled with deep affection. "Dad is with Mom and Mavuto now, Joel. They will be alright—they are together. And we'll be okay too, because they will be watching over us. Let's go, we will be alright."

She was the last person out of the house, and stopped to look at her childhood home, now a tomb for two of her family members. With tears in her eyes, she closed the door and left.

State House, Lilongwe city

There were four pairs of eyes in the room, three of which were focused on the tall, thin man in a grey suit. Limbani Maloto could not remember the last time he had seen the vice president. Chona had lost a lot of weight, a fact accentuated by the large chair he was sitting in.

The speaker of parliament spoke first. "We really don't have time to waste, so I'll get right to the point. The country has lost its leader. Now the constitution dictates that the Vice President takes over, but personally I have my reservations."

Vice President Chona's demeanour suggested he was not surprised. A faint trace of amusement shimmered in his eyes as the speaker continued.

"You have been charged with treason. Under the circumstances, we feel that letting you lead the country would not be the prudent course of action."

"If that's how you feel, gentlemen, then why am I here? Did you make me leave my residence and travel through the madness in the streets, just so you could ask me to step aside?" Vincent Chona did not wait for an answer. "I am well aware of the chain of command, Mr. Speaker. If I were to decline the presidency, then you would be next in line to take over. I will not let that happen, I assure you."

The fourth man in the room, the chief justice, detested politicians. "From a legal point of view, Vincent, nothing can stop you from ascending to the presidency. You have not been convicted of anything yet. Innocent until proven guilty."

"You have, however, made many enemies in the executive. Not many would be willing to work with you." Limbani Maloto's tone was accusatory.

"I have driven through the streets, Limbani. I have seen what those things are doing. We need a coordinated response. So you will forgive me if I do not give a rat's ass about who likes me or does not." Vincent Chona relished the shock on Maloto's face. "Our people need a leader. They need to know that the government is intact. Most important of all, our country must be defended. We need to show those bastards that they cannot just come to our planet and play God. So for now, I suggest we put our political differences aside and fight together." He smiled, pointedly, at Maloto. "The firings will come later."

The chief justice sighed. "First things first. I am going to need a bible."

Chileka, Blantyre district
The desultory movement of the military vehicle belied the urgency of its passengers' thoughts. None of them could take

VIII

their minds off what had happened within the past few hours. Worse still, everyone was afraid of what was about to come.

The truck ground to a halt at the makeshift roadblock. They all disembarked, ignoring the dead bodies, including the little boy and a tall, fat corpse perched on the metal rod blocking the road, its mouth a permanent sinister grin. They also ignored the dead soldier who was locked in a seemingly post-coital embrace with a hulking figure that still had its hands around his throat. What did get their attention was another military man, alive and in the company of spear and machete-wielding civilians.

"Glad to see you're still alive, Corporal," Onani spoke with genuine sincerity. Corporal Lanjesi Chimanga only gave a slight hint of a smile. "I had a little help staying that way, as you can see. Your car is still intact too."

"Enough of the chitchat, Corporal," the sergeant barked. "Where are our reinforcements?"

"There aren't any, sir," the corporal replied. "We have been ordered to return to the cities. That's where most of the trouble is. Closest city to us is Blantyre."

Onani spoke up immediately. "We're going with you."

"Like hell you are," the sergeant gruffed matter-of-factly. You have been reunited with your girlfriend, now get in your car and go home. Don't be in the way."

"This is not just your war, Sergeant." Nina's voice startled everyone. "These things have destroyed our homes, our families. They say they want to kill us, but I'll be damned if I'll just stand by and let them!" That brought a few cheers from the crowd.

The sergeant looked like he was about to blow a gasket. Corporal Chimanga spoke before the sergeant could. "Actually, sir, President Chona has authorised civilian involvement. He urged them to mobilise themselves and fight for their country."

"President Chona?"

"Yes, sir. He was sworn in about an hour ago. President Moto died of a heart attack."

331

"Well, that's just fantastic!" The sergeant then uttered a few unpalatables before continuing. "Fine, the civilians can come, but keep in mind that you are no longer my responsibility." To Onani, he said, "Follow us in that little white car of yours." Then, loudly enough for everyone to hear, "Let's kill these bastards!"

This time the cheers were louder. Even the soldiers joined in. Everyone was caught up in the euphoria. Everyone, that is, except Joel. He silently moved away from his sister, walking towards the smiling figure slumped over the roadblock. He was still looking at it when Nina noticed his absence and ran to get him. His little mind was fixated on the sergeant's words *'Let's kill these bastards'*.

War had begun.

VIII

Andrew Dakalira started writing in his teenage years. Some of his stories have been published by *Brittle Paper*, *Fundza*, the Africa Book Club website and africanwriter.com. His work also appeared in the first Africa Book Club anthology *The Bundle of Joy and Other Stories from Africa*. A three-time winner of the Africa Book Club monthly short reads competition, he lives in Malawi's capital city, Lilongwe.

An Indigo Song for Paradise

Efe Tokunbo Okogu

Dedicated to all those who've ever felt unloved, disrespected and/or profaned by wrong thoughts, false words and/or wicked deeds. The Devil may be happy but The Lord ain't never gonna be sorry. May we all know our true wealth, manifest the best of our ancestors and attain our true heart's desire. Big up your true self! Ashe!

#Hi5# *Message Begins*

WonCelo8 => HQ:

The following is a selection of the mind states of certain individuals we recorded during our latest visit to Planet Terra, in the reality we have designated RX42373, along one of the time-lines that we have been unable to track fully due to a temporal interference upstream.

As per the request of the Lady during our last gathering, we have presented this report in the fictional style common amongst the people of the space-time in question. We hope it is both entertaining and educational, if only as a snapshot of certain levels of vibration.

Message Ends **#FistBump#**

Efe Tokunbo Okogu

Prologue

Gutter Dice

In Paradise City there lived a rather odious little man by the unlikely name of Ohnoly Bab, whose function in life was to facilitate certain transactions which the authorities though profiting from, did not wish to seem connected to. We decided to scam him by posing as the perfect marks of a scam, the idea for which would magically appear in his mind as if inspired by the muse.

Unbeknownst to him, the muse in question was in fact my crew and I, performing with multiple props and the city as a backdrop, a finely choreographed...dance shall we say. A dance that his mind interpreted as a sweet little con, which when played out was designed to leave him and his employers considerably poorer.

The ensuing casualties, shortly after we vanished, would not be missed by the world. That was the plan in any case. What we failed to factor in was random collateral damage, though I suppose if we had, we would have been in a different line of work entirely.

My crew and I made the decision long ago to live as Kings and Queens by convincing people to give us whatever we wanted, in ways that made it seem as if the giver was choosing to do so and if they ever got wise, we always had numerous exit planned out. It was beautiful...for a while. And doomed to fail for all such beauty must wither, age and die.

The problem with any perfect plan is the unexpected.

As for the solution...well, that is the divine mystery within the heart of it all. The master key that unlocks all doors. (Un)fortunately it is hidden from view like a skeleton buried deep in the sand in the interzone between the City and the Wasteland, staring blankly into eternity. Can you imagine the light that those empty eyes see? The path of unconditional love manifesting through respect for one's true self and reverence for the ALL. I couldn't back then. But after our last score everything changed. I am no longer in the life. I am now truly alive for the first time, ever, experiencing a whole new reality full of magic and wonder, the illusions of which I used to employ in mesmerising my unsuspecting victims.

The way I see it, I'm already dead and all of life is a dream. The only question is how lucid I am. Perhaps it is all a con but if it is a cosmic con*spiracy,* the only thing the devil seems to want is to empty my soul that there might be space for it to be of use to the ALL, like an empty bowl whose functionality is in its open space which can be filled with whatever is necessary.

I am the rice bowl and God is the rice bowl maker. I am a fractal of the source of the rice, the bowl, and the very concept of the maker, the eternal mystery known to the ancients as the Dao. The word conspiracy means to breathe together. It means that we are the mysterious wizards behind the curtain, whose breath of life sends ripples through our perceptions.

Miss Took

Religion says know God and thus gain clues as to the nature of one's environment and true self. Philosophy says know thyself and thus gain clues as to the nature of one's environment and the ALL. Esoteric Science says the truth is out there and in you; seek and ye shall find.

Mainstream Science says it's all an unfathomable accident of some description which is probably this or that particular theory which will probably be disproved at some point in time if history is anything to go by. History says the theories are not theories but the facts according to the victors. His story: his version of events.

Fiction says when you're inspired by the muse and discovering another world, anything can happen, including the impossible. And what is more impossible than the fact that we even exist at all? Is it not a genuine miracle?

Before the beginning and after the end; before all beginnings and after all endings; exists the source of the primordial AAAUUUMMM, the vibration that creates the illusion most

337

call reality. In comparison to the source, we are as children playing at the bottom of a garden, glimpsing, but barely comprehending the mystery which makes the plants grow.

Perhaps the greatest crime ever pulled by Ignorance and Deceit in the name of Science and History is the perpetrating upon the minds of the people, the meme that life is not sacred. In the name of Religion and Philosophy, THEY managed to make the people believe in dogma over living divinity, thus losing faith in the power of the heart and forgetting that we are the mystery.

Tell me, hueman, can you conceive of anything more beautiful in all the cosmos than the mysterious?

As for fiction, at its best it can shine a light upon the strange dream we call reality and illuminate for the conscious mind, that which the soul already knows. At its worst? Well, the state of Babylon, our sworn enemy, is but the reflection of the worst in us all. It only exists because we created it, just like fiction. Paradise, they call this city-state. What a bad joke. A state cannot be governed without a heart. And a heart is more than flesh and blood; it is emptiness powered by pure love.

An Indigo Song for Paradise

1: You know the score

Ecila

My name is Ecila and I'm not from the city. Let me repeat that, I'm not from the city. I grew up in a village surrounded by wild fields in an abundant valley. I value the memories of those days like a bee treasures honey or TerraCorp loves money.

I often spend my time remembering and daydreaming of the day when I finally return. Everyone will be there to welcome me. Especially Chi. Sweet Chi. But it's been so many years since the storm hit the village and washed my happy little life away.

I know it is folly, to waste my life away on such daydreams but it is my sweetest vice in this strange new world that feels older than the gods; this mechanical jungle full of beasts in the sleeves of men.

The village was spared the brunt of the storm. No one died and there was little irreparable damage. But the next day, while surveying the aftermath from the top of Turtle hill, I saw a strange glint in the distance.

It was only a couple of days away so after repairing the roof of my auntie's house and helping my neighbours clean the wreckage from our village, I decided to go and explore. I went alone as I have done many a time.

I arrived at the source of the glint, a large metallic structure unearthed by the storm which had clearly been far fiercer here than in my village. Fierce enough to excavate this strange leftover of some lost civilisation from within its tomb in the earth.

Who knows how many aeons it had lain there under the earth, slowly dreaming in the soft womb of creation. It looked like a cracked dragon's egg glinting in the morning sun. The dammed thing should have stayed buried. Or I should have been less curious, less adventurous. I was a man but I was young; little more than a boy. I had not yet made love to a woman but I was looking forward to that changing. Chi and I were… Not that it matters now. All that was years ago and worlds away.

As I walked around the artefact, I began to hear strange sounds: voices, echoes, warbles, and other unfamiliar noises. I turned around attempting to tune into the source and suddenly I was somewhere else.

Here.

To say it was the greatest shock of my life would be like saying Para City is a fucked up place. Nothing but the goddamned truth. I thought I had entered the land of the dead. But where were the ancestors and Orishas?

I was standing at a crossroads not meant for mortal men to cross. Large insect-like beasts breathing foul smoke were whizzing by, their translucent bellies filled with people.

Giant metallic men strode around streets overshadowed by buildings so tall their roofs were lost in the clouds. There were other people at the crossroads, dressed in strange garments made of unfamiliar materials in odd designs. Several were looking at me as if I had just appeared out of thin air. I stepped backwards and onto another man's shoes. He glared and shoved me away.

I bounced from one person to another till I emerged onto the path of the beasts and they were racing towards me. I froze like a rabbit or deer startled by lightning. As I did so, one of them almost crashed into me. I could see the faces of the people it had consumed distorted behind its translucent face. It squealed to a stop a mere hand's breadth from me and screamed. A long loud HOOOOONNNK!

My heart leaped ten feet into the air and took my body along for the ride. More of the beasts stopped and the people began to walk across the white lines of the crossroads, many looking at me like I was crazy.

The noise in the air was deafening. A cacophony of strange trills and howls. I was swept along by the people. Everyone was in a rush to get somewhere important. I had never seen so many people, all different shades of melanin from ebony to tanned leather—though in my village we have a much wider range of hues, all colours of the rainbow, I myself am blue-black.

To the streets, I was just another lunatic and it wasn't long before they locked me away. The police beat me to a bloody pulp then dragged me off to an insane asylum. I told them my story and they pumped me full of drugs that clouded my mind and weakened my body.

They tortured me for months with electrical shocks and strange music played at random intervals, feeding me at odd times, turning on the bright lights for hours then leaving me in darkness for what felt like days. Eventually I lost all sense of reality.

One day, it was suddenly over. I was moved by two huge attendants with electric batons to a ward with other patients, where natural sunlight filtered through the windows and there were pleasant nurses and doctors. It was mostly peaceful but I remained on edge. The disparity between the two worlds was almost worse than being in the dungeon. It was as if the world was pretending it never happened.

Afterwards, they calmly explained to me that I was delusional. "There's nothing outside the city but a wasteland. No hueman being could survive out there. Your memories are false, an elaborate fantasy created by a mind that can no longer cope with reality.

"While we admit that it's odd you are unregistered, such things are not unknown. Perhaps you were abandoned as a child and grew up underground. That might explain the strange bluish hue of your skin. But you are from the city. After all, you do speak Engrish even though your accent is funny."

Maybe they're right. Maybe I am crazy. Maybe the language I'm speaking is Engrish and not !#$&%=?*¡. Like the doctors said, either I'm insane or the rest of the world is. "But this city is crazy," I replied. That roused a small chuckle from the strangers who held my fate in their hands.

It was at the asylum that I heard the tale of Paradise City. But first they showed me a map that had no place for peaceful villages surrounded by lush nature. On their map, there is one city, home to several hundred million souls. Para City squats like a parasitic insect in the trigger of a vast gun-shaped continent.

The rest of the world is a desert, surrounded by dark oceans that look like congealing blood. It was once the greatest city in the Empire of Man, a great civilisation that flourished across the world. But when the last emperor departed Terra in a spaceship along with his entire court to colonise a distant planet, the empire fragmented into city states constantly jostling for supremacy.

The emperor took with him the greatest minds in their respective fields from science to philosophy to the arts, as well as the most gifted athletes, along with many secret technologies no longer operable now that the operators were gone. The war amongst those left behind for the few remaining resources was inevitable.

When the dust settled, Para City was all there was left standing. She defeated her enemies but nearly destroyed the planet in the process. The city was a semi-autonomous colony of machines that managed themselves as best they could alongside the people.

One day in the future, when the open wound of radioactive wasteland healed and receded, huemen would once again venture out of the city to reclaim the desert. One day... so they say.

For now, Paradise City aka God's Clock, aka the PC, aka Amerika, is my home. Officially I am of 'no fixed abode' but I spend most of my time in Freaktown, a barrio full of hustlers, musicians, bums, poets, geeks, griots, healers, preachers, dealers, players, gunslingers, gangsters, fiends, stick-up kids, hookers, clowns, revolutionaries, and freaks of multiple denominations, all loving and warring each other and the world in which they live, some taking the game seriously, others taking the game real seriously.

I like Freaktown for a few reasons, number one being it's got a free park; some local kids hacked the force field, the city occasionally fixes it but Freaktown kids got skills. There's an energy down here that you don't find in most of the PC. Folk in Freaktown are off the clock. Period.

Seven years I've been here in Amerika. Seven long years of dodging death, duelling with fate, battling my own heart. I've killed three times since I've been here. Three hearts that will never beat again, three pairs of eyes and ears that will never see another sunrise or hear the sound of a loved one breathing. The first man was a drunk by the name of Catswail who came after me because I was talking to his lady. He took me by surprise at a dice game and I shot him in the belly with his own gun as we rolled around in the dust.

I had no interest in his woman whatsoever. No one has yet to replace Chi in my heart and I doubt anyone ever will. I knew, even then, I knew that I ought to let her go. That holding on to her was the source of all my misery and pain. That I would never find her in the bottom of a cheap bottle no matter how hard I looked.

The second man was also a drunk. A man called Deal who mistook me for another man who owed him some money. He had a switchblade but poor balance; I threw him off the roof of an apartment building that was days away from being knocked down. I remember Big Bola wouldn't stop complaining for days that I'd ruined a perfectly good barbeque.

The third time was a trio of rich guys who liked to set bums on fire and post the videos on WhoTube. A group of us caught them pouring gasoline over Busqrat one night. Two got away; we beat the third one to death. It didn't take long.

It's taken me a while to accept the nature of my new reality. Sometime after I first got here and before the boys in white took me to the asylum, I remember kneeling down in the middle of an abandoned lot, screaming at the sky.

Why me!? Tears streaking down my face. *What have I done to deserve this fate!? Am I cursed or simply unlucky? Sometimes I feel schizophrenic, unsure as to the true nature of reality. Is this all a strange dream?* I was giving up all hope. It was like dying, a deep well of nothing in me waiting to be let out.

I was in the asylum for almost nine months. When I got out, I was a new man. A registered citizen. They gave me a bed in a halfway house for a few weeks then I was back out on the streets. They were no longer confusing to me. It was simple: I was in a jungle made of concrete, glass, and steel, far from home. A jungle full of burning unrestrained life, all running towards death like blind bulls towards a heifer in heat.

Or maybe I was amongst the walking dead, huemen somehow tricked and bullied into living like animals. Worse even, for animals are innocent whereas huemen ought to know better. And I was one of them. Wandering like a ghost, daydreaming of being back with Chi.

The only way out of the city was to go into the city of my heart. If the village was lost to me forever then the city would be my village. I wandered her streets and listened; for the silence that I knew lay behind her chaos; for the rhythm and rhyme in the gaps betwixt gunshots and wet thuds; for the music of her soul.

Deep within me, at a crossroads in the middle of nowhere, I hear the sound of a lonesome wind howling in the wasteland beyond. I have been all over this city. Roamed from one barrio to the next until I ended up here in FreakTown. I guess my legs finally got tired.

Babylove Brown

I pressed my back into the wall blending into the shadows of the alley, my gun gripped tight in my fist. I was breathing hard, sweating from the run. I didn't dare pop my head out yet to see what was going on so I took a few deep breaths to calm my racing heart then opened my mouth slightly, sent out an ultrasonic burst then listened. I could see-hear the sound of sirens and the tell-tale clanking of a cop in a mecha running through the streets looking for us as my echo returned with the locations of various objects. I'm no mutant, I don't think, but I learned from some of the best as a child.

An Indigo Song for Paradise

I hadn't been spotted yet but there were airborne drones searching for me and the rest of the crew. I was wearing camo and an airfilt mask, but the drones had gait recognition software and we'd all been captured on camera back at the TerraCorp labs.

As the sound of the mecha moved away, I popped my head out of the alley. It was a fairly busy street and I blended quickly into the crowd. At the corner I saw a TerraCorp mecha heading my way and I spun around then ducked into the corridor between two shops selling electronics and mystery meat.

The corridor led to stairs which I followed till the seventh floor where I emerged onto a mezzanine overlooking an exogene fruit 'n veg market. I walked to the doors at the far end which led me into a food area. I wove my way through customers and staff, then through another set of doors and into an area full of artisans with their clever little contraptions, all wonderful colours, melding modern technology with traditional designs. I walked past the elevator and took the stairs back down towards street level.

My phone beeped on the third floor and I clicked the stud in my ear.

After a moment of silence, Low's adrenaline charged voice said, "Three minutes," then he hung up.

Two minutes and forty nine seconds later, I walked out onto the street just as the van we'd jacked for the job pulled up. The side slid open and I jumped in. We rolled on like nothing was nothing.

Low and Casey were in the back and Tealson was driving. Moha was still out there somewhere. As we threaded our way through traffic, I pulled out a small black bag from inside my jacket and tossed it to Low. We made eye contact. Respect. Bless. One of his long lanky arms snaked out and caught it in mid-air, his dark angular face expressionless. Casey was dialling Moha on the screen, his high yellow face a little red from the run, his brow creased in concentration, the corners of his mouth expressing a touch of worry. Moha picked up and the sound of his breathing came through with sirens in the background. His position popped up on the screen. I leaned over to look.

"Motherf..."

Moha was in an office building, trapped inside a cordoned off area. Police and corp security were searching and people were being slowly evacuated and searched.

"Drop the bag, preferably somewhere hidden and retrievable and walk. We're on the corner of Desolation and Fourth. Don't forget to walk funny," Low said, ended the call, and the little red dot vanished from the screen.

Tense minutes passed.

"Maybe we should call him again," Casey suggested.

"Let's wait a few more minutes. Don't want the cops or TerraCorp to track the signal," Low answered.

We waited. It was almost a game, seeing who would crack first. Two minutes later I said, "Call him."

Low dialled the number again. Moha picked up the phone, his breathing erratic, his location barely changed from the last call.

"I been shot," Moha's voice sounded weak and in pain. "Didn't say nothing cause I thought I could make it... {huff huff}...There's a lot of blood and a lot of mechas...I ain't gonna make it. Get the fuck out." We listened to the wet sticky sound of Moha coughing. It sounded like his lungs were leaping out his chest, one grisly chunk at a time.

"We're not going to leave you," Low said, "just hang tight, okay?" He disconnected the call and turned to face us. His eyes were grim, stress bruised.

"We need him. We all got out of TerraCorp with a different piece of the device. We need his part for the damned thing to work."

"What you saying, Legs won't pay?" Tealson asked from the front seat.

"Oh he'll pay. But without Moha's piece, he'll try to stiff us."

"Fuck we gonna do?" I asked.

346

"How 'bout we drive in, grab him and drive out. Shoot down anyone gets in the way," Tealson said.

"You seen how many mechas there are out there?" I asked. "What you got a death wish or something?"

"Look, we can't sit here all day with our dicks in our hands," Low said. "We gotta do something."

"What about the device?" Casey asked.

"What about it?" I asked.

"Let's put what we got together and see what it does." Casey suggested.

In response to our curious glances, he said, "Reality displacement. In the lab where I got my piece of the device, there was a bunch of equations on a screen. At the top of the screen it said 'Reality displacement.'"

"Reality Displacement? What the fuck is that?" I asked, "teleportation?"

"There's been a lot of street-chatter about that lately actually," Tealson said, swivelling around to present us with his broad face, wide nose and thick lips, peeking out from his immaculately groomed beard that blended in with his large afro. "Black tech alphemists have been vanishing. Some heavy paranoia underground. You know how many players would give half their kingdoms for that kinda edge?"

We all looked at each other. We had to get Moha out somehow. When in doubt think outside the box. After all, his part was connected to ours. Maybe we could just magic him home.

We began opening the little black bags containing the pieces of an experimental machine we'd stolen from different labs in TerraCorp's labyrinthine R&D department. The operation had gone smoothly except for the most important part. Our getaway.

After a few false starts, we managed to piece the thing together, the hole where Moha's section should have been, *clearly* visible. The thing looked like a mix between an organic saxophone, a fat man's exotic staff, and a melted bazooka made of calcified alien flesh.

"What does it do?" I asked.

"Don't know," Low replied.

"It looks like…I don't know what it looks like," I said.

Obram

My old man always said, 'No one owes you a living.' I took that to mean 'fuck off kid', so I did. Signed up to TerraCorp straight outta high school. I joined the security department because I always wanted to ride my own mecha. Sure, I could wait until I was as rich as I planned to be, but aside from the cops, the only folks I'd ever seen ride mechas were actors in the movies and corp security guards.

If you've ever seen my ugly mug you'll know, a dead pig's got a better shot in Stellarwood than I do. As for the police department, let's just say they ain't popular in my barrio, Jugglers Pass. My aunty Bonnie also works at Terracorp. She's upstairs in admin. We have lunch together sometimes which is nice.

I come from a family of vampires on my mother's side. A lot of folk hate us. They call us palefaces and whitey and cracker and blame us for every goddamned thing wrong under the sun, including funnily enough, depleting the ozone layer and altering the electromagnetic field in such a way that most vampires were killed off. A low melanin count is not conducive to health in the twentieth century.

According to most history books, my ancestors were responsible for nearly destroying the planet. Maybe so, but what's that got to do with me. I wasn't there. I'm just a nigga like everyone else, trying to survive in the PC.

Growing up as a kid was hard. We lived in Romania for a while then moved on to Jugglers Pass when I was eleven. In Romania, we were treated differently. No one really messed with me but I didn't really have any friends either. On the one hand I was popular but on the other I wasn't close to anyone at school. Was it because I was half vampire, half negro? I guess so but to tell you the truth I have few memories of those days. In Jugglers things were different. I had to fight.

348

An Indigo Song for Paradise

My folks were both blues musicians. Papa sang and played the guitar. Mama sang too and played the harmonica. They spent a lot of time in FreakTown. I loved going down there with them. If it was a school night, they'd usually leave me with Mrs Gonzalez, the Witherspoon's maid, and her twin daughters, Mona and Mango. I still see them now and again. But on the weekends, Mom would use her natural sunscreen concoction—brewed by an old witch who was friends with Pops from way back—and we'd get in the old junker, drive out of Romania through Dhoti, then take the Nawa underpass to Jugglers up through Ozu to end up in FreakTown.

Out of all their songs, my favourite one recorded, with my father singing in a hiccupping staccato style and my mother backing him up with her sweet barbershop croon, went like this:

> *Baby, when you're sad (don't wonder why)*
> *I swear I hear the angels cry (love don't die)*
> *Threw a spear into cupid's heart (screw that baby!)*
> *Now his head's on a stick just for you (love you babe!)*
> *and now his heeeaaad (yeah he dead)*
> *is on a stiiicckkk (now that's sick)*
> *just for you! (thank you!)*

My parent's story is one of love overcoming the odds. She lived in privileged Romania, one of the last vampire enclaves. He was a handyman straight outta Jugglers, where in the words of Old Devil God 'We always go for the jugular/slash open arteries to reveal the art of murder.'

When her folks found out, they were upset. There were tears, raised voices, threats, attempted bribery, and more tears. In the end it was decided that the young couple would marry and live in a small house in Romania that belonged to an eccentric uncle who recently died without any children of his own. It was conveniently out of the way. I went to an exclusive private school and was the odd one out. A drop of colour in the privileged world of the last vampires.

Grandpa died when I was eleven. Grandma basically threw us out. She'd had enough of the embarrassment. It hadn't diminished with time as she'd hoped but had grown into a most burdensome sore that refused to heal. We'd had enough of Romania by that point anyway. In one way or the other, we were all ready to leave our gated community.

It could have been a paradise if we were not reminded regularly in some small way or another that we were not truly welcome. The only reason my parents stayed so long was for me. They wanted me to get a good education. My favourite classes were Philosophy, Martial Arts, and Engineering.

School was different at St James. The work was easier and I blended in a lot more because Jugglers was a multicultural community. I spent a lot of time in the sun in Jugglers and my skin darkened to the point where a lot of kids looked like me. My schoolmates eventually found out that moms was white though and I got teased…bad.

"Nigga's Mama look like a pus bag! She one big ol' pimple! No wonder he an only child. His papa scared to squeeze her too tight! Afraid she might go splat! Got Milk! Ha ha ha!" Shit like that. I got into lots of fights defending my mama's name but then so did a lot of kids. 'Your Mama' jokes were a common game. The trick was not to get riled up but come back with a badass response like, "Yo mama so fat, her waistline is the equator," or "Yo mama so scary, she give xombies nightmares," or "Yo mama so nasty, she gave your pops a blowjob then kissed you goodnight."

Most kids were cool with me though and I eventually made a few friends. And despite the teasing, everyone who got to know my Moms loved her. She was the kindest soul in all the world, her heart open to all who needed love, from stray kids to lonely old folk.

We lived in an old building that Death Star—the department of services—had given up on, so the residents fixed it up themselves. We were one of the first to stop paying council taxes and get away with it.

After graduation, I considered college because my grades were pretty good and a scholarship was a genuine possibility. Then I found out about the fraternities and their *paleface parties*. Racist niggas would paint themselves to look like vampires, straighten their hair if they hadn't already, and pretend to walk, talk and act like white folk. Fuck that shit.

TerraCorp training was hype. We started out with exoskeletons and those of us that passed moved on to the mechas. I was a natural, top of my class, and they assigned me to the xombie squad. My team and I spend most of our time out in the desert hunting xombies. The eggheads in the lab prefer we bring 'em in alive; they're trying to isolate the agent that animates them.

There's fame and fortune waiting for the corp that figures out what makes xombies tick. How do they survive out in the desert without succumbing to radiation poisoning? How do they sustain their population out in the wasteland? Can we train them to perform tasks for us? Why do they all die so soon after arriving and being caged? These were their biggest questions.

As for commercial applications, xombies were good for several things. Medical students trained on their corpses. After all they were no different from huemen physiologically but for their skins which were grey and had the ability to lighten and darken into beautiful fractal patterns suggestive of many 'scapes and levels of worlds.

Xombies have superior physical abilities, though my Martial Arts instructor would have said that anyone could do what they do if they believed in themselves and worked relentlessly for it.

Xombies communicate by a combination of strange resonant sounds that mimic nature and the city. If it is a language, it must be one of subtle metaphors where a tree falling in a forest and a bell tolling combine to represent some unstoppable force composed of love or something.

As for their genes, all attempts to observe their DNA have led to strange results. According to the scientists, instead of DNA they have strange micro-singularities that pop in and out of existence. The scientists have dubbed it metaronin.

Automobile companies used them as crash test dummies (they damage similar to huemen but can heal from multiple compound fractures and bleeding, both internal and external, within hours). Pharmaceutical companies harvested their body parts and extracted various elixirs for use in a multitude of products, including, if the urban legends are true, food for the masses.

I reckon xombies must live on cactus and lizards which are poisonous to huemen, but no one has yet to see them eat, drink, shit, or fuck, and no traces of any such activity have ever been found, out in the wasteland or in their bodies. One thing's for sure. No matter how many we bag, more keep popping up out there. They're not really dangerous or ugly like on screen.

What I mean is they don't attack huemen like in the movies and their flesh isn't all rotten and falling off. That only happens to them after we give them over to the white coats upstairs. Everyone's seen the videos on WhoTube of caged xombies acting like the ones in the movies, but they're not actually like that in the wild.

Xombies are incredibly strong and fast and do defend themselves when our crew rolls up, but we're heavily armed and good at what we do. Our kill to capture ratio is just over 1:1 which is better than most crews. Some of the other crews regularly kill twice as many as they bag alive.

Fanta reckons xombies must have some kinda super sense that lets them douse hidden underground sources of water. He says he saw what looked like the entrance to an underground tunnel once but it was during a sandstorm and the cams were malfunctioning.

Some scientists believe they're able to metabolise the energy of the sun in some way. Others claim that xombies don't actually exist. That they are in fact empty spaces of grey nothingness that just happen to be shaped like huemen. Why? According to this faction, because we huemen observe them. They claim that the patterns we sometimes observe in xombie skins are simply reflections of our own inner psyches, like inkblot tests; that xombies are quantum phenomena of our strange reality, conjured up by the ghosts of sins past, wandering the wasteland. Like the desert was more than a desert or something. Crazy shit, right? I've heard them arguing in the cafeteria about all sorts of weird ideas.

Our mechas are top of the line, equipped with a wide range of weapons as well as a state of the art life support system that takes care of all our basic needs. We go out on ten day patrols, the four of us, Padox, Fanta, Killer, and me, living in our giant mechas, tracking xombies. They come equipped with rations and supplies that can last a fortnight so we plan our ops carefully to make sure no one dies out there. Xombies tend to be solitary creatures by nature and it takes time to track and bag 'em.

We'd just returned to the city from a patrol on which we'd bagged four and were planning to go out celebrating when the alarms went off and Mack burst into the changing room out of breath, his fat face streaked with sweat, his double chin bouncing around.

"Gunslingers have broken into the labs and stolen a prototype. Killed one of the guards. They're going nuts upstairs. You're all on overtime. Triple pay and six months wages as bonus to anyone who bags the bad guys. Back in your mechas, now!"

This was not good. I had a meeting with a very dangerous man known as Legs, a Freaktown hood who'd recently bought out my bookie. My old bookie was a decent man who gave a man a chance to pay off his debt. He rarely got violent. Legs, on the other hand had threatened to break my legs if I didn't pay him back yesterday. I only had half the money but I was hoping he'd give me an extension. After all, I couldn't pay if I wasn't mobile.

"Did you say six months?" Killer asked.

On the other hand, if I got that bonus, I could afford to pay Legs back and pocket a touch on the side. I really needed to quit gambling. It wasn't good for my health or sanity.

"Yes, you heard me, now back in your mechas, all of you!"

"Back in my mecha? Man, fuck you! I got a date tonight. You know how long I been waiting to bang this bitch. A month, nigga, a month!" Padox shouted.

"You talking about Rhonda?" Killer joked "Sheeeit nigga, I banged that gal the first night I met her. You need to step up your game, son."

"Man, fuck you. I know she ain't even fucking with your stingy ass. Jerry curls dripping all over the place. You so stingy, I bet you use engine oil on your hair. Get the fuck outta here, you banged Rhonda. Old men in retirement homes get more play than you do!"

I kissed my teeth. Dumb niggas elevating pussy while disrespecting the womb. Didn't they know Rhonda was someone's daughter, someone's sister? Didn't they know she could have been their Mama in another life?

"Look I know y'all just got back from the outside but this is big. When's the last time anyone got triple pay?" Mack asked.

"But only the cops are allowed to ride in this zone."

"Don't worry, this is bigger than the cops. We're talking government contracted tech here. Suit up, mount up, and ride out people."

We looked at each other and shrugged. I got out of my civvies and back into my suit then joined the rest in heading to the hangars. I saw panic on the faces of some of the folk upstairs and we grew grim.

"What got taken?" I asked.

"Don't know. They're not saying. But we got the perps on cam. We'll patch 'em through to you once you're mounted along with a proximity sensor that'll activate if you get within a hundred yards of any of the pieces that got taken," Mack answered.

"Listen Mack," Padox said, "our mechas need to be overhauled between missions."

"We don't have time for that. If you don't feel your mecha is up to it, you can ride a spare but I know how you riders feel about your mechas so it's up to you. In any case, they're already fuelled and waiting."

"Hey Bra," Fanta's voice called out as I climbed up my mecha's right leg and swung myself into the cockpit, "I ain't never hunted a hueman before."

I said nothing as I strapped myself in, closing the chest casing. The goggles on my flight suit went dark then lit up with a view of the hangar from my mecha's perspective. I cycled through the cams then ran a quick systems check.

"Alright my niggas," I called out. "Let's see what we're up against."

I activated the profile sent by Mack. It had five clips of different individuals breaking into different labs, stealing specific machines and escaping via multiple exits. They were good, fast and efficient, professional gunslingers.

2: Protest

Ecila

As a child we did not go to school, or rather school never ended. We learned all we needed to know by observing our environment. We could and did ask many questions of the world; we spoke with the elders and watched the masquerades—which one day we would also dance. We told each other the stories of our favourite characters, and played wonderful games.

Life was simple. We lived in tune with our nature and our world.

The people of this city on the other hand are strange and twisted. Many are clearly insane, little more than meat robots programmed and conditioned by their schools and screens to fulfil certain functions. Powerful wizards and their invisible demons keep them mesmerised with infernal devices. Or so it seems to me but then maybe I'm just paranoid. On the other hand who isn't in Para City. The people here do not know how to use the tools they possess and are thus possessed by them.

There was some kind of protest going on in the free park in FreakTown, people are waving placards and agitating. Chants of "TerraCorp is a terrorist! They got all our names on the death list!" and "No Justice! No Peace! Fuck the Police!" Some kids were breaking, stomping, krunking, and tricking; there was a live band and a couple of sound systems clashing and melding; also a table laden with free food and juices— fresh and wholesome, cooked with love. Freaktown is a green place and the communal lots feed a lot of folk. I walked past some MCs freestyling, taking turns to flow over a megaphone.

> *What we even doing in Para city?*
> *(The nitty gritty but pretty*
> *Where people nice then do you dirty*)*
> *(*Offstage:Verse Supreme)*

An Indigo Song for Paradise

Big Birds packing heaters
KKK-dicts and their dealers
lost my papers, chased by mechas
got evicted, making no paper…

I have learned a lot from these urban griots over the years as I roamed from one barrio to another; the best of them hardly get any play on the radio. A troupe of youths painted grey like xombies, with fractal patterns that looked like trees and coastlines and ghost-like dancers passing through each other like the wind, began to perform a co-ordinated routine.

Sitting on a corner, smoking trees don't wanna
do a goddamned thing but be a King,
Hanging with my boys just got out of sing-sing,
What the fuck you want pig, we ain't got no bling!
Scoping the street life, too wise for the strife,
But it's time to make a choice,
Brother roll the dice…

They gambled with our lives,
Sold our futures to feed their tribe
Why we acting the fools?
Getting used like bad tools?
They living it up in Romania
We down here in Transylvania,
Being bled to feed the greed of the system
I hate all 'em vampires - I say we just kill 'em.

As one, the people began to walk the streets slowly weaving their way into increasingly commercial areas. The rundown apartment buildings and abandoned properties were replaced with more gloss and shine but the corruption within was still evident.

On the news, they say the city is running out of resources. So why don't they stop throwing away what little they have? Why do they waste their diminishing resources on killing the

357

competition when they could be co-operating. Why waste time, money, and honour, gambling on a system that regularly throws away as waste a third of all it produces, cutting corners and valuing cash over lives, as if there aren't poor and hungry folk that should reclaim their stolen inheritance.

We crossed a large roundabout, Trapper Joe's Circle, and I began to appreciate how large the crowd truly was as more people converged from various side streets.

This ain't got nothing to do vampires, son,
We all responsible for this planet we on;
While TerraCorp be out there terrorising the planet,
They smiling in our faces like we was some punk ass bitches
How about ya stop treating Pacha Mama like a ho?
Nasty motherfuckers worse than the po po!

You got fluoride in our water calcifying our pineal glands
Closing up our third eyes like rusted clams
Chemtrails in the air poison the atmosphere
GMO food rots our guts – it just ain't fair!
The same folk that be fucking up Paradise
Are basically raising our kids – do that sound wise?
When we gonna wake up and take back what's ours?
Do we really wanna wait until the final hour?

We were in the Jekalo, a semi-industrial neighbourhood full of warehouses. Some police had shown up but they were keeping their distance. We were being joined by more people all the time as we went along.

All sorts of folk, different ages and dark races—I even spotted a few palefaces, I mean vampires, merging with our mob. It was as if they'd been all waiting for this moment, stewing over their rage, waiting for the coming release like an alien vomiting up so called hueman food, pumped full of our clever poisons that killed us slow while preventing the crops

358

from withering in their proper time, fattening up the animals
and keeping them from showing the signs of their internal rot
as they rooted in their own filth in our dungeons and awaited
their own slaughter.

> *TerraCorp is the evilest gangster that ever lived,*
> *a wild beast mutated into a money-making machine,*
> *hunting in the city in the middle of the night,*
> *an armed robbing serial killer, you ready to die?*
> *Cos it's your money AND your life,*
> *Won't ask you twice...*
>
> *Modern day slavery*
> *but niggas got no bravery -*
> *You got children making sneakers*
> *and mining for minerals,*
> *sent by grown men acting like infants*
> *with toys that can destroy planets*
>
> *An adman's a mask for a completely mad scientist*
> *implanting memes in minds like trojans and viruses;*
> *fucking with your software till your hardware is*
> *divided,*
> *pillaged and conquered like your very brain was*
> *guided*
> *to your own destruction by a completely one-sided*
> *bullshit tale sold to colonise your mind dead.*
>
> *Stay cool, baby, we rugged and raw*
> *Swarm like killer hornets, wave crash on shore*
> *TerraCorp going down, break down the door*
> *Rolling with the braves, tooled up for war...*

By the time we arrived in Orelem there were tens of
thousands of us. Around me I saw people filled with a
combination of elation and grim determination. There was
music and chanting in the air and a masquerade was dancing

through the streets, the multiple huemen that animated the spirit leaping up and down in wild but co-ordinated movements.

A large float rode by powered by a dozen pedalling teenagers, their muscle power generating and giving life to an elaborate diorama that told the story of the tragic death of another innocent young man murdered at the hands of the police. Other teens were handing out IPGs, Improvised Protective Gear, I helped myself to shin and forearm guards, and a chest and back plate attached with thick cord and a crash helmet.

> *Are we really living or we just slowly dying?*
> *Are we thriving or we just surviving?*
> *While they play mind games and get lost in illusions*
> *We be switching masks, fuck you and your delusion*
> *No I ain't your slave, I'm a free man, Terra!*
> *You step to my set, you get took, Corp!*
>
> *Fuck you TerraCorp, we don't co-operate*
> *We ain't buying your products,*
> *We know about your tax deducts;*
> *First driving the prices down*
> *undercutting the local shops,*
> *then driving the prices up*
> *and feeding the poor folk your slop;*
> *Little babies dying cause your milk gave 'em*
> *cancer!?*
> *Die motherfucker, you unnatural disaster!*

We were almost downtown. Shouts of "Po Po" and "Watch your back," filtered from the front lines.

> *What a waste of talent, a low down dirty shame,*
> *How many niggas lost seeking fortune and fame?*
> *I know life's a game, can't afford to be lame,*
> *So I embrace the pain like she was my dame;*

An Indigo Song for Paradise

Kane slew Abel while Seth led to Enoch,
Righteousness was born when the Dao was lost,
We fucking up the world – it's crazy to me
How beautiful a rainbow on an oil spill can be;
Will we ever have our fill of making the planet ill?
Are the old gods gonna have to rise up and kill...

...huemanity – does that word mean nothing?
Were we really fronting when we took over like god-
kings?
Top of the food chain, the planet is ours
Got no more predators so now we warring on Gaia?
Bunch of dumb monkeys trying to murder our
mama?
I don't think she wanna but what choice but the fire?
Armageddon baby – Apocalyptic shit
Talking the four horsemen like in the Holy Word,
innit?!
Time to break free from the corporate machine,
Better wake up sucka, fuck the Amerikan Dream.

I heard a strong woman's voice on a loudspeaker:
"TerraCorp, you sick son of a perverted mind...we the people
whose babies you murdered cast a simple spell on you. That
these trials and tribulations that we're about to unleash lead
shortly either to your motherloving enlightenment or to your
death! Amen?"

"Amen!"

"All the crimes you perpetrate on the streets, backed up by
the lying murdering brutal Gestapo tactics of the politicians
and pigs in your pocket, you turn around and blame on the
streets! Well you can't put this one on us so you better watch
out cos the straw don drop! You just went and broke the
camel's back...fools!"

Efe Tokunbo Okogu

Babylove Brown

Moha was still out there and we were no closer to saving his black ass. Caught between fight and flight, we didn't know whether to storm the rock or flee the hard place.

There was a button by the side of the machine. It didn't look like the main button to activate the machine, but it was a button nonetheless. The only one without Moha's piece. We looked at each other in silence. Watching, waiting for the energy to spill forth in words from someone's tongue.

"Push it," I said

"Cool it Babylove, let's think this through," Low said

"Fuck you Low, I am cool. We don't even know if Moha is still alive. We need to do something. Anything. Push it."

"Yeah but we don't know what this motherloving thang do neither. For all we know, we could blow ourselves up. And the whole of Amerika too!" Casey said, exaggerating as usual.

"So!" I snapped. "Look, Moha's dying! We gotta do something and I'd rather go out with a bang not whimpering like a little bitch! You were the one talking 'bout riding in guns blazing like Takeshi Adeju but now you scared to push a little button?"

"But Casey's right. It could blow up," Tealson said. "Like I said, the van's preliminary scans are picking up some strange and potentially volatile readings."

"Fuck it," I said and pushed the button.

Nothing happened. Nothing at all. Except for a moment I smelled something wonderful, like freshly made bread or was it some cold dish, sweeter than honey.

"You know you're crazy don't you Babylove?" Casey asked letting out his held breath.

"Guess we need Moha's part," Tealson said.

"Let's just go get Moha," I said.

"You got a plan?" Casey asked.

"Improvise," I said.

"Alright B, get up on a rooftop and give me a visual. Case, I want you to-" Low began.

362

"Wait a minute," Tealson said, flipping up his right earphone. His legs were prosthetic but he was a great driver. In a sense he was our van. That's why he always wore headphones and spoke through the mic. While communicating with the rest of us he was also listening to a whole bunch of other frequencies.

"Luck of the devil," Tealson whispered, his voice reverberating a little, "there's a goddamned protest heading our way."

We took a moment to contemplate this turn of events. For an instant, I had the strangest sensation that I had called up the protest by pushing the button but that shit didn't make no goddamned sense and I shook my head to clear it.

I saw this documentary once on quantum mechanics and that shit blew my mind. There's this famous experiment where you take subatomic particles and shoot them like bullets through two vertical slits and against a photographic plate on a wall. If one of the slits is covered then you get a single line where the particles have passed through the slit and hit the wall.

So far so good.

The strange thing is that when both slits are open, instead of two bands hitting the wall, you get multiple bands called an interference pattern, even if the particles were fired individually, one after the other. According to the scientists, this means that each individual particle not only passes through both slits simultaneously, it also takes every possible trajectory to get there.

Baffled as to how they do this, the original scientists decided to place a device next to the slits that would observe which slit each particle went through.

That's when the shit gets freaky.

When placed under observation, the particles behave like you would expect them to and create two bands of light, not multiple ones, almost as if they know they're being watched. Almost as if they're magicians who refuse to reveal their secret methods to our spying eyes.

The upshot of all this is that subatomic particles exist as waves of probabilities that only coalesce into possibilities when observed. I even did the experiment myself with Tealson so we could see the magic hiding in the mundane with our own eyes.

Then it gets even weirder.

Let's say you take two cameras and place them on opposite sides of the galaxy in order to film a photon that was travelling towards the Earth from the other side of the Milky Way. Due to the curvature of space, the photon can either curve left or right. If you choose to observe it through the camera on the left, then the photon will appear on the left and if you choose to observe it through the right one, the photon will appear on the one on the right. But the decision to curve left or right took place billions of years before you were even born which means that consciousness has the ability to influence events in the distant past.

Freaky shit, right?

So maybe I did call up the protest by pushing the button. The idea of it frankly scared the crap out of me, and I'm Babylove Brown, I don't scare easy.

"I feel the hand of fate," Low said. "Okay, here's how it's gonna be. Babylove's gonna be our eyes, scope the scene. Tealson, circle round to the east side closest to where Moha is then sit tight. You're our ears. I want you on the cops and TerraCorp like a flea on a dog. I want to know what they know before they do. And see what you can do about that force field." Tealson nodded, flipped his headphones back down and swivelled to face the dash. His hands began turning dials and flipping switches. "Casey, you and me are going after Moha. You're distraction and backup. I'm on point. All good?"

We nodded. "Alright, bring it in," Tealson turned round on his chair to face us and we all bumped our fists together, forming a hard-edged circle of power.

"Seventy-three! Do or Die!" we said and made an explosion of our fingers. They'd all grown up on 73rd street. Casey uptown near Hallway, Low and Tealson down by the rail yard. As for me, Babylove Brown, I grew up underground but spent a lot of time on 73rd.

Don't ask me why. I'm just another abandoned baby flushed into the sewers and raised by mutants. Maybe my real folks were from the area and it smelled familiar or something. Who the fuck knows?

In any case I was lucky, could just as easily have been eaten or worse in the city underground. The first time I saw daylight I was maybe four years old. A crew of us went out picking pockets just like the elders taught us. I'm still a big sister to the little ratz but I haven't been down there in a while.

No one gives a fuck about people like us. We're little different from animals in a zoo to them. They just like to hear our stories in pop songs or watch cops chase us in screen versions of our lives. We are their dark fantasies come to life but they forget that their collective shit was the fertiliser that bred us. One of these days, they'll have no choice but to care.

"Don't forget to walk funny," said Low.

I slid open the door of the van and Casey stepped out followed by Low. I jumped out last and slid the van door shut. We didn't speak. We didn't need to. We were connected on a fundamental level. One blood, like siblings. Our hearts grooved to the same beat. We hugged each other and moved out.

Low vanished. He was a straight up ghost, just dove into the crowd like he wasn't even there. Casey crossed the road and hit the corner; scan, one, two, three…then through a gap in the cars, on to the other side.

I walked down the block and waited for the lights then crossed when the green man flashed. I walked past an ice cream stand and a bookshop, then smelled the sour scent of piss. An alleyway, sweet Lord. I ducked into it and made my way down carefully, past the trash cans at the back of the establishments in the area.

I walked passed some boys smoking a joint in the back of a restaurant. Sister Louise from the orphanage was always trying to save kids like these. Underage workers hustling to get paid. In some ways being a busboy or a dish-pit jockey was better than being a runner for a dealer. In some ways, it was the same thing, especially considering what they put in the food in some of these culinary establishments and what they paid the kids.

They turned to look at me as I walked past but they could not see my face beneath my shawl. I turned a corner and climbed the wall till I hit the roof, my treaded gloves and shoes sticking to and unfurling from the concrete. I pulled myself over the edge and rolled into a low crouch.

Before me lay the scene.

The downtown area spread out in concentric circles around the zocalo. There was the tower of TerraCorp, hundreds of stories high. Its middle floors were made of polygon-shaped glass angled to reflect the sky and a shimmering mesh net interwoven with tiny screens that shifted every few microseconds in response to the changing light.

It created from ground level, the illusion of a beautiful sky. But from my vantage point, I could see the city overground, hidden from the streets below. Only the rich have the toys to play such games with perception. They want their workers to feel as if they are in a vast cloud floating far above the disasters they game over.

The rest of us have no choice but to watch their symbols of power shit radioactive waste all over us. Their fantastic worlds advertised on billboards to mock us, beautiful lives of others in some pimper's paradise of fancy toys and people whose expressions made it clear they were full of drugs and having pornographic sex on a regularly basis.

There's Sofia on a luxury yacht advertising MuGu up there. She's ridiculously attractive, like a goddess amongst mortals with her luxuriously silken straight hair, though you know her hair just was just as nappy as the rest of ours when she was a child, and her slender yet oh so womanly physique, that tempting smile and those oh so bright eyes.

I don't want to be her. I want to be her character, the one she plays in the movies. The one that lives in paradise and can not only afford to sail on the lagoon at the heart of the city, stud on her arm, but doesn't have to wake up to a city full of devils and demons when the director yells, cut!

But to get there, we had to hustle. We were close to our target; almost had enough to afford a lifetime pass to Lagoon, the heart of the big Clock. Finish this job and home free Babylove, home free.

I looked for Moha first thing. I couldn't see the building he was in. I did see a couple dozen or so mechas searching the streets within the cordoned off area, looking for him—several grouped around the TerraCorp building.

I scanned the scene, spotted Casey straight away. He was clowning around for some cameras, hiding in plain sight. It took me a few moments to find Low. He looked like just another worker on his lunch break, milling around the edge of the cordon, rubbernecking on the excitement. This was better than the screen. This was live.

The sun was high in the sky, blazing down on us all, mercilessly baking the city like a hot plate in the desert. The only thing keeping us from popping and exploding was the Lagoon. I could see it in the far distance beyond the towers. Just the edge of it, shimmering like a mirage behind the legendary un-hackable force field.

Years ago, I murdered a hard man to kill and in payment received a very rare and highly illegal piece of tech known as a phase transducer. It can get me through any force-field, including Lagoon's. Unfortunately I can only use it once because the phase transducer has a bad habit of casting the user's aura onto said force-field thus ensuring that the user could never pass through another force field in the city without alerting every cop in shooting distance.

I picked up the phase transducer when I was young and dumb enough to believe I could just break into Lagoon and hide out. I've never used it but I keep it on me as a last resort for emergencies. You never know when you're gonna need that ace up your sleeve.

I walked backwards until I reached the other edge of the rooftop then crouched slightly, my focus on the horizon. A bird wheeled past in the muggy sky, a slight breeze gathered and I was up and running, straight at the edge, a joyous gleam burning in me like a bolt of lightning about to shoot into the sky. Some days I do love Amerika... ;)

Obram

"Okay guys!" I said. "Spread out through the zone. We've got seventy square blocks full of nooks and crannies so use a wide sensor range. Study the vids of the perps we got. Watch how they move. They will be camouflaged. Remember you are hueman and can see things our mechas cannot. They are machines and their job is to alert us if and when the gait recognition or heat signature software picks up one of the perps. Move out!"

I was walking down 23rd street heading past the huge statue of the last emperor when I stopped at the intersection with Du Pont. There were many people around being led away by strategically placed policemen in their pig and dog mechas. As I scanned the buildings around me for the perps, I observed the crowd.

The financial players and their support staff, the men and women who worked all day every day shuffling numbers for their bosses in Lagoon and externalising as much shit as possible to feed the hungry beast sitting on the bottom line; the temporary employees of the coffee shops and restaurants; the bums that ate out of their garbage, a whole mess of huemanity guided by men and women in giant robots.

I moved on towards the edge of the cordon scanning buildings as I walked. Eventually 23rd street became Osiris Boulevard and I was at the palm tree fringed border of

Downtown and Orelem. Beyond the crossroads lay a huge crowd of people. It looked like there were thousands pushing up against the force field of the cordon.

Lines of police stood between me and the crowd, the black metallic hulls of their mechas glinting in the afternoon sun. They were different from ours. While ours were more like big dogs or cats, theirs were stout like armoured pigs.

If my folks were alive, they'd have been down there along with all the freaks and geeks, the workers and the students, the artists and the dropouts, the fed up and the revolutionary. Freaktown had descended from her narcotic heights to pay the penguins a visit along with a whole bunch of other folk from dozens of barrios.

I felt a thrill run through me, nostalgia tinged with sadness and a hunger or thirst I'd suppressed. It was like being homesick for a place and time that no longer was. I could see huge flags and banners waving in the air along with a forest of placards inscribed with all sorts of anarchist and anti-capitalist slogans. I zoomed in on a few signs and faces. For a moment I saw Mona or was it Mango and then she vanished back into the crowd, submerged like a teardrop in the sea.

The twins. The loves of my childhood years knew the meaning of sexuality. Wow. Crazy to think but we were once like brother and sisters. Now they were almost strangers to me.

I replayed the tape and it was definitely one of the twins. The WorldHum tower had a mecha ladder. I climbed it in order to get a better vantage point. I went up five stories then swivelled my mecha's hips to face the other way and added the twins to the mecha's list of targets, but in a separate category marked friendly.

The crowd looked ready to riot. I could see exoskeletons, IPGs, and potential weapons. Wasn't this excessive? Not that they didn't have legitimate complaints. On the contrary, the city was fucking up. No doubt. Just that Freaktownians for all their flamboyance were a pragmatic people. I knew this was as much an excuse to loot as anything else.

So did the city. Let the rioters have their fun, release their energy. When they were tired out, the mechas would move in and clean up. A few arrests would be made and the mayor would have another excuse to take away a few more rights. As long as they were contained, riots weren't always a bad thing for the brass. Especially in these days of improvised protective gear or IPGs. I just hoped no one got killed, especially not the twins; strange to say but they were my oldest friends in the world.

I know this one guy. He's one of my ex-girlfriend's younger brothers. Little guy has got the brain the size of an apple. I've seen scans of it. Yet he acts no different from anyone else. I mean yeah, there's something a bit strange about him but it's subtle, you know, like you can't really tell if you're imagining it or not just because you know he's got a tiny brain.

I can't help fucking with him sometimes. I like to ask him philosophical questions or Zen koans. What's the sound of one hand clapping, shit like that. I once asked him, Doug, his name was Douglas, I said Doug, what's the meaning of life and he looked at me like 'are you joking?' then cracked up laughing.

Then he answered "41.9 recurring."

"Recurring? What's that supposed to mean?"

"There's 41.9 recurring things a person has to do before they die," he answered

"Oh yeah? What are they?" Doug actually went on to list them one by one, pulling out a little scroll from his jacket pocket. I can't remember what they all were except 'to understand your life's story' was one of them, 'to face the trickster at the crossroads' was another and the last one was 'to die.'

"Why is that last one, point nine recurring? Why not make that forty two things?" I asked

"Shoot," he said "that's because we ain't dead yet. And most folk have to keep on coming back to life, reincarnating again and again before they finally learn to die properly."

An Indigo Song for Paradise

I don't know why looking at the crowd made me think of him. Maybe because people in mobs often have the intelligence you'd expect from someone with a brain the size of an apple, unless you actually knew one. Or maybe the real truth was most people only used an apple-sized portion of their mind's potential. What a frightening thought. What were the rest of us up to while we wandered around lost in this rat maze? Maybe we were the xombies.

I watched a small group of people going wild, smashing and breaking everything around them seemingly without rhyme or reason, and sighed. The damage was limited to a few stores in the process of being looted. Surely the twins would have the sense to get out of there. In any case I couldn't see them or the gunslingers and I had to move on.

"Anything yet, guys," Mack's voice crackled over the intercom.

"Nothing," Padox said.

"Nada," Fanta said.

"Nope," Killer said.

"Not a goddamned thing Mack. We'll keep you posted," I said.

I walked along the edge of the force field, still scanning, and the rioters gave way to protesters. As I got nearer I saw a man with a big white afro and a bushy beard standing on a raised platform close to the edge of the cordon. He addressed the crowd, "They've gone too far! Nine hundred and eleven children dead from drinking tainted milk! Shame on you TerraCorp and shame on you Para City for allowing such a travesty of justice to take place! What they do, milk a xombie's titties? Sick fucks!"

Some people in the crowd laughed and others booed. Someone shouted "Power to the People!"

"Power to the people!" the afroman responded raising a right fist. "And we the people demand justice! Of course TerraCorp claims that they're investigating and have recalled the bad milk but this ain't the first time them gangsters have killed our babies.

Efe Tokunbo Okogu

"Remember back in seventy-three when that flu epidemic turned out to be some kinda experiment escaped from their labs. That was quite a few years ago so I don't know if all you folks remember."

Someone shouted out, "I remember, brother! That flu killed my mama!"

"I'm sorry to hear that brother, I truly am. Now if I were to kill somebody's mama I'd end up on death row or in prison for the rest of my natural life. So how come TerraCorp gets to kill folk and all it has to do is pay a fine. I thought corporations were legally hueman. What are we then, second class citizens?"

There were shouts of "Tell it brother" and "You said it" and hums of "Mmmm mmmm."

"And that's why we're here today. To let TerraCorp know that we know they ain't nothing but terrorists. And we're gonna let the whole world know, right here, live on screen," he said waving at the floating cameras that were recording the scene.

"Now before I leave, I wanna talk to all y'all about Christmas. I know how you just *love* to give huge chunks of your hard earned money to the corporations every year as a way of showing your love to your families and friends. How about this coming Christmas, we cut out the middleman and you show your love with the true spirit of the holiday.

"Fuck Santa Claus, that cracker, breaking and entering into your homes down the chimney every year to rob you blind. Let's take back Christmas for Christ, a negro just like you, who was murdered for preaching that we oughta love each other as we love ourselves. True love, unconditional love.

"Did you know Santa Claus was made up by the corporations? Did you know his props: the red and white, the socks above the chimney, the reindeer, all of that was stolen from shamanic culture? See, back in the day, way up north, when some white folk—I don't like the word vampire even though so many of them use it themselves—still lived in harmony with nature.

"Their shaman lived apart from the rest of the people and once a year he would visit to gift the people with red and white magic mushrooms which they would hang above the fireplace in socks to dry. The shaman's gift was a ceremony that opened the doors to the spirit world and the main spirit animal of these people was the reindeer.

"Now y'all may not know this history on a conscious level but the information is in your genetic memory. You see, the first people on the planet were negroes and they were fruitful, spreading across the whole world and multiplying, and over time some of them turned white.

"Even though you may not be directly descended from those particular peoples, their connection to the planet is something you resonate with on a subconscious level, deep in your bones. Your ancestors know the shaman and thus so do you…somewhere in your heart.

"Knowing all this, the corps manipulated the symbols for their own profit, like a wolf dressed up as your favourite grandma, only her teeth suddenly grew real sharp. If y'all really wanna take down TerraCorp and all the other corps, quit giving them your money!"

He stepped off and out of the amp zone, hugging a woman on his way down. She was in her thirties or forties and real pretty with long braids down her back. She took his place on stage and addressed the crowd.

"Brothers and Sisters! My name is Silva Kalim and I work for Onyx and Associates. My team and I are representing the families of the victims. The nine hundred and eleven tragic victims of corporate greed! Nine hundred and eleven innocent lives, plucked like grapes from the vine to brew the evil wine known as profit at all costs!

"How long shall we feed this beast of Babylon! How long shall we suffer under slave conditionalities and fucked up externalities? Must we sacrifice our very flesh and blood to satisfy a hunger that can never be sated?"

The crowd cheered and booed simultaneously.

I once asked a Rastafarian what Babylon was. He laughed and said 'open your bladht claht eye, fool!'

"We have subpoenaed all files and records pertinent to the case but as usual they are delaying us with injunctions. At this very moment, in that great tower behind us, they are probably shredding the evidence that we need as we speak!"

Another man jumped onto the stage and began talking in terse whispers to the lovely Miss Kalim. "You can't say that. We could be held in contempt for inciting a riot!" he hissed.

"Inciting a riot? You think these people need inciting?" she answered and they both turned to look at the crowd.

Okay, so TerraCorp makes mistakes. I'll be the first to admit it. What I want to know is why those mothers weren't breastfeeding their babies? Why trust a corporation to do for your baby what Mother Nature does infinitely better?

I shouldn't be saying this but the truth is people could get along perfectly fine without TerraCorp's products. But then if they did, I guess I'd be out of a job.

An Indigo Song for Paradise

3: Blood on the streets

Low

He looked like a low level worker losing his life away in some bland office or something. Probably hated his job on a subconscious level but he kept a glimmer of hope alive. Kept his nose clean and went for the promotion. The ladder sure looked high from down here but…

Low emptied his mind and stepped into character. He flowed with the people past all the fancy downtown stores and towards the cordon. As he drew closer, he could see the shimmer of the force field. He looked up and watched the twin towers of WorldHum vanish along with the top halves of all the scrapers, replaced by a beautiful blue sky, soft wisps of white clouds overhead. The air was different too. Fresher and cooler. The micro-climate downtown was pleasant. Not the paradise of Lagoon but pleasant nonetheless.

Lagoon… He sighed. Soon they'd all be safe in paradise and the first thing he was gonna do was let Babylove know he was ready to take their relationship to a whole other level. She knew how he felt about her and he knew she had love for him. Why not make it official? But before that could happen, they had to get Moha and the last piece of the device. All that stood in his way was an impenetrable force field and dozens of mechas. He sighed again and tapped the stud in his ear.

"Tealson?" he sub-vocalised.

"Yeah."

"Force field?"

"Working on it and I'm not alone. There's another crew out here."

"You sure?"

"Either that or I'm better at this than I think."

"Could be our employers got us some hidden backup."

"Could be competition, could be protesters."

"Okay. You catch that B?"

"Yeah. I'll keep an eye out," Babylove said.

"Can you see Moha?"

"No, but I'm looking at the building he's in right now. Tealson sent me the plans already. Only thing stopping me from starting my run is the force field."

"Mmm mmm," Low replied thinking about her phase transducer—Babylove didn't know he knew she had one. "Casey?"

"So I told that motherfucker, hold on a second...wassuuup baby, never guess where I am. I'm on Screen with...who you again...that's right, Jai News, and I was telling them about the time I had to take down two cops, and they were in exoskeletons too, and all I had was my fists but I'm from Afghanistan 73rd don't be scared I know ya heard...kn'am-sayin' and we don't play like that so I had to show them niggas the truth. So I dropped the first sucker, kicked him like this, Pow! Right in his motherloving glass jaw. Yeah bitch! Then when the second, wait, what, where you going, listen don't forget, buy local, buy organic... Wassup Low?"

"Once this force field is down I want you to create a distraction so I can sneak in. Then circle round to the van."

"Cool."

"Tealson?"

"Working on it. Boy, these motherfuckers got some sharp code but they don't know who they fucking with."

Low smiled and surveyed the scene. All the pieces in place, ready to be played. Nothing to do now but wait; adrenaline pumping, breath regulated, heartbeat steady, ready to jump the...

Ecila

...Gunshots followed by screams and I smelled blood on the air. People ducked and ran for cover. More gunshots followed. I watched a man get hit twice in the chest. He did not stand up again.

I dropped low and ran for the nearest corner where a group of folk were already hiding. The streets were filled with people running for safety. Bullets were flying like they cost pennies to keep us on lock-down. After a couple of minutes a few of the young boys ran up crouched low and dodging between burning cars and upended kiosks.

"What you got there, son? Molotovs. Yo, little man here got some of that loon-shine!" a bearded man said.

"My nigga! Go on back there and get us some more of those," another added.

"Three fifty," the kid said

"What?"

"You heard me nigga, three five oh. Matter of fact make that four hundred for wasting my motherloving time. They deading niggas out here, man. I'll get you some more loon-shine but it's gonna cost you... My crew came prepared, son."

A tense moment followed then the kid said, "Just fucking with ya," and the two of them handed out the cocktails and soon their backpacks were empty. As he did so the bearded man began to laugh quietly from deep in his belly followed by a few others.

"Funny kid," a skinny guy muttered not sharing in the hilarity.

"Gonna re-up. Stay strong. One," the kid said, and they loped away staying low.

Almost everyone had one including myself. I looked at the bottle. This was escalating fast. I could see my reflection sloshing about inside like a dreamer about to wake up to find his house burning. Someone flipped open a zippo and we leaned in to light up, a circle of heads throwing up shadows against the walls.

Moments later, I was racing round the corner and flinging the bottle from my hand onto the policemen, skidding to a stop behind an upturned bus as bullets whizzed past my head. The molotovs soared through the air, some sailing, others flipping end over end to crash onto the shields of the policemen and against the carapaces of Mechas, exploding into acid and flame on contact. I could hear screams of panic and pain.

Not for a moment did I stop to question my actions. As far as I was concerned, the police were dirty filthy criminals whose job was to keep the negro down for the benefit of the vampire elite and it was our duty to destroy them.

There's a game they like to play here in the city. It's called do or die. Everyone out there chasing after the prize: cold hard cash. Why? Cause you wanna eat, don't you nigga? Unless you wanna eat out the garbage or some shit. You want to have nice things for you and the family, don't you? Then you gotta hustle, my nigga, get yours while the getting's good, ya dig? You can take the man out of the jungle but you can't take the jungle out of the man! Do or die, nigga, do or die!

My hustle is simple. I just follow my nose, sniffing out the places that remind me of the village. I have slipped through the cracks of this city and discovered the earth is still there, ready, willing and able to be a home, even here in the heart of this concrete jungle. Somehow, most days, I find food and shelter worthy to be called such. When you ain't got nothing but breath to sustain you, you come to understand the power of breath.

Whenever I can, I plant seeds in empty spaces to thank the Earth for her kindness to me. What Mother Nature truly desires from those she loves is for them to manifest the courage and wisdom to finish what she started. If we can't do it, she'll find another way. If only we mortals were like the heroes of our legends. If only we could rise up and live up to the promise of who we were meant to be.

But what can I do about Paradise City? It is too big and I am too small. All I can do is plant my seeds, pray for rain that the plants may grow—perhaps lightning that Babylon may burn— and cultivate my gardens, and be satisfied that some poor folk get some healthy food to eat every once in a while. I'm not the only guerrilla in the city. There are others and we are slowly but surely making a difference.

I have lived on the margins and been to the edges of the city and stepped in the interzone. Not long after I got out of the asylum, I stood facing the endless desert beyond. I wanted to walk off into the territory and disprove their maps. But looking into the vast wasteland crushed that dream like an ant beneath the cruel foot of a selfish, spoiled child turned rotten in need of serious discipline. According to everyone, if I started walking in that direction, I'd end up a xombie.

I ran through the streets from one barricade to the next, surrounded by death and carnage. I was slinging rocks at the cops, dodging between safe spots. It would have been a mismatch but these were no ordinary rocks. The Freaktown boys had worked some alchemy on them and the rocks exploded into acid when they hit the cops, melting through exoskeletons and the carapaces of mechas to burn the flesh within, that the motherfuckers might feel the pain of our suffering.

The village and the city are very different. Back there, everyone did everything, more or less. I mean, we farmed together, built together, hunted and gathered together. Everything was communal, everyone had enough and there was always plenty in storage for lean times. The only schedule we followed was that set by nature and our reward was a long, healthy and prosperous life. Of course people had their own specialities but we were all jacks of all trades.

Here in the city, people are far more specialised. They fulfil certain functions like interdependent organs, some cancerous. The street-sweeper, the doctor, the bookie, the policeman, the dealer, the lawyer, the pimp, the whore, the teacher, the hitman, the mayor... They follow the schedule set by supply and demand which follows a nature of its own, influenced as it is from on high, or is that down low, by the super-rich.

Money is like stained glass in a whorehouse whose reflected light throws up hypnotic illusions. I have seen them sell their bodies and their souls for money. I have seen people lie, steal, cheat, and kill for money, as if it were a god and not a tool.

That's another difference from the village, people kill each other all the time out here. Maybe it's because there's too many of them. Of us. Or is that what the powers that be want us to believe?

Innocent folk stopped, searched, harassed, beaten, arrested, incarcerated, gunned down, or worse, by trigger happy cops, or taken out as collateral damage in wars between gangsters supplied by spooks and sponsored by secret societies. Everybody know who did it, but no one never do shit about it unless they after some player or other so they can rob 'em. The whole city is a warzone full of filth and corruption. How many times have I stood on the street, watching the flashing lights and listening to the crying mothers and angry brothers? How many…

Something exploded next to me and I ran for cover.

Babylove Brown

The contours of my run lay out before me like prescience. The ledges and balconies, the contraction and the explosion, soaring over pitfalls and death-traps like gravity was my biaaatch.

There were other people on the rooftops besides me. Police and rioters playing sniper but when I'm on the edge, touching the void, I'm like the shadow you don't see when you blink your eyes.

On the streets below it was carnage, but controlled. I could see the people working together to build barricades and advance forwards. Many were fleeing back towards Freaktown and other barrios and they weren't being stopped, but there were several core groups serious about this fight.

The timing was perfect. I felt a little tingle as an invisible eel swam over my skin. Was it all a coincidence? Maybe. Maybe not. I mean, there's always something going down and every once in a while, a whole bunch of somethings go down at the same time, you feel me?

There were five main groups of rioters that I could see and many individuals scattered between them. The one furthest ahead was trapped behind several overturned public buses. Another two groups were flanking their position. I sailed past them and towards the police line. I was going fast and keeping out of sight but I could see only two choices ahead of

380

me. One, drop down to the street and sneak through or keep on going knowing I'd probably be spotted when I crossed the lines. My heart said to keep on going. My right hand tapped my earstud and my vocal chords said, "Tealson?"

"I'm almost there...{screeech!}...circling round to the east side of the cordon..." I could hear the van skidding and gunfire from his location.

"Low?"

"I'm with Casey...[huff huff]...we're a little busy." It sounded like close quarters combat, exoskeletons clanging and fists pounding, a few gunshots, and the sound of men grunting and breathing heavily.

"I got a clear run," I said. "I can get to Moha and get him out but the mechas are a little too close for comfort. I need you to create a ruckus, distract the motherfuckers and cut out. Head for the van."

"Em...Okay...One"

"One."

I watched and waited. A couple of minutes later there was an explosion towards the west. A mushroom cloud blossomed from atop a building. Sirens blared and the people cried out in alarm. The flames licked the building like a plasma tongue licking an ice cream then spread to the next. Soon half the block was on fire and a third of the mechas turned to investigate. I took a deep breath and leaped into my run.

Obram

They were killing each other out there. The police and the people were killing each other and I was caught in the middle of it. Mack was telling us to ignore the chaos and focus on finding the gunslingers but that was easier said than done.

We were too big to enter some buildings but TerraCorp teams in exos were on it. Just to be sure we scanned them all as we walked using infrared, heat, and motion and gait-recog detectors. Twice I'd spotted something and radioed it in. The exos had investigated but each time it had turned out to be a false alarm.

My team had swept most of the area by now. If we didn't find them soon it meant they were long gone. Other teams were no doubt out there scouring the city but that wasn't my concern. I was striding down the centre of the street, picking my way over the wreckage of vehicles and the occasional corpse when I turned a corner and saw Fanta battling with a small group of rioters.

"What the fuck are you doing, Fanta!" I shouted running towards them. The rioters saw me and some turned to face me. I know why they fired. They thought they were cornered. They saw a second giant mecha and opened fire. It was my fault. I shouldn't have run. I should have walked. Actually it's Terracorp's fault. None of us should have been out there. We were trained to bag xombies not deal with rioters. I responded instinctively and shot back. Fanta and I caught them in crossfire and blew them away. It was all over in seconds.

"Holy fuck! Did you see that?!" Fanta was yelling, his face aglow with exhilaration. "That was straight up slaughter, son!"

"What the fuck were you doing? We're here to catch armed robbers not kill people!" I screamed.

"They shot first! Man what was I supposed to do, just die? Fanta don't go out like that. They was shouting 'Kill TerraCorp' and shit like that. Well I am TerraCorp and you're dead, biatch!" Fanta stamped a mechanical foot on a dead man, breaking bones and splattering blood onto the concrete streets and stainless steel walls.

"For fuck sake Fanta! Let's get the fuck outta here!" I backed my Mecha away from the dead and swivelled to walk away. Fanta followed.

"We are not TerraCorp, Fanta, we're just mech riders, okay and we are not authorised to murder civilians!"

"We work for TerraCorp therefore we are TerraCorp, Bra. A corporation is nothing but its constituent workers doing their job just like a machine is made up of all little parts doing their thing. These people were attacking TerraCorp and TerraCorp

defended itself. That's all that happened here. Don't feel bad
about it."

"Fuck you Fanta! Those weren't xombies, man."

"No shit. If they were xombies they wouldn't be shooting
guns at me."

"And besides, we're expendable, Fanta. Think! They'll
throw us to the wolves. The last thing they need, what with all
that tainted milk on the screens is more scandal."

"What, you think we'll get fired?"

"Fired? nigga, if news of what we did ever leaks, we're
spending the rest of our lives trying not to drop the soap!"

"No!"

"Man, you got blood all over my fucking mecha!"

"Fuck, I don't wanna go to jail, man!"

"The only people who know what went down are me and
you."

"Yeah. And any cameras in the vicinity."

"Shit, let me think. You know Barrie, right? My wife's
cousin's husband, the policeman. He got busted down to
surveillance for some shit, anyways I can ask him to find and
delete any footage for us."

"He'd do that?"

"I don't know, man. Maybe."

"You guys close?"

"Nah, but I got some dirt on him that his missus don't know
about. He's batting for the other side."

"Man, let's just get the fuck out of here."

A few minutes later...

"Obram?"

"Mack?"

"Round up your team and bring them back to base."

"What about the gunslingers?"

"The sector's clear. They're long gone."

"Roger that…. {sktch]… Alright guys. We're heading back
to base," Padox and Killer responded.

I turned back to Fanta.

"No, that's bullshit Fanta! They are not our enemies and we are not at war!"

"Are you kidding me Bra? Look around you! Of course we're at war. There's too many people and not enough resources. Everyone wants to make it to Lagoon but Lagoon is only big enough for the rich, right? I don't know about you but I ain't bagging xombies for nothing. I'm never going to live in Lagoon but this job means that I can afford somewhere nice like Latier one day. These rioters want to shut down Terracorp. If they do, I'm out of a job, so fuck them and fuck you. They shouldn't be shooting at me."

"Fuck me? Fuck you! I have friends out there Fanta! All I know is I don't want to kill no more people. You sure they shot first?"

"Look, I'm no fucking psycho aiiight? I don't want to kill nobody neither. But life is tough. Everybody's looking for something, Bra, but only a few make it." Fanta shadow boxed with his mecha as we turned the corner and entered the TerraCorp plaza. Padox and Killer were already there with another team of four mechas.

As we joined them in front of the TerraCorp building, the low rumbling I'd been dimly aware of grew louder and exploded into several hundred rioters running towards us, pouring out of the side streets like some amoeba squelching its way through the clogged arteries of the city.

What happened next changed my life forever. I saw one of the twins running towards me, her face contorted with rage. I saw Fanta firing his guns into the crowd and the other riders followed suit. I saw Mona or Mango falling down, shot or not, I know not, one of a multitude of bodies dropping like flies before the guns of my fellow mecha riders.

My mecha meanwhile was identifying multiple sources of gunfire from the crowd heading in our direction. I could feel bullets bouncing off my mecha's shell. Almost before I knew what I was doing, I aimed my guns and fired… at the other mechas.

An Indigo Song for Paradise

Why? I don't really know to be honest. It was instinctive, like smacking yourself in the face to kill a mosquito. Was it the right thing to do? I don't think there is such a thing as the right thing anymore. One thing's for sure, no one was expecting it. Not them, not the rioters, not me.

High powered explosive tipped bullets and fragmentation grenades blasted out from my mecha's guns and shredded through the other mechas. I aimed for their weak spots at point blank range and fired with everything I had. My fellow riders, my colleagues and friends who would have given their lives for me, were dead before they really knew what was happening.

Two of them managed to spray my mecha with bullets and I got hit twice in the left leg. My mecha was already working its micro surgery on the wounds but I was dead as well. Or I would be when the cops showed up.

The crowd was shouting like I was a hero as I walked to the side of the TerraCorp tower and climbed up the mecha ladder. I didn't feel like a hero. It was black on black crime and I hated whoever or whatever had led me to this space-time where I was faced with such choices.

I moved fast, hoping I was fast enough. On the roof I stepped into the cupped hand of the catapult and pushed the release button without bothering to adjust the direction. I could hear alarms ringing and the sound of retribution coming after me: the piston-clank of mechas and the low whine of drones. The catapult needed a few more seconds to load and I kept my guns trained on the edge of the rooftop.

The chrome hull of a drone poked its head over the side just as a little bell rang. I blasted it away and a moment later, was hurled into the dusk sky. At the height of the arc, I spread my wings and ignited my thrusters, speeding towards the edge of the city.

Paradise City is beautiful from above, an iridescent scarab beetle made of flowing neon, amber, and silver lights. As I soared through the sky, I felt a wave of despair wash over me.

My life was over. I knew it like I knew the desert was my destiny.

I passed over an area where the lights and terrain combined to form the face of a grumpy old man. Suddenly I was laughing, for no reason but that it reminded me of my old man, pulling faces to make us laugh, Mom and I, making fun of people who didn't know how to have fun. Pops was dead but it was like his spirit was still with me, using the city itself to make me laugh.

My despair leaked away from me like gas till I was empty. I felt a strange calm wash through me as I aimed my mecha towards the desert and rode a gust of wind out of Paradise for the last time. I knew they'd come after me. I knew I'd die somewhere over the wasteland, shot down by missiles and drones.

And I knew what they'd say about me too. 'What do you expect? He was half white. Can't trust them vampires, man. Turn your back on one and they'll bite you in the ass.'

4: Food-stamps, Loot, and Dr Guff

Legs

"You know the problem with you Bobby. You're a big guy but you got no heart. Where's my money?" Legs said, then bitch slapped the fat man in the face with the back of his right hand, his ring bruising Bobby's cheek.

"I'm a get it for you Legs, I promise. I just need a little more time," Bobby snivelled, sniffing back snot and blood. He was sitting down in a chair in Legs' office, behind him stood Lil'T and JoJo two of Legs' larger enforcers.

"I gave you more time already. How many times I give you an extension Bobby?"

"I know. I just had some bad luck, that's all. Come on Legs, we all have bad luck sometimes. I mean, look at this fucking situation right here. But please, Legs, believe me. Just a little more time and…"

"Enough already. Listen Bobby. I'm a reasonable man. I don't want to break your legs but you're not leaving me a lot of choice here."

"No please! Legs! Don't do this!" Bobby cried out. He tried to stand but Lil'T's heavy hand on his left shoulder planted him back in the chair.

"It's your own fault Bobby. What I say when you come to me asking for thirty Gs to invest in…what the fuck was it…who gives a fuck? What I say to you Bobby?"

"You said you didn't care I was married to your cousin, you'd still fuck me up if I didn't pay but listen to me, Legs, just listen to me! Aight. I've got this guy. We met down at the Tropicana. He works in Death Star! So I've been hanging out with him, showing him a good time, you know, getting him girls and drugs and whatnot. He's almost ready Legs. Just a little more time and I can flip him."

"Flip him?"

"Yeah get him working with us. He's got access to food stamps, man!"

"Food stamps? Do I look hungry to you, Bobby? What the fuck I want with food stamps?"

"We can sell 'em man. Make some money and I can pay you back."

"Food stamps? Who the fuck gonna buy food stamps, Bobby? They're free. Somebody get me a baseball bat."

"NO! Listen Legs! Just listen, okay! A lot of folk are hungry out there. There's a whole untapped market of working folk who make a little too much to qualify for food stamps but not enough so they don't need 'em."

"But the margins Bobby. They sound kind of small."

"Small multiplied by the whole city Legs. I'm talking monopoly 'cause no one's figured this angle man."

"Hmm. What's your guy's name?"

"Miguel. Miguel Hermossa."

"You better be right about this Bobby"

"Trust me, Legs. You won't regret this."

"Any regret will be shared by the both of us. Okay, bring him down to Dark Fantasy, Saturday night. I wanna meet him."

"Saturday? Legs, listen, I'm going slow with this guy. Don't wanna scare him off."

"Scare him? Shheeit, I'm gonna seduce the motherfucker. Show you how it's done. Alright, get the fuck outa here."
Lil'T hauled Bobby to his feet by his shirt then walked him out the door.

"Food stamps. Hmmm? What you think Armand?" Legs asked Armand, his right-hand man who'd been facing the arched window that overlooked Freaktown's park. Armand swivelled round to face the boss.

"Food-stamps could work I suppose, if we deal in volume. Wouldn't be bad for PR neither. I'll check the numbers," he replied. "The mayor recently cut welfare again. Anyways, we got bigger fish to fry. Those Jugglers motherfuckers hit us again. If we don't do something soon, we're gonna look weak. I know you said hold back but…"

"Let me worry about those clowns. Have you heard from Low?"

"Yeah."

"And?"

"They got most of it. There's a missing section somewhere out there in the city."

"Call them."

Armand nodded and dialled Low from the screen that floated above the table.

After a few rings, Low's low voice said, "Pepe's Pizza. Can I take your order?"

"Low," Legs spoke, "talk to me. Where's my machine."

"We're working on it. I lost one of my crew out there. By the time we got to him, he was dead and his section of the machine was gone. Someone must have looted it."

"Just come in with what you got."

"The money?"

"The money was for the whole machine. I'll give you a quarter."

"I can't do that, Legs."

"What you mean you can't do that?"

"I mean I can't do that. I'm sorry Legs. I got bills to pay. Look we'll bring you the whole thing once we find the missing part."

"Listen to me, Low. Some very important clients want that thing so don't fuck with me or I will burn you to the ground like Christ on Judgment Night!"

"Don't threaten me, Legs. I'm not in the fucking mood. We'll get you your machine, we just need a little more time."

"Yeah, you and the whole dammed world. How you gonna find the missing part anyway?"

"Let me worry about that. Just have our money ready."

"Low! Just bring in what you got, okay. How about a third?"

"No, Legs. We need it all. I'll be in touch," Low said and hung up

"Motherfucker…" Legs said.

"Indeed," Armand said.

"I want you to find that fucking thing wherever it is. Put the word out on the street. I want our guys checking out every pawn shop in the city, especially the ones that are connected. If we're lucky whoever found that thing is gonna try and sell it."

Legs walked over to the window and looked out across the free park, his gaze roaming over the neighbourhood. Several of the buildings on the high street were nothing but smouldering husks and cinders. Last night's riots had spread from downtown to several barrios including Freaktown.

"Damn!" Legs said shaking his head. "Who the fuck burned down the barbershop? Like we livin' in the last days or some shit."

Ecila

I stood in front of the warehouse wondering if I had the right place. Word on the street was there was a hacker in here by the name of DevilDog. I'd seen the tag around FreakTown and a few other barrios but had never thought much about it.

Paradise is full of graffiti 'pon the walls and trains, esoteric hieroglyphs encoded and deciphered by street shamans engaged in neuro-linguistic hacks into the programming of the masses.

I pulled the little device out of my jacket pocket and stared. It was real. I wasn't imagining it.

During the riots, I had heard Chi's voice on a hooligan wind saying 'go south,' so I did. As I was walking down a temporarily deserted street filled with trash and a few burning fragments of the city, I saw this unobtrusive looking box the size of a large book, clutched in a dead man's hands, and for some reason picked it up.

There was something strange about the machine. It seemed to have more corners and folds than an object ought to have. Was I seeing into the land of the blind, the one Harmony the shaman often spoke of? There were several buttons of unknown functions marked by strange symbols. Symbols I had not seen in seven years; not since the cracked dragon's egg that somehow brought me here. I'd almost begun to believe I was crazy. But these symbols were proof. Of what, I wasn't quite sure, but I was going to find out.

I stared at the strange swirls and sharp angles till my head began to spin because it was as if I knew what the symbols meant on some level that my conscious mind could not access. It was frustrating.

The machine looked like the control panel of a larger machine. It had moulded bits sticking out that looked like they connected to other sections. I'd pushed all the buttons but nothing happened, except for a strange moment I smelled something similar to fried plantain.

I needed to find someone who was good with gadgets and my friend Big Bola suggested I come here. I put the thing back in my jacket pocket and walked through the car park. The sun burned down with the heat of a thousand djinns, burning away all desire for anything but water.

The concrete was all cracked up, and there were shopping trolleys lined with cardboard and filled with brown caked dirt everywhere, as I walked up to a large industrial door that looked like it might be an entrance. It was made of a heavy metal and painted black. I knocked. There was no answer. I knocked louder and called out but still no answer.

I walked to the side of the warehouse and down a garbage strewn alley, looking for another way in. All I could find was a cast iron drainpipe that led to a toilet window several stories above. *Fuck that!* I walked back to the door and banged loudly, yelling out "Heeeelllloooooo!" Nobody answered so I sat down in the shade, figuring someone would show up eventually.

The asphalt of the lot looked like it was melting, heat waves warping the light passing through the air, the photons filled with information awaiting to be decoded, and in the distance, the high towers of the city shimmered against the pale blue sky. A giant mecha flew by overhead, casting a dragon's shadow across my noon.

Half an hour later I returned to the drainpipe, bored of banging on the door and throwing stones into trolleys. What were they, some kind of art piece or something, or were these fuck-the-system types actually going to grow something useful?

I gripped the drainpipe and began to climb, keeping my limbs straight and my body relaxed. I climbed till my head almost touched the overhanging roof then reached out and grabbed the window ledge.

The toilet window was fairly large and I stepped through easily though there was a moment when I was almost entirely suspended in mid-air. There were a few toiletries, a dark towel of indeterminate colour hanging on the wall, and an incense stick burning beside the statue of a laughing fat negro with dreadlocks sitting cross legged on the back of a turtle. The inside door of the toilet had 'Welcome' stencilled on it. I opened the door and stepped out into a corridor.

"Hey dude," someone said. I turned round to see a man with long hair and a joint in his mouth, a large hat flopped lazily on his head.

"Yeah?" I said

"Up the drainpipe huh?"

"Yeah."

"That's cool. I still come and go that way sometimes when I don't have keys. I'm heading down to the basement. Want a hit?"

"Sure," I said and he passed me the joint. "Thanks."

"My pleasure, dear fellow," he said and laughed. "Dear fellow, ha! You know like Old boy says on Gatman. Do you watch Gatman? Yo reckon anyone is actually that deadly with a gat? I mean, like in real life? I mean like Babylove Brown or Silly the Kid, Scorpionisis, Leftie Biggles, all them slingers…" He walked down the corridor towards the stairs and I followed past walls covered in graffiti, paintings, and posters.

"I don't have a screen," I said as we walked past a broken screen stuck on the mannequin of a child's shoulders, "but yeah, I reckon there's folk that fast."

"Sleeping rough, huh? Well you're probably welcome to crash here for a few nights as long as you're not a psycho or a cop? You're not are you?"

I shook my head.

"Good. Yo Navi, this is…"

"Ecila."

"He came up the drainpipe. I'm Bone," the long haired guy said and we bumped fists. I turned to do the same with Navi but he crossed his arms instead. He was about my age and height, maybe a little younger and taller, dressed in expensive clothes, a fur coat, and platinum chains around his neck.

"What the fuck you want?" Navi asked.

"I'm looking for Devildog. Big Bola told me she stay here sometimes," I said.

"You friends with BB? How the lady doing?" Bone asked.

"What you want with the Devil? Free inet?" Navi asked simultaneously. We shared one of those silent moments of looking at each other knowing we were all thinking the same thing, but that the thing, whatever it was, couldn't be expressed in words, we then all laughed a little at the same time.

"Yeah. BB and I go back. We both used to sleep under the Nawa overpass a few years back. She's aight, her back don't hurt so bad now that she eating healthy and doing yoga. And no, I don't need free inet. I found something last night."

"You mean looted," Bone said then frowned. "I can't believe I missed that shit man."

"Ha Ha!" Navi laughed. "I got me some nice loot. One of them new floating screens and a whole new wardrobe. Check out the free shop."

We reached the ground floor and walked through a set of swinging doors into a large space. It was filled with piles and stacks of… almost everything. Clothes, jewellery, tools, gadgets, screens…unopened boxes piled high next to racks and piles on tables and rugs.

"Help yourself to whatever you want. We gotta get rid of it all as soon as possible, man. And these damned communists are against selling it to make a buck. If the cops come calling we'll just leg it underground, eh?" I snatched a funky looking black hat and placed it on my head at a rakish angle then kept walking.

"Nice," Bone said, leading us through another set of doors and down a staircase into the basement, ducking a little to avoid hitting his head. Someone had scrawled 'Ouch!' in red crayon and a stick figure with a lump growing out its head. The stick figure had big ol' titties, hairy balls, and a thick penis longer than its arms and legs.

The basement was filled with machinery, all sorts of mechanical devices and screens. They looked like they'd been cobbled together from a thousand different parts from as many different sources. There were about a dozen people down there, some working on the machines, others smoking out of a large and intricate bong.

"Yo Deedee, someone here to see you."

A young woman on the far side of the room flipped up a visor and looked up. She was in her twenties, chubby and pretty, in good shape with a ring in her snub nose and another in her upper left eye-lid. Her hair was dreadlocked but shaved on the left side.

"I know you?" she asked pointing at me with the soldering iron in her hands.

"No," I answered, "I'm a friend of Big Bola's and she told me you might be able to help me out with this." I pulled the machine from my jacket and held it out.

She put down the soldering iron, and took it in her rough hands. She caressed it and again that strange glitch, that twitch of the eye and I was seeing other angles of the machine, parallel to reality.

"Hmmm? Where'd you get this?" she said walking over to a workbench.

394

"Downtown," I said. "You know what it is?"

"Not yet. I don't recognise these symbols. Hold on."

She pulled out some jump cables and clipped them to two of protruding knobs, one of which I'm not quite sure was there before.

She flipped a switch and a floating screen appeared above the workbench. She tapped on a symbol and lines appeared, mapping some sort of frequency.

"Hmmm…let's see." She played around some more then looked at me and said, "This might take a while."

"That's cool, I can wait. Does it look strange to you?" I asked her, wondering if she could see the shifting nature of the machine as I could.

"Yo, come say hi to the lady Jane," Bone called out.

"Yeah, go on. I'll let you know what I find," DevilDog said.

I was reluctant but she was insistent. After a moment of silence, I nodded and walked over to the circle. I flopped down on an old car tire and looked around.

The guy sitting opposite me was talking. He was bare-chested and well built, covered in tattoos that danced like flames on the surface of his ebony skin. "I know we're all committed to the cause but there's never going to be a revolution."

"What! The way the world is fucking up, a revolution is inevitable," the girl to my left answered. She was petite with a big afro, dressed all in black, sitting cross-legged on a sheepskin rug.

"If it was inevitable, it would have happened by now," Tattooguy replied.

"What about last night?" a male voice asked from behind me.

"The riot? Look, when Old Devil God said 'We the people take back what's ours,' I think he was talking about the freedom to be our true selves, free from oppression…not a new gold watch," Afrogirl said, flashing her brand new gold watch and a big gap-toothed smile that made her suddenly glow.

"We're giving most of the loot away," Tattooguy said, "what more do you want?"

"What more do I want? Let me break it down for you, Jack. I mean, don't get me wrong, it's great all that we do. Food not Bombs, the free shop, raising awareness about modern day slavery, the guerrilla gardening, the workshops, Copwatch, the boycotts, the protests, supporting the free clinic and the work-trade centre, all of it is good stuff. But I'm tired of being a band-aid soaked in blood. I'd rather be the flame that cauterises the wound," said Afrogirl.

"What do you suggest exactly?" Tattooguy said as Afrogirl passed me the pipe. "I mean, what can we really do? Change will come eventually with or without us. I'm not so arrogant that I think I can change the whole world. Besides, the people are too paranoid to stand up. Or too scared. "

I took a hit from the bong as the man continued. A long cool stream of marijuana flavoured with cloves and cinnamon wound its way through the glass spirals and loops to fill my lungs. I held my breath as Tattooguy kept talking.

"But then who isn't paranoid in Para City. You'd have to be brain dead or a xombie not to be. I mean everyone knows that corporations are run by parasitic psychopaths and the government is their puppet but still they vote and pay taxes, work their lives away and die soon after retirement of some catastrophic organ failure 'cause they were too addicted to the poison of their choice."

My breath let go in a series of little hiccups. Smoke rings coiled before my eyes and then I let go. Dragon's breath streamed from my nostrils and mouth. A lightness opened up in my chest, spreading to encapsulate my whole body in a sweet high. It sure tasted niiiiice.

"It's not arrogance. One individual can change the world. You just have to be at the right place at the right time. You just have to be ready, willing and able to do the right thing and I ain't talking about those riots last night neither," Afrogirl said as I passed the pipe, "right?"

An Indigo Song for Paradise

I turned to look at her and a strange thing happened. My mouth was speaking, "I don't know, unless you got a time machine, it's impossible to know what really caused what to happen," but at the same time I was thinking no doubt and Afrogirl smiled and mouthed the words, 'no doubt.'

"Okay, my turn to read a poem," she said.

"It's not about God again is it?" a female voice called out from behind me.

"Well he's in it," Afrogirl replied then added with a pout, "Just because most of y'all are a bunch of heathens don't mean I'm gonna stop loving the Lord. One of these days I'm-a save all your souls, whether you likes it or not."

"I'm sorry to break it to you, sister, but God ain't gonna save us," the youth to my right said, lifting up his cap and speaking for the first time. "We have to do it ourselves."

"I know that, but without the Lord, nothing is possible and with the Lord, nothing is impossible. Look, you wanna hear it or not?"

"I do," I said and a few of the others made assenting noises or nodded their heads.

"Okay. It's called 'Re-colonial Mentality.' It goes:

> *Coloniser:*
> *It's your own fault for wearing that tight resourceful dress;*
> *I know you wanted it, deep down in your breast;*
> *now take all that pain and make sure you repress*
> *the truth – bitch-ass-niggers, you better hate yourselves!*
> *Just keep on sucking the shit out of my ass*
> *and say, "Thank you sir! Best I ever had!"*
>
> *(I love trees)*
>
> *Colonised:*
> *I don't know why I'm so scared all the time -*
> *sometimes it feels like I'm going out of my mind;*

397

was I really that evil in a past life
that I gotta suffer through all this sorrow and strife?
Why can't I be like my heroes on screen then?
Am I nothing but ones and zeroes, screaming?

(rise again)

Free:
Lord, I pray for that glorious day
when all my people no longer turn away
from the clear light of love and intelligence;
let's make it happen – Jah Bless.
May we master ourselves and ascend
To the promised land when you descend
Like a meteorite from outer space
To smash to dust the Babylonian phase.
It's about damned time we colonise our own minds -
and wake up to the true meaning of man (is) kind

"Holy fuck!" DevilDog called out.

"What?!" I asked, jumping up. I was at the workbench in three strides, "What is it?"

"Where did you say you got this again," she asked looking at me intently. "And don't give me no bullshit about looting it neither."

"But I did loot it downtown."

"Where exactly?"

"I don't remember. It was out on the streets in the hands of a dead man."

"But what made you take it? For real man, tell me."

"The symbols. I recognised the symbols."

"You know what they mean?"

"No, but I've seen them before. A long time ago. In another... place"

"They mean something to you," she said. It was not a question. I wanted to say more but my time in the nut farm had taught me to be wary. She seemed to sense my caution and did not push it further for the time being.

"So what is it? The machine, what does it do?" I asked.

"I don't know. I mean it's like nothing I've ever seen before or even heard of. These readings I'm getting are frankly impossible but I can't tell you much more than that right now. I need more time. And a second opinion... mmm, let me see... yeah, my old professor at the university, Dr Guff. We should go talk to him and I happen to know where he'll be tonight."

Babylove Brown

"Honey, I'm home," Dr Guff called out as he walked into his comfortable three bedroom house in a gated community in the heart of Latier.

"Welcome home, Daddy," I said placing the business end of my pistol against the back of his head. "Don't be stupid or the family gets it." He turned around, saw my masked face and screamed all high pitched like a little bitch. I pistol whipped him to shut him up. Not hard enough to knock him out. Just enough to silence the bitch. He spat out a bloody tooth and looked at me incredulously like he couldn't believe I'd just stolen his ice cream or something.

"Listen Daddy," I said, "Mommy, Becca, and Junior are in the living room with my associates. Why don't you go say hi."

His eyes widened and he scrambled to his feet and ran into the living room. He began to whimper when he saw his wife and kids hogtied on the living room floor. They started crying.

Casey turned up the volume on the screen he was watching.

Last night's riots spread out from the downtown area around TerraCorp plaza to many of the city's barrios. Police say the worst is over and the clean-up is already underway. A spokesman from the Department of Services had this to say: "The damage done last night was extensive. Property damage to the tune of tens of millions not to mention the

399

many lives lost. Today is a sad day for the city but we at the department of services are working overtime to ensure things get back to normal as soon as possible."

"Stay cool, Daddy," I said, "don't want to lose no more teeth now, do you?"

Low came out of the kitchen with a plate full of sandwiches and placed them on the coffee table. "Professor," he said, "we need your help. No harm will come to your family as long as you co-operate."

"What do you people want?" Guff blubbered. He was getting on my nerves, acting like a little bitch. His fat face jiggled like one of those toy dogs you see on the dashboard of cars and he was shaking like a leaf.

"Glad you asked," Low said, taking the man's arm and leading him through to the garage. Guff hesitated at the threshold looking back towards his family. They were scared, imploring him with their eyes.

On screen the mayor appeared, solemn and dressed in a traditional green and gold agbada, his trademark hat held in his hands.

Mayor of Paradise City, Mr Obvious Beastedy commented:

"My heart goes out to the tragic victims of these criminals who do not respect hueman life. Looting, arson and murder have nothing to do with civil liberties. Rest assured justice will be as swift and as severe as the sword of Damocles! I say this to the families of those who were brutally slain, go home and bury your dead. To succumb to vengeance is to say they died in vain."

Mr Mayor, will you still be attending the World Music Awards on Saturday? Your daughter is nominated for several awards including best new artist.

"Yes, I will be attending the awards. In these difficult times, it is more important than ever to carry on with our lives and I for one could do with listening to some good music. Now if you'll excuse me, I'm very busy."

"Don't worry Daddy," I said, "We ain't gonna hurt your sweet little family." I shoved Guff into the garage where the van was parked, slid open the door, and Low stepped inside. Guff hesitated and I shoved him again. He climbed in after Low. I leaned in through the passenger's side and smiled at Tealson. He was taking a nap.

In the back of the van, Low uncovered the machine from under a tarp.

"What is it?" Guff asked

"That's what we want you to tell us. All we know is it came from TerraCorp's labs and is worth more money than you'll make in a lifetime."

"How am I supposed to know?"

"You're an expert on quantum dynamics," Low said. "We did some research. You wrote a paper on reality displacement. I couldn't understand all of it to be honest but this machine has something to do with that."

"That's impossible, we're years away from even detecting the morphogenic field let alone experimenting..."

"Looks like someone at TerraCorp beat you to the punch."

Guff looked at Low then turned his attention back to the machine. It looked like a gun to me. Some kind of blaster only there was no trigger. But it also kind of looked like a saxophone, and as I thought this, I could almost hear a strange sound like low strains of a lonesome howl somewhere far out in the wasteland. What was that about?

The room began to shake, just another earthquake. We all rode it out without speaking. A painting fell off a wall and some screws rolled around on the floor but otherwise it passed without incident.

After a few moments Guff spoke up. "I can't help you from here. I need the equipment in my lab. There is a science fair at the university and I'm expected to be there tonight."

"Yes, we know about the science fair. Okay," Low said then turned to me. "Get everyone." I nodded and walked back into the living room where Casey was munching on a sandwich.

The screen was playing a music video, Johnny Toxic singing a love song and I couldn't help thinking of Low. His firm hands and strong presence. You always knew you were safe with him.

We caught up with Johnny Toxic, who is rumoured to be dating the Mayor's daughter.

"Too fucking right the people are pissed off man, I mean have you been down in these streets Miss Screen Reporter, bitch get the fuck out my face!"

"We gotta roll," I said lifting up the boy and girl, one in each arm. They looked at me with frightened pleading eyes and I smiled at them to calm them down. It had the opposite effect and I sighed as first the boy and the girl began to cry afresh. I'm no good with kids. "Bring the woman," I said to Case.

Casey turned the screen off and hefted Guff's wife over his shoulder.

We took the hostages into the garage and dumped them in the back of the van. I jumped in the front seat next to Tealson and nudged him awake. His left prosthetic leg spasmed as he woke up. "The university," I said. He nodded and started up the engine.

An Indigo Song for Paradise

Intermission

Gutter Dice

We live in a corrupt and savage world,
full of murder and betrayal.

On dark and lonely nights
I often wonder,
what manner of soul
throws the dice of their lives
into such a place?

Is it merely to marvel at the beauty of rainbows in
gutters?

I used to be a good for nothing son of a gun who
didn't give a damn about no one but number one.

Now I wander the streets: a man with a purpose,
delving underground into subterranean realms
amongst the lost and found,
soaring across alleyways in broad daylight
don't worry - it's a rare sheep that looks up,
searching for answers.

I was born here but do I belong?
What accident of fate -
what synchronicity
led me to this reality?

Who are my ancestors:

The divine archetypes?
The primordial Nagas?
The ancient Africans gods and heroes of myth and
legend?
The (un)known(?) builders of the great pyramids

from Egypt to Cambodia to Machu Picchu?
The lost tribes of Israel?
Adam and Eve, who for all I know are still tripping
on the forbidden fruit,
falling to the grass of Eden while dreaming our saga,
observed by the serpent?

And what's with these strange plastic people
popping up all over the place?

Who do the parasites of Pacha Mama work for?

Do they truly seek to replace Love with the
Machine?
Respect with Institutions
run behind the scenes by cabals
following diabolical codes designed
to enslave the people,
corrupt their minds
and destroy their very souls?

Is Reverence for the source of all Life truly beyond
them?
Is that why they seek to keep us locked down in fear,
leading by example and expecting us not to care?

What are we even doing here
racing around like rats in this crazy maze?

Is this all some grand cosmic experiment?

Who decided to take a divine being,
place him in a body that's mostly water
on a world that's mostly water,
then raise him up in a culture where
the greatest aspiration of the majority
is indulgence in sensuality and shameless decadence

An Indigo Song for Paradise

built on mountains of filth and toxic corruption?

Who, God, who!?

Think about it and let me know if you figure
something out.

Lately, I've been imagining reality as some giant
Casino
and our lives as one big roll and tumble across the
green
on our way to the final reveal.

(sevens or snake eyes,
luck, strange skill or blessings in disguise,
all eyes focused on the prize,
devils become angels and lovers grow wise,
nature do love courage, it does or dies)

Who threw the dice if not us?
Yet why would we do such a thing?
The gods must be crazy!

Neither Church nor State have any answers for me
and the economy is one big old pyramid scheme.
The reality of money is in the words, honey
listen careful now, "e con me..."

And that's why I became an outlaw ;)

I'm not in it for the cash, the thrills or fame;
I do this because I'm good at the game.

Fucking with the Man is just a perk;
to fund spiritual growth,
I'm happy to be a jerk.

Efe Tokunbo Okogu

So I levitate across a highway
to the rooftop of my penultimate destination
where my partner for the low down awaits:
Miss Took, dressed all in black, smiling
like she was lady death's finest gunslinger herself.

Crouching low,
we peer over the edge and scope the scene,
flipping up our hoodies
as acid rain begins to fall.

They call me Gutter Dice
and I'm here to play.

Miss Took

This world is nothing but a low down dirty shame,
full of cowards and fools,
trapped by ignorance in fears and desires,
deceived into valuing attachments over the freedom
which is their birth right...

yet we fell willingly,
unknowingly...

Oh denizens of Paradise City,
To paraphrase one of your prophets:
May all your passions become virtues
And your devils, angels.

The enemy is dastardly indeed
and I fear it may be too late for this world.
We fight for justice from the shadows
unknown and unseen; a worthy cause -
but I long to go home.

If I could ask every man woman and child in
Paradise

406

An Indigo Song for Paradise

some questions, it would be these:

Have you ever looked in the mirror
and failed to recognise the one staring back?

Have you ever been to the crossroads
and realised there was no turning back?

Have you ever wrestled with darkness
or fought to tame a shadow?

Have you ever said no to low fruit
then risked your neck for woe to the foe?

Have you ever looked on your death without fear
or wagered on the outcome of the eternal war?

Have you ever given everything you got
only to find out you have to give more?

Have you ever perceived beyond good and evil,
grasped both worlds and strove for greatness?

Have you ever truly felt alive
or known deep in your soul what it means to be
blameless?

Have you ever wondered why
in the first place you chose to be born?

Can the depths of your true self be fathomed
or must the gods forever mourn?

I wish I could ask these questions
but would it make a difference?

Forgive them father for they know not what they do;

They are blind and deaf to their own divinity,
gods with their tongues cut out,
unable to smell what the third rock from the sun is
cooking.

I would despair had it not been foretold:
Babylon will burn to never rise again.

And we will finally be free.

I wish it were today,
but that's an ion quest
for trumpets players and other aficionados
of the sound of real brass.

Not my will but the Most High be done.
Right now, we've got work to do.

"Yo, Gutter Dice."
"What's up?"
"Care for a little joyful participation in the sorrows of the
world?"
":)"

Meanwhile, twenty one floors down below...
A certain intrepid young reporter stands on an empty street
chewing on a stick of ginseng flavoured gum. A monkey the
size of a young boy swings through the alley behind her and
drops to land by her side. It has indigo fur and is wearing a
necklace, tin-foil hat, dark leather trench-coat, and dungarees.
The reporter steps back startled as they both study each other
closely.
  "Are you my contact?" she asks feeling ridiculous even as
she does so. Nevertheless, events of the past few weeks have
opened her eyes to a whole other world she never suspected
could exist and at this point, she has suspended all disbelief.
  "Who are the Kings and Queens?" the monkey asks.

408

"Em…the rich and powerful?" she answers.

"No. The Kings and Queens are those who have in common with the Earth, the spirit of natural leadership and their true wealth and power is not measured in the material, though of course the Earth always recognises royalty. Tell me, who is God?"

"I'm God, you're God. It depends on your level of awareness, I guess. We are all infinitesimal fractals of the infinite and eternal One that is ALL."

"Do you know why a full third of the host of angels rebelled against God?"

"Em… I haven't read my Holy Word recently but isn't it because they wanted to be rulers in heaven and not servants?"

"That's the official story. The real truth is found in the setup of any good game. For it to be satisfying, the opponent must be powerful enough to challenge you into becoming a better player, but not so powerful that you cannot overcome. Tell me, who is your opponent?"

"My opponent? Well I'm a reporter so I guess my opponent must be lies."

"What of the lies you believe to be true? What of the lies you tell yourself? Tantric practitioners in their sacred ceremonies, take off the mask of their temporal personality and wear the masks of the gods. It is a way for them to see that both the gods and themselves are masks worn by God. If you know you are God, why not take off your mask?"

She is silent as she contemplates his questions. A soft breeze blows by, whipping dust and discarded newspaper pages into mini twisters. For a moment, the debris is shaped like a man sat cross legged in the air. The monkey is also silent, watching her face with an inscrutable expression. After a while she asks, "Tantra is about sex, right?"

"Tantra is a spiritual science. Sex is a part of it, but far from all. But before you get into tantra, first you must get into yoga which is the science of the mind. And before yoga, you must be healthy in body for which the science of ayurveda is most useful."

"Why are you wearing a tin-foil hat?"

"It is lined with thin strips of an advanced form of magnetic orgonite that protects me from negative vibrations. My necklace is also made of it," he says pulling it out from within his dungarees to show her. It is translucent and shaped like a pyramid, filled with bubbles and layers of different materials of varying colours and textures that she can't identify.

"Come," he says, reaching out a hairy paw. "Let me show you the city underground and reveal the true nature of your enemy. Do you know what a friend you have in the Lord? He ain't sitting at the right hand of the Father for nothing. Motherlover's creating new worlds. Come, there is much I would like to show you."

As he gently holds her hand, acid rain drops reflecting neon playing a staccato beat on their clothes, and the metal, glass, and concrete surfaces of the dark alley, she realises just how strong the little monkey is. He could snap her arm like a twig if he so chose. But she feels no fear, no hesitation. Her strange path had brought her this far and she intends to see it through.

The Network is Real. It is not just some conspiracy theory or SF fantasy. It is her destiny. Most folk believed in the illusion that they were separate entities. She was entering deeper into the knowledge that all is one. This she felt in her bones.

5: Who's the man?

Lil' T

What is the value of a hueman life? Let me rephrase the question. If the only thing standing between you and your goal is some motherfucker continuing to breathe then what would you do? Well, you've got three choices really.

One: you turn around and walk away. Take the hit and go down. Live and let live. But what if you're desperate? Why? Who can say? Life has a way of pushing you to the edge of the abyss sometimes. Don't get caught slipping 'cause it's a long way down.

Option two is to take the motherfucker out yourself. Get tooled up, find the guy, drop him and get away clean. That ain't easy for most people.

That's where option three comes in. If you can't put in your own work, you call me. That's who I am. That's what I do. I am a powerful tool, use me wisely.

I am currently in the hands of an employer who rules much of the street level of criminal activity in this city from his base in Freaktown. I deal with life and death every day. It's cold out here, son. Don't step up if you ain't got what it takes.

So what is the value of a hueman life? Is it measured in the number of heartbeats per lifetime? Do you count those moments when the record skips? All I know is if somebody wants your corpse donated to medical science and my employer doesn't need you breathing, then I might just be the last face you ever see…depending on how I kill you.

"Yo Tone," JoJo said. "Let's check out a university, bro."

I stopped writing and turned to look at JoJo driving, the city lights flashing behind him, harsh reds and bright greens, slashes of purple and yellow lighting up his dark face, square jaw, scarred cheek, and nose that had been broken and reset one too many times. We were in the west end where all the theatres, cabarets, and speakeasies played out their narratives amidst the glow of flashing lights and razzmatazz. I like showbiz people. They know how to have a good time.

"A university?" I asked

"How many pawn shops we checked today? How many guys Legs got out here doing exactly what we're doing right now. But think about it. This machine or whatever it is that we trying to get so bad, it's some kind of advanced science type gadget, right? So maybe someone at the university might know something."

"What, you wanna go now?" I asked. "Who's gonna be there at eleven in the pm."

"I don't know. Don't they got mad scientists and shit doing secret experiments late at night when no one's there to know they're breaking the code of ethics or some shit."

"Man you watch too many movies but okay, what's the closest university? Wait, hold on a moment." I pulled out my pocket screen and activated it. An oval of light filled with data organised in a hexagon appeared before my eyes. I clicked on the GPS and quickly located a few universities in the vicinity.

"The closest one that seems relevant is the Obatala Institute of Learning. Here." I flicked the information onto the windscreen and he headed uptown.

"Obatala? Wasn't he like a gunslinger from the vampire days?"

"You've never heard of Obatala? Wow nigga wow, where'd you go to school? Obatala opened up the world's first university, only back then they called them mystery schools. I'm talking about thousands and thousands of years ago, long before the emperor. There were many levels and you had to study for like, forty years, before you could read the secret scrolls. Obatala was so wise a lot of people believed he was an alien from a race so far advanced people worshipped them as gods. Some even believed that they created hueman beings.

"Aliens created us? I thought we evolved from monkeys."

"Well, they took some apes and used their own DNA to genetically modify them to create us. We're all hybrids essentially."

412

"And forty years in school?" JoJo exclaimed incredulously. "That sounds like a long fucking time, man."

"Yeah but by the time you graduated, you were like, a Jedi master. You could levitate and see halfway round the world and blow shit up with your mind and cure diseases and read people's thoughts and all sort of cool shit like that," I said.

"Man, I can do all that with technology and as for reading people's minds brother, that's easy. All you gotta do is watch how a nigga moves and you'll know all you need to know. Anyway, fuck that. Did you hear the one about Mr No-one?"

"Mr No-one?"

"Yeah, Mr No-one."

"No."

"One… Okay so Mr No-one is like a nobody right, a regular invisible man who becomes so good at it that he disappears. I mean he's still there only no one sees him. Unless he chooses to be seen. I mean this guy's a ghost, no one knows he exists. So after awhile he decides to sell his services to get paid. I mean he's also just a regular guy you know and he needs money so he becomes a private detective.

Of course he's good at it. Efficient. Reliable. Discreet. Makes a name for himself among those in the know, you know? Then one bright and early morning, Mr No-one gets a client who asks him to help him find himself. 'You want me to help you find yourself? What are you, lost? You're right here, ain't ya?' 'No I'm not,' says the client, 'I only think I am but I'm really somewhere else entirely.' 'Where's that?' asks Mr No-one. 'I don't know. If I knew where I was, would I be paying you to find me?'" Jojo chuckles to himself then continues.

"Mr No-one can't argue with that kind of logic so he says okay. He figures he's got a lunatic on his hands, probably a rich eccentric or something. If the fool wanted to pay him, what harm could it do? He could always give some of the money back if a relative complained. Besides, it'd make a change from the usual dirt chasing he was hired to do."

We pulled into the university's parking lot. It was filled with cars, mostly practical fuel efficient little numbers. The campus was one of several spread out within the neighbourhood.

"Let's take a walk around. There sure are a lot of cars. You think there's something going on?"

Jojo was checking on his screen. The ball of light hovered in front of his eyes as we walked, bobbing up and down to match his movements so that the image remained steady for him. "Yeah, there's some kind of science fair going on."

As we approached the building I saw a security checkpoint. No doubt they'd have weapons detectors. We stopped walking. We were both strapped.

We ducked around the building, casing the joint for other points of entry but all the windows were closed and there were cameras everywhere.

"Okay," I said as we stood under a tree round the corner from the entrance. "I'll go in, you stay out here." I passed him my weapons one by one, the twin sub-machine guns in my shoulder holsters, the quickdraws strapped to my forearms and the grenades in my boot. I kept my ceramic knife tucked into the small of my back. I was wearing an exoskeleton but I had a license for it.

"So what happened to Mr No-one," I asked as I walked away.

"Right. So Mr No-one has this cush little earner right, he don't have to do nothing but sit back and let the money roll in," JoJo's voice was clear in my earstud, audible only to me. Unless another hueman being was standing with our auditory passages cocooned by the cave of two ears physically touching, they wouldn't hear a thing, and even then it would sound like a whisper.

"There's only one problem. The client. He comes in once a week pestering Mr No-one for answers. It gets to be a real pain in the ass fobbing this guy off. I mean he's a nutcase and he's convinced he doesn't really exist or something. And the madness starts to rub off a little. Mr No-one finds himself

414

contemplating the nature of reality. Asking questions he'd never asked before like 'Who am I?' and 'Why do I exist?' I mean, he was just a nobody, a regular guy who happened to have a knack for being invisible and a mind clear enough to figure things out. Then a funny thing happens. He starts getting answers."

I walked up the stone stairs that led through a marble archway into a lobby area.

"May I have your ticket?" the security guard asked.

"I should be on the list," I said a little breathlessly like I'd just jogged here, "I'm helping with one of the exhibits but I'm late. It's been a nightmare. My uncle got hit by a bus and the whole family's been going crazy with worry. I just came from the hospital. He's alright but I have to get back. I just came to help out with some settings on the flux capacitor."

"Who are you with?" he asked

I glanced up at the corner of the room as if seeing something startling, he turned to look and as he did so I took the opportunity to check out the list.

"Class 2B," I answered, "Dr Maria Hoon."

"Let me see…okay, here we are…and what's your name?"

"Justin Thyme."

"Justin Thyme? I don't see your name here."

"What, did they fuck up again? I told Dr Hoon to get a new intern. Look, there's been some kind of mix-up. Here's something for your troubles. Just let me in and you'll be doing a lot of people a favour." I pulled out my billfold and peeled of four high notes for the man. He looked into my eyes for a moment and I added a fifth, threw in a rich kid smile for free. He took the bills and turned around without even asking to see my exo license and I walked into the main hall.

It was filled with people walking up and down the corridors between the various displays that filled up the space. All sorts of gadgets with screens full of schematics and equations and vids filmed out in the field. Directly opposite the door was a huge banner. It showed a blue skinned female child with a dozen arms, each one playing with different items ranging from the nucleus of an atom surrounded by whizzing electrons to a hueman heart with wings.

DevilDog

According to *The Art of War* by Son Tzoo, what the ancients called a clever fighter was one who not only won, but excelled at winning with ease. Hence her victories brought neither acclaim for wisdom nor credit for courage. She won her battles by virtue of making no mistakes, conquering an enemy that was already defeated. This is my inspiration. To be that good. To be a Master.

We live in a world without heroes so who's gonna step up if not us. If not me. After all, I do believe in certain principles like freedom and honour, principles sorely lacking in Paradise. How great do I have to be to actually make a change in my world?

In the real world, everyone makes mistakes of course. Nobody is perfect, at least that I've ever met, but I believe it is within us to strive for impeccability. Life is simple really, perfectly imperfect; somehow the great invisible machinery of the cosmos keeps on rolling and our crude souls are the fuel which we refine by living our lives like a Fibonacci sequence approaching the golden ratio. Why else would we choose to be born? By luck or fate, I'm ahead of the curve because I know who my enemy is and what my true heart desires.

My enemy is me. Devildog. A hueman being who likes to play games. My true heart desires to be my best friend, to nourish and support my healthy growth.

There are no such things as external enemies. I am a living breathing woman, manifested in this reality, which wise ones say is little more than a dream. I see the elegance of the game and I know real life is beyond the material, beyond all abstract concepts. All that matters is here and now. Live. Not on a screen, though the infernal devices have their uses.

An Indigo Song for Paradise

This is first and foremost, a universe of energy. Matter is an illusion. It's all magic and we are gifted with many tools. Some are fools, blind to reality, others are wilfully ignorant.

Am I a fool to hunger for revolution? Even after the riots last night? Even after all those dead people. Perhaps. But then the real revolution has ever been within, found in our beating hearts and inspired by cosmic winds.

A non-violent revolution would be ideal but can we afford to wait? Wait a minute, what am I saying? Afford to wait? Why do we speak of time as money? Why do we spend time and save time? Is it because our time is the real wealth and money is just ones and zeroes running through the mind of a computer somewhere like a daydream, or perhaps a nightmare?

Maybe the whole city, God's clock, is nothing but a complex machine designed for the sole purpose of stealing our time and converting it into energy for the machine to feed on while giving us the illusion of wealth in return.

Maybe it poisoned the natural world so we'd have no choice but to live in symbiotic relations with it like some sort of insane psycho control freak partner that can't let go of a bad relationship because of the fear of being alone.

Maybe the machine tells itself on those long dark nights of the soul that it loves us. That getting us hooked on sugar, fat, sex, violence, celebrities, politics, consumption, money, and all the inanity of modern culture, was for our own good. That hijacking our natural desires and turning them into addictions for poisons only it can provide was its way of being a member of the family.

There's a theory that the whole world is nothing but a simulation being run on some sort of hyper-dimensional computer. If so then maybe we're not stuck in this reality, this doomed megalopolis on this dying planet of Terra.

Maybe there's a way to hack into the operating system and free ourselves from the clutches of the machine and its cultural memes that masquerade as our gods. Maybe one day we'll wake up from this nightmare into a new world, one where man is no longer enslaved by the whips and chains in our minds. A world where our souls can roam free of all limitations.

Maybe...

We were standing in the middle of the annual science fair at my old university. Dr Guff was probably around somewhere but I hadn't seen him yet. I could see many other faces I did recognise though; academia is a small world. I'd dropped out of my PHD in Abstract Metamathics seven years ago but I occasionally came back to, ahem, appropriate material for the cause.

I dropped out because a handful of cactus seeds blew my mind one mad summer and I became allergic to hypocrisy. It literally makes me want to hurl. Who knows what cosmic energies were at play that summer, but suddenly a whole generation of us were dropping out and experimenting with the hallucinogenic cacti growing in the interzone between civilisation and the wasteland.

It was like talking to the desert and discovering that it knew your soul better than you did. It was like crossing a burning bridge just to see if you can fly. The next six months were strange, to say the least; causality revealed itself to be multidimensional and ancient stories began to whisper to newly awakened lobes in my lucid dreams.

After a while I adapted to my new reality and discovered that science was merely one aspect of magic; that magic possessed a science and mathematics to it, a meta-logic that decoded reality to create keys which in the right hands could unlock the door to...

Let's just say to see something you haven't seen, you have to do something you've never done. For the past seven years I have been experimenting with energies that mainstream science does not acknowledge. Or so I thought until Ecila showed up with his almost luminescent blue skin and a device labelled 'Prototype: Property of TerraCorp.' A device that, if my interpretation of my preliminary readings were correct, was older than the universe itself.

I was excited. This was a genuine mystery. Either our estimates of the age of the cosmos were wildly inaccurate or something else was going on. Could the little machine in Ecila's jacket really have sidestepped the big crunch and bang? Could it exist outside the eternal wheel of destruction and creation? That was impossible. Only God could do that. Something else was going on, but what? The existence of the machine hinted at something incredible.

Let me explain.

They say a lot of knowledge and wisdom, scientific, metaphysical, and magical, was lost when the last emperor took to the stars. I'm sure it's true, but this machine was evidence of something many of us had long suspected, that the emperor did in fact leave a fragment of the empire behind. I believed the machine to be one such relic, probably one of many scattered among the power players or lost and hidden on Terra.

It also hinted at something far greater.

Most scientists now believe seventy-three percent of our universe to be dark energy, and twenty-three percent dark matter. The distribution of dark matter is in fact similar to hueman cells and networks, almost as if the universe were a vast living brain or perhaps beating heart and its network of arteries, veins, and capillaries. Only four percent is ordinary, what we call matter.

Numbers are a funny thing. I believe they are alive in some way and exist in a meta-reality connected to ours. I believe that on their plane our lives are the result of calculations made by entities so complex our ancestors could only envision them as the machinations of gods.

For example, 4 is not only the percentage of atomic matter in the universe but also the same number of points which the simplest form of matter, a tetrahedron, requires to be perceivable and thus exist in the three dimensions of space. In both cases less than 4 and we enter into uncertain territory. 4

is also the minimum number of castes prescribed by the ancients for a functioning human society: priests, warriors, farmers/merchants, and labourers.

I dream of a world with no castes. Or perhaps an infinite number of them.

Then there's 23, the percentage of dark matter in the universe we previously considered to be empty space. It is also the number of chromosomes in gametes, all other cells having 46 in pairs of 23. The average hueman biorhythm is 23 days and Terra is inclined on its orbital plan by 23.5 degrees, the point five may be represented as $5 = 2 + 3$. The number 23 also pops up over and over again in connection to strange coincidences throughout Terran history, while 'Psalm 23' is the most quoted verse in the Holy Word.

> *The LORD is my shepherd, I shall not be in want.*
> *He makes me lie down in green pastures, he leads*
> *me beside quiet waters, he restores my soul.*
> *He guides me in paths of righteousness for his*
> *name's sake.*
> *Even though I walk through the valley of the shadow*
> *of death, I will fear no evil, for you are with me; your*
> *rod and your staff, they comfort me.*
> *You prepare a table before me in the presence of my*
> *enemies. You anoint my head with oil; my cup*
> *overflows.*
> *Surely goodness and love will follow me all the days*
> *of my life, and I will dwell in the house of the LORD*
> *forever.*

I love those words. I used to be an atheist because I did not like the dogma and hypocrisy of organised religion. But after those cactus seeds opened the doors of my perception, I now see that the Lord is a fractal concept, a state of mind that we can all attain if we but strive for it. A state of mind that is there for those who listen deeply in the silence, without fear.

An Indigo Song for Paradise

As for 73, it's probably the coolest natural number out there. Its constituents, 7 and 3, are both considered to be magical numbers by many ancient cultures. There are 7 chakras, 7 deadly sins, 7 heavenly virtues, 7 days in a week, 7 colours in a rainbow, while 3 represents the trinity, a fundamental concept in all religions. Ask the average person to think of a number between one and ten and most will choose seven followed by three.

73 is not only the percentage of dark energy in the universe but also a prime number; a star number; the same number of books as in the Holy Word; and an emirp, meaning that the reverse of 73 is 37, also a prime number and a star number. Plus 73 is the 21st prime number while 37 is the 12th prime number.

The number 21 has 7 and 3 as its prime factors. The number 21 in binary is 10101; 7 in binary is 111, 3 in binary is 11, and seventy-three in binary is 1001001. All of these are palindromes. In addition, of the 7 binary digits representing 73, there are 3 ones.

Also, $37 + 12 = 49$ (seven squared) and $73 + 21 = 94 = 47 \times 2$, $47 + 2$ also being equal to seven squared. Additionally, both 73 and its mirror, 37, are permutable primes and they both form the centre of sexy prime triplets.

There is more. Much more. The deeper I dig, the more I find.

What does it all mean? I'm not sure to be honest. Putting it all together is almost like...remembering...rather than discovering. I don't know how else to explain it.

What I do know is that prime numbers are the building blocks of mathematics and they exist at the sea level of a 2 dimensional map of numbers, matching the quantum nature of atoms exactly, which means that they are spaced out in a grand pattern which we do not fully grasp as of yet but evolve ever closer to understanding.

I also know that 73, 23, and 4, all came up a statistically significant number of times along with, to a lesser extent, 8, 12, 21, 37, 46, 47, 49, and 94, in the various readings I took from Ecila's machine. Playing with numbers can be fun and/or dangerous to one's mental health but doing so is taking my meta-mathics into uncharted territory—especially relating to fractal fluctuations in the morphogenic field, and what are we if not pioneers.

There be monsters out there and I'm hunting the largest and oldest ones. Considering that the least advanced huemen only use four percent of their cerebral capacity and the most advanced mind ever studied, the famous child prodigy, River "Bongo" Congo, used twenty-three percent, I believe it is all significant somehow. Bongo's death was such a tragedy. He could have single handedly saved the world.

I sometimes wonder what the majority of our minds get up to while we dream in the darkness. Perhaps the world is so fucked up because we exist in a state of ignorance. Perhaps the more aware we are, the less evil is manifest.

I was four years old when I found out that the stories my parents told me at night about Santa Claus where not real. I was twenty-three when I first realised that Santa Claus' props were all stolen from Shamanic culture, that the advertisers were weaving magic spells on people not for their physical, mental, and spiritual healing, but to sell them poisonous products while tempting and bullying them into bad lifestyle choices.

That was back in '73, the summer TerraCorp tested one of its biological weapons on the populace—pretended it was an accident when they got caught, and of course got away with it. The courts are run by the same folk who run the corps. Like with the police, when the same folk who terrorise you write up the reports, don't expect to find the truth anywhere but in between the lines.

The numbers are trying to tell us something; probably many things. All I know is that we exist in a dark world. We are in fact the darkness from which the light arose as well as the light illuminating the darkness. In this time of mass extinction and numerous crises, I believe it behoves us more than ever to increase our awareness and level of consciousness before it is too late.

An Indigo Song for Paradise

Shakespeare's Sonnet 73 ends with the lines:
This thou perceiv'st, which makes thy love more strong,
To love that well, which thou must leave ere long.

The bard was right. Time waits for no one. Better to spend it sharing love and cleansing karma than waste it chasing temporary desires or fleeing illusionary fears. Space and linear time are illusions, space being the construct that creates the illusion of separation, time being our perception of events as being subject to linear causality. This means that I can warp space. This means that I am time. Thus I can bend space-time at will. We all can. After all, consciousness, awareness, the self, is all that truly exists, here in the eternal and ever changing now. It is however one thing to know, another to do.

To attain to my full potential and become my true self, I know I must undergo an inner revolution, destroying the false state of my conditioning with its limited conceptions of reality, and co-create a higher state of being, one with the divine spirit which vibrates at such an infinitely fast rate, it appears to be perfectly still, the Most High being another name for God.

Revolution demands Love which demands Courage which demands Strength which demands Wisdom which in turn demands Revolution. Spiralling ever upwards and outwards, we witness and experience, learn and grow on our way home.

I couldn't see Dr Guff anywhere. Ecila, Yolanda and I were walking around in a group observing the exhibitions. We stopped in front of a stand where a young guy was hovering in the air with a pair of bio-mechanical wings strapped to his back. Wow! He looked and sounded like a hueman hummingbird as he moved gracefully through the air.

He hovered up towards the roof of the atrium, dodging past other flying contractions. It caught everyone's attention and a crowd gathered around as he came back, touching his feet lightly upon the hardwood floor like a barefoot ballerina. He was young, maybe sixteen, one of those child prodigies OIL University is so proud to nurture.

423

"The geometry of the wings changes moment to moment," he explained taking off the wings and placing them on the table next to his display stand. "Each polygon makes up an interdependent plane that generates energy by vibration. The wings then flutter as a whole."

"What's the power source?" someone called out.

"The vibrational frequency of the interdependent polygons themselves creates a field which can be activated with a simple tuning fork. That field is the energy conduit let us say. The source would be everything...and nothing.

"I prefer to look at it like this. The energy field already exists like a fat lady singing in a room connected to ours by a closed door. All I do is open the door for the music to come in loud and clear." He pulled out a shiny tuning fork and held it up to the light.

"Each polygon is of a different shape and size, like snowflakes, no two are alike. More than that however, each one is in itself in a state of constant fractal flux. The only constant in this universe, ladies and gentlemen, is change. Vibration, resonance, motion." He struck the tuning fork and the wings began to hum like a sweet chorus of background vocalists harmonising, then suddenly leapt alive.

"Once flapping, you can fly for as long as you yourself are able to before getting tired. There are no controls but the inside of the harness is lined with sensors that transmit neural signals from the flier's back muscles.

"It takes some adjusting to but once you get used to it, it's like," he smiled, "well it's like flying. This is the only prototype and we're a long way from being able to a mass produce wings but my team and I believe that in ten years from now, we will all be flying through the skies."

There was a loud murmur of excitement. 'Oh my gods' and 'That's incredible' and 'How much to let me try it out?' Wild chatter and all the sounds of a crowd of people dreaming a brave new world where they were no longer huemen but aermen or something like that. I was already in the skies looking into that boy's smiling face. He knew he'd just blown our minds.

A spontaneous round of applause broke out that lasted for several minutes. The crowd had chosen their favourite. Even if the wings didn't win first prize, they'd won our admiration.

Legs

I'm at the spot overlooking the club from behind half reflective glass. Dark Fantasy is packed as usual, the players all pimped out grooving to the house band, Slip Top 'n Cream, backing Sister K'Rude crooning her twisted blues. She's been with me for years. I know she hates my guts for what I did to her and her family but then it is this very hate that inspires so much of her music. She thinks I don't know about her schemes and plots but I got it under control. Girl actually imagines she's gonna have me killed and take my throne or some crazy shit like that. Talk about dark fantasies. It's not real sport but toying with the little people does keep life entertaining.

Whatever...it's all in the game, anyway. I can see them but they can't see me. I am less than a gleam in the eye, I am more than any of them can imagine. They believe I'm a mere gangster and I admit it's a role I play very well. The devil makes it easy for me. All I have to do is use the tools gifted me by God.

Can I help it that I am a wolf surrounded by sheep? There are many creatures in this world, if you have the eyes to see.

My current clients for example remind me of giant insects, sophisticated in their communal theory, elegant in their design, cold as a crater on the moon, evil as a fiend koked out on KKK trying to rob you for a quick fix. They're spooks of some description, feds whose interests lie in the acquisition of power beyond the ken of the common man. Not the same feds who supply me with my drugs and weapons but feds nonetheless.

They frighten me, to be honest, and I don't scare easy. The way they always manage to get the drop on me is infuriating.

425

I have the best security money can buy but these spooks are clearly using the kind of tech money can't buy. I turn back from the club scene to look at Mr Fin in his impeccable black suit and tie, eyes hidden behind dark shades that are no doubt linked directly to some command centre somewhere. One thing's for sure, this room isn't the only thing those eyes are looking at.

"Relax Mr Fin," I say pouring myself a drink. "Don't flip out or anything." He just sits and watches me impassively. "That was a joke. You guys never get spooked right?" He still doesn't say anything.

"Look, what do you want from me?" I say, downing my thousand-dollar-a-bottle rum on the rocks and pouring myself another, savouring its fierce elixir, the refined spirit burning through like a slow explosion. "My men are out there scouring the city. Give me one of those magic suits of yours so I can teleport myself out there. How many times I gotta tell you, just give me one chance and I can do some serious damage. Really get some work done. You know?"

"We don't have magic suits, Mr Elegance, and teleportation is nothing but science fiction. If we did, we wouldn't have hired you to steal the device for us, would we?"

"Then how did you manage to sneak in here? I know you're not a hologram because I already shook your hand."

"As I've explained to you before Mr. Elegance, you rely on .trick.nology to protect you and we are experts at manipulating the flaws in .trick.nology."

"Everyone relies on technology. Everything is technology. Without technology we're just animals. Come on tell me the truth, did the aliens give us technology? They did, didn't they? Come on now, we're in this together, son. We're partners, you can tell me... Man, fuck you nigga!"

I throw my glass against the wall. It shatters onto the carpet. A little robot emerges from an alcove and cleans up the mess. Mr Fin doesn't even flinch. For a moment I have the feeling he isn't really there in the room with me.

An Indigo Song for Paradise

"Okay," I smiled, "no worries, level six security clearance and all that. Above top secret. I get it. I'm down with need to know. I just want you to know that I'm capable. Otherwise we wouldn't be doing business." I walk over to a cabinet and pour myself another rum.

"Listen player. I'm the master of this level of the game. Why else you talking to me? You know and I know that I'm pimping this bitch out. Getting paid. Do you know how I got here? I was hungry and I didn't take no for answer. I'm still hungry, Mr Fin. So come on, throw a nigga a bone. You won't regret it. I got skills."

I poured another drink and took a sip, looking at him across the table. I know I cut a nice figure in my zoot suit, the colour of midnight. I'm young, strong, and healthy. The ladies love me and I'm making bank. I paid the most expensive interior designer I could find outside Lagoon to Feng Shui this room. It's got a micro-climate designed to keep me calm and alert including subliminal sound-waves that replay a mantra reminding my sub-conscious that Julian Elegance is the greatest Caesar of them all. Thames Pond ain't got nothing on me.

"I am only here to remind you, Mr Elegance, of our agreement. We have paid you a lot of money already and we will pay you a lot more. We have fulfilled our end of the bargain. Now it is up to you to deliver. Give us the device. There are no other options. *trick.23.*"

"Don't worry, Mr Fin. You'll get your device."

I turned round to face him but he was gone. Motherfucker! I froze. There was no way. There were only two ways out of here. One was the door which I was standing next to. The other was the window which was rigged to shatter at the push of a button. Sure a few niggas might get a few cuts but let's just say, that's the price I'm willing to pay. I was also wearing a lightweight bulletproof vest and an exoskeleton beneath my zoot suit, the latest slim line model upgraded by my guys at the chop shop. Ready to rock and roll at any moment.

427

If I went out, it would be with a bang Freaktown wouldn't forget in a hurry. Boom! Bye bye baby blues... I won't miss you so fly away. Children will sing dark nursery rhymes about me for generations to come.

I went over to check the cameras. On one of the old tapes, you can see something flicker like a shadow, as if the screen had briefly caught in its invisible net some fleeting imprint, the edges of a trail of a man who moved so fast the rest of us were like statues. I couldn't understand it. If Mr Fin could do that, why come to me?

Mayor Obvious Beastedy

He looked into his exhausted bloodshot eyes; his whole face was haggard and falling apart, losing cohesion. Goddamn, he was weary of life. He was still young, forty two at his last birthday but he looked and felt twenty and a deuce years older. God, he was tired of dealing with the filth and scum of society.

He came from a prominent family. Old money from the days of the Empire. The Beastedy fortune could be traced to a certain Olmon Beastedy who had been a minor bureaucrat in the empire, a position that allowed him to embezzle a small fortune for his descendants.

It was true that Obvious had come further than any other Beastedy. He was, at least in theory, ruler of the world or at least what was left of it. The city state of Paradise was his personal kingdom. He was the most powerful public figure on the planet. He should have been luxuriating not staring into the mirror wondering what it was all for. Like the old song said, *I've reached the top but I had to stop and that's what's bothering me...*

He was tired of waiting for the true reward. At the rate he was going, he'd be dead of a heart attack before he retired.

"The reporter might be a problem," Adam was saying, "she exposed the chemical dumping that affected the city's water supply last year and now she's investigating VIBRA."

VIBRA was new tech from TerraCorp being secretly tested on the population. It was early days but the old boys in white claimed it could be used to implant subliminal suggestions in people's minds.

"Hmmm, let's put a scare into her. If that doesn't work..."

"Understood. Now about the poster. Now is the time. The people are enamoured with such gunslingers and ghetto superstars as Babylove Brown and Silly the Kid. We need to show them your tough side. The Sheriff, riding into town to clean out the trash, vigilante justice, that kind of thing."

Obvious looked at the poster. It was done in the style of street art. His face, half in shadow painted in dark colours overlooking a stencilled city of bright lights seen from some mystery location in the hills, a revolver in his hand.

Was Adam being serious? They'd laugh him out of town. He looked at Adam's bright shiny teeth grinning with an enthusiasm Obvious did not feel. He looked back at the poster. "I don't know."

Sometimes Obvious felt like a painted skeleton on marionette strings, controlled by little more than instinct. He had a sharp intellect but right now what he needed could only be found in a purple pill. He turned his back on Adam and popped one. The moment the gel sac touched saliva it began to dissolve into liquid intuition. This was one of his secrets. A drug from the old boys at TerraCorp. You couldn't buy this stuff with money.

It didn't even have a name, just a long string of numbers. He carefully placed the little vial containing the pills back in the leather pouch around his neck next to his little gold cross and tucked them back under his shirt. A few seconds later...

..

.

.:.

;. [his body accepted the virus]..

[for a second he felt as if something threw up in his guts then it passed in a wave of chemical sensations]

..

Tic toc
The King of the Clock
…

..

.

He sat down in his ergonomically grown semi-organic chair and relaxed. One of the pleasant side effects of the purple pills was colours. Their vibrations now spoke to him on a deeper level. It was like everything was suddenly alive. Vivid images jumped out at him, accidental confluences of light and shadow creating a sort of meta-landscape.

It was like being in a sumptuously designed film and his office was suddenly revealed to be much more. Everything in his field of vision was an extension of his true self. Everything seemed to dissolve into everything else. His office was the whole world and it was made of nothing but light and air.

He knelt down and threw up. Great globules of ground up meat and vegetables from his exquisite lunch earlier in the day, now converted by his stomach acids and enzymes working with the various bacteria and other life-forms that inhabited his guts, the throne of intuition, into a homogeneous slop.

He stood up and took a few deep breaths. He walked away from the mess as a droid designed to look like an anthropomorphic puppy came out of her little closet and cleaned up the mess in the most realistic imitation of a naughty French maid. Sometimes when no one was looking, he fucked it. Real nasty like. She was his personal little midget sex toy. She was realistic in that aspect too, physically simulating sensual reactions from her bouncing titties to her moans, her dirty talk to her juices. If she was a touch cold and mechanical, it was little different from making it with the social climbers that he often bedded. As mayor, he was King of the Clock and he enjoyed fucking around. Sad puppy just happened to be his favourite little kink. At least she wouldn't ask him for favours or connections afterwards. He knew it was technically not normal behaviour but he hadn't risen to the top by being normal.

The whole world was one big con and the vast majority of people were fools. Only those brave enough to be their true selves, however warped that may seem in the eyes of others, had the stuff it took to make it on this half-dead world.

He looked at the poster again. What was his doppelgänger looking at, off stage and page? What other world? Was it the same world shadows gaze at with no eyes? It did look good, he had to admit. Mayor Obvious Beastedy, avatar of justice, neither young nor old, neither handsome nor ugly, an everyman graced by the gods, doing his duty. He could be your brother, uncle, nephew or cousin. He could be your neighbour or colleague, your best friend. He could be you.

His common appeal had helped him blend in all his life, the ambition that burned within him, brighter than the solar flares that beat down on the city, hidden behind his friendly smile. Quietly, unobtrusively, he had risen up the political ranks.

Then one fine day in his home in Lagoon, he had been invited by an orb of light to meet with certain ladies and gentlemen. Invisible to everyone but himself, the orb had led him to a light-golden sailboat on the lagoon. He sighed in memory. It had been one of those perfect days, the sky a soft blue, the clouds like wisps of pure imagination.

The orb led him indoors and the hatches sealed themselves. The sails furled and put themselves away and the sailboat transformed itself into a yellow submarine. It had dropped like a slow anchor to the depths of the lagoon past the multicoloured little and big fish to land on the bottom of the lake.

The submersible attached itself to a portal hidden on the lagoon floor and he was led into some sort of underground station where a silver bullet the size of a car hovered, waiting for him.

The plush interior was made of a luxuriant fabric he'd never seen before. The door sort of melted shut and the bullet shot off at a fantastic speed but inside it was as if nothing was happening. He'd have believed it all to be a giant screen

431

illusion had he not actually arrived at a destination at the end of the improbable journey.

Inertia dampeners: he'd heard of them but wrote them off as an urban legend. Obvious was a keen racer and he'd actually searched for them, going deep with his people into the black markets where mutationists and alphemists dealt in illegal technologies. He'd found some weird stuff, some of it useful, some of it frightening, but no inertia dampeners.

As he remembered, he visualised what his eyes saw back then; thanks to the purples he was able to remix reality. Adam's face was now swimming faintly behind the window to the tunnel, whizzing by so fast it became something else entirely, a giant underground snake, whose skin was the very skein of life, coloured with the various treasures won in countless battles, and dotted with the dark patches of exits not taken. A great serpent whose slithering caused earthquakes beneath civilisations.

He smiled remembering his shock and awe when he realised he'd travelled far beyond the boundaries of the city, still deep underground. Eventually the bullet slowed down and came to a stop in an underground station made of solid gold interlaid with precious jewels of all shapes, sizes, and colours. He had ascended the golden staircase and entered another life.

They, the mysterious elusive THEY, had given him a glimpse of another world full of sumptuous gardens and fabulous wealth. A glimpse, and nothing more, of a world that made Lagoon look like a trash heap.

Pleasure domes that held the last treasures of the Empire set amidst forests where animals he'd believed extinct were hunted, and incredibly nubile young men and women, sex slaves of great attractiveness and skill, were available for *any* game he desired to play.

If he played his cards right, one day he too would live among the chosen ones. Of course they were mostly vampires and occasionally engaged in blood sacrifices but hey, no one was perfect. That THEY believed in such superstition was almost endearing in a sick and twisted way, felt Obvious. Their victims were probably unwanted by society anyways or perhaps even bred to be killed. In any case, all he had to do was keep the drones on the surface working the cogs of the complex machine that the unseen and unknown lords and ladies of creation might feast in decadent luxury and one day he'd be one of THEM, and they had access to anti-ageing technology that would extend his lifetime three-fold.

His campaign for mayor had been planned and orchestrated by experts and he had won in a landslide, taking over from the last mayor who portrayed himself as being exceptionally incompetent. Obvious had been the obvious choice, the golden boy, a bright and shiny antithesis to the corruption and muck of the last administration. The people had bought it, hook, line, and sinker.

His campaign logo had been "Yes, We Are!" The people chanted it at his thunderous speeches where he asked, 'Are we masters of our fate? Are we lords and ladies of our destiny? Are we the chosen people, inheritors of the Earth? Are we guardians of tomorrow? Are we free women and men?'

"Okay, run the poster. Anything else?" Adam's grin grew even wider as he walked out.

"You won't regret this sir," he said.

Obvious Beastedy was impotent. He could get it up but this sheriff was firing blanks. No souls chose to be born through any cosmic portals anywhere near the vicinity of his testicles. Many years ago, he had formed an alliance with an ambitious young lady, a rising bureaucrat named Milo Upyors. She had been disappointed for she found Obvious to be a perfect husband in all but the one respect.

Fortunately THEY had been involved in his life ever since he took his vows as a member of the Furs and Fangs in his first year of college and had stepped in with a surrogate. A man who looked very similar to Obvious in a certain light. The man had made love to his wife once and left.

Obvious had asked the obvious question. "Why not artificial insemination?"

The man had replied, "No *trick*, it can only be this way."

Obvious remembered there had been something weird in the man's accent when he pronounced the word 'trick', almost as if it had some other esoteric meaning Obvious could not grasp.

As the course of nature took her turn around the sun, Milo grew large and gave birth to their daughter, Sofia. They'd been happy…for awhile. They would be happy again…he hoped. Right now, his family hated him almost as much as the rest of the city. He hadn't made love to his wife in several years and as for his daughter, Sofia was lost, utterly lost.

Maybe he should have been more like his own father. Maybe he should have kept his family in constant fear, then at least they wouldn't constantly embarrass him.

Now Sofia had taken up with that musician, Johnny Toxic. Lord, what a nightmare that was turning out to be. Johnny was an outspoken critic of all politicians and his bad boy devil-may-care attitude won him a lot of admiration. The boy was all front of course, but still Obvious' PR people were working hard on finding solutions, the latest of which was to hire professional seduction artists to break them up. What a fucked up world he lived in where he was reduced to contemplating such measures. What had happened to his sweet little Sofia? When did his little honeykins grow up into a nineteen year old bitch whose mission in life was to ruin his career?

Obvious turned on the screen and there she was, his beautiful daughter dressed like a prostitute singing about broken hearts. Did she know she was breaking *his* heart? Actually it was a pretty good song. Sofia had genuine talent; why did she have to expose so much skin?

6: Free Energy

Legs

I was still in the office ten minutes after I wanted to be. I looked impatiently at the seconds ticking by on the watch tattooed on my left wrist. Armand was still talking, going on and on about every little problem under the sun. Was he trying to drive me crazy? I was going to have to give Armand's knuckles a rapping soon. *Armand...* Pff! What a gay name.

"Okay, a couple more things. One, we've got to do something about them Big Birds," Armand said.

"What did the Jugglers boys do this time?" We'd been feuding with the Big Birds for awhile now. It all began when they refused to pay their taxes. I run this town but those motherfuckers seem to think they're above my law. They'd recently hijacked several shipments of ours in a row suggesting they had a mole in my house. We managed to block their planning permissions when they attempted to build some kind of after-school club for kids in a rundown section of Dhoti where I happen to own a lot of property.

Not that I have anything against children, but I needed the area to stay poor a little while longer till I bought out a few more people. Dhoti is strategically placed for redevelopment and the profits will be huge when the time is right. The Big Birds tried to muscle in on us with their fake-ass save the children routine but they failed.

"It's Johnny Toxic. They're trying to steal him from under us. One of their guys from Talisman Records is wining and dining him right now."

"So what? He's signed to K'Racked Pipe Entertainment, right?"

"It was a five year contract and we signed him four and a half years ago."

"He hasn't re-signed yet? Hmmmm. It's probably nothing. Nigga know he got a good thing with us. Why jump ship? We're all making bank. He's killing it on the charts. 'Ballad of Babylove Brown' is at number two; 'Slo Dance in hell' is what?"

"Number nine."

"Yeah, number nine. He's up for best artist, best album, best song... Just pay him whatever he wants. Is he trying to squeeze us, the little bastard? How much he want?"

"It's not all about the money Legs."

"Whachoo talking 'bout Armand?"

"I talked to him a few days ago and that's what he said to me. He was pissed off about something."

"What else he say?"

"Just that there was more to life than money and art shouldn't be caged."

"Little prick! Okay, forget about it, I'll deal with it. It is Bad Money's birthday party on Friday, right? The night before the awards. Johnny and Bad Money go way back so Johnny'll be there. I'll talk to him, sort this mess out." I stepped around him and opened the door.

"Now if you'll excuse me."

"Wait. What you want me to do about Bobby?" Armand asked.

"What about him?"

"He vanished. I ran the numbers, Legs. There's no profit in food stamps."

"He vanished?"

"Yeah. Your cousin Olive's been going nuts. She's saying we killed him."

"We didn't, did we?"

"No. The fat fuck just ran. She's downstairs right now."

"Who is?"

"Olive, your cousin? Bobby's wife?"

"Oh for fuck's sake! You didn't tell her I was here did you?"

"I said I'd look for you but I reckon she knows you're here Legs."

I looked out the window and there she was, sitting at the bar, watching the window to my office like a hawk. I jumped a little. For a moment it looked like she could see me. I went to

436

my desk and laid out some lines of KKK. This shit probably killed more niggas and their communities than Paradise City did when she killed the rest of planet Terra.

"Damn! I hate that bitch. She always used to make fun of me when we were kids." I snorted two lines, one into each nostril and leaned back into my chair, feeling that familiar stinging sensation followed by the incredible rush... Fuck that was good. A pure high. The best money could buy. I felt ready to headbutt a bull.

I looked at my watch again. There was still time to make it.

"Shit! Okay, send her fat ass up. Tell her I'm late for a meeting and can only spare her five minutes."

Lil' T

The science fair was incredible. The theme for the year seemed to be free energy. There were all sorts of inventions revolving around energy harvesting, optimisation, conversion, and utilisation. Solar arrays designed in fractal patterns, artificial octopi whose waving limbs harvested wave energy underwater, a plasma field generator, a giant vat of water filled with some sort of blue light, a generator than ran on piss, another which ran on water, an engine that tapped into the planet's electromagnetic field, and many more.

"This is the end of all our problems," a man was saying loudly to a group of listeners. "With free energy finally within our grasp, we will easily tackle all other problems facing society.

"After all, energy is neither created nor destroyed, simply transformed from one form to another. Thanks to the recent simultaneous breakthroughs, we now have the ability to access far more energy than ever before.

"Energy that can be harnessed to power fantastical new inventions. Mankind will never want for anything again!" There was a wonderful infectious excitement in the air. The crowd around the speaker grew louder.

"This couldn't have come at a better time in hueman history. The very last uranium deposits in the world lie not far from the city and we long ago passed peak. I predict a great change in society, ladies and gentlemen, now that we have crossed this scientific thresh-hold. In fact, I will go so far as to say today heralds the end of war and all forms of crime and violence. What need a man for violence against his fellow if he hath everything his body and soul could desire?

"The fact that all the inventors have decided to give away the plans for free across the inet further means that there will be no pretence at monetising energy. With the end of war, comes the end of the economy. No more shall he con me, that masked devil known as capitalism. No longer!"

Groups of people were speaking excitedly, others were using their various devices to broadcast their reactions live onto the inet where news of this unprecedented event was disseminated across the city.

The flying man soared into the air again making loops near the high roof of the auditorium.

"We have come, ladies and gentlemen, to the end of an era. Let us call it the Psychopathic Era and have entered a new era. The Empathic Era. It will take a while for us to become accustomed to this new paradigm. At moments like this, it is impossible to predict what great changes huemanity will undergo.

"What new cultures and sub-cultures, styles of poetry and art, waves of innovation in music and technology await?

"Ladies and gentlemen, we are in for one heaven of a ride!"

There was a thunderous round of applause and the people pressed forward to speak to the man. People pushed past me and then a gap cleared in the crowd and I did a double take. Some motherfucker with skin so black it looked blue was standing right there, holding the machine I was looking for in his hands.

Babylove Brown

As we rolled to the university area from the north side, the radio started playing 'The Ballad of Babylove Brown'. The guys began hollering and cheering as usual; they love that

tune. I have to admit its pretty good apart from the line about
me being the baddest witch in town. I mean it's true but the
way he sings it, stretching out the '*Brrrrooooooowwwnnn*'
always gave me goosebumps like some feline devil was
jonesing for a fix of my soul.

> *Bullets flying in the noonday heat*
> *Sirens wailing as the shots ring out*
> *Babylove Brrrrooooooowwwnnn, hit me!*
> *The baddest witch in town!*
>
> *The cops have got her whole crew on the run*
> *But no one's faster than Miss Brown and her gun*
> *In shootout after shootout, she out-slings em for fun*
> *Babylove Brrrrooooooowwwnnn, two time!*
> *The baddest witch in town!*

We listened to the rest of the song and then I said, "He make
it sound like we out here just partying with guns or some shit.
Outslings 'em for fun? One of these days I'm gonna shoot
that motherfucker Johnny Toxic in the face." As if in
response the DJ said, "No doubt about that, 'The Ballad of
Babylove Brown' holding steady at number two. That was
Johnny Toxic and you're listening to Tribe Vibes, the last
refuge for the soul. I'm your host DJ Connect. Caller, you're
on the air. Who are you and what do you have to say to the
members of your fellow tribe of man on this beautiful
evening in Paradise?"

"My name is Lo-rize, representing El Cabron. Big up to the
Permies, Osayin, and The Seed Savers. Ashe! First up I'd like
to give a shout out to my shorty Lulu. Thanks for having my
back when no one else gave a damn. Second, I just wanna say
to the families of those who died in the riots, be they
policeman or civilian, that you are in my prayers. Last but not
least, can you play *Dom, the Devil and John Brown* by
Chango?"

"Sure thing, you have a good evening now."

"You too," said Lo-rize and a moment later and the beat kicked in with the sound of a gunshot accompanied by a wailing blues harp like a train howling into the distance and Chango's old-timer sing-song rhyme schemes.

> *Free Dom - the brother's innocent;*
> *he didn't shoot no deputy – the Law's out to get him.*
>
> *He only sought for peace of mind*
> *by showing true love and being kind,*
> *but one moonlit night out by the tracks,*
> *he crossed paths with the Devil*
> *and Sheriff John Brown.*
>
> *Now the Sheriff had always hated Dom,*
> *been jealous of him since they was young;*
> *and despite now being the big man in town,*
> *the people still respected Dom more than John*
> *Brown.*
>
> *So John looked around to make sure they was alone,*
> *no one to see what was about to go down;*
> *he smiled a mean ol' evil frown*
> *and said "Dom, your time has come!"*
>
> *As the Sheriff pulled his gun,*
> *Dom kicked up gravel and moved like light from the*
> *sun;*
> *Brown got shot and thought he was done;*
> *and the Devil cried out, "Boy, what have you*
> *done!?"*
> *Well, better kill him off, it might even be fun*
> *to blast the head off that son of a gun!*
> *They'll hang you fo' sho' if you let him live*
> *it's you or him, one life's gotta give!"*
>
> *Dom ran straight back into town*

An Indigo Song for Paradise

And told all the folk the Sheriff was down
by the tracks and bleeding out;
"better send a doctor before you need a devout
priest to read the man his last rites;
even that dog deserves to face death with a fight."

As the deputies arrived, Dom fled the scene;
they shot at him but couldn't capture him;
Four of them chased him into the forest;
Three came back claiming John killed the fourth.

Now I don't know what happened out there;
When it all went down I was sitting in my chair,
rocking on da porch, smoking my funny pipe,
watching the blue moon all full and ripe.

But if you ask me my opinion,
I reckon you must be smoking opium;
Whatever happened to that deputy
had nothing at all to do with Dom being free.

See the thing about Dom and I pray me and you
is we got the light so there's no need to rue
doing the right thing - it's always rewarded
in this life or the next, it's all recorded.

So please take the bounty off our brother's head,
Free Dom or you'll have us to deal with instead.

As the song finished, Tealson drove us through the campus and parked as close to the auditorium as he could in an unblocked spot advantageous for a quick getaway. He turned off the radio and we both swivelled round to face the others. The family were sat with their hands tied in their laps and their ankles bound.

"Alright Professor," Low said. "We're going to go for a little walk. Your family will stay here in the van so don't worry

441

about them, okay. They'll be safe. All we want from you are two things. First and most importantly, we want you to see if you can find the missing section of this machine somehow. My partner," he nodded towards Tealson, "has picked up a signal within the city but is unable to isolate the exact location due to its strange nature. Secondly, we'd like to know what the machine is. If you think you can handle that, your family has nothing to worry about."

"I'll do my best," Gruff said.

We stepped out of the van, Tealson staying behind as usual. Gruff stopped to look at his family for a moment before Low gently nudged him away.

"I really should pop my head into the science fair," said Gruff. "If I don't someone will start looking for me. Tonight is a special night for the university and the city. I don't know if you are aware but there have been a series of incredible scientific breakthroughs, by different teams simultaneously. The synchronicity of it is astounding."

"So?" I said.

"So there's a lot of press in there and I'm expected to give a speech. If I don't show up…"

"Okay, we get it," Low said. "Just don't do anything stupid."

"I won't," Gruff said.

As we neared the stairs leading up to the auditorium Casey stopped us. "Hold on. Weapons check."

It was true, there were several security guards with scanners. We looked at each other and shrugged, then placed our hands together and played a round of rock, paper, scissors. I lost. I sighed as Low and Casey took off their weapons and handed them to me. I unzipped a side pocket and unfurled a large kleptodethrene shoulder bag to carry them in.

As they went into the building I found myself a good vantage point close to the entrance, hidden in the shadows of a corner. If they needed me, I'd be there in six seconds tops.

Seventy-three! Do or Die! Our code ever since we were kids running wild on the streets. Meeting each other had been like

An Indigo Song for Paradise

God herself was saying to me, *I know how sad and lonely you've been. Here, let me make it up to you. You look like you could use some friends.*

I met Casey first when I was twelve. I hadn't been underground in a minute but I was surviving. The mutants had taught me well. Casey and I were working the same trick ass marks and mark ass tricks in the same streets so after awhile we figured, why not rob them together.

It was great or at least round the corner from greatness. We worked our way up to hit the rich neighbourhoods, sniffing out the ones who liked them young, pretending to be lost jailbait. While one of us distracted them, the other would sock them over the head. Then we'd take 'em for all they had.

Casey had a home but he was always running away. His old man was real violent. Burned him with cigarettes and shit like that. He once tied him up in the basement for three days with no food or water, used his skinny pre-teen body as a punching bag. Casey's mama died of an overdose when he was real young.

I had no idea if my folks were dead or not. They probably just didn't want me. There's files on me but I never bothered to look them up. Who gives a damn, right? What difference would it make to my life if I was able to trace some blood relatives? After all it's not like we're family anymore. Fuck 'em, they don't want nothing to do with Babylove Brown, that's for damn sure.

Tealson and Low were brothers. Tealson was older by a couple of years but he'd lost his legs in a car accident and was in a wheelchair, his promising boxing career amputated before his prime. Low robbed his first bank a few weeks later with his friend Moha and paid for Tealson's first set of prosthetic legs. By the time Casey and I met them, they were on their third bank job together and looking for more gunslingers. A mutual friend introduced us and the crew was born.

We've done everything from theft to armed robbery, hijacking to kidnapping, and elaborate scams to straight up

443

assassination. We're good. Real good. We're even famous, Babylove Brown and her badass crew, even though I'm not really the leader. We don't have a leader though Low is often on point. Everyone just does their part, you know.

But that's just the way the media is; they tunnel vision on the most sensational aspects, in this case, me. It's not always a bad thing, the publicity. Men look on me with a form of awe. I think it's because the male psyche knows it has brutalised the female and fears retribution. So it idolises the bad-ass female as a way to appease the gods.

Most men are a bunch of sissified punk ass bitches with no balls these days anyways. As for my fellow sisters, too many are still waiting on that special man who's gonna be the hero. They have yet to learn what I knew ever since I was flushed away like a used tampon. There are no heroes in Paradise. Only winners and losers.

Amerika is a rigged game in an illegal casino and no one understands the rules because there are none. The House makes it up as it goes along and yes, the House always wins. Sure they'll sell you a song about how you might just be the one lucky or smart enough but it's different for people like us. We know we're coming to the table with a bad hand and no money to re-buy-in. That gives us three choices.

One: play it safe and hope to get lucky after spending our entire lives struggling. Two: bluff but don't get caught or lose all credibility. Three: cheat and run the risk of being locked up, fucked up and/or killed.

My soul cries out for a fourth way. But no one hears my song. So I give them gunpowder instead.

"Help! They've got my family!" It was Gruff, I could hear him in my earstud. Damned hostages. Most of the time they're easy to control but every once in a while shit hits the fan. Nothing to do but roll with the punches. I was already running towards the stairs.

"I'm on my way," said Tealson.

"They kidnapped my family! Those two and others outside in a van! Help me!"

I leaped up the stairs three at a stride.

"Wait now, there must be some kind of mistake, what you been smoking Professor?" Casey buying me some more time. I raced past security and burst into the auditorium. The alarms began to ring and the two guards behind me shouted out for me to stop.

I scanned the room and spotted Low, Casey, and Gruff, standing in a loose crowd of people. I swung the bag round a few times like a ball hammer then released it. It sailed high over the heads of the gathered people, knocked a flying contraption out of the air and landed in front of Low and Casey.

As this was happening I turned to face the two guards who were approaching, hands hovering above their hip holsters.

"Freeze! Security! Don't move!" one shouted.

"PCPD!" yelled a voice somewhere behind me in the auditorium. A shot rang out and the rent-a-cop in front of me reached for his gun. I drew both pistols from my hips beneath my light trench-coat and blasted the guard in the chest. As he dropped, I put a bullet in the second one's head. Bullets whizzed past me and I twirled to shoot a cop in the throat then ducked behind some kind of flying saucer.

I hung onto the side of the floating disc and peeked my head under it. I spotted Low and Casey shooting it out with security and cops, and Gruff, dead on the floor, a hole in his head. *Dumb motherfucker! We would have let y'all go, you and the family. Now you got me out here deading niggers again.*

I righted myself and my weight moved the disk. I bent my knees slightly and rode my steed into the fray, bullets bouncing off its metallic surface.

Holding on with my left hand, I reloaded with clips of fractal bullets then fired round the right side and blasted a policeman in the legs. They exploded in a red mist and a chunk of gore splattered onto my face.

As I wiped the blood from my eyes, the disk began to crack from the pressure of gunfire and I jumped clear to roll behind a machine that looked like a cross between a giant hedgehog and a film projector.

Across from my position, I saw a dark skinned man standing over a dying man that I recognised. The dying man, one of Legs' strong-arm men, was saying something over and over again that looked from the movements of his lips and mouth like 'No-one loves you' and the blue skinned guy was nodding. Then I saw the device in the blue man's hands. It was the section Moha had died for.

I was on my feet and running over when one of the walls exploded and our van flew through the hole, knocking over stands and displays and skidding to halt in front of me. I flung open the side doors and dove in, dodging bullets.

I grabbed the crying little girl and tossed her outside. She landed and rolled, screaming from behind her gag as she tried not to injure her tied limbs when they twisted beneath her body.

"Cease fire or the family dies!" Tealson's voice boomed out over the van's loudspeakers. I grabbed the boy, put a gun to his head and crouched low, using him as a hueman shield. His eyes rolled wildly in his head and I could smell the acrid odour of piss rising from his trousers. His mother jumped to her feet and hopped past us, out of the van and towards where her daughter lay.

I scanned for Low and Casey, my mind urging them to hurry the fuck up. Then I spotted them, lying dead in pools of blood, perforated and torn apart by numerous bullets, the jagged edges of blasted exoskeletons sticking out of their corpses like the bones of some beast not yet born of Terra.

"Cease fire!" a few voices shouted repeatedly and the bullets stopped flying. The dark-blue looking guy was right there, a couple of meters away, huddled beneath a display with Moha's section in his hands.

"You!" I shouted. He looked up at me and the gun I was pointing at his head. "Get in the van!"

He looked in my eyes for a few moments then stood up and walked over. As soon as he stepped inside, Tealson took off,

reversing then spinning round and flying back out the hole
he'd blasted in the side of the auditorium.

I threw the boy out of the van and closed the side-door as we
crossed the threshold out into the night air. He landed badly
and I saw his neck snap like a twig just before the van door
slammed shut. I was silent for a few seconds. *Damn! That
wasn't supposed to happen...sorry kid...I've killed a lot of
people in my life but you're the first child I've ever taken out,
that I know of... Low, we fell real low didn't we? Maybe we
didn't deserve to be happy ever after...but then, does anyone?*

We bounced and jangled around, thanks to Tealson's
shortcut, down a hill, my gun still trained on the blue skinned
man as my thoughts moved on to Low and Casey. My
friends, my partners, my brothers, now deader than the desert,
deader than a gunslinger's heart.

We'd been so close to getting out. The mutationist who was
going to alter our features was waiting and our passports to
Lagoon were already prepared. All we had to do was show up
with the money.

Fuck! I know what Low would say, 'Live by the gun, die by
the gun. Drink a toast to me and move on. Just another day in
Paradise.' At least they went out blazing. We could still make
it, Tealson and I. We just had to stay alive for a little while
longer. Our new hostage was looking back and forth between
the machine, the section in his hands and me.

"You've been shot," he said. I looked down at myself and
saw blood soaking through my left side. It looked bad. I
pulled out a monocle from a jacket flap and affixed it to my
left eye then scanned the wound. I was bleeding internally
and my guts were all torn up. I could see blinking red lights
highlighting the numerous micro-surgeries I needed to
undergo within the next half hour if I was to have any hope of
making it. *Shit!*

The cold hard decision no gunslinger ever wants to face: jail
for the rest of my natural life or death. There were too many
of them out there.

Low was dead and with him any chance that he and I would one day live like the celebrity couples on screen. Beautiful Low who could slit a man's throat without moment's hesitation but was too shy to ask me out on a date. He was waiting for us to get out the gutter first. Or maybe that was just another of the little lies I told myself to keep going.

And Casey, my oldest friend in the world, who showed me how to have a little fun after taking the money and running. My boys were dead. All but one.

I watched the back of Tealson's big head and wide neck as he made our getaway and a tear bubbled close to the duct before dissipating back in a mist of emotion, spined with nano-steel. A moment later, I smiled grimly.

The ballad of Babylove Brown was coming to an end and I was not sad. Not really. No sadder than a broken heart. No sadder than a cum stain on a grown man's pants in public. No sadder than you were, the last time you cried over some big deal you can't remember anymore.

I popped open another flap on my jacket and pulled out an emergency shot. It was a cocktail of antibiotics, pain meds, stimulants and sundry exotics that would keep me going for a while. I plunged the mini hypodermic needles into my side and tossed the empty casing aside.

"Put it together," I said to the blue man. He just kept staring at me with a funny look in his eyes like he was a fan or something. I pointed my gun at him.

"Put the machine together or I'll give you a reason to feel blue," I said.

"I must be crazy but is that you, Chi?" he asked.

DevilDog
It all happened so fast. One moment I was in a group talking to Deph, the kid who'd invented the wings, and the next moment people were shooting guns at each other. I dropped down behind Deph's display then pulled him down out of harm's way.

448

"Easy cowboy, you're not bullet proof," I said then peered round to see if I could find Ecila. He was being chased by a real big guy. The man tackled Ecila to the ground and then they were struggling. Ecila got to his feet first but the other man quickly followed. The big guy was moving in that exaggerated manner people in exoskeletons have. He was clearly a trained fighter. I saw him slash at Ecila, the flash of a blade in his hands and I gasped involuntarily. He was trying to kill Ecila!

Luckily he missed. I had to do something, but what? I looked around frantically for anything that might be of use. My eyes jumped to the flying devices in the air and then down to Deph's wings. They looked like an origami dragonfly, folded glass encrusted with a filigree of intricate metalwork. I grabbed them, slung the hoops over my shoulders and began to attach the harness to my rib cage. They fit like armour.

"What do you think you're doing?" Deph asked

"I have to save my friend," I said, adjusting the wings to settle comfortably on my back.

"You don't know how to fly," he said. I grabbed the tuning fork and stood up. It was made of a humanium, a rare metal that constantly vibrates on audible frequencies. I could hear it singing softly as it moved through the air.

"How hard can it be?" I asked, being far more flippant than I felt, then struck the tuning fork with my finger. The wings leapt alive in a wonderful chorus of ethereal song and I began to float upwards.

"Imagine you're a fish swimming with a great current," Deph called out. "And don't let the wings face downwards too long!" I nodded and ascended quickly into the air.

Below me to the left were three shooters fighting against a dozen security guards and police. To my right, Ecila was dodging and evading the big man with the knife. Ecila was fast but it looked like only a matter of time before the knife took his life. I could see blood on his cheek from a cut he'd been too slow to dodge. I spun out of the way of a dirigible and swooped to grab a flying machine. It was shaped like a very long and sharp needle.

My fingernails were painted with nanocircutry which I proceeded to activate. A screen appeared floating above the toy aeroplane. I hacked into the crafts mainframe within moments and reprogrammed it into a missile targeted at the big man's back. Ecila was still dodging the knife attacks, using the small machine in his hand as a shield.

As all this was happening, a part of my mind took the time to question if I was truly ready to kill another hueman being. It was like a voice was silently whispering direct to my third ear as I hit the final sequence and my improvised missile flew down at close to bullet speed, aimed to pierce the man's back. He didn't die however. His exoskeleton must have been real good quality from the way he stumbled and fell.

The knife was suddenly in Ecila's hands and then in the man's throat. The big man spun around with a choked cry and crashed onto his back. In that moment I felt no guilt, no elation, but in my breast there was an ice-cold sliding sensation that burned like lava.

Ecila kneeled over the dying man, placed his hands on either side of his head, and broke his neck with a viscous twist. Then he proceeded to place his left ear onto the other man's right ear. It was one of the oddest things I have ever seen but in that moment it felt right, like some form of esoteric ritual, an acknowledgement of life and death, as if to say 'I hear you, I understand, you are not alone. Now walk towards the light.'

A van exploded out of one of the walls and skidded to a stop not far from Ecila. One of the shooters dove in and a few seconds later she threw out a little girl bound by her wrists and ankles. People started shouting "Ceasefire!" and the guns briefly shut up.

A woman hopped out of the van and across the floor towards the little girl, also bound hand and foot. She looked kind of funny, like a worm trying to walk like a man and then Ecila was kidnapped at gunpoint.

The van's tires squealed and it sped off, flying out of the auditorium and off into the night, spitting out a little boy before it vanished. The guns started firing after them. I dropped low and flew out of the doors, into the reception area then out through the main doors.

For some reason, I was clumsier closer to the ground and it took me a while to navigate. I was losing precious time but eventually I was out and up in the night sky. There was no moon and there were no stars. Just a heavy blackness illuminated by the bright lights of Paradise City. I rode the winds up and spotted the van cutting diagonally across a two lane road and then down the side of a hill.

I flew over the city, watching the van fishtail and almost roll over then skid to barrel up an exit to the freeway, vehicles crashing violently as they got out of the way.

Synchronised with the wind, I drifted closer, watching the play of lights, each one illuminating the world of man whilst blocking out the natural light of the night sky.

It suddenly struck me that the city was hell on Earth. Literally. A vast prison where we souls of the dammed were being punished for our one true sin, only we were too feeble minded to see the truth of it and too weak hearted to change the situation.

The van with Ecila in it was tearing down a highway, weaving in and out of the other vehicles. Police in mechas, assault vehicles, and helicopters, backed up by drones were swarming in from all directions converging on the van. I saw a news helicopter fly past with the words 104.9 painted on the side so I tuned in with my earstud.

"We now bring you live to the freeway where a high speed chase is underway. Babylove Brown and her crew are being hunted down by the police and oh my god, that was incredible! Did you see that?"

It was incredible. Like something out of a movie. Babylove Brown leapt out of the back of the van and onto the front carapace of a mecha. She emptied a full clip of the machine gun into a single weak spot and the mecha crumpled to the

451

ground, the rider dying as her bullets pierced through. She clearly had experience in killing machines.

As the mecha was going down she was going up, using her momentum to bounce onto another mecha then onto the roof of a cop car. The second mecha fell dead from an explosion in its chest and the cop car flipped over as she pumped several bullets into the tires. It looked like she was using fractal bullets.

Fractal bullets are very illegal, each designed in such a way that they fragment into deadly patterns that infiltrate structures on a fundamental level, causing cascades of massive damage. Anything hit with fractal bullets is blasted apart from within.

I watched Babylove Brown surf aboard the upended and skidding cop car as she fired at other vehicles and mechas. She leapt clear as it crashed into the side of the freeway causing a huge traffic accident of vehicles, both cop and civilian.

Vehicles exploded and I rose a little higher as the heat struck me in a wave. I spiralled out of control and fell like a stone, my wings facing down but I managed to right myself moments before I landed on the roof of Ecila's van which was still being chased by cops. I crouched low as bullets whizzed past me, some striking the van inches away from me.

We were speeding down the freeway curving east even as Babylove Brown was running on the rooftops of the buildings that bordered the road, heading south west. I was pulling the tuning fork out of my jacket when a couple of bullets hit my wings. They made a terrible crackling and crunching sound, sparks flew into the air and I felt the weight shift.

I lost my grip on the roof of the van and almost fell off but was able to grab on again, my fingers gripping the raised edges on the sides of the van's roof.

At the same time, a light began to emanate from inside the van, some kind of fierce illumination that peeled back the colours of the world turning everything translucent. I could see the man driving and Ecila huddled over the machine, the source of the light.

All three of us were glowing with refracted light, our skins semi-translucent. I could see my heart popping in and out of vision in time to the beat. The arteries and veins, the nerves and bones that made up my flesh, all pulsating together as one with the whole world, overlaid with strange patterns and veves.

The road suddenly vanished and deep beneath us I could see some vast crystal also pulsating to the same beat and far above us, beyond the skies, some sort of structure many times the size of our sun, like a brilliant glowing egg with uncountable strings reaching out in all directions, also pulsating.

Then in a sudden flash of darkness, all the colours were gone and for a moment there was nothing at all, not even me. I opened my eyes and we were somewhere else entirely.

Here… *Wow! Is that a motherloving dragon!?*

7: Curtains

The Xombie formerly known as Obram

He died somewhere over the desert, his mecha shot to burning pieces, his body crashing to the earth like a meteor penetrating the ionosphere. It lay in the wreckage for four freezing cold nights and three blazing hot days, a burned and blasted carcass slowly submerging itself beneath the surface of the desert by the simple act of being there.

On the fourth day he rose again, crawling from his shallow grave to stand in the sun. He was newly born, no longer a man but a xombie. The exotic and strange radiations in the wasteland had burned through his flesh, excavating all traces of the city from his system.

His body had reacted by producing large quantities of metaronin turning his skin into a deep fluctuating greyness that danced with layers upon layers of fractals. He held up his hands and saw infinity and eternity in the fractals that played through his skin, like music composed by a great unseen conductor, or instructions being downloaded via the sunlight.

He looked up and stared into the sun; his mind empty, his blank eyes watching solar flares explode towards the Earth, tracking photons and dancing particles, watching the colours his mind had never dreamed of make music with cosmic rays.

The internal dialogue which had been his constant companion most of his life—as it is the constant companion of most huemen—was now silent. The sands of the wasteland had scoured his internal landscape, scrubbed him clean of all traces of Obram. He was now something other, both less and more than a man.

He took a deep breath, turned away from the sun and began to walk with neither a destination in mind nor a doubt as to where he was going. He simply walked. He could feel the energy of the sun soaking deep into his skin and the soles of his feet as they left footprints in the sand.

He walked for days, taking long full strides, not once tiring, until finally the city rose from beyond the curvature of the

An Indigo Song for Paradise

Earth like a mirage, like something dreamed up by the desert to while away its long journey through the cosmos.

Sofia

It was Bad Money's birthday party and he had a surprise for us all.

"From now on, I shall no longer be known as Bad Money aka Mad Monkey for I renounce the wicked ways of my youth. I know many of my fans will be disappointed with my new material for I no longer glorify in the sins of Babylon. All I can say to these shallow individuals is they can go fuck themselves. Furthermore, kiss my black ass.

"From this day forth, I shall be known as Welfire! Yo DJ McGuffin, drop that beat, time to show these fools what time it is:

> *Your whole life's passing you by*
> *like a pretty girl on the stairs*
> *but you too scared to say hi;*
> *instead you waste your time battling day-mares*
> *lost in illusions like your mind was not worth the care*
> *so beware before you lose your soul in some evil dare*
> *no fear, that's just the devil in your ear*
> *no fear, that's just the devil in your ear...*
> *Trying to come on with that same old shine on*
> *Talking about "can't we all just get along?"*
> *While plotting to backstab you – you know he wrong*
> *Warring with the enemy till I am forever one!*
> *Your choice son [singing]*
>
> *(Chorus) Babylon or true Corazon*
> *Eternal life or annihilation*
> *Listen to your soul's song*
> *free your mind before kingdom come*
> *Aaauuummm*

Efe Tokunbo Okogu

Yo check it check it, it's time we blessed it
Speaking truth straight from the heart now test it
You guessed it: don't test me or vex me I'm a nutter
Put a hex on you like Harry Potter,
Shazaam, yes, I am a bad man
Snake up your spine making you divine;
Cause a glitch in the matrix
destroying all fakeness
my mental is contagious
enlightenment spontaneous
Dreading the dreaded? We blameless -
Deading the dead at heart? We infamous
They fear us coz we dangerous,
punk ass hos be acting shameless.

(Chorus) Babylon or true Corazon
Eternal life or annihilation
Listen to your soul's song
free your mind before kingdom come
Aaauuummm

Several folk joined in the chorus and Welfire sang it thrice with his backup singers till the whole room was in on the act before ending on a long sustained AAAUUUMMM.

There was a moment of silence followed by a round of applause, then Welfire continued speaking. "I will be performing more of my new material later on tonight but for now let me just say, welcome brothers and sisters to my humble home; may this night be a celebration of our communal huemanity and one motherloving party none of y'all will forget in a hurry! Oh yeah, it's on!"

Bad Money, I mean Welfire's pad was in the old heart of Freaktown. A brownstone round the corner from Ol' Patch theatre, the stage that had nurtured so many great musical talents over the years. I remember the first time I performed there, the magic of the space was pure electricity, like the gods were watching the stage too, and maybe jamming along once in a while.

"Give it up for Welfire." There was another round of applause as MC Ng took the mic on the stage and Welfire returned to his table. "And now, the lovely but twisted sister K'rude…"

I'm coming for you baby, gonna be real nice,
I made a deal and our souls are the price
fall with me into sensual delight   (come on baby)
eat of the fruit before they turn on the light

I walked through the archway into the next room, her voice trailing her words away into a low croon. Johnny was still talking to Legs, so I wove my way through the people towards the bar.

"Hey Sofia, love the dress," Hola called out from the bar and I walked over. She looked classy, a slinky little black dress showing off her curves.

"Thanks babe, love your show," I answered, leaning on the glass surface of the bar and looking at the exotic fish of multiple colours and patterns that swam within. I turned to the bartender. He was a good looking kid, probably another aspirant to the dizzy heights of Stellarwood.

"I'll have an Afterlife with a twist, easy on the lime," I smiled.

"You should come on the show some time," Hola said. "We can talk about music and life, a little politics but I want to focus more on the spiritual side of Sofia. You do know your name means wisdom?"

I nodded and accepted the drink from the bartender. He gave me a friendly smile.

"I'll put you on with Guru the seventh, have you met Um?" she said sipping from a straw bobbing out of a bottle. There was some kind of glow-worm in her alcohol.

"Um?"

"'Guru the seventh is called neither he nor she but Um? because the guru alone knows if he's a woman or she's a man.' That's from their literature. Can you believe it? In this day and age of scanners that can tell you what your mama had for dinner the night your papa knocked her up, not one person knows the gender of Guru the seventh. Every machine scan has revealed confusing results."

"Um? Pronounced with a question mark at the end? Sounds kinda off to me. No, I haven't met, um, the guru," I said sipping my drink. It was good. A warm creamy melt of caramel and fire. "You could hire a private detective," I suggested, arching an eyebrow.

"I did," she answered mirroring my expression.

"And?"

"He joined the Guru's cult. Come on my show and I promise you, your eyes will be opened." Hola opened her eyes wide to demonstrate and smiled. She was very beautiful. Her hot chocolate skin and amber tinged eyes, her long dreadlocks with their little bracelets made of wood, crystal, shiny metals, and ribbons made of silk and leather and other cloths. "Do you want to meet the guru now?" she asked.

I looked over at Johnny and he looked like he needed rescuing. Legs was chewing his ear off about something and poor Johnny boy looked bored out of his skull. "Sure, can I bring Johnny?"

"Actually Um? would like to meet Johnny as well," Hola said standing up.

We walked over to table where Johnny sat flanked by Legs and one of his men, Chuckles or something. On either side of them were two of their plastic whores, all sexual artifice and no soul.

"Johnny baby," I said. "Hola and me were wondering if you weren't too busy," I paused and made my lips into a cute O, "maybe you could *come* upstairs for a little private party. We need you to make love to us Johnny. The both of us, right now."

Everyone fell silent. Johnny was looking into my eyes with a little smile on his face and then Legs burst out laughing, followed by Chuckles and the two girls.

"Well you heard the lady. Go on now, just don't forget what we talked about," Legs said as Johnny got to his feet and walked around towards us.

"Room for one more on that train?" Legs asked as we each took one of Johnny's arms.

"I don't think so," said Hola and the three of us walked away.

"Thanks babe, that guy's really starting to piss me off," Johnny said kissing me on the cheek.

"What's the matter?" I asked

"Like I was saying last night, I can't stay at K'Racked Pipe. It's time for a change. The whole post ironic hardcore thing is played out," Johnny sighed. "Whatever, I just have to survive another five months and then I'm free. The bastard actually thinks he can convince me to stay."

"Don't worry, there's nothing he can do babe," I said kissing him on the cheek. "I'd kill him if he hurt you."

"I'd be careful, Sofia, mayor's daughter or no," said Hola. "I've heard some awful stories about that man."

"They're all true, I assure you," said Johnny, "He gave me my break, it's true, but that break could have come from anywhere. I mean my talent didn't come from Mr Elegance. It's not that I'm not grateful, but K'Racked Pipe is holding me back creatively. I need some new energy but they just ain't hearing me.

"I told that motherfucker just now that I wanted to record some tracks with The Chango over at Talisman and Legs started going on about how they were all a bunch of snakes who couldn't be trusted. I mean, what the fuck? I just wanna make music and he's trying to tell me who I can and can't do that with? Uh-uh, fuck that shit!"

"Hey Johnny, I heard that Babylove Brown was gunning for you," Hola said. "Are you worried?"

"Gunning for me? Where'd you hear that?"

459

"On the grapevine. In your song you called her '*a bitch out of hell, with balls bigger than her bazoongas.*'"

"Don't remind me, please. Man, I don't even remember recording that song and it's a hit. You know my favourite track on the album, 'Everyone Zero', didn't even chart?"

"I know, baby, I know. The game's all fucked up. By the way, Hola's got someone she wants us to meet," I said.

"Wait a minute. Have you lured me under false pretences? What happened to the threesome?"

"Sorry Johnny," Hola smiled with sweet mocking sadness, "not tonight. Have you met Guru the seventh?"

"Guru the seventh? I think I saw a video on WhoTube. It was...um, interesting. A whole bunch of conspiracy theories and shit about aliens and interdimensionalites or whatever."

By this time, we had walked through several rooms and ascended a few flights of a spiral staircase to find ourselves outside a dark wooden door on the top floor.

"The guru is a guest of Welfire. It was in fact the guru's influence that led to Bad Money's change of heart and name. These are Um?'s rooms," Hola said, knocking on the door.

A voice called out, "Come in," from within.

Hola turned the brass knob and opened the door.

"Oh yeah?" Johnny said, "I was wondering about that. We haven't had a chance to talk much recently."

It was a fairly large room with a queen-sized bed, a work table covered in books and papers, several comfortable looking chairs, a large window overlooking a garden and doors leading to a balcony.

"Welcome," said the guru as we walked in, standing up to greet us. He was a short and sturdy person with close cropped grey hair and very dark skin. I couldn't place her age or gender. He could have been anything from a twenty-nine-year-old woman to a sixty-year-old man. It was a little eerie.

Not that there was anything spooky about him. (S)he was clearly a hueman being. It's just that somehow the guru managed to look like no one else entirely. I suddenly

460

understood why they called the guru, Um? I didn't know what to make of...it.

Um? had a certain...aura. It was almost visible, like a glow. It was as if Um? had decided to shed all barriers between Um? and everyone else. Or (s)he had some very fancy toys, the kind daddy used to manipulate people in his political games. I was probably being paranoid but then only the paranoid survive in Para City.

As for Stellarwood...all you gotta do is give up a piece of your flesh to the devil. Like the cops rent out their blind eyes and deaf ears, their loose tongues and jack-booted feet, their truncheon-gripping fists and their trigger fingers. I never used to think about stuff like that before I met Johnny. He's into all that anti-establishment stuff. I like it because it pisses Daddy off something fierce.

"Come in, please, make yourselves comfortable," Um? said, ushering us into the room. "Would you care for drinks or snacks?"

Soon we were all seated with our chosen drinks. A sublime little cake made of nuts and berries layered with chocolate was melting into my mouth and Johnny was holding my hand. Hola was on his other side smoking haze out of a vaporiser.

"Your song, Sofia, 'Inspire', the one in which you sing, ahem, forgive my interpretation..." and then the guru sang my words in a strong sweet voice, and I had that lovely feeling inside knowing that a fellow hueman being knew where I was coming from. The same fucking planet, right?

> *If I knew how to be free*
> *Would I be in this cage?*
> *Would you still desire me*
> *If I turned the page?*
> *Why do you fear me,*
> *Like the end of an age?*

461

All three of us clapped our hands together. Um? sang beautifully, with a deep clear voice that could guarantee success in show business if Um? so chose.

"Thank you. You wrote that song, did you not?"

I nodded.

"As I thought. Sofia, would you and Johnny be interested in starring in a movie I recently wrote?"

"Really?" asked Hola, "you didn't tell me about this before."

"It was a surprise. Would the three of you like to hear my pitch?" Guru the seventh asked, "I assure you it won't take long."

"I don't believe it, I'm getting pitched by a saint," Johnny burst out laughing and hugged Hola and me close to him. "Pitch away, sir, err, madam, pitch away."

"Thank you," the guru said standing up and facing us, "but if I'm a saint today, know that I too once such a sinner. All the world's a stage. Maya. Illusion. Overstand your role and you awaken the infinite dreamer. First contact, second chance, third eye open, fourth wall breached, fifth dimension visible, sixth sense aware of the seven tales unfolding. The observer changes and is thus changed. Just remember there is always a higher level, a perspective beyond your blind spots."

Um? took a deep breath and began his pitch. His voice had a rich and deep timbre to it and she held us spellbound with the weaving of a tale.

"Imagine, if you will, that you were alive during the last days of the empire. Imagine suddenly waking up and discovering that the emperor was leaving Terra for greener pastures, another shore far from the planet. Most of the berths in his spaceship are already taken but the emperor in his generosity has left a thousand and one spots open to the victors of The Final Games."

"The Final Games?"

"Yes. There are actually records that suggest this took place. As you know, much of our history was lost during the wars, destroyed along with countless lives and uncountable treasures of the past. In any case Johnny, you will play Ecila, a young fellow competing in the Final Games and you, Sofia, will play Chi, a young woman who is one of the few to decline the emperor's offer to emigrate to the stars."

"Okay," said Johnny, standing up and walking over to the minibar. "I can dig it. We're talking the last days of the empire. The end of the Golden age. Beautiful sets and fantastical machines. All that wealth and decadence."

"Well, an austere form of it," said the guru. "Now, focus on the pathos for a moment. Imagine what it must have been like for the people. Those staying on Terra knowing they had been judged to be second class citizens, unworthy in the Empire's eyes.

"Some accepting their fate or creating their own, some fighting for a berth in the spaceship, some denouncing the emperor as a cold hearted son of a bitch. Imagine the lifelong friends and families saying goodbye, loved ones who would never see each other again."

"Why does my character, Chi is it? Why does she choose to stay on Terra? Is it for a man or family or something?" I asked.

"Chi wants to stay because she doesn't like the idea of what will happen to huemanity if the best of everyone leaves. Chi wants to stay to stop the war."

"But we know the war happened. So Chi fails?" I said.

"Yes and no. Meanwhile Johnny, you're competing in the most challenging games ever designed by mankind. We're talking about mental and physical challenges that kill many competitors and drive others insane. The whole world is watching via screen and you are suddenly a celebrity.

"In the mean-time, Sofia, you are being wooed by the emperor himself for he needs your genius in bio-morphology. You ask him how he can be so cruel as to abandon the people and he replies that huemanity must take responsibility for itself.

"You reply that you are hueman and will not abandon your fellow man. He says that there is nothing you can do to help them. Even if you stay, they will hate you for being one of the chosen ones, and they will complain that you are not doing your job well enough. And without the infrastructure of the empire, you will be reduced to basics, meaning your ability to help will be limited.

"Perhaps, you say, but something is better than nothing and I could teach the people what I know. In any case, who are you to decide who stays and goes? You ask. Well, says the emperor, wear this invisibility cloak and we shall go amongst the people we are to leave behind.

"If you can show me just one hueman who deserves a berth but was neither given one nor the chance to win one, I shall delay my departure until ships are built for rest of the entire population. If however by the end of the movie, one such man cannot be found, then you must sever your attachment to huemanity.

"In a series of twelve long scenes, each one shot in one take, flashbacks and dream sequences included, Chi and the emperor meet twelve archetypal personalities of huemanity and the stereotypes they have degenerated into as well as their hope for redemption.

"The spontaneous and trusting innocent who ends up living in denial; the streetwise and accepting orphan who turns into a perpetual victim; the heroic warrior who ends up a villain; the caregiver who ends up a guilt-tripping martyr; the brave seeker who ends up a castrated perfectionist; the lover who becomes addicted and uses sex to manipulate; the destroyer who instead of destroying that which no longer serves life in order for new life to grow, engages in self-destructive and psychopathic behaviour; the creator who becomes too obsessive to truly create; the responsible ruler who ends up the ogre tyrant; the magician seeking to make inspired visions a reality who ends up the evil sorcerer, transforming to the ill with negative thought patterns and bad intentions; the wise truth loving sage who becomes the cold unfeeling judge; the fun loving fool who becomes the glutton, sloth and lecher without dignity or self-control.

An Indigo Song for Paradise

"Mankind, having forgotten that the archetypes live through us, is demonstrated to be a broken machine; the living dead, the damned, and the lost, all locked in eternal cycles of karma, unable to transcend to dharma. In the same scenes we also see the beauty of man's struggle to overcome the world she herself has helped create.

"As for myself and my court, says the emperor, we are not simply leaving behind the planet but an entire noosphere of negative thought patterns. We intend to push beyond the very boundaries of space and time itself. I have moved beyond good and evil, Miss Chi, says the emperor; come with me if you are ready to take the same leap.

"In the end, Johnny, you fail to win a berth by the narrowest of margins. On a night out with your friends to commiserate, you meet Sofia and spend a night of passion together. The next day Sofia boards the emperor's spaceship."

"That's kinda sad," I said.

"And kinda beautiful," Johnny added.

"Yes, but that is just the beginning of your characters' arcs. The film concludes in a montage of the war and the various cultural milestones of the past two thousand years leading right up to the two of you, today, living in modern times.

"Like I said, that's the end of the first film. The two sequels will…"

"Sequels?"

"Yes, it's a trilogy. The ultimate goal of which is to show that it doesn't matter who went with the emperor, slave owning son of a bitch that he was, to explore the stars and who stayed behind on Terra, for the energy and ability to do incredible things are encoded within us all. Once the Buddha achieved enlightenment, it became possible for all to do the same. People have to learn to believe in themselves again.

"This truth is the heart of the entire trilogy and shall be the subtlest and most powerful of all the messages, revealed allegorically side by side with the simple fact that for all the machinations of powerful entities, we are our own worst enemies for we let it happen. It's time we let go of all the bullshit in our heads that tells us in one way or another that we, in our natural honesty and commitment, are not good enough.

"Tell me, Sofia, why do you straighten your naturally beautiful hair, turning God given roots into bad copies of the white woman's hair-do? Why do so many negro women and not a few men use harmful chemicals to bleach their skin, even in these dangerous times when melanin protects you like your mama's love?"

I shrugged, embarrassed, then sighed in relief when Johnny interrupted and said, "For some reason, that reminds me of one of Chango's tracks, the one where he goes..." Then Johnny drawled out in Chango's signature half-drunken style:

> *Babylon's got the brothers out there mercing each other*
> *while the sisters turn ratchet lined up twerking together;*
> *inspected by policemen like cattle led to slaughter -*
> *Niggas so scared, the enemy don't even gotta bother*
> *Life in Paradise sure is one hell of a mother...*

"Yes, I like that. Paradise is indeed one hell of a mother. Or should I say, 'one hell of a motherboard'. You see, Paradise City is an illusion, a simulation on a hyper-dimensional computer. That's why we call it the PC. Your task in the game of life is to save your life and your soul. Unfortunately, the game being played on the PC's mainframe is Empire. The Graphic User Interface displays Paradise but deep beneath the City, a ravenous beast of a machine seeks the corruption of your mind and the destruction of your soul.

"Our task in the game of life is to save our lives and indeed, souls. We have to become our own heroes, for all our sakes. We have to become our own superheroes, for all our sakes.

"Now in the game, there is a minority population, the vampire elite, who effectively control the majority through imperialism, the original schism founded upon deception. An empire only lasts as long as it is able to maintain, in the minds of its subjects and slaves, the belief in its almost divine right to kill, rob, divide, conquer, exploit, and oppress the people. 'Manifest Destiny', they call it.

"Another way of saying we can do whatever we damned well please so fuck you and your sacred connection to the planet. Once people no longer believe in an empire, it collapses. That's why propaganda is their most effective tool. Control what people think and believe and you control the world. They're so good at it the people don't even realise they're still slaves.

"The empire that currently runs what is left of our world was founded on the theft of indigenous land, and the kidnapping, mass rape and murder, extortion, and enslavement of the indigenous population. The genocidal emperor may be long gone to live in the stars but that original crime is still a part of the empire's nature, its code.

"That's what the superheroes in the comics never understood. The only real enemy is within; and if you but surrender to the Lord, the state of mind which was in the Christ will arise in you. Then you become the guru on the way to the superhuman. Then you can finally realise that you are the one you've been searching for all your life, all your countless lifetimes, often without even realising you were searching.

"The Christ was a negro just like you, the latest and greatest superhero to bust out of the PC and he now sits at the right hand of the father. God became man so man can become God. And thanks to the Lord's infinite grace, we can all achieve Christ consciousness.

"When I say surrender to the Lord, I don't mean run out and join your nearest church, though I'm not saying you shouldn't do that either. As long as people gather in the true spirit of the Lord, the church is not made of wood or brick but salvation itself.

"Unfortunately, the world *is* full of superficially *good* people who blindly follow the herd as it stampedes off the edge of the cliff. Even the temples are full of middle class negroes singing *Halleluyah* on Sundays while spending the rest of the week working to aid and abet the same motherfuckers that are exploiting and killing them, their loved ones, and the whole planet. They don't realise they still slaves.

"But if you remain in the herd heading for mass suicide, are you any different? Will you blame the steer in front of you for leading you to your death or the steer behind you for pushing you over the edge? Will you turn to the steers on either side of you and say, 'Um? I don't think this is the right way guys, there's a really humongous cliff up ahead and I don't think we've evolved the ability to fly just yet. How about we,'…*[moooooo, splat!]* Or will you do something about it?

"Meanwhile the justice system and the media collude to make criminality appear the norm for negroes, until the people not only accept it, but buy into the false mythology and lifestyle.

"As for the failing educational system, it helps to perpetrate this false consciousness and perpetuate the situation by glorifying the horrific criminal exploits of vampires past, while insinuating that negroes are three-fifths of a hueman being! When the truth is the paleface evolved from some of our ancestors, those randy niggers, *ha!* indulging in a bit of the strange with Neanderthals. Did you learn *that* in school? No? I wonder why?

"The first man was a negro. We are the original hueman race. Let me make one thing clear, anyone can be saved, black or white, but *we* were the chosen people and *we* fell off. Do you know why the elite want us to call white folk, vampires? It is because they wish for the common man to fear the blood-sucking elite, who are predominantly white folk, as they, the elite, fear us. As they fear our potential to ascend, which they, in their lust for material pleasure and power, have apparently lost.

"The elite wield their weapons from afar, playing complex PC games and piloting drones, be they memetic, robotic, paperworked, or indeed hueman, all from the comfort of their homes, jacked into the matrix with VR headsets that normalise their utter lack of empathy. And y'all want your kids to grow up to be like them…*(tut!)*…as if psychopathy were an admirable trait. Culture is not your friend, trust me!

"But fear not. If God did not love you, you would not exist. And if you do not love God, by which I mean if you are not thankful for the air, the plants, the sun, this glorious gift of life as a living breathing human being, aware of the glorious possibilities inherent to ascension, then you just ain't paying attention. You lost, too busy disappointing your own soul. Witness and experience, learn and grow. That's the way home for all of us."

Guru the seventh indicated she was finished by raising and opening his hands, as if inviting a response.

"That's quite a story Ms…err…Mr the Seventh," Johnny said.

"Please, call me Um? Not Err? For I do not."

"Do not what? Err?" Johnny asked.

"I strive each day for impeccability in order that I might know true humility. It is my only possible response to this great gift of life," (s)he answered.

"Like this: breathe in the prana of the universe, full and deep for it sustains your life; breathe out all that no longer serves you, that it might be of use elsewhere. Contemplate the reality in which you live and meditate on the source of it all. Ask yourself, 'who am I?' Pray. It really works. Speak from the heart and be clear in your prayers; your higher self will respond.

"Serve Life and I promise you, the Lord will reward you in this life and the other. Eat healthily and exercise, and do good work that benefits the All, in order to sustain yourself and the All, even as the Lord sustains the entire universe.

"Did you know that if you so chose, you could reach out your arms and touch infinity? Did you know that in this lifetime, you could attain immortality? Let the mind that was in Christ arise in you. Be inspired by the Holy Spirit. True love is within. A man once said, 'the Soul is always lovely, full of love. It is the Mind that likes to play games of creation and destruction.'

"The mind is so tricky, it's not even funny. Many have said that the greatest trick the devil ever pulled was making the world believe he doesn't exist. The truth is that it is the ego that wants you to believe it doesn't exist. It invented the devil and the system in order for us to have someone else to blame for our sins, or mental mistakes if you will.

"The very same devil that people unfortunately fear and admire as the prince of lies, blowing smoke in everyone's eyes; the very same system that raises our kids, indoctrinating them into accepting less than the freedom that is their birth right.

"Intentions and thoughts have power. If we are controlled by our egos, we are doomed to live in a world full of vice and apathy, filled with tyrants and slaves, all dominated in one way or the other by lust, envy, pride, hatred, greed and delusion.

"Those who overcome the ego are the enlightened souls who live in peace and love, free of sin, while simultaneously following a disciplined and integrated spiritual practice, happiest when serving selflessly, sharing love and elevating their people, empty so as to be filled with the clear light of natural intelligence, each blessed by power in their own unique way, each a blessing onto their worlds. The secret is to use the gift of your Free Will as an arrow aimed at Destiny.

"Listen, Sofia and Johnny. Have the strength, courage, and wisdom, to love all life, respect those that serve life, and revere the source of life.

"For when death comes to whip away the veil, the manner in which you dance with her will determine whether you graduate or repeat this school of life. Transcendence or re-incarnation? She is a friend but death ain't no joke and most minds are simply not prepared for the reality beyond the veil.

"Death is a doorway, a transition, the most elegant foe you will ever face. Will you have fears and doubts? Will you succumb to them and fall off the path? Or will you have the strength, courage and wisdom to walk the road into the clear light. A strength, courage and wisdom that you ought to begin cultivating right now.

"Being born a hueman is a rare privilege, so don't waste it. This plane of reality has awesome potential for spiritual change yet most folk waste it craving material things and sensations, or fearing the loss of them, unable to detach from the causes of their suffering."

"Can you tell us how old you are?" Hola asked.

"Older than you can imagine. Would you believe me if I told you I once met the emperor when he was but a boy?"

"Did you?" Johnny asked.

"It doesn't matter. Suffice it to say that I am a child at heart."

"Do you eat meat?" I asked. "I've been thinking of becoming a vegetarian or a vegan or something."

"Our diets are far too acidic. Alkalise yourself and you'll see great benefits. All you need are fruits and vegetables all colours of the rainbow. As for meat, it is not necessary to our diet but neither is it harmful in moderation. Eat healthy free range animals, be thankful of the gift, the sacrifice made by your fellow life-form, and use it wisely.

"Stay away from milk and dairy, though. Milk is for infants and advanced yogis; it infantilises the adult mind, keeping us dependant on the false authority of the elite, like genetically modified factory farmed animals sucking on artificial teats.

"As for water, considering what Death Star puts in the taps, I would buy it from a reliable source. Of course I'm sure you two have good filters in your homes.

"I personally like to pour my water into glass containers with crystals in them, which change the structure of the water into healthy configurations, then drink it with chlorophyll.

"Truer words were never spoken: health is your true wealth. Health in body and mind. I remember the day when I realised I had to become my own mother, my own father, my own child. Before then I lived under the spell that so much of mankind live under.

"Huemanity's fundamental problem is we believe ourselves to be separate entities when in fact we are all cells within a vast and complex super-organism. Unfortunately we have been conditioned to value separation and competition over unity and co-operation, turning many of those cells cancerous.

"This mind-set is unsustainable and Terra has little choice but to restore balance. It's going to get a lot worse before it gets better. A cataclysm is no doubt coming soon. In the meantime, we must continue to strive, for none know the day, none know the hour. Huemanity has migrated from the heart to the brain to the machine... I say it's time to return home.

"Think on this. Every single atom within your body contains enough energy to blow Paradise to Kingdom-come. Imagine what you could do if you had access to that energy...as a force for positive change. You could reshape the world into an actual paradise. A Topia, if you will, for the definition of Utopia is a place that does not exist.

"You could become who you were truly meant to be, who you came to Terra to become. This is the true knowledge which the educational system spectacularly fails to teach and in fact attempts to obfuscate. Self-knowledge of man's godlike nature is traded away for the ability to memorise and regurgitate a colonised mind, a slave mentality.

"We groom our children to conform to the evils of the age rather than be transformed by this reality's awesome potential for spiritual change. Time to flip the script!

"So what do you think? Are you interested? You don't have to answer now, of course. I know I've given you a ton of information all at once and it will take time to digest. Unlike most people, however, I can tell the two of you have incredible powers of focus. All I suggest, is you use that same gift to focus within and arise to becoming your greatest possible selves."

An Indigo Song for Paradise

The Xombie formerly known as Obram

The xombie formerly known as Obram stood in the blazing heat of the desert, one of dozens of xombies staring at the sinkhole. Fractals flowed through their grey skins like falling leaves, ethereal wormholes and hyper dimensional spaces opening and collapsing. There was a collective pattern evident that spoke of natural law and meta-intelligence.

In the sky above, several birds wheeled about waiting for a giant iguana to die. It had crawled out of the hole and was now slowly lumbering away from the city. It was very old and did not have much longer to live. Obram knew without knowing that the iguana would live longer than the birds hoped but would eventually perish and be eaten by a multitude of creatures, great and small, leaving behind its bones to slowly bleach in the sun.

A xombie dropped down into the hole and landed in a tunnel. Obram could feel him walking towards the city, the same place that called him inexorably forwards as it was calling all the xombies across the wasteland. Why, he knew not—but he could no sooner deny this impulse than a fish could deny the existence of water, or a true hueman the power of love, respect, and reverence.

The xombies dropped down into the tunnel and began to walk, widening the hole as they did so. More were coming.

Babylove Brown

I am dying. The bullets in my guts have done a righteous number on me. Fucked me up real good. The drugs will keep me going but I'm as good as dead. Just like Casey. Just like Low. I don't know what happened to Tealson. I remember seeing a flash of light and then the van was just gone. Only for a moment, I thought I saw something in the light. Some place full of trees and clouds under a loving sun. Maybe when you know you're gonna die you start seeing things. Who can say?

I am dying but I'm going out with a bang. In a few moments I'm going to step out of the shadow I'm hiding in, leap off the

473

edge of this building and glide down onto the force field of Lagoon. My phase transducer is going to get me through. It's my one way ticket into Lagoon and I'm gonna make it count.

I am dying but when I land onto the roof of the Shadow Theatre and Grand Opera building where the Melodium awards are being held, I'm going to drop into the building via a vent and trigger a mini EMP device that will short circuit every electronic device in the building for several seconds. Enough time for me to merge with the crowd. My camo automatically cycles my heat signature and as long as I walk funny, their gait recog won't catch me. I'll be a fox in the chicken coop—if chickens ruled the world.

I am dying but then so do we all. In my line of work it's always good to have an ace up your sleeve. Mine is a neutrino bomb the size of a grain of rice embedded in my lower left back wisdom tooth. One hard bite and the mental decision to die and boom and The Shadow Theatre along with all its occupants will be no more. I found the bomb on our last job and decided to keep it for myself rather than share with the crew. I know I'm a bad person, I know.

I am dying but when I go I'm taking the richest and most powerful citizens of Para City with me. They say there's not enough room in Lagoon for the people... Well, I'm making room.

Babylove Brown is coming to town, motherfuckers! Let's find out who's been naughty and nice.

Johnny Toxic

The Melodium Awards. The big time. Big production, no expense spared. A vast and overarching dome with incredible light and sound effects that change from segment to segment, the stage designed like some sort of ancient sacrificial altar around which numerous stars have performed and gyrated sexually around tonight, Sofia and I included.

So this is it? This is what I struggled all these years for? So I can sit here with all these rich and fancy folk masturbating our egos? There's gotta be more to life than this. I've done

474

everything I always wanted to do. I'm rich, I'm famous, I have the hottest girl in town and my music is top of the pops. So why does it all feel so...pointless all of a sudden? Am I just another rebel without a clue?

There was a sudden round of applause and Aso Prelax came back on the stage. "Give it up once again for the lovely Delilah and the Ladies of the Weave. Keep your weaves tight, ladies. Wouldn't want to look like savages, now, would we? Ha Ha Ha! Alrighty then! Now that's what I call music. You know, ladies and gentlemen, in these troubled times, it's good to know that some things never change.

"Delilah, who received a lifetime award last year, remains one of the most talented musical visionaries our world has ever known. And despite the many grave issues that our city faces, Mayor Obvious Beastedy remains a great leader. A round of applause for our mayor!"

The mayor walked onto the stage to moderate applause and took the stage. Sofia held onto my arm as her pops began to speak.

"Thank you. Thank you. Ever so kindly. I won't take up much of your time because I, for one, came here to partay, ha ha, as they say, but allow me to share a few words."

Sofia smirked a little and the cameras lingered on her face for a moment as she composed herself and smiled the kind of smile every guy wants to have in his life.

The mayor continued. "There are those who claim that our city is falling apart. While it is true that there is too much violent crime and far too many folks live below the poverty line, I urge you to remember that the situation is improving.

"Our various drives and initiatives have been largely successful in cleaning up the city and creating jobs. I know things aren't perfect but I have a little something called faith. And the great thing about faith is it can move mountains.

"Together, we *will* salvage what is left of our world and one day reclaim it as the veritable garden of Eden. In the meantime remember, we do this not for ourselves but for those yet to come. Thank you, and may God bless Paradise City!"

While the audience erupted into more applause, a dark figure dropped down from the walkway high above the stage and landed on the stage next to the mayor in a dramatic crouch. The figure stood up and pointed a gun at the mayor's head.

Was this part of the show? People looked around at each other and confused murmurs rippled through the room. Sofia clutched my hand and held on tight enough to hurt.

The mayor turned to walk away and the figure pistol whipped him. A woman screamed somewhere behind me and we all began to panic and scramble to our feet.

"Sit the fuck down or everyone dies!" a she-demon's voice thundered and there was something in her voice that left no doubt in the mind and no room for argument. That's when I clocked who it was: Baby motherloving Brown!

Sofia and I sat back down and turned to look at each other. That damned song popped into my head again. Man, I should have been paying more attention. I was high when I wrote, recorded and signed away the rights to that shit. KKK ain't no joke. Thank God I gave that shit up, for real.

I pulled my baseball cap down low over my face and hoped she didn't see me. The problem with being famous though is that Sofia and I were seated right where we would be best seen.

I wondered what Um? would say about all this. Earlier tonight, backstage, I saw he, she, it, or whatever, talking to Mr Fin, that creepy hood Legs has been dealing with recently. *What in this world or the next would the two of them have to talk about?*

Mayor Obvious Beastedy
Fuck! This can't be happening! Just before I got on stage, my head of security whispered that xombies had been spotted in numerous locations across the city. I didn't want to cause a panic and Special Forces were on the case so I said nothing. With any luck we'd be able to cover it up. After all, this

wasn't the first time xombies had made it past our defences though never in so many numbers. Those damned tunnels were too numerous to be mapped. Now the side of my head is throbbing with pain and bleeding thanks to Babylove Brown standing with a gun pointed at my head and I can hear death knocking at the door.

Dear God! This is happening. I'm going to die right here. I can feel it. Unless one of my men can take her out before she pulls the trigger. Maybe if I make a move and distract her…but who am I kidding? I'm frozen here, sweat dripping down my face and there's a sudden itch in my balls I need to scratch real bad.

"Ladies and gentlemen of the one percent. My name is Babylove Brown and I'm here to play a game. It's a simple game really. You see, one of you is sitting on a bomb. Now don't panic. It's a small bomb and is only going to kill the person sitting on it. Those to either side of our lucky volunteer might get a little singed but I promise you'll live with no scars a cosmeticon couldn't fix in a jiffy. Now, the rules of the game are simple. As we live in a democracy, all of you get to vote. Who lives and who dies? The choice is yours.

"What I want is a simple 'boo!' Either 'boo' yourselves or 'boo' the mayor. Whoever gets the loudest 'boo' wins a one way trip to the next life. Are you ready?"

"Now wait a minute!" I shouted. "That's not democracy! What is this, a demonstration of craziness? You're insane!"

"Maybe, maybe not. Let me ask you this, what are your objections to our little game?"

"That someone might die," I spluttered, then regained my composure. "Listen Miss Brown. I'm sure we can work this out. We all understand you come from a deprived environment. That you were failed by those entrusted to protect you. We have all heard 'The Ballad of Babylove Brown'. But believe me, this isn't the way."

"We all die mayor. Those are the rules of the game of life. And you make decisions that cost the lives of countless people all the time."

"That is my job young lady! To ensure the safety and well being of as many people as possible. Do you think that it's an easy task?"

"Someone put a gun to your head and forced you to become mayor?" she asked. "All you politicians are corrupt and all you rich motherfuckers who hog the water and the wealth while the rest of us suffer and die are just as culpable. You know you couldn't be luxuriating up in the clouds without the broken backs of the common folk to stand on.

"Whatever, time's awasting. This is just the first part of the show and you don't want to miss what comes next. If you don't play this game, we all die. There's another bomb hidden somewhere in the building and it's got enough juice to wipe us all out.

"On the count of three, 'boo' if you feel that one of yourselves deserves to die. Ready? One two boo!"

There was a single solitary "Boooooooo," long and low from somewhere in the back followed by a smattering of nervous laughter like static electricity.

"Hmmmm. Not looking good for you there Obvious. Not looking good at all. Just be steady, it'll all be over real soon. Now everyone 'boo' if-"

"Wait! This isn't fair! These elections are rigged! You can't ask someone to choose another's life over their own," I interrupted.

"I thought you were a believer in the prophet. Does it not say in the Holy Word that 'unless a leader is willing to sacrifice all for his people, he is not fit to enter the kingdom of heaven?' Were you lying when you said you were a man of the people but a servant of God? Or are these fine folk not worth the sacrifice?"

Did the prophet say that? I honestly couldn't remember.

I realised then that my team wasn't speaking to me via my earstud. Had Babylove Brown murdered my personal staff?

She smiled like she was reading my thoughts. "I don't believe God wants anyone to die here today," I answered.

"Well, we'll have to see about that."

The strangest thing happened to me then. I had nothing to say. I never have nothing to say. I'm the mayor of this motherloving city not some chump. Who did this bitch think she was?

"Cat got your tongue?" she asked, not even bothering to look me in the face, the gun never wavering.

"You kn-kn-know what young la-la-lady, I've had eno-no-nough of y-y-y-your lip," I stammered in rage.

"What you gonna do? Spank me?"

"No. But you know this is a waste of time don't you?" I asked, stalling for time, wondering why someone hadn't shot the bitch yet. "Do you really believe killing anyone in this room will change anything?" *Do you really believe the secret rulers of the world are hanging out at an awards ceremony? Foolish child! We are sacrifices to their dark gods, nothing more, nothing less...*

Babylove Brown

"Save it. Interrupt me again and I *wi-wi-will* put a bullet in your head. Go ahead, call my bluff. Now on the count of three, whosoever believes the responsibility for our failed city state lies with our fearless leader say 'boo'.

"Remember...in the old days, when shit was just, life fucking up, you know, kinda like what's happening to the world, the King sacrificed himself to appease the gods. So let me ask you fine upstanding citizens, when you look upon our devastated world, is it not clear the gods are pissed the fuck off? Okaaaay, here we go…"

I bit down hard and repeated my secret mantra to myself in my mind activating the neutrino bomb then I began my countdown. As the word 'two' emerged from my mouth, a sniper's bullet entered the top of my head, bored a hole through my brain, nasal cavity, and mouth to emerge and unhinge my jaw as it blasted through to embed itself in the floor, now splattered with blood, bone, and meat, that formerly resided inside my skull.

In my final moments of life I thought of my parents and wondered who they were and why they abandoned me as a baby. They were probably babies themselves, like so many on the streets, addicts of one description or another, fated to a life of cheating, robbing, whoring, and killing, all for the right to mainline another hot-shot of the Amerikan Dream, the greatest drug ever designed by man.

A moment later, the Shadow Theatre and Opera House vanished from the face of the planet, taking everyone within her on a one way trip into the unknown, leaving nothing behind but a dark smouldering hole in the ground.

The Xombie formerly known as Obram

The xombie formerly known as Obram walked through tunnels made of rough-hewn stone embedded with crystals. He was one of many xombies making their way through these ancient arteries that connected to the sewers beneath the city.

All the xombies could feel the energy of the people above. It was what was calling them. For what purpose they knew not but they were drawn inexorably onwards and upwards, ever closer to their cousins on the surface.

Eventually they came to a ladder that led up to a grate. There were people walking past above. A xombie stepped up to the ladder and began to climb followed by others. Soon they pushed the grate aside and emerged onto the street. They swarmed forth from the sewers to stand under the dusk sky and newly lit streetlamps.

A few people stopped and stared but there was strangely no panic. Obram looked at the huemen around him and saw their connection with the other huemen on the planet like a fine network of fungi, winking as luminescent as otherworldly fireflies. He felt their suffering. He could see their fears and cravings riding them. He could smell their demons and angels waging war. He could hear their souls crying out to be set free. Not all of them, but the majority.

A few were different. They were...Om be; not xombies but neither were they like the rest of the huemen either. Their presences were unclouded. They were not to be touched. As for the rest, they were zombies feeding on the bounty of the planet and giving nothing in return.

Their brains were filled with such a variety of exotic illusions and waking dreams that the xombie formerly known as Obram couldn't help but wonder what they tasted like. After a moment, he decided to find out.

He approached a middle aged man of average height with sad eyes, dressed in a suit and tie, standing at a bus stop. The man flinched when he realised that Obram was a xombie before dying a moment later from a single blow to the head that caved in his skull like a bullet striking a watermelon.

As it happened, a ferociously bright little light exploded and swirled deep within the grey mass of the xombie formerly known as Obram's skin, like a dying star or a galaxy being born, spreading out to fill his ultra-dark skin with Fibonacci spirals all colours of the rainbow. The greyness vanished in an instant and his skin was suddenly fire and smoke, clouds and nebulae, galaxies and stars, infinite worlds in a simple yet complex design wrought by no mere mortal hand.

The xombie formerly known as Obram looked at the pineal gland he had plucked from the man's head. It was calcified, a third eye blocked from seeing the light by mankind's clever poisons.

The truth was as clear as the light this man had once seen as a new-born baby, before being corrupted by Babylon. It wasn't worthy to feed on. None of them were. It changed nothing however. Their time had come. He crushed the pineal gland to dust in his fist and moved on.

Soon people began to panic.

Efe Tokunbo Okogu

Gaia

Ecila, DevilDog, and Tealson, stood on the edge of a cliff high above the clouds. The van they had recently leapt out of was still plunging down the side of the mountain and had yet to hit the bottom.

Behind them and all around stood a thick forest. The air was a little thin due to the altitude and in the distance a glowing dragon flew across the early evening, a sliver of rainbow colours snaking past through a sky ablaze with a fiery sunset, like an epic poem.

Ecila looked at the strange machine in his hands then at the other two; the man with the mechanical legs and the girl with the broken wings. They looked as bewildered yet exhilarated as he felt. It was the air. It was so fresh it was almost unreal. Like he had never truly breathed before this moment.

In the far distance, a column of smoke rose into the air. Devildog wondered who they were and if they had any food. She was suddenly starving.

To Tealson, it smelled like gunpowder and blood.

Then Ecila looked up into the evening sky and suddenly he was laughing and weeping. The early stars were rising and he recognised them. There was the Butterfly and there was the Cosmic Trixter. He was home. Not in the village, but back on Gaia. Wherever this mountain on which they stood was, it was on the same world as Chi and he was going to find her.

That other woman in Paradise City who looked like Chi, she must have been a sign from the Ancestors and Orishas that they were soon to be reunited. The shaman of his village always claimed that huemen were but shadows of the gods.

Whatever dance they were performing that had flung him to strange new worlds only to return him home with no rhyme or reason he could discern, he was grateful. He whooped with joy into the sky as his two companions turned to look at him as if he was insane.

Maybe he was, a part of him thought. Maybe his insanity was so powerful it had finally come to life. For all he knew, he was this moment walking through the desert, having chosen to flee into the interzone and brave the wasteland rather than stay in the rotting cyborg corpse they called Paradise City.

Peace on Terra

The Xombie Apocalypse took the huemen of Terra by surprise. Within a few months, they were wiped out save for the few whom the xombies considered as Om Be. Many of the elite attempted to flee and hide but the xombies were relentless in tracking them down and not even the deepest nuclear bunkers offered any protection.

Afterwards, the survivors turned away from the corrupt ways of the last huemen and began the slow but steady process of living once more in tune with nature, as true huemen. After thousands of years of civilisation, huemanity finally learned that love was the answer all along.

They focused their attention on permaculture, silent contemplation, renewable sources of energy, mental technology, laughter, new genres, artforms and meta schools of dreams, styles of music and dance that were integrated into games and sports unseen and unheard of before. The innovation of artistic, physical, and mental acts of spiritual creation unfurling like petals following the rising sun, revealing the exploration ever deeper into the fractal depths of transcendence, ever pioneering towards new frontiers, ever refining, ever vibrating higher towards at-one-ment with the Most High.

Over time, life awoke in the wasteland until Terra was, once more, a veritable Garden of Eden.

The xombies, their purpose fulfilled, returned to the desert and became one with the landscape of the planet that had spawned them, their skins fragmenting into multi-coloured fractals which scattered onto the wind and disappeared as suddenly and inexplicably as the xombies had arrived, as if their fractals somehow merged into the fractals of the world and thus vanished *from* the world, to enter into the myths and legends of the peaceful inheritors *of* the world.

Efe Tokunbo Okogu

Epilogue

"Welcome to your new life," Miss Took said to a certain intrepid young reporter, "I'm happy to see that you survived the xombie apocalypse, but the journey has only just begun."

The two women took a moment to gaze around them at the field filled with thousands of folk; men, women, children, negroes, vampires (though in the post xombie era they were no longer called such), and other hueman races, mutants, and a few visiting aliens, all awaiting the solar eclipse.

Some were sat on the grass while others were running, leaping, levitating, throwing and catching balls, boomerangs, frisbees, sticks and other objects made of fire, water, other elements and forms of energy; or relaxing on magic carpets powered by their own mentally generated forcefields, drinking floating bubbles of fresh water, healing herbal teas and delicious blends of juices; or smoking holy chillums in circles and chanting sacred mantras, surrounded by larger circles of dancers moving to the rhythmic pluckings, tappings, poundings and auralisations of improvised tunes, weaving around primordial standards on strange new instruments.

"Huemen are now aware that in addition to the three dimensions of space and one of time they are so familiar with," Miss Took continued, "time also possesses three dimensions. I am happy to see that more huemen are gaining control of the third spatial dimension and overcoming gravity with the power of their minds.

"Linear time is analogous to moving forwards and backwards, though of course the vast majority of huemen can still only move forwards. You are learning to *bend* time though, which is very good."

As she spoke, the young lady responded by slooowwwiing down time and Miss Took's words stretched out without losing coherence, but rather subtle nuances could now be heard that revealed all the sounds around them as being dialectic with her words.

"Stay aware and focused in the present moment. Remember that Here and Now are all that exist. You are eternal... you can touch infinity..."

A flock of birds arose from a tree in the distance and spiralled out, moving as one being towards the sun.

"Access to horizontal time or the fifth dimension gives one the power to move between parallel realities, some hellish, far worse than the empire or Paradise City ever were, others akin to 'paradise on earth'. The sixth dimension or vertical time allows one to actually ascend to the realms of the gods or descend into the hells."

Miss Took was silent for awhile, her eyes focused on a flying red kite swirling and twisting through the air in the deft hands of the wind and her accomplice, a young laughing boy floating in the distance, one of many gambolling through the air. As expected, the youths were learning to fly faster than the adults.

It was such a beautiful day, the sun high was in the blue sky, smiling upon the wide open field of grass dotted with people and a few trees, and flowers all colours of the rainbow.

Miss Took smiled and breathed in deep as she took it all in.

"What of the seventh dimension? And how many dimensions are there?" the young reporter asked after a while.

"The seventh dimension is a door, but to cross that threshhold, one must let go completely," Miss Took answered, refocusing on her young friend.

"Let go of what?"

"Everything. Especially that which you hold most dear to you."

"What's on the other side of the door?"

Gutter Dice smiled as he listened to the women speak. He passed the joint he was smoking to the indigo furred ape who sat on its haunches to his left, toes nestling luxuriously into the earth.

"The answer to your second question. To all questions in fact. There are an infinite number of dimensions where the ancestors dream and the arch-angels sing. We are their dreams and we both inspire and dance to the divine tune. On the other side of the door, your higher self awaits you in your true home, and the beauty and mystery of it all is that you are already there. Now all you have to do is walk the path."

"The path?"

"Within your heart of hearts there is a pure light gifted to you by God. Devote yourself to that light with the innocence and unconditional love of a child. Serve the source of that light with strength, courage and wisdom, with every moment of every breath. That is the path. Are you ready?"

"It's simple," Gutter Dice added, "Think of it as a three step program where you do all three steps simultaneously: One – Love yourself. Two – Be present and aware. Three – Manifest positive energy. Every blessing you put out into the world comes back to you ten-fold.

"Once you know the path, ain't no good reason to deny yourself the incredible awesomeness. And if you ever feel blocked, see it for what it is and if need be, push on into the darkness, all the way through and out the other side into the light. No fear. All the way.

"We got you, God. Trust," he touched his chest over his heart chakra. "He got you." He pointed up at the sky to indicate what lay beyond it and indeed the entire cosmos.

"Hey check it out," the indigo furred ape spoke up, stubbing out the roach between the thumb and middle finger of his left paw. "The eclipse is about to start."

An Indigo Song for Paradise

Efe Tokunbo Okogu is a Nigerian writer who was born in the UK on *Dia de los Muertos*. He now lives in Mexico where he is developing various projects in the areas of holistic health, body-mind activation, spiritual science studies, and multi-disciplinary artistic expression. His words have been heard live and published in digital and print form. His novelette, *Proposition 23* was nominated for the 2013 British Science Fiction Association awards, translated into Italian, studied at various universities, and is available online. He believes that life is real SF and far stranger than anyone can conceive.